About *Stolen Boy*

"Basically, Mic did all the hard work, and I got all the glory. I couldn't have even thought about making the film without Mic's help, and as always, he went beyond the call of duty to search out the truth in why things turned out the way they did …"—From the Foreword by Nick Cassavetes

"If there was ever a true-life drama tailor-made for a celluloid adaptation, it's this one."—*VCReporter*

"Cassavetes and Michael Mehas … cut a wide swath in amassing the details that would give texture to the script (and book), which sticks closely to the devastating story."—*Los Angeles Times*

"It's a tale of boys gone bad to the level of *The Last Detail* meets *Lord of the Flies*, Santa Barbara style."—*Ventura County Star*

"Writing the story as fiction gave Mehas a chance to get closer to the truth." —*Ventura County Star*

"Youngblood's tale is a house of cards constructed by the shaking hands of wayward youth so deeply self obsessed that it fails to see that pride comes before the fall. Deeply detailed and scatologically entertaining, *Stolen Boy* lays bare the consequences of callow thrill-seeking—and how the world of senseless excitement is one of the foundations on which rests cheaply available annihilation."—*Santa Barbara News-Press*

Stolen Boy

Stolen Boy

Based on a True Story

Michael Mehas
Associate Producer
Major Motion Picture *Alpha Dog*

iUniverse Star
New York Lincoln Shanghai

Stolen Boy

Based on a True Story

iUniverse Star
an iUniverse, Inc. imprint

iUniverse books may be ordered through booksellers or by contacting:

iUniverse
2021 Pine Lake Road, Suite 100
Lincoln, NE 68512
www.iuniverse.com
1-800-Authors (1-800-288-4677)

Because of the dynamic nature of the Internet, any Web addresses or links contained in this book may have changed since publication and may no longer be valid.

This is a work of fiction. All of the characters, names, incidents, organizations, and dialogue in this novel are either the products of the author's imagination or are used fictitiously.

ISBN: 978-1-60528-000-4 (pbk)
ISBN: 978-0-595-91870-6 (ebk)

Printed in the United States of America

For those lost souls whose energies merged into this tragedy of flesh and spirit, may you forever be blessed with peace.

Foreword

By Nick Cassavetes
Director: *Alpha Dog, The Notebook,* and *John Q*

Mic Mehas and I have been best friends since we were fourteen. We have played sports, chased girls, and tripped the light fantastic for thirty-three years. He has always been the better, brighter one: more athletic, smarter, funnier, kinder, and more diligent.

The funny thing about growing up is not that we go our different directions. It's that we get busy. We get older and so very involved with our own doings that we drift away. The location becomes more distant, but in our hearts, we remain present and inseparable.

I went off to make movies, and Mic went to law school. He became a fine lawyer, and I did what I did, but when I was presented the opportunity to make a film based on the real-life story of Jesse James Hollywood, my first phone call was to Mic. There were mountains of research to do, and I needed someone to digest and present the information to me in a way I could relate to.

I was surprised as Mic unfolded the story to me in intricate detail. Except for a few tragic twists and turns, what happened in West Hills and Santa Barbara was not too different from the way Mic and I grew up. Life for young people in the San Fernando Valley hadn't changed all that much, and the experience of growing up in today's modern, affluent society took on a particular universality that I hadn't seen depicted on film before.

Basically, Mic did all the hard work, and I got all the glory. I couldn't have even thought about making the film without Mic's help, and as always, he went beyond the call of duty (it's well documented how much material the prosecutor Ron Zonen supplied to him, ultimately leading to his recusal from the case) to search out the truth as to why things turned out the way they did, and for that I am eternally grateful. I don't know whether I've ever told him that, but maybe it's nice that it's now in print.

Anyway, somewhere during this process, two things happened. One, Mic decided to write a book, and two, he became the foremost authority in the world about the events surrounding and leading up to the crime. The following is the result of four years of exhaustive study, research, interviews, and experience. It is my distinct pleasure to watch this fine writer come of age. I couldn't be prouder or more pleased.

Sleep tight, Nicky. May your slumber be blessed.

Acknowledgments

Though there usually turns out to be only one name on a book's cover, every book is a collaboration of energy and effort, a statement that has never been truer than with this one.

Without the support and encouragement of certain blessed angels in my life, this project might still be alone and hidden, out of sight and out of mind, on my shelf of story inventories. For lifting it off that shelf and extending it into the light of day, my unending gratitude reaches out to my friend and editor, Cliff Carle, and to professor extraordinaire Harry Major, who still patiently teaches me the English grammar I slept through while in high school.

I must also extend my deepest appreciation to Santa Barbara County Senior Deputy District Attorney Ron Zonen, who went out on a limb—and felt it snap—by providing me with the information that stirred my mind with depth and clarity of character and plot. For their keen insight and healing support, I want to thank my kindred spirits Richard Evans, Lisa Schwartz, Yaneth Chavarria Piedrahita, Monica Amparo Chavarria Piedrahita, and David Duckwitz. Dear friends Yenka Honig, Bob Youngblood, Chris Kinkade, Owen Kugell, and Jolene and Eric Harrington also provided invaluable feedback on this torturous road.

To Jessica Cheng, I offer my deepest thanks for providing everything that was needed when the work was at its coldest and emptiest; and for his generosity and love, I thank my soul brother, Nick Cassavetes, without whose belief in me this project could never have materialized.

Most urgently, allow me to express my gratitude to my family for offering patience and tolerance, which were often in short supply; to my attorney (and mother) Donna Santo, who was always present to lend encouragement; to my namesake and father for continually offering an eager ear for my words; and to my sister Misty and her husband, Ernie, who provided me with the perfect gift in the form of two beautiful little nieces, Sequoyah and Tenaya, who, though they may not realize it yet, fill my heart and mind with the inspiration of love that makes up the universe.

Ventura, California

April 2007

Prologue

Saturday, July 3, 2001—12:01 a.m.

The explosion of shattered glass shook Mickey Youngblood to his very core. He jumped up in his sleeping bag but couldn't tell where he was or how long he'd been out. His head swam in a fog of booze and dope, and his heart raced as he realized that the shards of broken glass raining down upon him had once formed the front windows of his living room.

He'd been out partying late with his buddy John Barbados, when they came home and ended up passing out in sleeping bags in the middle of his living room floor. This was how Youngblood slept these nights. His house was empty, because he was in the process of moving out and selling it. Too many people knew where he lived.

His first thought was that someone had shot out his windows. But as he studied the shadows, he realized there were no bullet holes, only what sounded like muffled laughter coming from around the side of his house. Whoever had broken out his windows, he was pretty sure, was now in the process of trying to escape.

He reached under his pillow and tossed Barbados the black semiautomatic pistol he always kept for protection. After pulling on his tennis shoes to protect his feet from the broken glass, Youngblood pushed his muscular five-foot-four-inch frame into a crouch. Like a crab, he scrambled over to the closet, opened it, grabbed his pistol-grip shotgun, and pumped a shell into its chamber. His finger slid to his lips as he rose and slipped silently past Barbados and over to the jagged window frame. Youngblood gazed intensely out into the night. Seeing only darkness, he turned to Barbados. "Cover me."

Barbados nodded, and Youngblood skulked across the living room to the front door. He stood behind the door, grabbed the handle, and twisted it slowly …

When the door jerked open, Youngblood aimed his shotgun, and he could see that half his neighborhood had also been awakened by the attack. But the assailants were nowhere in sight. He yanked the gun back and stashed it inside the door. One of his neighbors would later tell him that she had two young daughters who had seen two guys with baseball bats climb into an old green pickup and speed off.

That's when Youngblood understood who had attacked him. He knew who the owner of that green pickup was; the same gutless wonder who owed Youngblood money from a failed drug transaction last year. It was the same clown who had killed Youngblood's dog, snitched him out to the insurance company, and even threatened to shoot him. It was the same jerkoff who would later phone in his signature to the crime.

But calling the cops on Rick Leblanc was not an option. It never had been. Because during their former days of dealing together, Youngblood had been an idiot and told Leblanc too much about his "operation." The feud had been raging ever since, but this time Leblanc had gone too far. The camel's back had been broken, leaving Mickey with only one real choice: he was going to have to punish his nemesis so badly that Rick Leblanc would never think about retaliating. If only Youngblood could figure out where the dickhead lived.

Chapter One

Twenty-year-old Luke Ridnaur ran around his house like a Mexican at a garage sale. People were coming over to score, and he couldn't find his pot or his scale anywhere. How lame was that? A stash of killer bud hid somewhere in his house; he just couldn't remember where. The party had rained on him so hard the night before, he just passed out, and that was all he could remember. He didn't know how he'd gotten to bed, or when.

He stretched his six-foot-four, one-hundred-fifty-pound frame under his bed and filtered through a pile of dust and spiderwebs—nada. He sifted through dresser drawers and found a couple dilapidated condoms and an old roach of killer bud that he'd totally forgotten about, but no scale or bag of pot. When his hand opened his closet, the stench of ancient parties overwhelmed him. An avalanche of stained T-shirts, slippery underwear, and dirty socks nearly buried him. He shoveled everything back, and that's when he heard the crinkle of plastic and, with it, his own sigh of relief.

He'd tossed the pot in there last night when he heard his old man creeping around out in the hallway. He'd waited as long as he could before opening his bedroom door to see if the coast was clear. But his old man had startled the shit out of him, his bloodshot eyes and bloodhound jowls staring right back. They exchanged awkward good nights, and then his old man staggered off to bed. That was when Luke got totally wasted and lost his scale. What a clown.

Now he wondered how a triple beam scale could just disappear into thin air like that. He needed to find it so he could weigh out the rest of his pot and unload it. He needed to get Mickey Youngblood paid off, which was what he was thinking when he remembered where he'd left his scale. He sprinted out of the room and almost ran over his dad, who stood loitering outside his door for the second time in less than twelve hours. It took a miraculous act of balance to stay on his feet and to keep the old man from falling and hurting himself. When Luke saw Fritz carrying three unopened bottles of red wine in one hand and his scale in the other, he knew his search had ended. *Fuck!*

"Lose something?" Fritz asked.

What Luke had lost was his patience with his father's attitude. His first thought was to deny any knowledge. But that wouldn't work, because when the math was said and done, there were only so many people in the house who might have a need for a scale.

His stepmother, Milsty Ridnaur, wouldn't be caught dead with pot. She was a religious woman who harbored the compassionate idea that all pot smokers should be taken out and shot. And it wasn't as if the woman ever stepped into the kitchen, let alone cooked anything, so she certainly wouldn't be considered a suspect for having a triple beam scale in the house. That left Luke and his dad, and since Fritz would know whether it was his scale or not—which it wasn't—that left only Luke. He thought about blaming it on one of his friends, but he didn't think that would fly either. He was going to have to cop a plea. But he was determined not to go down without a fight.

"What the fuck you doing searching around in my room, Dad?"

"I wasn't searching around in your bedroom," Fritz said, the left side of his walrus mustache shaved about an inch shorter than the right. "I found it in the pantry."

Fuck, that's right, Luke thought. Last night he had gone downstairs to weigh out a half ozer for his buddy, when he was suddenly struck by the munchies. He'd set the scale down and grabbed a can of tuna, which had fallen behind some pasta boxes, and that was the last thing he'd remembered until now.

But Fritz didn't even seem mad. "Look, uh, me and Milsty are heading out of town—"

"Have a nice trip."

"—and I don't want you having anyone over the house while we're gone."

Luke frowned at the absurdity of his father's statement. "What're you talking about, Dad?"

"I think you know what I'm talking about, Luke." Fritz leaned a hip against the doorjamb. "Milsty and I don't slave away all day so you and your freeloader friends can just hang out, smoke dope, drink all my booze, and eat us out of house and home. They make messes all over the place, Luke. I find beer bottles everywhere. You know how many cigarette butts I've had to pull out of my petunias?"

Luke hated his father's petunias. "You know what, Dad? You give me ulcers."

Fritz smiled a mouthful of brown-stained teeth. "You do the same to me, Luke."

"What is that supposed to mean?"

Fritz sighed heavily. "It means that when we get back, you and I are going to sit down and have a long talk."

"I don't want to talk, Dad. We got nothing to talk about."

Fritz leaned back and scratched his shoulder blade along the edge of the doorjamb. "Oh, I think we do."

Luke folded his arms in front of his chest. "Yeah, like what?"

Fritz moaned like a dog getting his belly rubbed. "Your pot dealing, Luke. It's got to stop."

Luke opened his palms to the ceiling, as if he had no idea what his father was talking about. *It's called denial,* he thought. *If they show you evidence, deny that too.*

"I don't know what you're talking about, Dad."

Fritz held up the scale. "Oh, I think you do." *Denial,* Luke told himself. "Your pot dealing with Mickey Youngblood is going to stop."

Luke's hands balled into fists by his side. He was again ready to jump on the denial wagon but had already lost the will to fight. There really wasn't anything to debate. The fact was he *was* selling pot, and his father had basically caught him in the act. But that wasn't the point.

"Dad, I'm an adult now. I can pretty much do what I want."

Fritz's head bowed with a chuckle. "Not while you're living under my roof, you can't."

"What about you?"

"What about me, Luke?"

The guy was being a total hypocrite. Luke's dad had a dozen seven-footers growing right now in the backyard along the fence, hidden beneath overgrown oleanders. "You fucking smoke your ass off every day, Dad. You grow pot out back. How can you even talk to me about it?"

"There's a big difference, Luke. I don't sell it."

Big fucking deal, Luke thought. *You're a stone-cold drunk who consumes enough alcohol to practically pickle himself, and now you're going to lecture me? What a jerk.* Luke yanked the scale out of his father's arm.

Fritz juggled the wine and nearly dropped a bottle, making a brilliant last-second save. "Luke?"

Luke turned his back to his father and scratched his shaved dome. "What?"

"I want the yard work finished while we're gone."

"I heard you."

"Don't yell at me. You spend all day drinking and smoking with your buddies, and you get nothing done. It's going to stop."

Luke pivoted to face his father. "Dad, I'm not your fucking slave, okay?"

"I never said you were."

"I'm going out tonight."

"That's fine," Fritz said. "You can go out as soon as you finish your yard work." Fritz then held out a sheet of paper he liked to call his To Do list. Luke glanced at it, and his first thought was that his old man had lost his fucking mind. When told this, Fritz assured Luke that he hadn't. He then slurred through the list, his trembling finger tracking down the page, telling his son to, "water and apply nitrogen fertilizer to the rose beds," when Luke lost it.

"You got to be kidding me, Dad. That'll take me forever." He ripped the list out of his father's hand. "Get the fuck out of my room."

"I'm not in your room."

Luke's hands gripped his father's shoulders and spun him around. He tried to guide his father away from his doorway, but Fritz pulled away and stumbled on his own.

Luke again peered at the list. It was three pages of illegible chicken scratch: an encyclopedia of every summer horticulture chore that ever existed, or that his father had ever imagined, and they all belonged to Luke.

"I won't finish this until November," Luke yelled. "Besides, Mickey's not gonna wait for me to finish this shit. He'll go to the party without me."

"Good," Fritz exclaimed. "I don't want Mickey coming around here anyway."

Luke bit his tongue. His old man was playing the hypocrite again. Fritz Ridnaur and Mickey's old man went way back to when Luke and Mickey played Little League together in the Angeles Valley, which everyone referred to simply as "the Valley." Fritz used to buy weed from Dick Youngblood and probably sold a little on the side, just as Luke was now doing with Mickey. But of course, Fritz **would never cop to it, because if he did, he wouldn't be able to say shit to his son now.**

"Dad, Mickey's my best friend." Luke zipped up the vinyl cover on the scale. "He's been my best friend for a long time. I'm going to have him over here whenever I damn well please."

Fritz's head shook. "No, you're not."

Luke nodded defiantly. "Yes, I am."

Fritz stared at his son in disbelief. His son gawked right back.

"What's the matter with you, Luke?" Fritz's jowls jiggled like gelatin. "Can't we just sit here and have a normal father-to-son talk?"

That would have been a first. Luke couldn't remember his father ever speaking to him like a son, or vice versa. There was too much baggage between them. The bottom line was that Luke acted as if he hated his father. He had ever since the selfish bastard destroyed his family by being an inconsiderate drunk of a father. But instead of telling him as much, Luke said nothing, which also might have been a first. He actually thought, for the briefest of moments, about what his father was saying. For probably the first time in his life, Fritz Ridnaur might have been right. If the truth were to be told—which it rarely was in his household—Luke was tired of dealing with Mickey Youngblood.

Mickey had been acting a motherfucker lately, and the dude was always uptight. Luke didn't know if it was the side effects from the Acutane or the excessive freebasing or what, but the dude was always getting upset over stupid shit. He was always yelling at Luke or one of the other schleps who did business with him to pay him back.

All Youngblood ever talked about was money. The guy rolled in it but acted as if he never had enough to be satisfied. He had also started hanging around some very strange people, unsavory people, people with bad reputations and little to lose. And to make matters worse, Youngblood had started spending a lot of time with guns. Buying guns. Playing with guns. Talking about hurting people with guns. And Luke knew, deep down in his heart, that it really was time to make a break from the guy, to stop dealing pot, and to get his shit together. He needed to get a job, as he'd promised his mom. He needed to go back to school, to make something of his life. But he would do it on his own time, not his father's.

"Are you finished yet?"

His father nodded. "For now."

"Good." Luke turned and stepped into his room.

"Luke?"

Luke stopped, eyes impatiently fixed on the bleached bush of the porn superstar plastered across his bedroom door. "Yeah?"

"Do we understand each other?"

A million smart-assed responses flashed through Luke's mind. But the truth was that he understood his father loud and clear. Besides, his buddy was due any minute, and he had to get the pot weighed out so he could sell it—so he could get Mickey paid off.

"Yeah," Luke said, and he walked into his room.

He smiled, because he liked the idea of getting Mickey Youngblood paid off for good. Then he turned and slammed the door in his father's blurry face.

Chapter Two

Saturday—6:47 p.m.

That evening, Mickey Youngblood blew through Luke's front door like a circus midget shot from a cannon. John Barbados and Hank Zitelli trailed him, laughing and shaking their heads as if they were embarrassed by the whole thing.

Everything had been totally mellow up to this point. With his folks safely out of town, Luke had the barbecue glowing and the beers on ice, ready for a sort of pre–Fourth of July party, when Youngblood flew by him into the living room, flinging a string of obscenities Luke had never heard before, without even saying hello. He yelled something about "The motherfucking bastard broke out all my fucking windows," and then he stormed off into the kitchen.

Luke started to follow him but thought better of it. *Let the little man calm down.* So he walked over to Barbados instead. "Dude, what's up with Mickey?"

John Barbados wore a wife-beater T-shirt and dark jumper-style pants and looked like a cross between a skateboarder and a gangster. Luke had known the psycho since they were both seven, when they met at a summer camp in the Valley. They reconnected a few years later in Little League, when they played on the Red Stockings with Mickey. They lost track of each other when Luke's parents divorced—Luke played musical houses between his parents' homes in the Valley and San Floripez—and they didn't see each other again until the last couple months, when Luke hooked back up with Youngblood.

Barbados shrugged. "You know Mickey."

Yes, Luke did know Mickey. He had been hanging out with him a lot lately. After not seeing Mickey for several years—other than a brief exchange of hellos in January—they ran back into each other about a week after Luke got out of jail for good from his DUI in April. Luke had been living with his mother in the Valley and was spending a lot of time at the skateboard park up by Johnson and Victoria. One day while working hard on a cool local backside slider on the rail, Luke heard the head-jarring thump of bass coming from someone's car stereo. When he looked up to see what all the racket was about, he saw a bunch of dudes gathered around a tricked-out, two-tone gray car.

All the commotion made him lose his concentration, causing Luke to fall off the rail and nearly break his ass. When he limped over to check out the action, he recognized the owner of the car. It was Mickey. He invited Luke over to party, and they'd been hanging out and partying together ever since.

When Luke sauntered through the living room about to enter the kitchen to see where Youngblood had disappeared to, the kitchen door flew back at him so hard, it almost tore his head off. Luke ducked away just in time, as Youngblood jetted back through the living room with a ducktail of steam shooting straight out of his ass. "The motherfucker's going to threaten my family? Who the fuck does he think he is?"

Luke pirouetted and followed him. He'd seen Youngblood go crazy on a number of occasions, but he usually identified the culprit. "Who you talking about, Mickey?"

Youngblood pivoted at the front door. "The motherfucker who broke out all my windows," he repeated. "Then sent me a fucking threatening message."

Barbados yawned and took a seat on the worn leather couch. He too had grown accustomed to Youngblood's ranting, and he helped himself to the bong sitting on the coffee table. Zitelli sat next to him and waited on deck.

"You said that, Mick," Luke said, waiting to see what might next pop out of Youngblood's mouth. "Who you talking about?"

Youngblood rolled his eyes as if that was the lamest question he'd ever heard. "Rick Leblanc. Who the fuck you think I'm talking about?"

Luke shrugged ignorantly. "Who's he?"

Youngblood started pacing aggressively across the living room floor, one five-foot-four twenty-year-old with a very bad attitude. "Some fucking motherfucker I'm going to fuck up."

"Oh, I see," Luke said, as if that had explained it all. "So what kind of message did he leave you, Mickey?"

Youngblood was on the move again, pushing past Luke, back into the kitchen, where he pulled the receiver off the hook. "You got to fucking listen to it." He punched in the numbers and handed the phone to Luke, who had followed him in.

Luke sighed and waited for the phone to pick up.

Suddenly, a high barrio Mexican-sounding voice appeared. "… This is Pistol Shooter. I'm the one who broke out your windows, you little dwarf. And this is just the beginning. You're fucking dead, you little midget. I know where your family lives. I know where you live. It doesn't matter where you go … And you better have a gat on you too. 'Cuz I'm coming over to get you. You're fucking dead, you little dwarf. And when I'm done with you, I'm going after your—"

Luke jerked the phone away from his ear, stunned.

"Can you believe that shit?" Youngblood said, hopping up and down angrily. "Can you fucking believe it?"

"No," Luke said. "Who was that?" Luke started to hang up when Youngblood yanked the phone out of his hand, hung it up, punched in several numbers, and handed it to Barbados, who'd just strolled through the doorway.

"That's totally fucked up, dude," Luke told Youngblood.

Youngblood ignored him and pushed back into the living room, where Zitelli was bonging out on the couch. When he finished, Zitelli handed Mickey the bong. Youngblood grabbed the bag of pot off the coffee table and loaded it.

"That's Rick Leblanc, all right," Barbados said a minute later, cradling a fistful of beers back into the living room. "Sounds like Ink Stain might have had a tad too much to drink."

Luke cast him an inquisitive eye as he took one of the beers.

"It's the nickname Mickey gave Rick Leblanc," Barbados said. "The dude's got tattoos like all over his body. More than even Ozzy Osbourne."

"That's a lot of tats," Luke said, this being more information than he really needed.

Barbados handed Youngblood a beer. Youngblood guzzled it down in one long swig.

"So there's something I don't understand," Luke said to Youngblood. "Why did he threaten you?"

Youngblood belched and said, "Because he owes me money."

Luke nodded but still didn't get it. It was usually the other way around. If someone owes you money, they shouldn't be the one doing the threatening. "He threatened you because he owes you money?"

"No, dickass. He threatened me because I tried to collect it."

Luke nodded, but his blank expression confirmed he still didn't get it.

"You know what I think?" Barbados said, handing Zitelli the last beer. "I think we should fuck his ass up. You know, teach him a lesson he'll never forget."

The room fell silent for a few minutes as everyone considered this. Youngblood flicked the lighter, and Luke, Barbados, and Zitelli watched in amazement as he knocked off six consecutive bongloads, without a breath in between. He was aqualung. When Mickey finished, his eyes were blood red, and he appeared calmer, which allowed everyone to relax—not.

"That's exactly what I was thinking," Youngblood said. "You with me?"

Barbados' bony fingers raked through his spiked raven hair. "Fucking aye."

They both looked over at Luke.

"Hey, guys." Luke tossed his hands in the air. "Don't look at me."

Youngblood handed Barbados the bong. "I am looking at you, dickwipe."

"I know you are, Mickey, but that's what I'm saying. Don't. I don't even know the guy."

Youngblood's face pinched like a prune. "So fucking what? The guy threatened me. What the fuck else you need to know?"

"I know, Mickey; that's what you said." Luke took the bong from Barbados and made a constipated expression. "Look, fuck him. You guys came out here to party, right? I mean, you didn't come all the way out here to fuck somebody up, did you? I mean, the whole purpose of tonight … the reason we made these plans last week was so we could make it a boys' night out. Go out and hook up with some bitches."

Barbados' head bobbed up and down. He was always into hooking up with bitches, girlfriend notwithstanding.

Youngblood's face puckered like he'd swallowed turpentine. "What the fuck's the matter with you, Luke? The guy fucking threatened to kill my family, and all you can think about is pussy?"

"Mickey, he didn't threaten to kill your family."

Youngblood threw his hands up furiously. "You heard the fucking message. What the fuck are you talking about? He told me he was going to kill me *and* my family. What the fuck you think I'm supposed to do?"

"Mickey, come on, man. Lighten up. He's probably just fucking with you. I'm sure he's not really going to do anything."

"The motherfucker already broke out my windows," Youngblood said. "He killed my dog and threatened my family. So I don't know what the fuck you're talking about."

"Whoa!" Luke said. "He killed your dog?"

"Yeah, motherfucker. What the fuck you think I'm talking about?"

"Zeus?" Luke asked. "He killed Zeus?"

"Yes!" Youngblood snapped the bong out of Luke's hand and hit it. He blew the smoke straight into Luke's face and said, "That's what I've been trying to tell you. He's fucking bad news. He's caused me a lot of fucking problems, and he needs to eat shit."

"Wow," Luke said. He looked stunned. He knew something had happened to the dog, but Mickey had never told him what it was, until now. Luke had loved Zeus almost as much as Mickey did. Youngblood had had him since he was a pup. But of course, the last time Luke had seen him, Zeus was the biggest, studliest Akita he'd ever seen. But he was dead now. How pathetic was that?

"I see why you're upset, Mickey," Luke said, absently picking at the cobra tattoo on his arm. "But it's not like he's going to come out here tonight and fuck with us. He's probably sitting at home waiting for you to make the first move. So fuck him. Let him just sit and wait. Let's not let him ruin our night. Let's go out and have some fun. That's what the plan was. That's what you guys are here for, right? What do you say, guys?" He glanced at the blank faces of Zitelli and Barbados.

Youngblood's gaze drifted over to Barbados, who nodded back while exhaling a string of gray smoke. He was game for anything Youngblood wanted.

Youngblood turned to Zitelli. "What about you, Zit?"

"I don't know, Mickey. I got a date tonight. I got to get back soon."

"Well, thanks for fucking telling me."

Zitelli's eyes dipped. "Sorry, Mick. I just didn't know we were going to be out here so late."

Youngblood's agitated eyes shifted back to Barbados. "What do you think, John?"

"Yeah, dude, to tell you the truth, I'm kinda burnt. Why don't we just do this tomorrow?"

Youngblood's gaze shot back over to Zitelli. Zit nodded. "I can do that. As long as it's in the afternoon."

Youngblood's little head bobbed as though his decision had finally been made. "All right, this is what we're going to do." He turned to Luke. "I don't feel like going to the party tonight either."

"Oh, dude …"

Youngblood quieted him with a wave of his hand. "Hear me out. Why don't you come on back to the Valley with us? We'll party the night down at my house. And then tomorrow we'll give Leblanc a little visit. And then we'll come back out and find some other party to go to."

Luke sighed as his arms folded across his chest.

"It'll be the Fourth of July, dude … fuck," Youngblood said. "There'll be parties everywhere. Didn't you say you had a friend down at the beach who was having a party tomorrow?"

Luke's lips parted and then closed. His head nodded slightly as he looked away.

"See, there'll be plenty of time to hook up with pussy tomorrow, dude. Come on—what do you say?" Youngblood gazed around at the others. "We'll fucking party it all down tomorrow."

Barbados and Zitelli nodded enthusiastically. Youngblood turned back to Luke. "How about it, Luke?"

Luke's head waggled. "Dude, it just doesn't make any sense. Why would you want to go near the guy? He's been causing you all these fucking problems. Why don't you just stay the fuck away from him? I don't get it."

Youngblood's emerald eyes nearly bored a hole through Luke's face. "Because the motherfucker owes me money."

Luke winced. "Well, what if he doesn't want to pay you?"

Youngblood turned to Barbados and Zitelli and laughed derisively. "Then I'll fucking shoot the bastard."

Chapter Three

When Luke opened the passenger's door to the white van in Mickey's driveway, the escaping rush of steamy air nearly blew his shorts off. He backed away and left the door open so the van could air out, and then he stepped over and kicked it back against the front fender. He pulled out a Mountain Red and lit it. As he inhaled, his eyes drew closed, and Luke could already feel the heat of the day enflaming him. It wasn't even noon yet, but the Valley felt like a blast furnace. Although he'd been back for only a night, he couldn't wait to get out of there, to get back home where the air was cool, where he could breathe.

The Valley was where Luke's family had originally settled and where he had grown up, yet there was something dead about the place to him now. His mom still lived there with her new family, and that was a good thing, because he'd always have a place to come back to if he ever needed it. But in a way, the Valley was all about Luke's past. His present now belonged to San Floripez, and who knew about the future?

He stomped out the cigarette on Mickey's asphalt drive and climbed into the passenger's seat. Although the air had cooled down, Luke's arm nearly melted when he leaned back against the scalding upholstery. He peeled himself off the seat, and settled back at a different angle and tried to avoid the burn.

Other than the fact that all his windows had been broken out, Youngblood's house actually looked pretty good. The lawn and flowerbeds were new, and the fence and house looked freshly painted. Luke was glad Mickey was selling the place, though, because he needed to get off to a fresh start in his life. Getting out of this place would be a good first step. They had come back last night around ten, with Youngblood still reeling about the Leblanc assault. He told Luke that Rick Leblanc was the reason he was selling the house in the first place. The guy had been harassing him for almost a year now, and Youngblood had to get away. That's why he had Bart Pray around all the time, to watch the place when he was gone.

Barty, as they liked to call him, was another one of Youngblood's buddies with whom they had all played Little League when they were kids. They were the same age, and although he wasn't as tall as Luke, Barty was much thicker. He was also one strange puppy. When the Red Stockings were playing, Barty would be lost out there at first base; his old man would sometimes show up for the games, and you could see there was something dead in the man's eyes as well, something that made you want to shove the look in a plastic bag and beat it with a shovel.

That's how Luke felt about Barty. He really didn't understand why Mickey didn't just fire his ass and send the clown packing. Youngblood was always bitching about Pray owing him money, yet the dude was always around. Mickey and the boys would be partying, and there would be Barty painting the fence, or pulling out weeds, or picking up beer bottles after everyone. The guy was totally a surly fuck, and Luke was glad he wasn't there now. But he knew Mickey had his reasons for keeping him around, those reasons being wrapped around the money Pray owed him.

Even stranger was the fact that Mickey had gone the whole night without mentioning the money Luke owed him. Normally Youngblood was tighter than a banker during foreclosure. Normally, he would never let Luke go a second without thinking he better get him paid off. Luke still owed him two thousand dollars toward the last pound he had fronted him, but Mickey hadn't said anything about it. What was up with that? He figured Youngblood was probably so preoccupied with moving—and with this Rick Leblanc thing—that he'd forgotten about the debt temporarily. But that wouldn't last long, and Luke really did want to get Mickey paid off as soon as possible. He didn't want to end up owing him forever like Barty did.

There was a knock on the back of the van, and Luke opened his eyes. He could hear the side door slide open, and John Barbados climbed in. The clock on the dashboard said it was a little past noon, and the hot August sun drilled through the front windshield like a burning laser. Luke felt like one of those bugs they used to set on fire with a magnifying glass when they were kids. It was probably karma getting back at him now. He was about ready to go back inside to see what was holding Mickey up, when he heard the front door slam shut.

"Move over," Mickey yelled as he traipsed down the front steps. "I want you to drive."

Luke thought Mickey was talking to Barbados, until he tossed Luke the car keys. Luke glanced at them dumbly in his hand. "Dude, I told you. I can't drive. My license is suspended."

Mickey acted like he didn't hear this. "Move over."

Mickey did the same thing last night when he tried to get Luke to drive back home from San Floripez. Then, Luke was stoned and weak and ultimately gave in to Youngblood's browbeating. Today, he had taken only a few bongloads and hadn't had more than two or three beers. He felt strong and wasn't about to let Mickey bully him again.

"I'm not driving, Mickey. You're not going to con me again."

Mickey leaned his squatty frame against the door. He had awakened this morning in his usual foul mood but had mellowed considerably since consuming thirteen bongloads and a half-sixer of beer in the first hour of his morning existence. His eyes were slanted, and Luke had to turn away from the glare ricocheting off his shaved head.

"You want a ride back to San Floripez, right?" Mickey's tone was mellow and stoned.

Luke wondered what the catch was. "Yeah."

"Then you're gonna have to drive. Now move over."

Luke frowned at his friend. "Mickey, I can't. My license is suspended. I don't want to go back to jail. Why don't you drive?"

Youngblood threw up his hands. "Dude, because I'm way too fucked up. Okay? You gotta drive."

It was the same lame-assed excuse Youngblood had given him last night, Luke being lame enough to go for it then—as if he were immune to DUIs or something—but not this time. He folded his arms across his chest. His head was shaking.

"Look, man," Youngblood said sharply, "if you want a ride home, you're going to drive."

Luke laughed at him as if he were nuts. But Youngblood wasn't laughing. If they were gambling, Luke would have bet the house that Mickey wasn't bluffing either. But then again, neither was he.

"Mickey, it's daytime. There's going to be cops everywhere. I just can't take a chance, dude. They'd put me in jail. Have John drive. He's got a license." Luke glimpsed over his shoulder. "You got a license, don't you, John?"

A Cheshire cat grin bit at the edges of Barbados' mouth. *Guess not.*

"Fine ... fuck it," Youngblood said, the mellowness suddenly drained from his voice. He yanked the keys out of Luke's hand and tossed them back to Barbados. "You drive."

Barbados smiled skeptically. "All right, boss. Whatever you say." He climbed over the console and up into the driver's seat.

Youngblood slid the side door shut and faced Luke. "Fine, you don't want to drive, then get the fuck out."

Luke blinked at him incredulously. "Excuse me?"

"You heard me." Youngblood yanked the passenger-side door handle, but it was locked. "Let's go. Unlock it. Quit wasting my fucking time."

Luke's head shook in disbelief. "Fine, dude ... whatever." He unlocked the door and started to climb into the back.

"No!" Youngblood shouted. "Get the fuck out."

Luke straddled the center console, one leg in back and one leg still up front. "What? I'm getting in back."

Youngblood scrambled over and quickly slid the side door open. Luke was already in back. "Come on," Youngblood demanded. "Get the fuck out."

Luke squatted down on the black futon in back. "What, Mickey? You're not going to leave me here."

"I told you, dickass. You want to go back to San Floripez, you drive. If not, you can fucking hoof it. Now get the fuck out."

Luke searched Mickey's eyes for the humor in them, but they were blank. "Mickey, I'm not walking home."

"I don't care what you do," Youngblood said, his thumb stabbing over his shoulder, the umpire calling Luke out. "Just get the fuck out of the van."

"Fine," Luke said, holding his palm open to Barbados. "You wanna be like that? Fine. Give me the keys. I'll drive." He reached for the keys.

Barbados squeezed his hand around the keys. He wasn't giving them up.

"Nope," Youngblood said. "Too fucking late."

Luke turned to Barbados. "Give me the keys, John. I'm driving."

Barbados' shoulders stiffened. "Sorry, dude."

"Get the fuck out," Youngblood said. "I'm not fucking around, Luke. I gave you a chance and asked you to drive. But you didn't want to, so get the fuck out."

Luke's head shook despondently, and then he climbed out of the van. Youngblood slid the side door closed and climbed into the passenger's seat. He shut the door and locked it, with attitude.

Luke just stood there on the hot asphalt, long in face, the sun blistering the back of his neck. What was he going to do now? His folks were still out of town, and it wasn't like any of his friends owned cars to even be able to pick him up if he called them. An empty betrayal gnarled his stomach, the same feeling he had as a kid when his mom spanked him. He moved into the shade and took a seat on the front steps. He was about to contemplate the seriousness of his plight, when he looked up and noticed Barbados sitting in the driver's seat, laughing his ass off. When Luke glanced over, Mickey was doing the same thing.

"You ready to go, ass-wipe?" Youngblood's mouth was sheathed in a sarcastic grin. He tossed Luke the keys, which bounced off his shin with a loud thud. As Luke leaned over to rub his shin, he picked up the keys and rediscovered his ability to laugh at Youngblood's lame-assed sense of humor.

✻   ✻   ✻   ✻

Luke Ridnaur blew west down Bradford in the white van at forty-five MPH, when Youngblood blurted out, "Take a right." Luke knew Zit lived off Triangle Drive, or at least he had the last time they partied at his house, which was about two weeks ago, but before he could confirm this with Youngblood, Mickey yelled at him again.

"I said right, motherfucker, are you deaf?"

No motherfucker, I'm not deaf, Luke thought but did not say. Instead, he spun the wheel sharply to the right, and the van lunged into a screeching, ball bearing-busting right turn through the intersection that had Barbados and all the shit in back tumbling assholes over teakettles to the left side of the van. Youngblood flew across the center console and nearly landed in Luke's lap. Luke straightened the wheel, barely avoiding the curb, and missed the little girl carrying the grocery bag on the bike by at least six inches before continuing down Ferndale. Youngblood hurled a string of expletives at him that would've made the *Goodfellas* blush. When he had finished, Luke compliantly asked, "Aren't we going to pick up Zit?"

"Take a left up here," Youngblood said pointing.

Luke did as he was told. He continued to follow Youngblood's directions, although he felt the way Bart Pray looked most of the time: totally confused. He had no idea where Youngblood was taking them. He had never driven down these streets before.

The quality of the neighborhood had changed dramatically in the last couple of blocks. Rather than the usual array of rundown paint-chipped houses, chop shops, and strip malls that typified the new Valley, they had suddenly journeyed upon a densely forested neighborhood lined with dead end cul-de-sacs, winding broad avenues, and freshly painted two-story homes surrounded by verdant lawns. Every corner had a lush park with swings and picnic tables and sandboxes for the kids to play in. Most driveways were filled with brand-new sedans or shiny new motor homes or both. Luke wondered when they had entered Oz. As he slowed for a stop sign, he could feel the moist heat of decay breathing down the back of his neck. He glanced over his shoulder and found himself face to face with John Barbados' crooked smile.

He returned the smile and twisted back to face the road, when something caught the corner of his eye, causing his brain to pause. He spun the gray matter into rewind and attempted to revisualize what it was he had just seen. When the composite sketch assembled completely in his mind, his heart skipped a beat. He turned back quickly a second time and noticed, on the floor beneath Barbados' feet, Youngblood's green duffel bag. Luke knew from Youngblood showing it off to him a million times that the bag contained his AB-10 assault pistol. Luke could feel his heart hammering inside his chest. What was Youngblood planning to do with the machine gun in the bag on the floor? Then he remembered being stoned out of his mind last night. And Youngblood telling him they were going to visit Rick Leblanc first thing this morning before picking Zitelli up. No wonder Mickey had sounded so anxious to have Luke drive. *Fuck that.*

When Luke took a longer glance back, he noticed that Youngblood's Winchester twelve-gauge shotgun with the pistol grip lay in Barbados' lap, and he was loading it. On the floor next to him rested the black vinyl top case that Youngblood kept his Colt AR 15-A2 semiautomatic rifle in.

Luke clutched the cramp in his side and breathed in deeply. He wanted to scream but instead glanced over, about to ask Youngblood what was up with all the guns in back, when he received the third-biggest surprise of his morning: Youngblood stroking his HK .40 semiautomatic pistol like a kitten in his lap. Luke's chest tightened like a frozen rubber. He had no idea what the fuck was going on, but whatever it was, he didn't like it. He knew Youngblood liked to keep guns around his house for protection, and with the tonnage of pot Mickey unloaded out of the place, that made perfect sense.

The man had to defend himself, his home, and his business.

Luke also knew Mickey carried the handgun on his person for self-protection. He'd done so ever since getting into a fight at the Flyntridge Mall over a territorial dispute with a couple teenage gangsta-wannabes. Luke had even gone out with Mickey and his girlfriend and seen him give her the gun to store in her purse for safekeeping, which she did willingly. In Mickey's line of work, and with the kind of cash he liked to carry around, there was always potential for violence, so Luke considered that smart business as well.

What bothered him now, though, was the fact that the shotgun and machine gun and assault rifle were no longer under Youngblood's bed, which was now in storage, but in Barbados' hands in the back seat. And to make matters worse, Youngblood held his pistol up front with itchy fingers and seemed on the verge of wanting to use it. Luke knew there had to be a very simple explanation; he just couldn't think of what it might be. He felt pretty certain that a daylight armed robbery would not look good on his resume, so he decided to find out what the hell was going on.

"Yo, Mickey, what's up with all the guns, dude?"

Youngblood's determined eyes bore straight ahead. "Don't worry about it."

Luke slapped both hands on the wheel, trying to stay calm. "No, Mickey, I'm sorry, but I am going to worry about it. I'm the one who's driving. And I know for a fact those guns have no place at my friend's Fourth of July party. So will somebody please tell me what the fuck's going on, before I have a heart attack?"

Youngblood said nothing, and Barbados sat expressionless in the back. Thanks to Mickey's excessive bragging, Luke knew the AB-10 carried anywhere from ten to fifty rounds, with the AR 15 having a twenty-round magazine, with fifteen more for the shotgun. Add to that Mickey's handgun, and that was a helluva lot of lead. "What the hell's going on, guys!" Luke screamed. "Will somebody please tell me?"

"Why are you yelling?" Youngblood asked calmly.

Luke lowered his voice. "Because, I want to know why I'm driving around with all these guns in the car, Mick. What's going on?"

Youngblood signaled for Luke to make another left. "Because everyone knows Rick Leblanc is a fucking pussy who has to carry a gun. And so does his little Nazi butt-buddy who's always hanging around him."

Luke slowed at the stop sign and tried the math in his head. He still couldn't solve the riddle. "Mickey, what're you going to do, shoot the motherfucker in broad daylight?"

"If I have to."

Luke groaned miserably, as Barbados leaned up between the seats. "We gotta do something to neutralize that animal, dude."

Luke turned away from Barbados' chorizo and tequila breath. Mickey's plan had been to exact revenge against Rick Leblanc "tit for tat," whatever that meant. The problem was, nobody knew where Leblanc lived. Leblanc used to live with his parents but had moved out over a month ago. Since they had no idea where he had moved to, they would start by driving by and breaking out his parents' windows. And then just sorta go from there.

But nobody said anything about guns.

It was now obvious to Luke that Mickey had brought the guns for protection in case Leblanc either happened to be there or showed up, catching them in the act. Either way, they'd be ready.

"Look, Mickey, maybe we should just forget about this, okay."

Youngblood snarled. "No, motherfucker, we ain't forgettin' about shit. The fucker owes me money. And he threatened my family! Fuck him. I'm going to get my money from that cocksucker. And when I do, I'm going to make sure he threatens nobody's family again."

It still made no sense. It was broad daylight. It was Rick Leblanc's parents' house, for God's sake. Mickey wasn't even sure Leblanc would be there. Besides, someone was sure to recognize either them or the van. This was a bad idea at the wrong time of the day, no matter how you looked at it. As the van approached the intersection, the light changed to yellow, and Luke punched it. The van entered the intersection with plenty of time to spare, until Youngblood's face twisted and he yelled, "Take a left."

The light changed to red as Luke cut the wheel hard. Tires screeched. Rubber burned. Bodies flew, and the blast from the shotgun nearly blew Luke's eardrum apart.

The hole in the ceiling was about eight inches in diameter, and right above the driver's seat. Luke's first thought was one of weighted relief that it had been the ceiling with the hole in it and not his head. He couldn't remember his second thought because of the severe ringing in his ear.

Youngblood had nearly jumped out of his seat. He cussed so loudly and incoherently—strands of saliva flying everywhere—that it was nearly impossible to figure out what he was saying. Luke could tell he wasn't pleased, though. He could make out bits and parts, like how Youngblood was going to have to "fix the fucking van" and how "you should fucking pay for it."

"Fuck that," Luke said attitudinally. "John's the one playing around with the guns. If anyone pays for it, he should."

Barbados slid up between the seats, his face a frown of displeasure, but Luke didn't care. He was tired of fucking with it. As far as he was concerned, he was ready to jump ship right now. Mickey could go on his little witch hunt without Luke; he just didn't give a shit. And it was then, at that very second, with Luke thinking of pulling over and bailing on everyone, with Youngblood screaming at the top of his little lungs about "the goddamned hole in the goddamned roof," with Barbados looking as if he wanted to put another hole in someone or something, that Youngblood again nearly jumped out of his seat.

"Isn't that Rick Leblanc's little brother?"

Chapter Four

Sunday—12:40 p.m.

"I don't know," Luke said, glancing over to see whom Youngblood was talking about. "I don't know Rick Leblanc's little brother."

"That's him," Youngblood squealed excitedly. "Pull over."

"For what?"

"Just pull over." Youngblood craned his neck to see the kid they had just passed. "Pull the fucking van over."

Luke checked his side view mirror, and pulled the van over. They had overshot the kid by a quarter block. The big yellow sign for Grant Market stood out a half block up on the corner of Splintura. Luke waited for traffic to pass, and he kicked it into reverse. As he backed up, he could see the kid walking on the sidewalk next to a white cinderblock wall. He was just a kid, no more than sixteen, wearing jeans, a flannel shirt, and wavy black hair, and for a second, Luke thought he recognized him.

When Luke stopped, Youngblood turned to him. "Get out and help me grab him."

Luke studied the side view mirror, all the traffic driving by in both directions. He rotated to Youngblood. "No, dude, I'm not jumping out and helping you grab him."

Youngblood huffed increduously, and pushed the passenger's door open. He jumped out and then started hopping around on the sidewalk like a kid who had just had his bicycle stolen. "Beat him up. Beat the kid up," he shouted frantically.

Problem was, Youngblood was the only one outside the van, and the kid looked as if he were about to take off. In back, Barbados was having a helluva time, repeatedly heaving his shoulder into the side door, but he couldn't get it open. He yelled for Youngblood to let him out. Youngblood whirled and yelled at the kid, "Don't run," and then he ran back to open the side door.

The kid looked away and turned off sprinting. Luke thought about doing the same. Instead, he jumped out of the van and yelled, "Hey, man, don't run."

The kid slowed to a brisk strut but kept moving in the opposite direction. Youngblood finally got the side door open, and Barbados jumped out. They sprinted up the sidewalk, and the kid started to run. But the speedy Youngblood caught him a quarter block later and took him down hard with a vicious horse-collar tackle. And there, on the concrete sidewalk, next to the white cinder-block wall and beneath the boiling sun, all the world witnessed Mickey Young-blood and John Barbados beat the hell out of Bobby Leblanc. The kid could only roll into a ball and groan, as he defended himself against the assault of punches and kicks to the body and head.

Out of breath, Youngblood then reached down and yanked the kid up by his shirt, flannel tearing in hands, buttons popping everywhere, and he threw him against the wall. "Your brother owes me money. Where the fuck is he?"

The kid's eyes filled with unbridled terror. "I don't know."

"I know he used to live with you. Where does he live now?"

"I don't even like my brother," the kid said. "I have no idea."

"Bullshit." Youngblood punched him in the shoulder with a thwop.

The kid yipped. "I swear to God, Mickey, I have no idea where he lives."

Youngblood grabbed the kid by the shoulders and shook him. He barked in his face, demanding the whereabouts of Rick Leblanc. But the answer remained the same. The kid had no idea where his brother was.

"Fuck me," Youngblood screamed as he pushed the kid to the ground.

"Now what?" Barbados asked.

Luke wondered the same thing. From the sidewalk, he could see cars driving by, cars with people in them, any one of which could pick up their cell phone and dial the police. From the left, Luke noted a particular light blue truck approaching slowly, and he crouched down near the front of the van. He nearly wet himself when he glanced up and made eye contact with the female driver as she passed. He rotated quickly. As the the truck sped away, he ducked his head into the crook of his arm, sprinted around the side of the van, and hustled back inside. He knew this place was way too busy to conduct this type of business from, but how did you tell that to Mickey Youngblood?

Youngblood must have been thinking the same thing, because he studied the traffic intently. After a couple irritable seconds, he turned to Barbados. "Throw him in the van."

Without hesitation, Barbados pulled the kid up off the ground by his shirt and pushed him toward the van.

"Your brother owes me money," Youngblood yelled; fire hydrant legs pumping feverishly to keep up with the kid's long strides. "So get your ass in the van."

Youngblood tried grabbing the kid by the scruff of the neck, but he pulled away. "I'm going, I'm going."

When they reached the side of the van, the kid started to climb in, but Barbados grabbed him by the shirt, and threw him in headfirst. Inside, the kid bounced hard against Youngblood's black futon. Youngblood climbed in behind him, his once-white T-shirt now stained dark yellow. "I'm not fucking around. Your brother owes me money. We're going to call him right now. What's his number?"

"I don't know," the kid cried. "I'm telling you, I have no idea what his number is. He comes by sometimes. We party, but that's it. It's not like we hang out together or nothin'. I have no idea where he is."

"How can you not know where your brother lives?"

"I know. Isn't it crazy? But I don't." The kid sat there shaking like a field of beaten corn.

"Fuck." Youngblood rabbit-punched the back of the passenger's seat. He crawled back out of the van and started pacing aggressively up the sidewalk.

Heavy Sunday Fourth of July traffic flew by in both directions, up and down Oleander. The sun continued to boil the van, and Luke just wanted to get out of there.

Barbados moved toward Youngblood. "Dude, why don't you just knee him in the head or something? You know, maybe it'll help joggle his memory."

Youngblood glanced over at the kid as if he were considering it. And Luke wanted to slam his own head off the steering wheel. What was Youngblood thinking? "Mickey, this is not what we came here for," he yelled out the passenger's window. "Your gripe is against Rick Leblanc, not his kid brother. Let's get out of here before the fucking cops come."

Youngblood cut Luke a glare but said nothing. He just stood there, studying the traffic, the sun bouncing off his shiny forehead and right into Luke's eyes.

Luke turned away and glanced back at the vibrating kid. "Jesus, Mickey, look at him. He's scared to death."

Youngblood stepped back over to the van and peered inside. What he saw was a shuddering teenager. A kid who looked and acted as if he were about to be executed. Youngblood climbed in and kneeled beside him. "Look, if I let you go, you better not go to the fucking police."

The kid's head shook wildly. "I swear to God I won't say anything."

Youngblood slapped the kid across his leg. "That's not what I said. Listen to me. I said, 'Don't go to the police.'"

"I won't, I swear."

"If I let you go …" Youngblood's voice lowered several decibels. "This is what I want you to do. I want you to find your assmite brother, and I want you to give him a message."

The kid swallowed nervously. "What do you want me to tell him?"

"Shut up, and I'll tell you."

The kid nodded as Barbados climbed in the van and slid past Youngblood, taking a seat next to the futon.

Youngblood continued. "I want you to tell Rick that we need to resolve this mess."

The kid looked at him quizzically.

"Don't worry about it," Youngblood said. "He'll know what I'm talking about."

The kid's chest rose and fell. "Okay."

"I don't want you to tell anybody else. Not a fucking soul, you understand?"

The kid nodded.

"You fucking tell anyone, and your brother's deadfuckingmeat. You understand me? I will have no fucking mercy on his ass." The kid's head bobbed, and a beatific smile bled across Youngblood's face. "Good."

The message had been sent, and Luke breathed easier with the realization that all would be well. Youngblood had scared the kid, and they would now let him go. The kid would go home and tell his brother what had happened. He would show Rick Leblanc how all-merciful Mickey Youngblood could be. The kid would tell his brother to settle things up with Mickey, and everything would be resolved without any bloodshed. How hunky-dory could it be?

Not very, because the very next second John Barbados took matters into his own hands by jamming the black barrel of Mickey's shotgun into the kid's ear. "You wanna fucking die?"

The kid's head waggled and his facial expression filled with the horror of one coming face to face with his own mortality.

"Then tell us where your fucking brother is, now."

Youngblood glared at Barbados like a man filled with malice aforethought. "What the fuck are you doing, John?"

"I think he's lying. I think he knows where his brother is."

"Who the fuck told you to think?"

Barbados' shoulders slumped. "I just thought we could, you know, find his brother. Get everything settled now."

"Shut the fuck up, will ya, John? When I want your fucking help, I'll ask for it."

Luke noticed a trail of moist sorrow trickling down the side of the the kid's face. The gun to the ear had to hurt, but the kid looked too scared to say anything. Youngblood seemed to notice it too, because he carefully placed his hand around the barrel of the shotgun, and pulled it away from the kid's head before nearly harpooning it through Barbados' chest.

"Real fucking smart, John. Now what the fuck am I going to do? He tells his brother we put a fucking gun to his head, what the fuck you think he's gonna do? Huh?"

Barbados turned away like a red-faced man with no good answers.

And Mickey was clueless as to what he was going to do. A second ago, he had been riding high with expectation. He'd seen the kid on the street and had visions of sugarplums dancing in his head. Mickey had known for a fact that the kid held the key to getting to Rick Leblanc, but now he wasn't so sure. It's one thing to beat a kid up to send a message home to his brother. At worst, what would Rick Leblanc do? Come and beat Mickey up? Hell, Ink Stain already wanted to do that—and much worse. The guy had flown over the edge when Mickey tried to collect some of his debt from Leblanc's fiancée. So Mickey could only imagine what the animal would do now, knowing that not only had his kid brother been beaten up, but he had had a shotgun buried in his ear tied to a threat to blow his fucking head off. *Nice work, John.*

Youngblood's inclination was to still let the kid go. Pin a warning to his lapel, and watch to see what happened. He knew he had to resolve things with Leblanc one way or another, and maybe this would bring the closure that he sought to the nightmare relationship.

Then again, maybe not.

They had been going at each other for almost a year now, with Leblanc exhibiting no sign whatsoever of backing off. And Mickey knew the guy wouldn't until he taught Leblanc a lesson he would feel all the way through his thick fucking skull. Mickey also knew he'd never have better leverage than he had right now in bringing the animal to stand for all the bullshit he'd been doing, because Rick Leblanc was the kind of guy who left very little room for maneuvering. Since Mickey had befriended him, Leblanc had ripped him off, reported him to the insurance company for insurance fraud, killed his dog, threatened his family, and broken his windows—all over a simple fucking drug debt.

But the weird part was—they used to be great friends. Maybe not best friends, but when Rick Leblanc wasn't stoned out of his mind, he could actually be a pretty fun guy to be around. He had a great sense of humor and loved to party, two qualities Mickey greatly admired in a man. Mickey could remember the first night they had partied together, sitting around his kitchen table pounding brews, when Leblanc got up and pulled out these two huge rocks of crack. The beer and pot party suddenly turned into crackhead city, and they had a blast.

"I could use someone like you," Mickey had told him.

But who couldn't? Rick Leblanc was as rough-and-tumble as they came. A street thug with no conscience, a man who feared no one and nothing. In turn, he needed someone like Mickey Youngblood—the Mac Daddy dope dealer who lived the kind of rich lifestyle Rick had always dreamed of having for himself. Besides, he had burned every other dope dealer in the Valley and needed a new bud connection. By the weekend, Leblanc had practically moved in.

Mickey had a full gym built in his house, and that's how they started spending their days: taking supplements, pumping iron, and peddling pot. With Mickey supplying him, Leblanc started pushing from one to three pounds a week in no time. Mickey's old man would come up with his usual inventory of between twenty-five to fifty pounds, and Leblanc would be on top of Mickey, moving it almost as fast as it came in. When Leblanc needed more, Mickey would just truck it on down to his dad's place, which was just a few blocks away, and be back with more stash in no time. It was a foolproof scheme from which they were both getting rich, only Mickey was getting much richer than Rick, and all it seemed to do was make Leblanc jealous.

Leblanc started coming over with this strange attitude, and Mickey started noticing shit missing from his house. Like his dope. One day he pulled a couple pounds out for a buyer, when one of them came up missing. No one had been in the house except for Leblanc, who of course denied knowing anything about it. But Mickey knew Rick was the only one who had access to it. He accused Leblanc of stealing from him, and Leblanc just told him to go fuck himself. This put Mickey in a bad way emotionally, and he started getting edgy with everyone he dealt with.

His dad would come over and ask: "What the fuck's your problem?" Mickey's dad never did like Leblanc. And he wanted to know why Mickey continued to hang around such a scumbag. He told Mickey that he should "get rid of the leech." And Mickey had finally found something he could agree with his old man about.

But he still had to get his money. He still had to deal with the fact Leblanc had threatened him and brought the shit straight to his house. He had personalized their ordeal by totally disrespecting Mickey; by trying to destroy the place where Mickey had once allowed him to live. And then he had the gall to threaten Mickey's family.

Motherfuck Rick Leblanc!

Mickey had a twelve-year-old brother of his own to think about. There was no way he would take a chance of allowing Leblanc to hurt him or his family; that's why he had to bring it all to an end. That's why he had to do it now. That's why he had to find Rick Leblanc. But Mickey knew he had to be careful. The kid was a Leblanc, after all. And like pit bulls and cheap whores, they could be fun to play with, but if they turned on you, you could be dead.

"Just let him go, Mickey," Luke said, yanking Youngblood out of the Doldrums.

"Shut the fuck up," Mickey said with resolve. He knew what he had to do. And letting the kid go was not the answer.

Chapter Five

Sunday—12:53 p.m.

Luke punched it all the way through Bentworth with a hot piercing wind whistling through the hole in the roof, searing the side of his neck. When he reached Ajax Canyon, he turned left and pulled up to the guard kiosk. A roly-poly guard stepped out of the booth, and Luke told him they were there to see Hank Zitelli. The guard checked the name against his list and then stuck an ID card inside on the van's dashboard. The wrought iron gate slid open, and the guard waved them through.

Hank Zitelli lived with his parents at their eleven-acre ranch-style home. The house sat atop a jagged precipice overlooking the entire Valley. An eighth of a mile driveway separated Zitelli's house from the main gated community thoroughfare. Since Zit's old man hated Barbados, due to all the dumb-assed trouble John had gotten himself into, Luke had to park the van at the bottom of the drive. When Youngblood jumped out, he slammed the door shut and then leaned back inside the window. He told Luke and Barbados to see if they could, "Try not to fuck anything else up while I'm gone, huh."

As Luke watched Mickey sweating profusely and walking up the hill, the three of them sat there baking like a soufflé at the bottom of Zit's driveway. Luke and Barbados twice met each other's intense gaze, then turned away without saying a word, just like a couple little bitches. Which was exactly what Luke felt like—a little bitch—for letting Youngblood get him into this situation in the first place. But of course, he didn't say that to Mickey, and look where it had gotten him. Barbados didn't say shit either. He just ran around licking Mickey's ass and doing whatever Youngblood told him to do. He chased and beat the kid, threw him in the van, and then nearly impaled his head with the shotgun.

Luke couldn't believe how his life had changed in an instant. One second he's all happy and shit, driving his buddies to a killer Fourth of July party, eagerly anticipating a fun afternoon of partying and skirt chasing. And the next thing he knows, Mickey and Barbados are out pounding some kid senseless on the street. What a fucking mood killer. The kid then gets his ass tossed in the van, and Youngblood yells at Luke, "Let's get the fuck out of here."

Luke was like, "Yeah, right," and he kicked the van into gear. He couldn't get out of there fast enough. His arm flew out the window and he cut into traffic. He headed straight down Oleander, when the kid leaned up next to him, grinning his ass off.

"Hey, bro, you left Mickey back there."

Luke's heart congealed. He glanced in the passenger-side mirror and saw Youngblood back where he'd left him in the middle of the street, his arms flailing frantically, screaking his head off. Luke grimaced and slammed on the brakes and kicked it into reverse. Laying rubber skid marks, he shot back to where Youngblood was going crazy. When Mickey climbed in, he looked like he wanted to asphyxiate Luke. "You fucking idiot."

Which was exactly how Luke felt now as he gazed back and saw the kid leaning peaceably against the futon with his eyes closed. They had met late last year, although at the time Luke had had no idea who the kid was. Luke had been staying at his mom's house and was over at a mutual friend's birthday party, when he and the kid just started talking. They went out into the back yard, smoked cigs and pounded brews, and talked about their favorite bands. They both pretty much liked the same kind of music, and Luke thought it was totally cool when the kid told him his favorite band was *Killer Pussy.*

Luke loved *Killer Pussy.* And he knew right away that he was going to like this kid. Later that night, they started wrestling around with some other kids under the Christmas tree. It was an evening filled with innocence, and a fun time was had by all. Now the poor kid just sat there quietly next to Barbados, drenched in sweat and probably wondering what the hell he had gotten himself into.

Luke leaned back and closed his eyes tightly. He pressed his fingers to his temples and began vibrating his fingertips. He tried to imagine where all of this was taking him. All he wanted to do was turn the kid loose, go party down at his friend's house for the Fourth of July, and get on with his life. He hoped that Mickey was right now up at Zit's using the time to somehow get ahold of Rick Leblanc. Luke prayed that they would soon leave and be on their way to meet the kid's brother, to resolve things, to end this ordeal. Then they could go to the party and relax. They could get stoned out of their fucking minds, and do whatever they wanted to do.

When Luke's eyes flipped open a minute later, his hopes and prayers disintegrated like Nagasaki. He cringed as he watched Youngblood and Zit bouncing down the driveway, Zit carrying a blue bottle of gin in one hand and a roll of duct tape in the other.

A minute later, the side door to the van kicked open, and Zitelli stuck his head inside. "Let's party, dudes—doggito style!" He said it way too loudly; his elbows jamming into his sides like a man who had just scored sweetly—and everybody just looked away.

Hank Zitelli was a smart-looking twenty-year-old with light brown hair cut short on the sides. He wore Jesus sandals, a neon yellow bathing suit that rode down to thick hairy calves, and an unbuttoned Hawaiian shirt that was loud enough to blind you. His swimming blue eyes scanned the dull blue-gray of the van's interior.

The late-eighties cargo van had more rips in the cheap plastic upholstery than a ghetto whore's stockings. It had the side door and the doors in the very back for loading and unloading. There was no rearview mirror, only the two side mirrors. The back was crammed with a bunch of Youngblood's shit from moving. There were boxes and bags of clothes and the long black futon that Bobby Leblanc leaned against. Next to him rested the stack of blankets John Barbados used to hide the guns under.

Barbados and the kid slid over, giving Zit some room. The first thing Zitelli did after squeezing in was snigger at the hole in the roof.

"Don't ask," Luke said, and he wasn't laughing.

Zit's stupid grin flipped immediately upon surveying the long faces next to him. "Damn, dudes, who died?"

Youngblood climbed in behind him and crouched down in front of the kid. He held his hand out to Zitelli, who gave him five. Youngblood punched Zit in the chest with a loud thwack. Zitelli gasped and grappled his chest.

"Give me the fucking tape," Youngblood demanded.

Zit sucked in deeply and handed Youngblood the tape. Youngblood unrolled a six-inch section and ripped it off with his teeth. He started to lift it toward the kid's face, when the kid suddenly jerked his head back.

"Hey, man, you don't have to do that," Bobby Leblanc said. "I promise I won't say anything."

"Not a fucking chance," Youngblood said, slapping the tape across the kid's mouth, shutting him up, telling him he didn't want to hear shit from him until they found his brother.

"He said he's not going to say anything," Luke interjected. "Don't tape him up." Youngblood laser-beamed Luke an irritable look, but Luke acted like he didn't care. This shit was getting serious. But he knew you always had to be careful with the way you dealt with Mickey Youngblood. One misspoken word could send the dude off on one of his famous tangents. Taking the edge out of his voice, Luke said, "Take the tape off him, Mickey. He won't cause us any problems. I know him."

The kid gave Youngblood a tape smile of confirmation.

Youngblood scowled.

Zit frowned at Youngblood. Barbados did the same thing; everyone giving Mickey his best "What are you going to do now, asshole?" look.

And it pissed Youngblood off to no end. "Fuck you guys," he said.

Then he reached out and ripped the tape off the kid's mouth, causing Bobby to yelp like a beaten dog. His hand shot instantly to his mouth, attempting to soothe the sting.

"You fucking say anything …" Youngblood said, finger stabbing into the kid's bony chest. "I mean a fucking word, and you're dead—you understand me?"

Bobby nodded submissively. Youngblood then scurried back out of the van and shut the side door.

This time, Luke waited for Mickey to climb back inside before taking off. He then drove down to Triangle Drive, where Youngblood told him to catch the 203 north. "We're going to San Floripez."

Luke shook his head as if he didn't hear him right. "What the fuck we gonna do in San Floripez with a hostage, Mickey?"

"Just go," Youngblood spat disgustedly.

As Luke started to accelerate, he heard Barbados cry out from the back, "Shit guys, I forgot my medication." Youngblood twisted and cut him a loathsome glare, and Barbados shrugged apologetically.

Youngblood turned to Luke with the same abhorrent expression. "Turn around."

Which is what Luke did. And they shot back through Ajax Canyon and caught the 589 west to Mineral Valley. When they arrived at Barbados' parents' house, he hopped out and ran inside to grab his heart pills, something he took twice a day to stay alive. Two minutes later, he was back in the van, and they headed north.

It was an oven outside, with everybody roasting in dead silence inside. But things quickly heated up at the bottleneck in Linderbilt, where they were now stuck in standstill traffic.

"Your brother's a fucking snitch," Youngblood blurted out of the blue, corkscrewing in his seat, waking everybody up. His eyes were enflamed as he yelled: "He wants to threaten my family? He thinks he's going to fucking kill my family! He wants to fuck me over! He wants to break my fucking windows out ...!"

Luke sighed and wished Youngblood would throw on another record. Mickey had been ranting nonstop ever since they picked up the kid, and Luke was tired of hearing it. He was happy to see the kid playing it cool, though, just sitting there, his chin dug deep in his chest, with the up-from-under look of a puppy being scolded. "I'm sorry for what my brother did. My parents will pay for your windows, Mickey, I swear."

Youngblood snorted. "Your parents aren't going to pay for shit. The motherfucker threatened my family. Who the fuck's going to pay for that?"

The kid had no good reply.

"I'm going to get every fucking cent that snitch owes me." The kid looked sad and lost and just sat there, quietly acting the part of the bad puppy, while Youngblood got it out of his system. "And what about your fucking dad?"

Bobby's ears perked straight up at Youngblood. His mouth hesitated, and then he spoke up anyway. "What about him?"

"He's a fag, isn't he?" Youngblood roared and spread his arms as if that were national news. "The guy was a fucking faggot gymnast in high school. His event was the little faggot rings, right?" Youngblood's voice turned feminine and mocking. "Ooh, Olympic rings, how macho. Your old man's nothing but a big fucking pussy just like your brother."

Bobby glared at Youngblood furiously, and Youngblood didn't appreciate it one bit. "Yeah, what's the fucking look about, dude? You want it knocked off your face?"

Bobby swallowed the look, but not his words. "That's my dad you're talking about."

Youngblood's nostrils flared. "Yeah, and he's a big fucking faggot just like your brother!"

Bobby's uneasy gaze shifted over to Barbados and then to Zit. They both looked away.

"Your brother's going to pay me my fucking money," Youngblood continued. "And you're going to stay with us until he does. And if you try fucking around for a second, I'll break your fucking teeth. Do you understand?" Bobby frowned. "I said, do you understand?"

Bobby's head shook disgustedly. He again peered over at Barbados and then to Zit. This time they both glared right back with pleading eyes that appeared to say, "Just answer the little man, placate him, shut his ass up for the moment, please."

So Bobby did, by twisting back to Youngblood and nodding his acquiescence.

Mickey's arms folded across his chest in placation. He faced forward in his seat, finally appearing to be on the verge of relaxation, when suddenly his little body twisted in a knot, and his mouth formed this raged arc as if he were going to yell something else at the kid, and then he froze, as if unexpectedly confused by the thick gold ring centered with a huge black stone on Bobby's left hand. "Gimme that."

Bobby glanced around curiously.

"The ring. Gimme the fuckin' ring."

Bobby folded his right hand over the ring, as if to hide it.

"Don't make me come back there and get it."

"I can't," Bobby whined. "It's a family heirloom."

Youngblood looked like he was about to pounce on the kid.

"Please don't," Bobby pleaded, eyes beginning to water. "You can have anything else you want. It's just that, you know, my brother gave it to me on my birthday. And my father gave it to him on his birthday. And, and my father's father gave it to him on his fifteenth birthday. And so it's like, it's been passed down through my family for a long time. And I ... I even sleep with it on. So please don't make me take it off."

Youngblood smirked mordantly. "Give me a fucking quarter, and I'll call someone who gives a fuck. Okay? Now gimme the fucking ring."

Bobby's jaw trembled in defiance. And Youngblood nearly tore the seat off when he leapt into the back. He punched Bobby with such ferocity it echoed throughout the van. Bobby grabbed his chest and groaned as if he'd been shot. He rolled onto his back and kicked his size fourteens out in self-defense. Youngblood grimaced and punched the kid's leg and feet repeatedly. But Bobby was relentless. His lips quivered and wetness fell from his eyes, but he held his ground. He would not give up his ring.

Around him, a van choked full of anxious eyes rubbernecked at Youngblood, tensely awaiting his next move. They didn't have long to wait. As Youngblood's jaw tensed, and his hand reached into his waistband.

The kid's eyes nearly bugged out of his head.

"Motherfucker," Youngblood said, "I'm going to give you one last chance before I go crazy on your ass. And you know what's gonna happen when I do? We're gonna bury your fucking brother in a ditch. That's what we're gonna do. Is that what you want?"

Bobby whimpered incoherently.

"I said, 'Is that what you want?'"

Bobby wiped a stream of wetness from his trembling cheek, and then he yanked the ring off his finger as quickly as humanly possible, handing it to Mickey. Youngblood palmed it giddily, his head bouncing, and he climbed back up in his seat like a cock in command. Before he could examine the ring, however, Luke broke his silence.

"Give it back to him, Mickey."

Youngblood shot Luke a dismissive flip.

"Look, Mickey, that's not what we're here for, okay. We're looking for Rick Leblanc. So give the kid his ring."

"Shut the fuck up."

"Please give me my ring," Bobby begged.

Youngblood's head swiveled. "I said—shut your ass."

"Please, Mickey, it's like my favorite thing. Please give it back."

"What did I just say?"

"Mickey," Luke said impatiently, "what are we, a bunch of fucking animals here? What are we doing? Trying to find Rick Leblanc, that's what. The kid's not involved in this. Now give him back his ring."

"Fuck you," Youngblood said. And then he twisted defiantly and jammed the ring on each of his fingers, one at a time, trying to find the right fit. But there was a catch: the ring was huge, and his fingers were small. The only digit it came close to fitting was his thumb.

"Mickey, give the kid his ring back," Luke repeated.

"All you motherfuckers can eat my fucking ass, okay," Youngblood squealed, whipping around in his seat and chucking it as hard as he could.

The ring rocketed through the air and nailed the kid square in the meat of his upper arm. Bobby groaned piteously and grabbed his shoulder.

Youngblood yelled, "Fuck off and die, all of you," and he shrank back in his seat and hugged himself. His lip turned white from biting down on it so hard.

On the 203, traffic began to move again. They were now cruising through the bedroom community of Lantana, where green rolling hills sprouted majestically up from their right. The Paradise Islands, surrounded by the roiling blue of the Pacific Ocean, rode to their left. And everyone else just rode in muteness as the mean gangsta Mickey Youngblood pouted in the passenger's seat like an insolent little brat.

The silence ended ten minutes later, when Bobby pulled a blue denim pouch out of his pocket. He put it in his lap and reached inside it and withdrew a black glass pipe and a small baggie. He was now ready for an attitude adjustment.

"Anyone want to smoke some pot?"

Youngblood twisted his neck and his eyes locked on the dope like radar. "That better not be any of my weed."

Everybody's eyes were again open, and Barbados angled over and snagged the bag out of the kid's hand. He tore open the baggie, and the sweet aroma of skunk and wild flowers swirled through the van.

"Shit, no," Barbados said, pinching the green herb covered with crystalline red hairs. "This shit's *good.*"

Everyone laughed except for Youngblood, who reached back and ripped the baggie out of Barbados' hands. Barbados in turn snatched the denim pouch from Bobby and emptied it onto his lap. Out fell six more dime baggies of weed and another filled with little blue pills. He counted thirty.

"What else do you have in your pockets?" Youngblood demanded, as Barbados took a dry hit out of the pipe.

"Nice pipe, dude," Barbados said, and everybody just seemed to ignore Youngblood.

Bobby turned to Barbados. "Thanks."

"Let's see," Luke said excitedly, as if missing out on all the action. Barbados handed the pipe up to Luke, and he glanced at it. "Very cool, dude."

When Luke reached to hand it back, Youngblood seized it out of his hand and angrily chucked it out the window.

"What'd you do that for?" Luke cried.

"'Cuz I asked him a fucking question. And I want a fucking answer." Youngblood whirled to Bobby. "What else do you have? Empty out your fucking pockets."

Bobby dug in his pocket with his hand. "All I've got is my wallet," he said, and he pulled it out.

Youngblood snatched the wallet out of Bobby's hand and searched through it. School ID, library and video cards, condom. There were photos too: one with Bobby holding his sweet little tow-headed niece. Another was a school headshot of a stunning blonde and blue-eyed teenage girl.

"Who's the camel-herder?" Youngblood asked.

Bobby looked over to see what he was talking about. "Oh, that's my ex-girlfriend, Anja."

Youngblood nodded coolly. "I'd fuck her."

"Let's see," Luke said. Youngblood flashed him the photo. Luke nodded his approval. "Damn, not bad, little man." Youngblood cut him an angry sneer. "I was talking to the kid, Mickey, I swear."

"Let's see," Barbados said. Youngblood threw him the photo. Barbados picked it up off the floor and studied it. "Yep, I'd fuck her too."

Luke said, "You'd fuck a goat with anal herpes, John. Who you kidding?"

Bobby laughed as Barbados handed the photo off to Zit, who glanced at it quickly and frowned. "What?" Barbados asked.

"Dude, I wouldn't fuck her with your dick." Zit winked at Bobby and handed him the photograph. Bobby shoved it in his pocket.

Youngblood found four twenties, which he yanked out of Bobby's wallet and stuffed into his pocket. He glanced back. "Give me whatever else you got in your pockets."

Bobby sighed. He adjusted his baggy pants around his waist and stretched his long skinny legs. Reaching into his pocket, he pulled out a shiny and expensive knife. Youngblood extended two fingers and flicked them back. Bobby begrudgingly handed Youngblood his knife.

Youngblood studied it thoughtfully. "Nice." He shoved it in his pocket and again gestured. "What else?"

Bobby shoveled deeper into his pocket. This time he pulled out a little black book with the word "Address" inlaid on the cover in raised gold script.

And Youngblood's eyes illuminated like he'd seen the light. "Gimme that!"

Barbados snatched the black book from Bobby and flipped it to Youngblood. Youngblood's face brightened as if he were ready to explode with rapturous delight. The kid had his address book on him—which Youngblood now held in his hands—and Rick Leblanc would soon be his. He excitedly thumbed through its pages, stopping at the letter L. His right index finger scrolled down the page until he came across what he was looking for: an entry for Rick Leblanc. When he found it, he let out a cackle that could crack ice. "Yesss!"

Luke bounced nervously in his seat. "What?"

A demented smile creased the left side of Youngblood's mouth. And just as quickly, it disappeared. And his left foot slammed into the dashboard. "Fuck!"

"What?" Luke said.

"There's no fucking phone number here. Or address." Youngblood spun his head. "What's his fucking phone number?"

"I don't know," Bobby said.

Youngblood leapt into the back and squatted down in front of Bobby, scowling madly. "What's the fucking number?"

"I don't know."

Youngblood punched Bobby in the arm. Bobby winced and grabbed his shoulder. "I'm going to ask you one more time. How do we get ahold of your brother?"

"I don't even like my brother," Bobby appealed. "It's not like we hang out together or nothing. When he moved away, he never gave me his new number or told me where he was going. I've never been to his new place. I'm telling you. I have no idea where he is."

Youngblood punched him again, and the thud was twice as loud. Bobby's face cringed, and the red carriages beneath his eyes began to overflow.

"Listen, motherfucker. You don't give me Rick's number; then I think we're gonna go by your parents' house. Break out their fucking windows. Just like your brother did to me. What do you think of that?"

Bobby's head shook frantically, tears bouncing off both cheeks.

"Or maybe we'll just hunt your brother down. Shoot his ass when we find him." Youngblood's nostrils flared as he waited for an answer.

Bobby sniffled and wiped beneath his eyes with his fist, but said nothing.

Youngblood cocked his fist again.

"All right. All right!" Bobby said.

"All right, what?"

"I think I might know a number."

"Yeah, I thought you might." Youngblood reached over and grabbed a pen off the dashboard. He tossed it and the address book to Barbados.

Barbados ran the ballpoint of the pen across his white-coated tongue. He then ripped the L page out and tossed the rest of the address book out the window.

Bobby sighed despondently. "Oh, dude. What'd you do that for? That's got all my phone numbers in it."

"Not anymore," Barbados said. "Now what's your brother's number?"

Bobby's shoulders fell dejectedly. He inhaled gravely and told Barbados the number. Barbados scratched it next to Rick Leblanc's name then handed the page up to Youngblood, who studied it with smug satisfaction. Rick Leblanc would soon be his.

The van fell dumb again, everyone breathing easier at the prospect of the loose cannon finally calming down. That's how Youngblood was sometimes. He'd throw his little temper tantrum and then, when he finally got his way, he'd just kind of smugly retreat into himself until he focused on something else he wanted. That's how he was now. And just when it appeared as if everything had righted itself, when Mickey Youngblood would finally get ahold of Rick Leblanc, when they would finally resolve their differences, and the kid would finally get to go home, a strange buzzing sound fragmented the calm. It sounded like an amplified fly fluttering its wings, trying to escape the deadly clutch of a spider's web. To Luke, it sounded like a girl's vibrator, only louder. He turned to Youngblood. "What's that noise?"

"I have no fucking idea." Youngblood glanced into the back. "What the fuck is that?"

Barbados shrugged ignorantly. Zitelli's eyes searched for the sound.

"It's my pager," Bobby said.

"What?" Youngblood looked like he was about to have a seizure, again. "Gimme that thing."

Bobby snapped the pager off his jeans and handed it up to Youngblood. Youngblood studied it intensely. "Motherfuckers." His eyes lit up every time he hit the buttons, trying to bring the numbers to life. There were no less than eight calls, all but two from the same number, calling practically every ten minutes. "Why you got so many clients calling you all at once?"

"They're not clients," Bobby said.

Before Youngblood could respond the pager startled him by vibrating loudly in his hand, what turned out to be the seventh call from the same number. "Jesusfuckingchrist! This is one persistent client." Youngblood's face flashed a picture of pure amazement. Then his eyes ballooned with awareness. "Fuck, is this your brother?"

"No," Bobby said way too quickly.

"How do you know?" Youngblood shoved the readout into the kid's face. Bobby shook his head. "Then who is it?"

Bobby tried to smile when he said it. "My mom."

"Your mom?" Youngblood looked paralyzed. "Why the fuck does your mom keep calling you?"

"Probably because she's mad at me."

"Why the fuck's she mad at you?"

Bobby's eyes dropped to the floor. "Probably because I just ran away from home."

"Fuck." Youngblood's face wrenched. "You just ran away from home?"

"Yeah." Bobby's head bobbed but he wouldn't look up. "That's what I was doing when you guys picked me up."

Barbados started cracking up, shooting Youngblood a "that's what you get, dickhead" look. Which Youngblood melted with a demonic glare before turning back to the kid.

"So what the fuck does she want?"

Bobby swallowed hard. "For me to call her. So she can yell at me some more."

Youngblood's eyes narrowed. "And if you don't call her, what's she gonna do?"

Bobby's head shook as if the right answer might fall out, but it didn't.

"What? Call the police, what?"

"I don't know," Bobby said. "She's probably pretty angry with me right now."

"Fuck!" Youngblood threw the pager onto the dashboard. "Just what I fucking need. His mom looking for him. While we're out lookin' for fucking Ink Stain."

The van swelled with disquietude as Luke glanced over at Youngblood's stone-wide gaze. He looked as if the tension had frozen his brain in midstream. Luke wanted to ask Mickey if he knew where they were going, but he quickly decided against it. Mickey didn't look like he really wanted to talk.

Chapter Six

Sunday—2:48 p.m.

The pager buzzed nonstop all the way into Winteridge. There were now several different numbers calling, and every time the pager would go off, so would Youngblood—first kicking the dashboard, then picking up the pager and aggressively reading the number back to the kid, asking, "Is this your fucking brother? I'm going to kick his ass." The kid's answer would always be the same. "I'm telling you, I have nothing to do with my brother. It's my mom, and I need to call her back." Youngblood would again kick the dashboard, but Luke could see he really wasn't into it. Mickey was wearing down. And he wore an expression that typified the way Luke felt inside: as if he wanted to cry.

Luke was beginning to feel bad for both Mickey and the kid. Neither one of them wanted to be in this situation, but at the moment, they were like two copulating beetles—stuck with each other. As if worrying about finding Rick Leblanc and then figuring out what to do with him once they did wasn't bad enough, they now had to deal with the fact that Bobby Leblanc's manic parents were out searching for him.

"Your fucking mom's totally obsessed," Youngblood said. "What's her fucking problem, you know? If she wasn't so fucking obsessed and going crazy like every five fucking seconds, I might've let you go. But she is obsessed. And she is paging you every five fucking seconds. And if she hasn't already gone to the cops, she sure as fuck will when you tell her what you've been up to."

"No she won't," Bobby insisted.

"Why the fuck not?"

"'Cuz I won't tell her what happened."

"Yeah, right. Shut the fuck up."

"I'm serious, Mickey. I'll tell her I was doin' something else."

Youngblood flipped him off and pushed back in his seat. He rubbed his palms over his eyes, trying to bleed from his brain the answer to his dilemma. If he called the kid's brother and asked him for the money, what would Rick Leblanc do? He would call the kid's parents, that's what he would do. And if not, he'd call the cops, and Mickey would be shit-fucked either way.

"So what *are* you going to do, Mickey?" Luke asked.

"I'm sure as fuck not going to call Rick Leblanc. At least not right now. Fuck." Luke waffled a deep sigh as Youngblood's glare returned to Bobby. "Look, I'm not going to let you go until we find your brother, period. So you're just going to have to be fucking cool until we do."

Bobby met Mickey's glare. "No problem, Mickey. I'm actually pretty good at sittin' back and being cool. You know that. I'll do whatever you tell me. But can I at least call my mom, so she doesn't worry about me?"

Youngblood looked apoplectic. "No!"

"Mickey," Luke said, "let the kid call his mom."

"No! What the fuck's the matter with you guys? We're not calling anybody's mom until I get ahold of his brother."

The dread of silence kicked back in as they cruised past a green sign on the side of the 203 that said Mantalay Bay, an exclusive seaside community glazed with chic beachfront shops, expensive restaurants, and multimillion-dollar homes. Luke bit his lip for as long as he could before turning back to Youngblood. "So what *are* we going to do, Mickey? This is really getting ridiculous. We can't go to a beach party with a hostage."

"He's not a fucking hostage," Mickey snapped, "and we're not going to any fucking beach party."

"Well, thanks for telling me." Luke threw his hands up disconcertedly. "So where are we going then? We can't just drive around all day with the kid in the car. We need a fucking plan."

"I got a fucking plan," Youngblood said. "We need to take him somewhere until I can get ahold of Rick."

Luke shook his head disgustedly. "So where do you want to take him?"

Youngblood straightened in his seat. "Let's go to your house."

Luke snorted so hard his brain nearly shot through his sinuses. "My house? Mickey, why would we want to take the kid to my house?"

"Because we can't go back to my house. And we got to take him somewhere. And you're the only one who lives out here."

"We can't go to my house," Luke said, "my folks are there. I told you that."

"No you didn't. You told me they were out of town."

"Well, yeah, they are out of town."

"Then what's the fucking problem?"

"The problem is they're coming back today. I mean, they're probably already back by now. And I'm telling you, my fucking old man will freak if he sees all of us there."

"Well, then don't fucking worry about it. It'll just be you and the kid."

Luke's head shook emphatically. "No, Mickey. We can't go to my house."

"Then where the fuck're we going to take him?"

"I don't know. It's not my problem."

"The hell it ain't, motherfucker. You're involved in this just like I am. Figure out a place we can take him so we can tie him up … until we find his brother."

Luke shook his head in exasperation. The problem was simple: Mickey Youngblood was out of his fucking mind. And whenever he got like this, there was no talking to him. One second he wants to just scare the kid and let him go; then he wants to hold onto the kid until he finds his brother. Then he says he's not going to call Rick at all, but now he wants a place to tie the kid up until he can get ahold of his brother.

Which is it, dude? Get it together—fuck. "Mickey, why don't we just take the kid home?"

"I'm not taking him home until we find his brother."

Luke rubbed his eye and contemplated his lack of options. "I don't know then. You need to figure it out yourself, dude. I'm out of ideas."

"Don't be such a cuntass. You live out here—think of someone. What about your boys out on the west end?"

Luke rolled the question around the shell of his mind. "You mean Ernie?" Youngblood nodded. Luke tugged on his ear lobe, trying to decide what to do. "I can't. They won't be happy with me bringing over a hostage."

Youngblood cut Luke a sharp glare. Loudly, he said, "Did you bring your cell phone?"

Luke gaped at him as if he were on crack. "I don't have a cell phone, Mickey. You know that."

Youngblood glanced back at Zit. "Did you bring it?" Zit nodded. Youngblood flipped two impatient fingers and drew them back. "Let's see it." Zit slapped his cell phone into Mickey's palm. Youngblood twisted and handed it to Luke. "Fucking figure it out."

*   .   *   *   *

They exited the 203 at Mormon Street, and Luke took a left before turning right onto Cherokee. He then doubled back east where the quality of the housing continued to deteriorate with each passing block. By the time they reached his homey's neighborhood, one who didn't know any better might have believed they were entering the ghetto section of San Floripez—if there were such a thing—since no house in the area ever sold for under three-quarters of a million dollars anyway.

To Luke, that's what made San Floripez a paradise. Its worst areas were a zillion times more attractive than anything the Valley had to offer. Thanks to its incredible weather, diverse topography, and gorgeous ocean views, people flocked here from all over the world. People only flocked to the Valley to fill dead-end jobs or to buy drugs. San Floripez played host to some of the country's most renowned golf courses. The locals all carried this cool "there's plenty of wealth to go around for everyone" attitude, and Luke often counted his blessings for having been made to feel a part of it. The Valley had little in comparison unless you liked broken asphalt, burning concrete, and choking smog. The area they were driving through now might have been congested with houses, cars, and people, but that was part of its charm. Luke appreciated the uniqueness of each passing house, some having paint, others featuring paint cracks, with burned-out hulls of primer gray cars adorning every other overgrown front lawn.

The van tracked past his homey's house, but the street was so crowded with cars, there was nowhere to park. Luke drove around and finally found a place down on the next block off Eucalyptus. When Youngblood had insisted Luke find some place to take the kid until they got ahold of his brother, Luke almost told him to go take a walk. Who the hell did that little despot think he was, ordering Luke around that way? And what did he think Luke was supposed to do, just snap his fingers and come up with a hostage sitter? But the more he thought about it, the more Luke realized Mickey was totally in a pinch. He kinda even felt sorry for the guy—almost.

Youngblood had wanted to call Rick Leblanc as soon as the kid had given him the number, but he told Luke he had to be careful with that. So Luke called his homey, Ernie Armstrong, hoping that with a little luck they'd be able to kick it back for a while; long enough for Youngblood to get ahold of the kid's brother, collect his money, and end this little drama. Of course, there was a snag to that plan as well: Ernie Armstrong wasn't home when Luke called. Ernie's roommate,

Julio Maldonado, answered, and Luke spoke to him, with Youngblood haranguing him in the background; telling him to find out if they had a closet big enough to stick the kid in.

Ernie Armstrong's house was one of the nicer homes in the neighborhood. Most of the plants out front were still alive, although the yellowed lawn looked in desperate need of watering. The three-tone, brown-on-browner exterior appeared freshly painted. The windows were shielded with heavy metal security bars, which were covered by malnourished bougainvillea plants. The glass in the front right window had been replaced by cardboard, and the front porch tilted slightly to the north. But once inside, Luke felt more at home here than he did in his dad's house.

Luke's twenty-year-old buddy, Jaime Gabrial, was smoking a cigarette out on the front porch when he walked up. "What's up?" Luke asked.

Gabrial nodded but didn't say anything, which was the usual MO for Jaime Gabrial. He was short and stocky, with mud-colored skin and thick shoulders that looked fit more for a mule than a man. Stubby meat-slab arms with long scars and tattoos alternating down to the elbows protruded from the sleeves of an oversized black T-shirt. Crawling out from the collar onto his tree stump neck was a six-inch tarantula tattoo.

Luke had known Gabrial since last summer, when they worked together down at Ed's Car Wash over on County Street. Gabrial was pretty cool and unusually quiet until after work—when they started partying, and the booze started flowing—and then Gabrial's big mouth would never let up. The guy was a shit-talking party animal gone out of bounds. A full-fledged gangbanger who used the car wash, and then his most recent job as manager at Burrito Hell, as his office from which to conduct the business of dealing drugs. He lived just down the street from his homey Ernie Armstrong and was probably over finding out what time the party started. There was always a party at Ernie's house, and Luke was hoping today would be no exception. After the morning they had just had, a party was exactly what the afternoon called for.

Luke knocked on the front door but didn't wait long when no one answered. The door was unlocked, so he plowed inside. Gabrial stomped out his cigarette and followed. Ernie's place was neatly kept. Wooden floors, a few scratched antiques, and an old brown couch that looked like it had been thrown from a second-story fraternity window graced the living room. Luke took two lefts through the living room and kitchen, and then stuck his head out the back door, but nobody was around. He doubled back through the living room where he again said "Hi" to Gabrial, then cut through the hallway, and to the right, into Ernie's bedroom. Still nobody.

Luke pushed back out and down the hall, where he checked Armstrong's roommate Julio Maldonado's room, which also stood empty. His hand scratched his bony head as he tried to figure out what was up. He had just spoken to Julio not more than fifteen minutes earlier, but the guy was nowhere to be found. When he heard the wrenching sound of overhead water pipes, Luke stepped over to the bathroom door and pressed his ear against it. He could hear the spray of running water. And he knocked. But there was no response. So he rapped harder.

"Hurry up, Julio. I need to talk to you."

Still nothing. He pushed back into the living room and asked Gabrial if Armstrong was home.

"I don't think so," Gabrial said, "but he should be back real soon."

Luke didn't ask him how he knew this. But he was hoping that he might be right since he had no other ideas for places to take the kid. He pushed back outside and headed toward the van when he heard the loud thump of blown-out car speakers round the corner. He turned back to see Ernie pull into his drive in his green midsize sedan, with two sweet young things sitting by his side. *Way to go, Ernie.* Luke walked over to the car, where they exchanged greetings. When Armstrong climbed out, he gave his homey a big hug, the kind usually reserved for lost relatives or enemies you were about to stab in the back.

Ernie Armstrong was twenty years old and wiry thin, with cream-in-coffee colored skin and tight curly hair bleached out at the ends. He looked more like a surfer than the gangbanger Luke believed him to be. The two babes that climbed out after him were really young, but kinda cute, just the way Luke liked them. "So what's the story with the jailbait, dude?"

Armstrong explained that he had just picked up his cousin Marcia Bautista and her friend Donna Donkster, who were both seventeen and visiting from down south. They had arrived Thursday and had been over visiting his mother, but were now here to celebrate the Fourth of July weekend with Ernie. Relieved for his homey's sake, Luke patted him on the back. No need for them all to be in trouble with minors this weekend. Armstrong told the girls to come inside, and Luke followed.

"So who's up with you?" Armstrong asked, holding the front door open. The girls filed past him.

"Mickey Youngblood, John Barbados, a couple other dudes," Luke said, following Ernie's shapely cousin inside. "We're on our way to Buddy Floyd's party down at the Strand."

"Cool," Armstrong said, stepping inside, closing the door behind him. "It should be fun."

Luke glanced around the living room. "Uhm, dude, can I have a word with you …?" His eyes trained on the girls. "In private?"

Armstrong glimpsed his cousin and friend, and he nodded. He led Luke into his bedroom, and Luke shut the door behind him. Luke couldn't help but laugh again at the cardboard duct-taped into the busted-out window.

"Don't laugh, dude," Armstrong said, answering Luke's question before he could ask it. "Domestic dispute. My girlfriend went apeshit on me."

Luke took a seat on the bed. "Again?"

Armstrong sniffed his armpit and frowned. He yanked off his Hell's Angels T-shirt and tossed it into the closet. "Again."

Luke studied the window, amazed at how many uses one could find for duct tape. "Hey dude, would it be cool, you know, if me and my buddies chilled out here for a while?"

Armstrong shrugged. "Dude, we're going to a barbecue. Why, what's up?"

"Yeah, well, you know, we just need a place to hang out for a while. Until we go down to Buddy's later."

"Why don't you just go down there now, dude? I'm sure it's totally happening." Armstrong opened his dresser drawer, pulled out a pair of underwear, and sniffed it. "Maybe we could all meet up there later or something."

Luke watched his homey change his clothes, as he tried to figure out the best way to break the news. He'd known Ernie for almost a year, having met when they both worked at the car wash. After work, Luke used to come and hang out at Ernie's where they'd be joined by all his homeys, and they'd kick back and party, and they always had a good time together. Luke soon started selling Ernie the pot he got from Youngblood, and Ernie started selling it to all his gangbanger buddies, and before he knew it, Luke was the toast of the town for supplying San Floripez with the best bud she'd ever seen. Luke trusted his homey and considered Ernie a good friend, but how did you ask a buddy to help you do what Luke needed to be done?

"So, dude …" he began, wringing the sweat out of his hands while trying to figure out the right words to use.

Armstrong looked at him sympathetically as if detecting his anguish. "What's up, dude—what's the matter?"

Luke tried to swallow, but the lump in his throat wouldn't go down. "Oh, man, you wouldn't believe it. We were on our way up so we could go to the party, you know, and …" He sucked in deeply but couldn't catch his breath.

"And so Youngblood decided he needed to collect some money from this dude who owed him. So instead, he picked up the dude's brother, and … And now …"

Armstrong stuck up a hand. "Wait, slow down, Luke. What's going on here? You picked up some dude's brother?"

"Yeah, you know. And now we just need a place to chill for a bit until Mickey can get his money from him."

"From who?"

"From the kid's brother."

"What the fuck is up with that, dude?" Armstrong now sounded anxious. He sat back on the bed and pulled off his socks. "You telling me you kidnapped the kid?"

Luke jumped off the bed defensively. "No, man, I didn't. It's not like that at all. I didn't have anything to do with it. It was all Youngblood's idea. But the thing is, the kid's cool about it. He knows what's up. And, and he wants his brother to get things straightened out with Mickey too."

Armstrong went from nodding to shaking his head to looking totally dumbfounded. Then he slipped on a fresh pair of socks. "But you kidnapped him?"

Luke's head shook vehemently. "Dude, no …"

Armstrong's brow knitted into a V. "No?"

"Well …" Luke looked like he was suffocating on a mouthful of air. "Yes. But seriously, don't worry about it. It's … it's just until we find his brother, you know. It's not like we're going to stay here all day or nothing."

✳   ✳   ✳   ✳

As a kid growing up in San Floripez, Ernie Armstrong had a photo album filled with snapshots from holidays, parties, and celebrations. When he got older, indulgent memories of his friends and family members either dancing on the beach or watching the parades or eating tamales while barefoot in the sand often flooded his mind. His parents sponsored many of the events when he was a kid, and they had provided him with an opportunity to learn the history, customs, and traditions of his Mexican and early American forefathers, and how they had comprised the cultural heritage of San Floripez. It also provided Ernie with an opportunity to boast about his family, which he was doing with his cousin and her friend on the living room couch, when the front door burst open, and Mickey Youngblood marched in followed by John Barbados, Bobby Leblanc, Luke Ridnaur, and Zit.

Armstrong's eyes bilged. "Damn, Luke, that's a lot of dudes."

Luke closed the door and stood there, looking as unsure of what to do or say as everyone else. He gazed at his friend apologetically. "I know, dude, I'm sorry."

Without saying a word, Mickey Youngblood broke from the pack. He marched right past Armstrong, grazing his shoulder, and straight through the living room and into the kitchen, where his eyes furtively searched the room. Not finding what he was looking for, he charged back into the living room, his chest all puffed out, looking like a miniature bantam cock searching for a hen to jump. "If the kid doesn't show each and every one of you respect by calling you 'Sir,' I want you to tell me."

Luke watched Armstrong and his cousin's friend roll their eyes at each other, and Luke wanted to bury himself. Marcia glanced at the kid with distressed eyes. She seemed to take mental notes of his hands buried deep in his pockets, his ripped shirt with all the buttons torn off.

Youngblood then pushed back into the hallway, where he started pacing up and down, tearing open and slamming closed one closet door after another. Luke cringed with a red face. He avoided making eye contact with Armstrong or his cousin, while Youngblood ranted and cussed about how he was going to "fuck Rick Leblanc up" when he found him.

Luke and Armstrong followed Mickey when he marched back through the living room and into the kitchen, where he jerked open the broom closet door. Luke almost croaked when a landslide of brooms and buckets emptied out of the closet and crashed loudly onto the kitchen's spotted linoleum floor.

Armstrong turned his palms up. "Dude, what the fuck's going on?"

Youngblood scoped out the small closet. "I need to stick the kid somewhere. But this one's all fulla brooms and shit."

"Well, no shit," Armstrong said cholerically. "That's what broom closets are for."

Youngblood kicked the mop bucket into the cabinet and marched out of the kitchen.

Armstrong shot Luke an agitated look. "What are we doing, dude?"

Luke threw up his hands in exasperation. What could he say? Youngblood was Youngblood, which meant he was fucking out of control—again. Youngblood had an enormous anger management problem that was starting to irritate everyone, and Luke had no idea what to do about it. He had to try to stay cool and keep everyone else cool while Youngblood stomped around trying to figure out where to stick the kid.

Luke could see Armstrong starting to lose it. He didn't know where Ernie's roommate Julio was, but he knew there was going to be trouble if he didn't do something quick. He had to get Youngblood settled down fast, but first he had a mess to clean up. So he bent down and started picking everything up, when the kitchen door blasted open, and nearly tore the side of Ernie's face off. He ducked out of the way just in time as Youngblood came barreling back into the kitchen, breathlessly. He stood there dancing from one foot to the other like a little boy who was about to wet himself.

Ernie glared at Luke like he wanted to exterminate him. Luke literally wanted to bury himself in a hole. But before he could, Youngblood asked Ernie, "Hey, man, mind if we use your bedroom?"

Chapter Seven

Sunday—3:40 p.m.

Julio Maldonado was feeling Irish clean and Guatemalan refreshed. He had just showered, and he was now ready to chase some pussy. Maldonado was one of those non-athletic types, short on stature, but rich in appreciation of all things greasy and edible. He was light skinned and bowlegged. And as he stepped out of the shower, he wore an orange towel wrapped around his head like a turban and a pink one wrapped around his waist like a belly dancer. A jagged, purplish scar snaked from his groin upward in a circle across his swollen belly, which hung over the front of his towel like a crumpled pillow.

When the twenty-year-old stepped out into the hallway, he heard so much commotion coming from the living room, he wondered if he hadn't stepped into the twilight zone. It sounded like a fucking convention in there, and he wanted to know what was going on. So he took off down the hallway and peeked around the corner into the living room. What he saw literally shocked him: his living room was filled with half a dozen people he didn't recognize. People who were talking loudly and making a lot of noise. People who were smoking out of his bong and drinking his beers. People who weren't there a half hour earlier when he'd hopped in the shower.

Over on the couch, he saw his roommate sitting and talking animatedly with his cousin. If Maldonado didn't know any better, he would have thought Armstrong was upset about something. He tried calling his name, but Armstrong couldn't hear him through all the racket. When Maldonado whistled loud enough to attract dogs, he not only got Armstrong's attention, but that of everyone else in the room as well. He pulled the towel tighter around his waist but felt underdressed for the experience.

Armstrong finally noticed him, and he got up and walked over.

"Who the fuck are all these people?" Maldonado asked excitedly.

Armstrong shook his head and grimaced and threw up his hands in frustration. He then pivoted, and walked back into the living room without saying a word. Feeling his own sense of frustration, Maldonado wheeled around and headed back toward his bedroom. When he heard footfalls coming behind him, he turned to see Jaime Gabrial heading into the bathroom. He motioned for Gabrial to stop.

"What the fuck's going on with all those people?"

Gabrial looked at him like he didn't understand the question, didn't care, or both. "What do you mean, what the fuck's going on?"

Maldonado tried another tactic. "Who are all the fucking people in the living room?"

"I don't know what the fuck you're talking about." Gabrial then pivoted and walked into the bathroom, the door slamming and locking behind him.

Maldonado wobbled his head. He didn't really appreciate Gabrial's attitude, but then again, he never did. All the guy ever did was come over and mooch their food, booze, and pot without so much as giving a "thank you." And now he was going to dis Maldonado like this? And then go and stink up his toilet? Any other day, Maldonado might have pounded on the door and said something, or kicked Gabrial's ass, or told him to get the fuck out. But not today. Today Julio Maldonado had more important things to do. He had a barbecue to go to. He had pussy to chase.

So he turned and headed back toward his bedroom, when he stopped suddenly. And his head revolved. And he heard something coming from his roommate's bedroom. The door was slightly ajar, and he didn't think anybody was in there. But he figured he better go check just in case. So he tiptoed the length of the hallway, stuck his head in the doorway, and nearly suffered a cardiac infarction.

Sitting on his roommate's bed was a kid, no more than fifteen, maybe sixteen years old at tops, bound hand and foot with duct tape. A black and white bandana wrapped around his eyes. And there was a sock crammed into his mouth, sealed by duct tape.

∗　　　∗　　　∗　　　∗

"So what are we going to do?" John Barbados asked while peeling a scab off his forearm. Shaken badly by the unfolding of the afternoon's events, he and Zitelli had retreated into the kitchen to find solace in each other and to look for glasses for the gin.

Luke had soon joined them, seeking the same respite. "Oh, dude, you tell me." Luke couldn't believe how weak his voice sounded, as if he were already defeated. In a way, he was. Things had obviously not gone according to plan. Ernie had told Luke they could hang around until they found the kid's brother, but then they had to go. He had a barbecue he wanted to take the girls to, and he was anxious to leave. But that was before Ernie saw the kid tied up.

Earlier, they were dicking around in the bedroom when Youngblood tried handing Luke the duct tape and told him to tie the kid up. Luke acted as if the tape were electrified and told Youngblood he wanted nothing to do with it. He pushed the tape back at Youngblood, and Youngblood pushed it at Luke, and then Barbados stepped in and took it from both of them. He proceeded to tape the kid up, when Armstrong walked in and groaned loudly.

Luke did everything he could to calm his boy down. "Look, man, I swear to God we'll be out of here as soon as we find the kid's brother." He walked Ernie out into the living room and plied him with severe bongloads. This seemed to satisfy Armstrong for about two seconds, until Youngblood trucked back into the living room and asked him if he could borrow Ernie's phone. Like what was Armstrong going to say—*no?* Not with the way Youngblood was acting. So Ernie reluctantly agreed, the good nature having visibly drained from his face, and Luke rewarded him with another bongload. Then they had to sit there and watch anxiously as Youngblood paced back and forth through the living room, making one phone call after another, shouting angrily into the phone, gesturing wildly, his arms flailing through the air like a biblical farmer swatting locusts, trying to find out where Rick Leblanc was. The dude was totally stressing everybody out, and Luke's heart couldn't take much more of it.

When he had gotten off the phone, Youngblood screamed to himself. He then moved out back with Gabrial to smoke a cigarette while nervously pacing a trench through the backyard lawn. That was when things finally started to calm down inside. The decibel level dropped dramatically, as did the tension. Luke, Barbados, and Zitelli discussed their options over chilled gin and tonics in the kitchen. And Armstrong pounded heavy bongloads from the couch in the living room. Everything appeared cool for the moment. Luke thought they just might be able to slip out of there without any more confrontations, if Youngblood could only get ahold of the kid's brother. But all thoughts of their little drama coming to an end evaporated when Armstrong's red-faced roommate barged into the living room and right up to Ernie with an orange towel wrapped around his head and a pink one around his waist.

"What the fuck's going on with the kid tied up in your bedroom?"

Armstrong threw his hands up disgustedly. "I know, dude. Don't ask me. He's Luke's friend. I don't know what the fuck's going on either."

"Jesus, dude, bite my head off why don't you. Where's Luke?"

Armstrong pointed.

Maldonado turned to see Luke in the kitchen. "Dude," he yelled, charging in after him. "What's up with the fucking kid in Ernie's bedroom?"

"Dude, I know," Luke said, nearly hyperventilating. "Youngblood's tripping, man. He's totally fucking tripping. We were driving through the Valley, and we grabbed the kid. And … and I don't know what's going on." Luke glanced out the kitchen window and nearly jumped out of his skin when he saw Youngblood glowering right back at him. His voice lowered dramatically. "The truth is, we need to talk to the kid's brother, and then we're out of here."

Maldonado followed Luke's eyes outside, and saw Youngblood angrily stomp out his cigarette. "Who the fuck is he?"

"Oh, that's my boy, Mickey Youngblood. He's totally cool. You remember him."

"No, I don't," Maldonado said, returning Youngblood's scowl. He turned back to Luke. "Why do you have to talk to the kid's brother?"

"Because he owes Mickey money."

Maldonado nodded incredulously.

Luke again looked outside, but Youngblood wasn't there anymore. Luke sucked in air and said, "All we're going to do is wait to see if we can contact the kid's brother. And that's it. We'll leave and take him home once we talk to his brother."

The sliding glass door nearly shattered when Youngblood slammed it open; he charged through the kitchen and right up to Luke. "Shut your ass, and don't say shit."

Luke shut his ass and didn't say shit.

Maldonado gaped at Youngblood. "Who the fuck are you?"

"Don't fucking worry about it."

"Don't fucking worry about it?" Maldonado adjusted the towel around his waist. "This is my fucking house. You don't come in here and tie up a kid and tell me not to fucking worry about it."

"I just fucking did …"

Maldonado laughed tensely. His eyes widened as his gaze shifted around the room. Luke, Barbados, Zit, Gabrial, and Armstrong all stood there, looking like they were ready to take sides, but nobody moved or came to his defense. So he wheeled back around.

Considered short by most standards, Maldonado towered over Youngblood. "Yeah, I do have a problem with some little prick coming in here and telling me what to do." He pointed a finger at Luke. "I ain't your fucking boy. Who you think you can just boss around whenever you want."

Youngblood pushed his chest into Maldonado's. "So what?"

Maldonado swallowed hard. "So what?"

"Did I stutter, motherfucker?"

Maldonado broke from Youngblood's glare and again glanced around the room, as if waiting for *his boys* to back him up. But nobody flinched. They all seemed to be waiting for Youngblood's next move. Luke then noticed Mickey's hand slipping toward his waistband. Knowing what Mickey had down there, Luke felt the need to make sure it didn't come out. So he stepped in and put a hand between the two roosters.

"All right, guys, let's see if we can't resolve this amicably, okay?"

"What the fuck's there to resolve?" Maldonado's voice was high with excitement. "I want this guy, and that kid back there in the bedroom, outta here *now*."

"We'll go when I talk to the kid's brother," Youngblood said, his face pressed right into Maldonado's chin.

The room held its collective breath. Maldonado and Youngblood glared at each other, and Luke could barely swallow the lump in his throat. Then Maldonado blinked, backed away from Youngblood, and turned his anger toward his roommate. "And what the fuck's with you, Ernie?"

"What do you mean what the fuck's with me?"

"You're not going to say anything? You let all these people come in here. Smoke pot and drink booze. While they got some fucking kid tied up in your bedroom. What the fuck's the matter with you? You should be ashamed of yourself."

Armstrong's fists balled at his side. "I didn't fucking let them in—I told you that."

"Then who did? I sure as fuck didn't."

"Don't fucking worry about it," Youngblood said.

Maldonado turned to face him. "Fuck you and the horse you rode in on, dude. I'm not talking to you."

Youngblood again pressed his hand to his waistband. "Well, I'm talking to you, motherfucker. And I think you better calm your ass down. Go to your fucking barbecue before somebody gets hurt."

Maldonado looked dyspeptic. Youngblood looked as if he wanted to shoot him. So Luke again put a hand between the two. "Mickey, please, can we just do what we came here to do and go?"

Maldonado glowered into Youngblood's face. "Yeah, why don't you just fucking go?" He then pivoted to face his roommate. "I don't need this shit. You want to stay here with these fucking assholes, fine. That's your deal. But I'm outta here. And these fuckers …" He said it glaring directly at Youngblood. "Had better not be here when I get back." And then he turned and left.

Youngblood's face flushed red. Luke could see his hands shaking. Youngblood looked as if he were about to blow full tilt. Luke needed to calm him down—get him out of there to give everyone a chance to cool off. But before he could, Youngblood took off. Luke reached for him at the last second, but Mickey brushed him aside easily.

Youngblood caught Maldonado in the living room. Maldonado pivoted defensively—and tightened the towel around his waste. "What?"

Youngblood again pressed his hand into the front of his pants, making sure Maldonado could see what he packed. "If I were you, homeboy, I'd keep my fucking mouth shut."

Maldonado's mouth contorted, and he looked as if he were about to lay into Youngblood, but he said nothing. The message had been received. He pivoted and headed off into the hallway, tail planted firmly between legs.

Luke couldn't believe any of it. He needed bongloads—many of them. So he stepped over to the table to grab the bong, when Ernie Armstrong pushed up next to him.

"Dude, this is bullshit. I don't really appreciate your boys coming over here and trashing my parents' house. You know what I mean. Maybe it's time for everyone just to clear out."

His homey was upset, and Luke didn't blame him one bit. But it wasn't like they had just trashed the place. That was bogus. Yeah, they had raided the fridge and were drinking his booze. And there were a few beer bottles here and there. And they had hijacked his bong. But it wasn't like they were smoking his dope or nothing. They were smoking the kid's dope. And what did Ernie expect anyway? Eight dudes in any house were a disaster waiting to happen. And this motley crew was no exception.

"I'll clean everything up, dude, I swear. Just as soon as we get ahold of the kid's brother." Luke loaded another bongload and handed it to his homey.

Armstrong pressed his lips to the plastic mouthpiece, and then stopped. "You know, I grew up in this house. And when my parents moved out, I promised them I would do whatever it took to preserve the sanctity of their home."

Luke eyed the bong, anxious to see if he was going to hit it or not. "Hey, dude, I totally understand."

Armstrong flicked the lighter. "I think all that is in jeopardy with Youngblood running around here like this."

"Dude, I totally understand. We'll be totally cool with your place. I swear to you." Luke's eyes slid from the flame to meet Armstrong's gaze. "Hey, dude, you gonna hit that or what?"

Armstrong's head shook as he passed the bong and lighter back to Luke. Luke downed it immediately, loaded another huge hit, and downed that one too.

"I have no interest in helping Youngblood pull off his kidnapping, or whatever you want to call it," Armstrong said solemnly. "I just want to go out with my cousin and have some fun, you know. Without having to worry about the police showing up when I get back."

Luke nodded brightly, his face buried in a thick gray and white cloud of smoke. He understood completely. His homey didn't want any trouble, and he wanted them to leave. Luke didn't blame him one bit. And so he packed another huge hit, and contemplated how he was going to get Youngblood out of there, when Mickey tromped aggressively right up between the two.

"Quit your crying," he said. "We're gonna keep the kid here until we find his brother."

"Why?" Armstrong asked. "Why don't you just take him home?"

"Because I haven't gotten my money yet."

The underside of Armstrong's jaw twitched as he glared at Youngblood. Luke knew Ernie wanted to tell Mickey to take his problem elsewhere. That Mickey and his hostage weren't welcome in his house. That if Youngblood didn't watch his ass, Ernie might call up a few dozen of his homeboys to come and shut it for him. But he didn't. It was obvious Ernie understood the seriousness of the situation and wasn't going to force anything, yet. Luke knew he was doing it for him, and it wouldn't last forever.

Armstrong then turned to Luke, showing his back to Youngblood. "We'll be back in a couple hours. And I'm telling you, dude, I want you all out of here by the time I get back."

Chapter Eight

Sunday—4:57 p.m.

By the fifth bongload, Mickey Youngblood had lost his scowl. By the eighth, he almost actually smiled. And by the tenth, he was talking about going to the beach party again. That's when Luke poured them each a hefty shot of tequila, their third of the afternoon, which they washed down with ice cold brewskis.

Luke was thrilled to be out of Ernie's house, even if it was only a temporary reprieve. After Maldonado and Gabrial had split, and Armstrong took the girls, Youngblood told Barbados and Zit to watch the kid so he and Luke could go over to Luke's place to shower and get ready for Buddy's party. It was a bunch of bullshit for sure, but Youngblood needed some time to analyze his options, and there was way too much pressure going on over at Armstrong's for anyone to do any clear thinking of any kind.

Barbados and Zit both started bitching and moaning, claiming they just remembered they had dates with their girlfriends back in the Valley. But they didn't really have much of a choice, since at the moment, they were just like the kid in duct tape: along for the ride.

Luke sat across from Youngblood at his father's kitchen table. Youngblood's eyes were crimson, and his speech was slow and thick. The dude was wasted off his ass, and Luke loved it. The old Mickey Youngblood had returned, the one whom Luke grew up loving to be around—the one who was fun to be with, to joke around and kick the shit with, the one Luke considered his best friend in the whole world. And he was thrilled to have him back.

"You know, dude, we can't go to Buddy's party," Youngblood slurred.

"I know, man," Luke said, beaming.

It was great the conversation had gone light for the moment, because they both needed the breather. Things had gotten way too intense. Luke's folks weren't home yet, which was fortunate, but he expected them back any minute. He needed to get out of here before they returned. He didn't want his old man to walk in and see Mickey sitting here, because there'd be problems. For some reason, Fritz Ridnaur had soured on Mickey Youngblood, and Luke didn't really understand why. He wanted to avoid another confrontation if he could help it.

He drained the last of his ale and hopped up from the table. He tossed the empty bottle into the trash, grabbed two more out of the fridge, plopped one in front of Youngblood, and sat back down. It was now time to help Youngblood resolve the issue of Bobby Leblanc.

"So what are you going to do with the kid, Mickey?"

The lightness of being that temporarily hung over the room was sucked dry the moment the question left his mouth. Youngblood was back to being Mickey Youngblood, slamming his fist down on the table, scowling angrily off into the distance. So Luke just let the question hang out there to give the little man a chance to work things through his mind. A refreshing breeze gusted in from the Pacific, providing a semblance of coolness to an otherwise heated moment.

"I don't know," Youngblood finally said before guzzling his beer.

Luke was glad that he had gotten Mickey out of Armstrong's when he did, because it had given everyone a chance to mellow out. But he felt bad about the mess he'd made with his homeys and wasn't sure if Armstrong or Maldonado would ever speak to him again. He would have to make things right with them eventually, but his only concern right now was helping Mickey figure out what to do with the kid.

At Armstrong's, Youngblood had seriously considered calling the number Bobby had given for his brother but decided against it. That's when he tried calling everybody he knew who had ever known Rick Leblanc, but nobody seemed to know where the guy had moved to.

Luke wiped his nose on his sleeve. "Maybe you should just try calling him, Mickey—you know, see what happens."

Youngblood frowned. "See what happens?"

Luke tilted his wobbly head.

"And say what?"

"That you want your money. That you need to resolve things."

"Yeah, right," Youngblood said sarcastically. He lifted his hand and pretended to put a phone to his ear. In an effeminate voice, he said, "Oh—hi, Rick, this is your former friend Mickey Youngblood—remember me? I'm the guy who's gonna kick your fucking ass. Yeah, that's right. And by the way, I picked up your brother. Got him tied up. Stuck in a closet at a friend's house right this very moment. And if you don't come out of hiding like the big fucking pussy that you are, I might end up doing something I don't want to." Youngblood pretended to hang up by slamming his fist on the table.

Luke nearly jumped out of his tattoos. "Jesus, Mickey, don't do that."

"Don't be such a cuntass," Youngblood said, slamming the table again, twice as loud.

"Dude, come on," Luke cried, "you're gonna break the table."

"What do you care? You don't give a shit about your old man's table."

Mickey was right, of course. Luke couldn't give a flying fuck about his old man's worthless table. But that wasn't the point. So he shot Mickey that famous Mickey Youngblood scowl, couldn't hold it, and started cracking up. So did Youngblood. Luke then took a long guzzle of beer and let out a gizzard-ripping belch that stained the air.

Youngblood frowned. "Im-pres-sive."

"So, dude," Luke said, interrupting himself with another belch, blowing this one across the table at Youngblood.

Youngblood screeched his chair away from the table, fanning himself, clearing the spoiled air out of his face. "So, dude, what?"

"What are you going to do, man? You're going to have to do something. I mean we can't just leave him over at Ernie's forever."

Youngblood got up unstably and stumbled over to the fridge. He opened the door and started to reach for another beer, when he realized he still had a half-empty bottle in his hand. He upturned it, finished it, then leaned over and tossed the bottle across the kitchen, and watched it slam off the side of the counter and bank into the trashcan. Unfortunately, the force of the shot knocked the trashcan over, dumping everything onto the floor. He threw his hands up into the air as if he had witnessed a touchdown. "Goooal!"

Luke groused at the mess. "Ah, dude ..." Eggshells, wet paper towels, and coffee grounds littered the floor, but Luke was too fucked up to do anything about it.

Youngblood turned back to the fridge and snatched two more brews. He closed the door and tossed one to Luke. "Dude, truth is ... I don't know if I'm going to call him or not. I might just have to wait until I find him."

This was not the answer Luke wanted to hear. His folks were due back home any second, and he had to get Youngblood out of here. To do that, they had to figure out what to do with the kid. Luke's homeys would be getting home pretty soon, and he didn't want them to walk in with the kid still tied up in the bedroom closet, and Barbados and Zit lounging around the house like a couple dark-skinned lizards.

"Look, Mickey, we got to do something now, man. We got to get the kid out of my boy's house before they get back."

"I told you, I will find his brother," Youngblood said, taking his seat back at the table. "I'm just not going to do it right now." He flicked the beer top with his finger, causing it to shoot across the table like a hockey puck and smack Luke in the neck.

"Ow," Luke screeched. He rubbed the deep red scratch that resulted on his neck. "Why not?"

"Read my lips," Youngblood said. "I'm too fucking burnt, okay?"

"No it's not okay, Mickey …"

Youngblood threw open his hands. "What do you want me to do?"

"I don't know. Call him or something."

"You want me to call him? Right now?" Youngblood's voice was rising. "From here?"

"Yes. Let's get this over with."

"Fine, you want me to call him from here. No problem."

"That's what I've been trying to say, Mickey. Let's call him and see if we can get ahold of him. Let's just see what happens."

Youngblood drained his beer in one giant swallow and smacked the bottle down on the table. He opened his mouth and belched so loud it echoed off the oven. And then he blew the whole nasty mess right into Luke's face. Luke jerked his head back, gasping like he'd been fumigated. His hands flung frantically through the air, trying to rid the room of the toxic smell.

"Payback, dicknose," Youngblood said, standing unsteadily. He pivoted and wobbled over to the phone. He yanked the receiver off the hook and punched in several numbers.

Luke could hear the phone ringing from where he was.

"Yeah, and when I leave a message," Youngblood said, "I hope you won't mind there'll be a record from your house."

Luke squinted at Youngblood, trying to focus on his face. "What are you talking about, Mickey?"

"Nothing. Don't fucking worry about it."

Luke did worry about it. Whenever Mickey told him not to worry about something, Luke automatically sweated it out. There was something fucked up about the situation; Luke was just too messed up to figure out what it was.

"Mickey, what record are you talking about?"

Youngblood lifted the phone away from his mouth. "The phone record. There will be a record of this number calling Rick Leblanc. So when the cops come to investigate what happened ..." He let the words dangle out there like a carrot.

The carrot hit Luke like an anvil to the back of the skull. What a fryer! Beneath Youngblood's sarcasm was the point Luke had been missing all along. If the cops ever did investigate the kidnapping, they'd only have to get ahold of Luke's dad's phone records to know that someone from this house had called Rick Leblanc. One plus one would equal Luke's involvement in the kid's abduction, and that couldn't happen. Luke wondered how he could have been so stupid to forget that.

He scrambled to get up and out of his chair and nearly broke his ass in the process. As he rose off his seat, his bare chest caught the lip of the table, causing it to fly up on two legs. He watched in slow motion as first his and then Mickey's beers slid across the tabletop and crashed down onto the floor.

Luke reached out quickly and grabbed the side of the table before it flipped over. He pulled it down and leaned on it, trying to steady himself. The room spun circles around him. He gazed down and could see blood beginning to ooze from the gash across his chest. He felt lucky not to have scraped off his nipple. Gathering his balance, Luke leaned over and fisted a paper towel off the counter. He wiped the blood from his chest and threw the paper towel on the floor. He then staggered over to Youngblood and jerked the phone out of Mickey's hand. He hung it up and stood there, panting his ass off, trying to focus on Youngblood's distorted face.

"You can't call him from here, Mickey."

"Yeah, no shit, dog-sore." Youngblood turned and tiptoed through the spilled trash back to his seat. "That's what I've been trying to tell you. Now you know what the fuck I'm talking about."

Luke bent down and picked the trashcan up off the floor. "I don't know, Mickey. You're still going to have to call him from somewhere."

"I will, man, but later. How many times do I have to tell you that?"

Fuck me, Luke thought. More than ever, he understood Youngblood's predicament. If they were going to do this right and make sure they left no trails, they probably weren't going to be able to call Rick Leblanc at all.

"Fuck, Mickey. Then maybe you should just track him down."

"Track him down?" Youngblood spat the question while digging his pinky into his left ear like an ice cream scoop. "You mean like a dog?"

"Yeah, like a dog," Luke said, as he leaned up on his knees and grabbed the paper towels off the counter. He ripped several off, and handed one to Mickey. "You know, and then confront him like a man."

Youngblood balled the paper towel in his fist and shook it at Luke. "I'll confront *you* like a man."

"Yeah, yeah, right." Using the paper towels as a shovel, Luke began scooping the coffee grounds back into the trashcan.

Youngblood drained the last of his beer. "So how do you think I should find him when his own brother doesn't even know where he is?"

That was a good question, but Luke could think of an even better one. What would Youngblood do once he did find him? Rick Leblanc was one bad-assed hombre, and from what Luke had heard, the guy didn't really have a lot of respect for his own or another's well-being, especially if that other well-being was the one belonging to Mickey Youngblood. Youngblood would probably have a better chance of tracking down the Loch Ness Monster and arm wrestling it for the right to swim in the Loch Ness, than convincing Rick Leblanc to pay him back.

An even better question might have been: what would they do with the kid until Rick Leblanc could be found? But that wasn't Luke's concern. His only concern at the moment was getting Mickey Youngblood and his bad attitude out of his house before his folks returned and his dad blew a fucking hemorrhoid.

"All right, Mickey, so what's the plan then? Where you going to leave the kid while you're looking for his brother?"

Youngblood smiled effetely. "Here."

Luke laughed so hard he nearly choked on the punch line. When he gathered his breath, he said, "I told you, Mickey, I can't do that."

Youngblood leaned on his elbows. "You don't have a choice."

The smile vanished from Luke's face. "What do you mean I don't have a choice? Of course, I've got a choice. We've all got choices."

"How much you owe me?"

"How much do I owe you? What the fuck does that have to do with anything?"

"Just answer the question," Youngblood said. "How much do you owe me?"

Luke could feel the lurch in his stomach. He placed his palms on the table, trying to stay grounded. "I still don't see what that has to do with anything."

"It has everything to do with everything," Youngblood said. "Now—how much do you owe me?"

"Two thousand dollars," Luke said, standing a little too quickly, the blood rushing to his head a little too fast. "And I got it all right upstairs."

The truth was he really didn't have it all upstairs. Like the mindless wonder he was sometimes, Luke had gotten so stoned before he left his house on Saturday for the Valley, that he had forgotten to collect the rest of his cash from his friends for the weed he had sold them. Instead of having the money in hand to pay Youngblood, Luke's friends got the dope and the money. How lame was that? Add to it the fact that Luke's buddy Vegas owed him eleven hundred bucks; Luke was still four hundred short of having enough to pay Youngblood back completely. But fuck it. He'd give him what he had and give him the rest when he collected it. He turned and staggered out of the kitchen.

Youngblood got up unsteadily. "Dude, where you going?"

"I'm getting your money," Luke shouted.

"Forget about it man," Youngblood shouted back. "I need to talk to you."

Luke clumsily careened back into the kitchen. "I can't forget about it, Mickey. I'm going to get you paid off right now."

Luke swayed in the doorway, as Youngblood wobbled over and put his hands on his shoulders. He looked Luke straight in the eyes; as straight as two fucked-up numbskulls could possibly look at each other. And Mickey didn't even seem mad. If anything, he seemed sad.

"Look, man, forget about the money, okay. What I really need is a friend."

Luke nodded and pulled away from Youngblood, tottering over to the counter. He poured himself a huge shot and set the tequila bottle down. He picked up the glass, about to down it, when he stopped and set the glass back down. He poured a second shot into a second shot glass and immediately downed it. He then picked up the first shot, turned to Youngblood while offering the air a toast, and absentmindedly downed that one too. His mouth creased with the hiss of the dragon's fire-breath. How he loved that taste; the rush of the alcohol searing his gullet, paddling through his bloodstream, allowing him for just a second to focus on what he needed to do. "I am your friend, Mickey. And I want to do anything I can to help you."

"I know you are," Youngblood said unevenly, "and that's what I need. I'm going to find that motherfucker, Luke. I just need to buy some time."

"Mickey, I can't—"

"Shhh … Listen to me." Youngblood's finger pressed to his mouth. "I just need a little time."

"Where am I gonna—"

Youngblood shushed him again. "Dude, shut up and listen, will ya."

Luke's mouth was open, but he didn't say anything. He just sucked in deeply, trying to keep himself from floating away.

"You okay?" Youngblood asked.

Luke's head shook. He was dizzy as a motherfucker. "Yeah, I'm fine."

Youngblood set one hand down on the counter, trying to balance himself. "How much you owe me?"

"I told you, two thousand," Luke said.

"All right, this is what I'm going to do for you. I'll deduct a hundred dollars if you'll keep the kid overnight."

Luke laughed a drunkard's laugh, loud and obnoxious, right in Youngblood's face. He couldn't believe Mickey's nerve. A hundred bucks to keep the kid for the night? Did Mickey think Luke was a complete fucking moron? He was out of his mind if he thought Luke was going to hold onto *his* kidnap victim—whom he had kidnapped over a stupid, worthless debt—while Mickey just took off scot-free. It just wasn't going to happen.

"Mickey, which part of *no* don't you understand? The kid's not staying here. We've got to figure something else out. And we've got to do it fast before my folks get back."

Mickey Youngblood was no fool. He knew he was going to have to deal, and he was prepared to do just that. "I'll tell you what—let's make it two hundred bucks."

Luke croaked, and something caught in his throat. He coughed a dry hack that nearly made him upchuck. He swallowed something slippery and turned back to Youngblood. "Mickey, I can't do it."

"Sure you can. It'll just be for one night."

Luke didn't say anything. He just staggered around the table and sat back down, gingerly. He then absently leaned his chair back on two legs, and tried not to fall flat on his head. His brain smoldered. He tried to focus on the unfocusable, the room swirling around him. And he needed to slow it down. He needed to wrap his mind around the issue at hand.

"Just for the night?" he asked.

"Just for the night," Youngblood said smoothly. To make it official, he threw in a smile.

Luke dropped his chair to the floor. "Make it two fifty and you got a deal."

The words barely left Luke's mouth before Youngblood stomped them. "Forget it."

"Then take the kid, Mickey. I don't want any part of it." Luke tried standing again but almost keeled over sideways. He grabbed onto the table for balance and closed his eyes. He looked like he was about to pass out, until Youngblood punched the table.

"All right, fuck it, you win," he said. Youngblood did not like to be outnegotiated.

Luke's eyes slid open. "What, you'll take the kid home?"

"No. Two hundred and fifty bucks for the night. But that's it."

Luke smiled blearily. "And you'll pick him up in the morning?"

"I'll pick him up as soon as I find his brother."

"In the morning," Luke said, looking like a man who was about to crash and burn. "I can't keep him any longer. My dad will have a fucking hysterectomy."

Chapter Nine

Sunday—10:14 p.m.

Luke Ridnaur tripped at least fifteen times on the elephantine walnut tree roots that buckled the dark sidewalks of San Floripez and were proving far too dangerous for him to maneuver through in the condition he was in. He was so drunk, he could barely stand, let alone walk. Good thing he wasn't driving. Same could be said for Bobby Leblanc, who staggered next to him cracking jokes, singing stupid songs, and reminiscing about the *Mr. Toad's Wild Ride* kind of day they had just survived.

Luke still couldn't believe he had agreed to take Mickey's hostage home with him. *But it's okay*, he kept telling himself. Mickey needed the help, and that's what best friends were for. They helped each other out when things got rough, even if it meant keeping your buddy's kidnap victim over at your parents' house overnight. The still air was tepid and sticky. An occasional car or truck crept slowly down or up the darkened street they walked along. The moon hung upon the eastern horizon, and it reminded Luke of a splash of yellow paint splattered against a black starlit canvas. He had measured it before by car, so he knew the walk from Ernie's to his parents' house was approximately two and a half miles long. As wasted as they were, it could have been two hundred miles and they probably wouldn't have noticed the difference.

Luke had been pounding brews, taking shots, and smoking bongloads since eleven this morning. He'd started off with three beers and six bongloads at Mickey's, then dug straight into Zit's gin at Ernie's, followed by dozens more bongloads. By the time Luke and Mickey had reached Luke's parents' house they were both totally smashed. But that didn't stop either one of them from the tequila or more beers, not to mention another dozen bongloads, enough to intoxicate a small army.

For Bobby, the story was pretty much the same. Once Luke and Mickey had returned from Luke's, Youngblood untied the kid and took him into the living room. He sat him down on the couch, talked to him, and then plied Bobby with enough bongloads to launch him into a coma. Barbados then gave the kid back his little blue pills, and Bobby immediately downed two with gin and beer, the breakfast of champions. In between, they smoked the rest of Bobby's pot and at least fifteen packs of cigarettes. It made Luke's throat scratchy just thinking about it.

And then Youngblood hauled off and just disappeared. It totally pissed Luke off at first, because they hadn't worked out the specifics of when Youngblood would pick up the kid. They had loosely agreed that he would grab Bobby first thing in the morning, so Luke just had to live with the uncertainty of what "first thing in the morning" really meant to Mickey Youngblood.

When Ernie finally returned from the barbecue with his cousin and her friend, he appeared shocked to see Luke and the kid still there. "Dude, what's up?"

Luke explained what had happened and that he wanted to hang out until later, so he could take the kid home after his parents went to bed. Luke could not allow his old man to see him bringing someone home. That seemed to placate Ernie for a short minute. Luke's homey then grabbed a beer, took a couple BLs, and seemed to forget there was ever a problem in the first place. They played the latest Terrorist Catcher video game, and Luke got his ass kicked by Bobby, who dominated everyone in the room.

Not long after, there was a rap on the front door. Luke turned to Bobby worriedly and told him to "be cool." The kid shrugged, acting as if he knew how to play the part. Some friends of Ernie's from the barbecue came in to party, and the group drank and smoked for hours. Bobby Leblanc hung out with everyone just as if he were one of the gang. He again kicked everyone's asses in Terrorist Catcher, including Armstrong's, who later told Luke that he had never been beaten by anyone at the game. It sounded like a fish tale, because Luke remembered kicking his ass a couple times, but Ernie was probably too wasted to remember.

Then the asshole Gurrola brothers showed up and nearly started a riot. Frank and Mario Gurrola were the neighborhood bullies. They were loud and obnoxious and talked mucho shit from the moment their fat little pug noses arrived. Frank immediately took it upon his drunk-assed self to pick a fight with Bobby based on what he had heard Bobby's brother had done to Mickey Youngblood.

He threatened to beat the kid's ass, and Luke told the dude to lay off. Frank Gurrola just laughed. Then he started harassing Ernie's cousin Marcia and her friend Donna by telling the seventeen-year-olds they needed a real man to teach them how to be real women. That was when Ernie decided he'd heard enough.

He set his drink down and said, "All right guys, party's over. Time to go." He stuck an arm around each of the brothers' shoulders, and they both jerked away like they'd been stabbed. Ernie glared at them, and they stared him down, their wobbly heads all tilted, as if he'd just insulted their mother. Hostilities were exchanged. Jaime Gabrial stepped over, and the tension peaked. But no one was sober enough to throw the first punch. Armstrong eventually convinced them to "just go" and got them outside, but they still weren't finished.

As the boozed-up brothers stumbled out the front yard, Mario turned and ran back up to the porch. He pounded on the door, yelling for the "gutless motherfucker Ernie" to open up. Armstrong refused, and Frank picked up a rock and smashed the porch light, shattering glass everywhere. Ernie jumped on the phone and called the San Floripez PD, and Luke figured it was time to boogie. By the time he and Bobby left, the Gurrolas were nowhere to be seen. Luke wondered if Ernie would tell the cops that Bobby Leblanc had been there. Somehow, he doubted it.

When Bobby and Luke reached the bottom of Luke's driveway, they were both exhausted. They then hiked up the steep drive, breathing heavily all the way to the top. As they approached, Luke could see the house's exterior bathed in soft moonlight; the house's only exterior light; Luke's old man being way too cheap to ever bother leaving a real one on for him.

The house's architecture was Mediterranean style, and it was situated in the middle of an old organic fruit and vegetable ranch. There were plants and trees everywhere, and a detached two-car garage. The large wrap-around patio looked in desperate need of woodwork and painting. When Luke's dad had bought the place several years back, it had been in a serious state of disrepair. The house had been overgrown with thick vegetation, but Fritz was able to distinguish the gem from the crud, and, with Luke's help, was in the process of bringing it back to life.

Luke stared at the front door and willed it to tell him whether his parents were awake or asleep. With all the shit he'd been through lately with his old man and Milsty, it was imperative that the kid not be seen. At least not before Luke had a chance to talk with his old man and prepare him for the situation. Luke didn't want Fritz asking a bunch of the wrong questions until Luke had time to come up with the right answers. That's why he needed to get Bobby upstairs to his bedroom, where it would be safe. He turned to face the kid.

"So you got to be cool, okay? You can't say anything."

Bobby peered at him through red-stained eyes. "I'm cool, dude. I told you that. Mickey's going to find my brother. And I'm going to go home. I can live with that."

Luke nodded his satisfaction, and they snuck in quietly. Inside the front door, voices filled with laughter wafted through the semidarkness from the kitchen. And Luke's shoulders slumped decisively. He felt disheartened to learn that his father and stepmother were still up. And it sounded like they had guests.

*   *   *   *

"Luke?" The voice crept up the stairs like stale smoke.

Luke and Bobby froze in muted blackness halfway up the stairs. They had sneaked across the tiled floor, through the spacious living room, and past the wood-burning fireplace without an issue. They then tippy-toed past the kitchen and had nearly made it all the way to the upstairs landing, when Bobby stumbled. It was a slight gaffe, but it had cost them dearly.

"Shit," Luke said, turning to Bobby, finger pressed to his lips.

"Luke, is that you?" His old man had heard them. But Luke didn't think he had seen him or knew anyone was with him. And he needed to keep it that way.

"Be right there." Better for Luke to go down to meet his old man, than for his old man to come up and meet them. He rotated and whispered to Bobby, "I want you to stay here. And don't go anywhere. I'll be right back."

The kid nodded, or so Luke thought, the stairway being too dark to really tell, his old man way too cheap to keep interior lights on either.

Luke sprinted down the stairs, skipping every other one in the process. When he stumbled into the kitchen, an explosion of overhead fluorescent lights accosted him. He turned and blinked in an effort to mute the intense brightness. The room was a reflection in orange. Orange acrylic floor, orange tiled counters, **orange and yellow sunflower clock on the wall, orange table and chairs, orange curtains.** Luke had always hated the color orange.

Fritz and Milsty sat at the table entertaining their drinking buddies from a couple doors over, Charley and Ruthanne Corning. That's why Luke didn't see a car in the drive or suspect anyone else to be there; the neighbors had stumbled over on their own. He saw the sink piled high with dishes and knew his old man had been barbecuing. Satiated expressions covered everybody's faces. An empty bottle of bilberry brandy stood at the center of the table surrounded by red and droopy eyes, supporting the notion Luke had missed one helluva party.

"Luke," his father slurred, "you know Charley and Ruthanne."

"Yeah, hi," Luke slurred back, hand waving from his waist. The fact was Luke probably knew the Cornings better than they knew themselves. They had been his father's drinking buddies ever since Fritz moved to San Floripez when Luke was thirteen. When his parents' divorce had been finalized, Luke was given the choice of where he wanted to live. He agreed to go with his father, while his sister Zoe remained with Mom. Several months later, Fritz took the job with the winery and moved his son up the coast with him. Luke lived with his father most of the time ever since and had become quite familiar with his neighbors.

Fritz Ridnaur waved his arm across the empty chair next to him. "Take the load off, Luke. Have a drink with us."

The last thing Luke wanted to do was sit down and have a drink with his father. The reasons were obvious: Luke had to get out of there. Besides, his father was an abusive drunk, a rerun Luke had grown tired of years before. When he was just a kid, Luke's mom would always complain about his father's abusive behavior. Luke would see her sitting up alone at night crying. But at the time, he was too young to understand. He later found out that because of his father's alcoholism, Fritz would disappear for weeks on end, occasionally calling and telling his wife that he was "traveling with friends." His father's irresponsible lifestyle provided too much insecurity for an at-home mom with two hungry kids to feed. The family suffered greatly, with Luke's mother often forced to borrow from family or neighbors just to pay the bills.

Luke's head jounced when he smiled at his drunken neighbors. "No thanks. I'm kinda burnt out, Dad. I think I'll just go on up to bed now. Good night, everybody."

The Cornings said good night. As Luke turned to leave, his father cleared his throat. "Luke?"

The left side of Luke's unibrow tightened. "Yes, Dad?"

"You've got a lot of work to do tomorrow."

Luke stopped and swiveled to face his father. "I know, Dad. Like what's new?"

Luke had work to do every day of his life. It had been that way for as long as he could remember—his father shucking off his own responsibilities and laying them on someone else. Luke's mother had come to the same conclusion years earlier, reaching her point of no return after Luke's last year in Little League. That was when she decided she'd had enough of Fritz's mean and immature behavior, and she filed for divorce. This caused Luke's father to go crazy on the entire family. He refused to move out of the house and continually took his wrathful feelings out on Luke and his sister in emotionally harmful ways. Fritz told them that their mother had destroyed the family and that their lives would always be fucked up as a result.

His father's errant philosophy particularly wreaked havoc on Luke's self-esteem. By the time his mom was finally able to get Fritz out of the house—months later—the damage had already been done. Luke had become an emotionally-battered product of one of the ugliest divorces in history. It was as though something had changed in him. As if a dark and dangerous storm cloud had inundated every aspect of his life. Beyond the age of twelve, Luke would never be emotionally stable enough to complete a full term in school, a disability that still hampered him today.

"I suggest you go on up to bed and get some sleep," Fritz Ridnaur said. "I don't want you sleeping in until all hours of the day tomorrow. I expect you to get your work done."

Luke flashed a magenta smile. His father was acting self-righteously again. It was an embarrassment, but he wasn't going to get into it with him now. Communicating with his father had always been a difficult assignment—an impossibility, really—and Luke didn't have time to fuck with it. He needed to get Bobby into his bedroom, and he needed to do it now. Besides, his old man had drunk so much that his better judgment was probably miles away.

Luke never had that problem with his mother. The woman was a godsend who tried to live her life for her children. They spoke by phone several times a week, something they had done ever since Luke moved away. When he was a teen, Luke would be home alone, and she would ask him where his father was. Luke's answer would always be the same. "At the bar." When Luke would take the train to visit his mother on weekends, he would call his father to tell him good night. He always knew where Fritz could be found, having memorized the phone number at the bar.

By the age of thirteen, Luke began imbibing on his own. Not long thereafter, his mother married Chris Parker. This provided Luke's dad with the unique **opportunity to shift the focus of his anger away from his ex-wife onto someone new.** Fritz refused to allow Luke or his sister Zoe ever to speak positively about their new stepfather without treating it as a betrayal of their loyalty to him. Luke's dad would constantly belittle Luke's mom and her new family to the kids, telling them that their mother had a new husband and did not love or need either one of them any longer. It took a huge emotional toll on both kids.

Luke's sister became heavily involved with drugs and alcohol. She dropped out of high school, moved away from her mother, and lived with friends. She would bounce from one friend's house to another's, often going to her father's in between, where she never had to deal with rules or curfews or any kind of structure whatsoever. She could come and go as she pleased. From the ages of seventeen through twenty, Zoe allowed herself to lose contact with her family, never once considering how her lifestyle might affect her younger brother, which it did dramatically.

While growing up, Luke found himself constantly shuffling between both parents' houses, desperately searching for stability without ever really setting any roots. He was still in search of those roots.

"That's what I just said I'm going to do, Dad." Luke started to leave. "Now, good night everyone."

"Luke?"

"What?" Luke's voice lacked patience.

Fritz stroked his lizard skin neck. His mouth opened, and he looked as if he were about to say something negative, when his face scrunched in apparent confusion, and his gaze shifted away from his son. "And who do we have here?"

Luke stood stumped with basically no idea what his old man was talking about. Again. He glanced over at the Cornings and faked a smile, before assuming his father had been hallucinating again. Then he turned and saw Bobby Leblanc's red face and bloodshot eyes standing in the doorway. And Luke felt a total shat blast coming on. "Dude!"

"Dude." Bobby's eyes resembled a deer's stuck in headlights.

The kid either didn't hear what Luke had told him on the stairs, or he was too stoned to understand. Either way, Luke was rat-fucked. He scrambled to regroup. "Uhm ... uh ..." He cleared his throat into the back of his hand. "This is my friend Bobby from the Valley. He's going to, uhm ... He's uhm going to spend the night. And, uhm, we're going to go to like this sortofa Fifth of July party tomorrow."

There, he had said it. And he exhaled. And he smiled weakly at his stepmother. And nodded unconfidently to his father, as interminable silence pervaded the room. Seconds segued into minutes as Milsty's hand crept under the table and tapped Fritz's knee. Red eyes and righteous indignation was cast down upon Luke as if he were a Catholic priest with a new altar boy.

Chapter Ten

Sunday—11:36 p.m.

"Dude, you were supposed to stay upstairs." Luke yanked the rolled-up mattress out of his closet and tossed it on the floor. He also grabbed the blanket and pillow he kept in there for sleepovers.

Bobby stood at the end of the bed, still sporting that faraway glazed look. "I was?"

"Yeah, dickwipe, you were. What'd you come into the kitchen for?"

Bobby frowned apologetically. "Sorry, dude. I just ... I thought somebody called me. Hope I didn't cause you any problems?"

Luke tucked the blanket and pillow into Bobby's chest. "Nah, dude. They just think I like to fuck little boys, that's all."

Bobby pondered this as if it made perfect sense. Luke told him to take the load off. And Bobby did by plunking down on the floor like a sack of carrots.

Luke scooted past him and out onto the balcony, where he grabbed his three-foot tall, glow-in-the-dark skull and crossbones bong and brought it inside. He dug under his bed and found a *High Times* magazine. He then grabbed a jar jammed with green leafy matter out of his desk drawer, sat on the bed, and spilled the jar across the magazine on his lap. He wiped the sweat from his palms onto his jeans and began breaking up the skunk-smelling bud. His mind continued to spin wild replays of their insane day. He couldn't wait until morning, when Youngblood would pick up the kid, and Luke could get on with his life. After a day like today, yard work—even the massive projects his father had assigned him—actually provided Luke with a sense of normality he had never appreciated before. He scooted his butt to the edge of the bed. His fingertips lifted to his nostrils, and he inhaled an herbal fragrance that reminded him of cocoa and vanilla bean.

Luke's room was sparse but quaint. Two large mirrored closet doors with gold metal trim ran alongside his queen-size bed. His mom's scratched and faded cherry desk and dresser provided the only other real furnishings. Minimalist decorations consisted of a dried-out stick in a clay pot on top of the TV, two signed photographs of ridiculously posed porn stars with silicone balloons for breasts, and the Britney Spears-in-a-bikini poster glued to the ceiling above his bed that Bobby couldn't peel his eyes away from.

Luke snapped his fingers. "Hey, dude, wake up."

Bobby's eyes bloated with lust. "Oh, dude. You know what I'd do with that shit?"

"I give up, what? Jizz on yourself."

"No, dude, I'm serious. They'd have to pry me off her with a crowbar."

"Yeah, yeah, yeah. You and whose army, dude? Get real. A chick like that can't be satisfied with a little white guy. You kiddin' me? She's like Madonna. She wouldn't feel anything short of the Blazers' starting five."

Bobby's head bobbed with comprehension. "Yeah, I guess you're right."

"Of course I'm right, dude. So dude … tell me. What do you want—the bed or the floor?"

"It's cool, dude, whatever. The floor's fine. No problem." Bobby leaned over and unrolled the mattress across the foot of Luke's bed. When he finished, he got up on his knees and started smoothing it out. "So, dude … can I ask you something personal?"

"You can ask."

Bobby wavered a second before looking up. "Why does your dad think you're a fag?"

"Dude—he doesn't think I'm a fag."

"That's what you said."

"No I didn't. I said he thinks I like to fuck little boys."

Bobby's eyes narrowed as he considered this. "So what's the difference?"

"The difference is that I'm not a fag. And I don't like to fuck little boys."

"Then why does your dad think you do?"

Luke huffed as he handed Bobby the bong. "Because his wife's a fucked-up cunt who needs a dildo stuck up her ass so she has something better to do than make my life miserable."

Bobby's eyes blew into red oceans. "Wow, dude. But how do you really feel about it?"

"No, dude, seriously. The problem with my stepmom is simple. She spends just a little too much time with her Bible. If you know what I mean. It's like she thinks everything that's not acceptable by the scripture is a sin. So I'm one sinning motherfucker—if you ask her. Because I like to smoke pot and cigarettes and drink. She thinks that's all I do. So when my buddies come over to spend the night, in her Biblical little mind, I must be fucking them."

Bobby's head pumped with understanding, as he inhaled a huge hit. When he exhaled, he coughed up a cloud of spit and smoke that sailed across the room. And then he said, "Oh."

"She did get my dad to stop drinking, though," Luke said thoughtfully. "And that was a good thing—while it lasted. But it turned out my dad was a better teacher than reformer. So instead of letting Milsty convert him to the Bible, he converted her to the bottle. God works in mysterious ways sometimes, ya know."

"Amen," Bobby said wastedly.

Luke slipped the bong out of Bobby's hand and said, "You know, my dad can't even get his own shit together. But the dude's always on my ass about something. If it's not my friends, it's my partying. When he's not hassling me about getting a job, he's on my ass about going back to school. It's like fuck him. Who needs that kind of pressure, you know?"

"But that's what fathers are for, dude."

"What—to badger us to death?"

"Dude, you should see my old man sometimes."

"What—your old man's a drunk too?"

Bobby smiled. "No, he doesn't really drink that much. He's just sorta like totally outta touch with reality sometimes, you know. I think it runs in the species or something."

Luke nodded his understanding and hit the bong.

Bobby asked, "How about your mom?"

Luke coughed out a lungful of smoke and rocked his head as if he'd lost his mind. "What about her?"

"You know, I mean—is she cool? Is she like your dad, or what?"

"Yeah, she's cool, I guess." Luke was still sucking air into his lungs. "I mean she's not like my dad, if that's what you mean. But she's got problems just like everyone else, you know. But with her—it's like over when it's over. We can go on with our lives. With my dad—it's just the opposite. It's like this big poisonous cloud that just hangs over us. It never goes away. All his anger. And the nagging. It's just like this big continuous problem." Luke shook his head as he loaded the bong. "How 'bout yours?"

Bobby looked at him like his brain was dead. "How's my what?"

"Dude, have another bongload. I said, your mom—what's she like?"

"Oh, you know …"

"No, dude, I don't. That's why I asked. Tell me."

"Yeah, you know, she just—she likes to act like a hypocrite sometimes."

"Oh, dude, they're all like that. Can you be a little more specific?"

"Oh, dude. It's just that …" Bobby agonized as he shook the sleep out of his legs. "It's like you said. She's just like your dad, you know. Always gettin' on me for my partying. And shit like that. Even though she does it herself. And it's just like totally embarrassing sometimes."

"Why, what does she do?"

"Oh, you know …"

"No, dude, I don't. What?"

Bobby sighed and folded his legs in front of him. "Okay, it was like … I don't know, what was it … last Labor Day, maybe? We're all up—my dad rented this house for a week up in Poinsettia. And so we're all up there, with my brother and his girlfriend. And my mom and my dad. And it's like the day before my brother's twenty-first birthday. And I was like out there with my buddy. And we're in sleeping bags. Partying in this little like dinghy out on the beach. And it's like this really beautiful night out. And we wanted to, you know, we wanted to sleep under the stars. And so Rick and his fiancée are off to the side. Smoking pot. And drinking cans of brew. And my brother gives us some herb. And everyone's like totally ripped to the tits. And we're out there laughing and looking at the stars. When all of a sudden, I hear like this really loud scream. And we're like 'Oh, my God, you know. Something must've happened to her.' Then I hear her scream again. 'Maxy, Maxy—'"

Luke interrupted the story by jamming the bong in Bobby's face. Bobby groaned and pushed it away. "No more, dude. Come on. Enough, already."

Luke shrugged, and asked, "Who's Maxy?" and then hit the bong himself.

Bobby said, "Oh, that's my dad. He doesn't party or anything. So he was upstairs snoozing. And my mom woke him up with her screaming. So he gets outta bed, you know. And my dad comes running down the stairs. And then suddenly he comes running out the front door. And he's like, 'What's going on? What's going on?' You know my dad's like wearing kid gloves. He doesn't … He wants to keep the situation from escalating. So he's like being really cool with my mom. And my mom comes running up. And she's drunk off her ass. And she says, and she tells my dad, you know, 'These two dogs, they just tried to attack me.' And she's breathing all heavy. And she tells him, 'And you need to go over there and kick that guy's fucking ass.' And my dad's like, 'Oh my God, what's going on, what happened?'

"And then this guy comes walking up from the beach, you know. Up to my dad. And he's got these two dogs on fricken leashes. And, like I wanted to die. They were like these little Shitzus ... tiny little fricken' dogs. So my dad's like, he tries to patch things up with this guy, you know. While trying to calm my mom down at the same time. And the guy's like, 'Hey, man, I'm really sorry. But apparently she was passed out in the sand, and my dogs sniffed her out and scared her.' And my dad was like so embarrassed ... like totally red in the face, you know. He tried apologizing to the guy. But at the same time, he had to watch himself. And not apologize too much in front of my mom. Or she was like just going to flip. Which basically she did anyway, yelling, 'Kick his ass. Kick his fucking ass. You can't believe the way he talked to me ...'"

"So what'd you do?"

"What did I do ...?" Bobby asked breathlessly. "I—I hid, man. I was like totally embarrassed."

"No, I mean like did you say something to your mom afterwards? Or did you go blow the guy, or what?"

"Yeah, dude, that's what I did. I went over and blew the guy right in front of my parents."

"What a fag. I hope you brushed your teeth before you kissed your mom good night."

Bobby winced. "Oh, Dude. That's so disgusting."

"No, seriously, dude. I'm telling you, moms hate that shit."

"Dude, I'm telling you ... You are one sick fuck. You know that?"

"Thank you," Luke said, as he crammed another red-haired bud into the bowl. "I'll bet she was ready for margaritas after that."

Bobby looked shipwrecked. "Huh?"

Luke muttered, "'I said all queers are deaf!'"

"What?"

"I said, You know all fags are deaf!"

Bobby giggled wastedly at Luke's obnoxiousness.

And Luke lifted the bong to his lips, snorting in yet another behemothic hit. He smiled at Bobby as his lungs expanded and his eyes flittered joyfully. When Luke exhaled, he reached behind his back and made a roll of duct tape magically appear. He then said, "Dude, I remember seeing this movie one time. Where these guys, they like wanted to kill this other dude, you know. And so they like forced him ... you know held his head back. And forced him to drink like these bottles of straight alcohol. It was like so disgusting, dude. I mean even I … they made that dude drink even more than I could drink. Or me and my old man put together. It was like so disgusting, dude. Is that how your mom gets sometimes?"

"Nah, she's not like that," Bobby said; his eyes focused intensely on the object in Luke's hand. "But, you know, I mean like—I've been in my pajamas before. And walked past the laundry room. And she'd be like totally passed out while folding laundry … My mom's like not totally together sometimes, you know. So she gets depressed a lot. I guess because I like to talk back to her or something. And so she likes to drink a bottle of champagne. And then take a whole bottle of pills. And then before she gets sick or anything, she calls my dad up. And her doctor. And she tells them what she did. And then my dad comes rushing home. And takes her to the hospital."

"Dude, that's really sad." Luke sounded like a man who understood sadness. "Sounds your mom's totally crying out for help."

"Yeah, I guess she probably is." Bobby harrumphed. "She's definitely got some issues, dude. Like this morning, when you guys picked me up?"

"Why, what happened?"

"Oh, dude. You wouldn't believe it. So like I'm in the middle of this incredible dream, right. Dude, I'm telling you, it was the greatest dream. I was with my ex, right. And we're like, we're in the middle of doin' it on this incredible beach in Florida. And we're about to like, just totally, you know, nail it. I mean, you know how you just totally nail it with a girl sometimes. You're just so connected. And you just totally hammer it? I mean, well that was me, dude. Just totally hammerin' it. When all of a sudden, I just got like totally shaken back to reality by my mom. It was terrible, dude. She's got like this cackle, you know? That just makes you wanna, you know, die. And she's like, 'What're you gonna do, sleep your life away?' And I was like, Yeah, dude—that's exactly what I'm gonna do …

"But, so like I'm totally awake now, right. And my mom's had like way too much coffee. And she's like, 'Here, Grandma wants to talk to you.' And I'm like … My mom's words are shooting out of her mouth like sparks, you know. And I—I couldn't get away. And she's like hovering all over me. And she's not—my mom's not a small woman. She's got like this big ol' blonde hair all piled on top of her head. And she's like wearing these baggy pajamas. That I guess my dad gave to her or something. And she's like—she just stares at me like I'm this little baby in a crib. And I tell her, 'But I don't want to talk to Grandma.' And she's like—she doesn't want to listen to me. You know, and she just slams the phone in my face."

Luke flashed him a mock look of sympathy.

"I'm serious, dude. My jaw still hurts … And then she just buzzes right on out. Just like that. Saying that I, you know, should come down for breakfast. It was like 10:30. But I felt like I was still dreaming. I was like, 'What the fuck's she doing waking me up so early?' Then she pops back in and says, 'Your father's going to be home soon. We're going to have our little talk. And then we'll eat.' And then she buzzes her ass right back out. And I … and dude, I was exhausted just watching her."

"Me too, man," Luke said. "Jeez Louise. But I don't get it, dude. What was she in such a hurry about?"

"Oh, you know, we had this big fight. The night before. I had gone out to CountyWalk with a buddy of mine. And my ex-girlfriend. And of course, she ends up bringing her new nigger boyfriend. And I guess I … I guess I kinda got uptight. I don't know, I guess I talked some shit or something. And then, and then she told me to go take a fucking hike. And, you know, that's what I did. I went and found this place in the parking garage. And I smoked myself into oblivion."

Luke peered at Bobby sympathetically. "Damn, dude. I should hope so. That's just awful … Can you imagine? I mean I'm telling you, dude, it's that Blazers' starting five mentality. It's the new thing with all the white chicks. You should see the Internet, dude. It's all over the place."

"Yeah, I know, dude. Tell me about it … But anyway, let me finish my story. So, you know, we're like … I get home. And it's like midnight. And, of course, my parents are still up waiting for me. So I walk in. And I'm like just totally wrecked. And as soon as I walk in, they're like all over me. And I ran into the kitchen. And they like corner me. And start hassling me about my 'drug use.' And my dad's like, you know … He wants to know what's going on with the bulge in the back of my jeans. And I guess I freaked. And I took off."

"Dude, way to handle the pressure. Where'd you go—your brother's?"

Bobby's head wagged. "No, he wasn't home. So I headed down to the park, you know. Burned a couple bowls so I could relax … Ran into an old girlfriend. And I—I ended up getting a quick handy. And then I headed home."

"Dude! A quick handy in the park …? Isn't that illegal?"

"I don't know, dude, is it?" Luke shrugged as Bobby rubbed the corner of his slanted eye. "Anyway, so I tossed the pouch with my stash in a neighbor's yard. And I went home. And my parents were still up waiting for me. Only this time, I guess they finally figured out how to get themselves under control. A little bit, anyway. So my mom's like—she greeted me with this big hug. And a kiss. But my dad's like—he could barely control his anger, you know. And I told my mom, 'I hate it when you guys get on me about my smoking.' And my dad's all like, 'You know damn well we're not talking about the cigarettes. It's the drugs.' But my mom's cool, you know. She knows how to cool everything down just in time. Before everybody blows up again. And she says that we should just wait to talk about things in the morning. 'It's time for everyone to go inside and relax. It's late. If there's going to be any discussion about drugs, it won't be tonight.'

"So this morning you know, I jump out of bed. And it's like a quarter to eleven. And my dad's like gonna be back from his tennis match any second. And that's when I went with Plan B, you know. I knew last night's truce was history. That our 'little talk' would escalate. Like it always did. And we'd be screaming in no time. And one of us was gonna end up gettin' his ass kicked. And that was probably going to be me. And I didn't want any part of it. I didn't want to hear any of my dad's lectures. Or deal with his anger issues. I was sick of it. World War III at the Leblanc house is no fun, dude. I'm telling you. So I snuck out just before my dad got home. And then like five minutes later you fucking guys showed up."

Luke frowned pitifully. "Dude …!"

"What?"

"That's the most pathetic fucking story I've ever heard."

"Tell me about it."

"Your family's worse than mine."

Bobby wagged his head and frowned and leaned over to grab the blanket off the floor. He shook it loose and pulled it up over his legs. He readjusted himself on the mattress, and then he leaned his head back. He finally appeared ready to relax, and he closed his eyes.

Luke breathed into the bong like a saxophone. He held the smoke in his chest. He then set the bong on the floor and rested his hands on his knees. Twenty seconds and ten thousand brain cells later, the second biggest mushroom cloud Luke had ever seen erupted from his lungs. He sat there wide-eyed and mindless amidst a haze of smoke and silence, before the room started vaulting, and his eyes started rolling up into the back of his head like cherries in a slot machine. His body wobbled unsteadily, and then he toppled over onto his side, looking as if he'd been shot.

With stone-red eyes, Bobby blinked at what he had just witnessed. Minutes elapsed before Luke's eyes would flutter open again, and his body would resume a vertical posture.

"Are you okay, dude?" Bobby then asked.

Luke's head revolved as if nothing had happened. "Yeah, why?"

"Because like you almost passed out. Or you did pass out. I couldn't really tell." Bobby studied Luke's contemplative daze, and it took him a few seconds to notice the roll of duct tape resting in Luke's hand. Only this time the end of the roll stood peeled off with a four-inch section of gray curled tape sticking out and waiting for assignment. Bobby's eyes inflated like soccer balls.

"Don't look at me like that, dude," Luke said. "You know I got to do it."

Bobby popped up like a jack in the box, his head oscillating rabidly. "No you don't, dude. I told you that. I'm not going anywhere."

"I know you're not, little man. I just can't take any chances."

"What are you talking about, dude? I've done everything I told you I was going to do. I'm totally content just to kick it back until Mickey gets ahold of my brother. Rick was wrong plain and simple. I can see that. He needs to make up for it. And I know he will."

Luke gestured with the tape. "Come on, dude. Don't give me the puppy dog eyes. It's just for the night."

Bobby flung his wrists wildly and glared at Luke with emotion. "Dude, come on. This is fucked up, man. I can't believe it. You guys pick me up. And you kick my ass. Then you get me totally fucking stoned out of my mind. And now you're gonna tie me up like a dog. That's totally fucked up, dude."

"Sorry, dude. Maybe you shouldn't run away from your folks next time." Luke motioned for Bobby to put his wrists together. "Now come on, let's get this over with."

Bobby huffed discouragingly. "Look, dude, I'm very content with this. Come on. I got no problem just kicking it back, okay. You don't have to do this, Luke. I'm rolling with the punches. Fuck. It's not hard to do in these surroundings. You're cool. Your parents are cool. I mean I know I'm going home eventually. So I'm not going to call anyone. If my mom and dad need to suffer a little in wondering where I am, that's cool by me. Maybe they'll learn to appreciate me. The time away will probably be good for everyone. So please don't tape me up."

Luke met Bobby's tear-filled gaze. "Bobby, it's only for the night. I told you, dude. I can't take any chances, okay? I'm sorry."

Bobby exhaled and wiped the wetness from his eye. Submissively, he folded his tanned wrists together in front of him. Luke reached over and slapped the tape onto his left wrist. As he started to wrap it, Bobby suddenly jerked his hands away; his eyes expanding with concern and fixed on something over Luke's shoulder.

Luke twisted anxiously as he heard a strange bang coming from the hallway outside his bedroom door. It sounded like his father again. He pressed his finger to his mouth, and Bobby nodded his understanding. Luke hunched up and tip-toed over to the door. He leaned forward and clasped his ear against it, listening intently. Hearing nothing, he pulled away and carefully turned the knob. The door crept open, and Luke could see his father shuffling aimlessly across the upstairs landing. Luke couldn't tell if his old man had been hanging by his door, or if he had stumbled, or what—but none of that mattered now. All that mattered was that Fritz was off to bed and out of Luke's hair for the night. When he was out of sight, Luke shut the door. He then sprinted back through his room and fell across his bed exasperatedly. "Jeez Louise … I think he was creeping around my door again. Fuck. I don't know what I'm gonna do about it."

There was no response. A minute later, Luke opened his eyes and glanced down to see Bobby laying motionless on the mattress. His eyes were closed. And a tiny smile played at the tips of his mouth. He looked content, and Luke liked him that way. Especially after the crazy fucking day they had just experienced together. How it had begun with the idea of Luke and the guys going to a friend's Fourth of July party, yet it had ended with the twister of Luke keeping Mickey Youngblood's hostage and getting the kid stoned out of his mind.

Bobby was practically sawing logs now, and Luke couldn't imagine why he ever harbored the notion of taping him up. The kid had told him point-blank that he wasn't going anywhere, so what was the harm? Sure Bobby could get up in the middle of the night and sneak out and use the phone, but what would he do then? As far as Luke could tell, the kid didn't even know where he was. They had intentionally tried to keep it from Bobby, and he believed they had succeeded.

Luke desperately wanted to trust Bobby Leblanc. But the truth was he didn't know if he could. What he did know was that the stakes were too high for him to fuck up. If the kid somehow got out, everything would go up in smoke. And Luke and Mickey could both end up going to jail. Yet, Luke felt as if he knew the kid well enough to trust him. All day, Bobby had done exactly as he was told. He had followed through on whatever he had said he was going to do. There was no reason for Luke to believe he would do otherwise now. The kid knew what would happen to him if he did. So it was with that self-reassurance that Luke tossed the roll of tape under the bed and fell back onto the pillow. To his disappointment, he was way too crispy to grab the bong for one last nightcap.

Chapter Eleven

Sunday—Midnight

When Bart Pray was a kid, he didn't even know he had it. He didn't understand what was eating away at him—sucking the marrow from his mind, depleting him of joy and happiness—while others were allowed to experience the bliss of life on a daily basis. By the time he was eleven, Bart had learned how to evade it by drowning it with alcohol. It was the easiest method of avoidance: to find a new trap, to experience a new sensation that didn't hurt so completely.

When he turned fourteen, drugs filled the void, raising Bart from the lows of the violence and neglect that filled his existence to the highs provided by the drug of his choice. Tranquilizers eased the pain and allowed him to forget. Coke got him so high it made him want to hurt somebody or fuck something up. Ecstasy played with his mind, often allowing Bart to forget that he had one. Drugs became a means of survival, because in Bart Pray's youth, survival was no guarantee. Not for Bart, his sister, nor his brothers or his mother, or even his father. They were all trapped in the same shadow, haunting the same crevices of their own sick minds.

Pot became the ultimate solution to Bart's emotional declination, but it was usually too expensive for a young man with limited means of subsistence. For a while his best friend—Mickey Youngblood—filled the void by providing the best green herbal medicine Bart had ever laid his lungs on. But once they had their falling out, Youngblood stopped providing the medicine, and the condition worsened. The shadow grew darker, and with it, the consumption of Bart Pray's self-identity grew complete.

Sometimes it would get so dark in the eye of his mind that he just wanted to turn it off. The feeling became almost overwhelming, and it affected everything he did. His moods would become so unbearable that he couldn't even stand to be around himself. He could isolate himself and stay away from others until *it* passed, but he could never escape who he was. And he hated that person whenever it hit him. He hated what he had become in life, and he feared that one day he might become his mother.

That's why he liked to stay over at Mickey Youngblood's house whenever he could. So he could read Stephen King. Through the master of horror's books, Bart had discovered new routes for escape to worlds far crazier than his own, where the characters inhabiting those worlds do freaky shit that often leads to disastrous circumstances, yet they somehow learn how to grow through it, how to survive until another day, how to lay the shadow on the line, and how to step over it. Bart hoped that he too would one day learn how to lay it on the line and how to step over it.

He breathed in deeply and stretched his six-foot-one frame. He felt strong as he glanced up at the cottage cheese ceiling from the middle of the living room floor in Mickey's empty house. He felt good to be alone—to be at peace with himself—even though he knew it would be short lived.

When Mickey had called him this morning at his grandmother's house, Bart had hoped he was calling with an invitation to join him to party. Instead, Mickey had told him to come on over and watch his house. Bart said he wanted to go with him to San Floripez, but Mickey had other plans. He needed Bart to stay at his house to make sure there wasn't another attack.

Mickey had complained about it to him over the phone, but it wasn't until Bart came over and saw all the damage—the shattered windows that Mickey had paid thousands of dollars to install—that he realized how serious it was. Mickey was furious, and Bart didn't blame him one bit. Leblanc had come over to his house and practically destroyed it. And the worst part was that Bart somehow felt responsible for the whole thing. After all, he had been the one to introduce Rick to Mickey in the first place. Bart knew Leblanc to be an extremely reckless man, so that's why, even though he had desperately wanted to be a part of the gang going to San Floripez, he agreed without hesitation to guard Mickey's place.

Bart also knew the extra time alone would give him more freedom to be with his favorite author. Through his works, Stephen King had proven to Bart that even in a world filled with despair and cruelty, it was possible for a person to find love and to discover unexpected resources within himself. Bart was searching for those same unexpected resources, as he dog-eared *Carrie* and set her on the floor. He peered over at the clock by the fireplace and realized it was getting late. He had spoken to Mickey several times during the day, but he forgot to ask him when he'd be back. The last time they spoke, Mickey had told him that Barbados would be bringing the van back later and asked if Bart wouldn't mind running it over to his godfather Denver Mattson's house when he got there. Bart shrugged his shoulders as he always did when subjected to difficult questioning and said "fine."

Barbados stumbled through Mickey's front door an hour later, totally wasted off his ass. He dropped heavily to the floor in the living room and tried leaning back against the wall, only to have his head crack against the doorjamb, and his eyes roll up in his head like a dead fish. It had sounded like a cantaloupe splitting on a sidewalk, but Barbados didn't even flinch. He didn't reach for his head or say ouch or ask for an aspirin.

Bart got up and went over to see if he was okay, or if he was bleeding, or if the wall needed replastering. He had spent all day—really, the better part of the last week—cleaning Youngblood's place to the point of scrubbing his fingers raw, and the last thing he needed was for Barbados' fat head to get blood, or scalp, or grease on the freshly scrubbed paint. Mickey would take one look at it and throw a conniption fit. He'd accuse Bart of derelicting his duties and threaten to kick his ass.

Mickey was always shitting on Bart, or having Bart pick up the shit, and Bart was getting pretty sick and tired of it all. Mickey needed to learn to pick up his own dogshit and start treating Bart with some respect, instead of always yelling at him for not getting paid. He knew Youngblood didn't really mean most of what he said—mostly just shooting his mouth off before he had a chance to think. But that's the way Mickey was sometimes. Flying around in a blind rage before realizing what he was actually doing.

Bart often felt that same rage. It would build inside of him, lurking beneath the shadow, waiting for a trigger to spring it to life. Just like in the book. Only Carrie White's rage manifested itself in supernatural powers that allowed her to get back at those who hurt her. All Bart Pray had to hurt people with were his fists, and unfortunately, most of the time, it was he who ended up being on the wrong end of getting hurt. When he felt as he did today, there were many people he wanted to hurt, and some of them very badly—like Luke Ridnaur for instance.

And he wasn't even sure why. But there was something about the guy that just bugged the shit out of him. Maybe it was Luke's sense of entitlement. The way he would come over to Mickey's and kiss his ass, snuggling up to the comforts of Youngblood's home without doing any sort of work whatsoever. Luke never picked up a beer bottle, or sanded a fence, or cleaned up the dogshit. All he ever did was come over with that smug surfer-wannabe look and leech off everything Mickey had to offer.

And that was the worst part of the whole thing—Mickey never seemed to mind. Youngblood was just like that sometimes, accommodating to a fault. And it destroyed Bart to watch Luke get away with it. Just once, he wanted to take the guy by the neck and wring it until his lights dimmed. But whenever he tried to do or say anything, Mickey was always there to yell at him. He never yelled at Luke. Bart knew there was no question he was going to have to do something about his choice of friends, but then was not the time to deal with it. He still had another chore to do.

"Come on, John, get up."

Denver Mattson lived less than five minutes away. By the time they had arrived, Barbados was snoozing in the passenger's seat like a baby. Bart grabbed the keys and left him in the front seat. He'd grab him on the way out, when they'd walk back to Mickey's together.

Mattson's was an old tract home in a family neighborhood loaded with big, old trees out front; every one of them seemingly dropping their leaves in Mattson's front yard. His house was painted two-tone blue, and it was topped by a slanted tile roof that was also drowned in leaves. *The guy desperately needs a gardener*, Bart thought, as he walked through the front gate. To his surprise, Mattson stood at the front door waiting for him. He acted as if he'd been expecting Bart all day.

They had met only once, but Mattson seemed like a decent enough guy. A thick, rounded man who could lose a hundred pounds, and you'd never notice the difference. Mickey had always referred to him as his godfather, and he looked the part, only heavier. He looked like the kind of guy who could order a hit just as easily as pulling one off himself.

When Bart handed him the keys, he noticed ham-sized hands extending to thick sausage-fingers. Mattson then thanked him, and asked if Bart wouldn't mind pulling the van closer to his house.

Now, as Bart reached over and grabbed the black cordless phone off Mickey's floor and punched in his mother's number, he realized how empty and alone he was. He would miss Mickey tremendously. But he thought he would miss staying at Mickey's house even more. Where Youngblood had become anxious to move out—and seemed content on staying away for good—Bart never wanted to leave. When he was alone, he sometimes found himself wishing Mickey would never come back. Not that he wanted him to get hurt or anything. He just wanted to be able to stay at Mickey's forever. With nobody ever coming around to molest him. Then he could just lie there on the floor and read his books and never have to explain anything to anybody ever again. But that wasn't going to happen, Bart knew. Mickey was soon going to sell his house, leaving Bart to stumble on his own path of personal instability.

But that will change, he kept telling himself, *as soon as I get my debts paid off.* Then Bart would be in a position to help his mother, who was in desperate need of her own professional care. The only person in the world who could now save Cyndy Pray was her son Bart. Sure, Bart's Auntie Linda would visit and help whenever she could, but she was a very sick woman herself, who didn't need the additional burden of worrying about her fucked-up older sister. As far as Bart's brothers and sister were concerned, they wouldn't be helping anybody for a while. Bart's younger brother Shawn was just finishing up the first three years of a nine-year tour of duty with the state corrections department for a home invasion robbery. His older sister Jenny had spiraled out so deeply that she had been living underground until a recent arrest on heroin charges. She was now serving eighteen months on a probation violation. And his eight-year-old brother Jimmy was being raised by their abusive, alcoholic father, Bart's equally abusive alcoholic stepmother, and her sickly brood in Brownsville, Texas, where the boy had been unable to avoid the violent pitfalls that had previously befallen his older siblings.

After thirty-one rings without an answer, Bart finally hung up. He had been trying to reach his mother for the better part of the last two days without success. The woman was not doing well, and he couldn't imagine her having gone anywhere, especially this late. She was usually too sick to leave her apartment and had been on a downward spiral ever since she stopped taking her medications. He wanted to visit her just to make sure she was okay, and if she didn't answer the phone by tomorrow, he would get on his heels and hoof the three miles over to her apartment. He often did that, just hike over, usually from his grandparents' house, and would just show up unannounced. Even if she wasn't doing well, just sitting with her was usually enough to get her out of bed and to start talking.

Her place usually had no food in it, so Bart would somehow scrape together a few bucks, maybe borrow it from Mickey under false pretenses, and take her out to lunch at her favorite restaurant, Burrito Vic's up on Douglas Way. Unfortunately, at the moment, Bart was a little low on cash, with no real prospects of getting any between now and then. But who knew? Just like in the books, anything could happen. Maybe Mickey would come back. Maybe he'd be in a great mood, appreciate all the hard work Bart had done for him, and give him a few bucks to hold him over. And then again, maybe Bart would win the lottery, hell would freeze over, and Santa Claus would want to adopt him.

Chapter Twelve

Day Two
Monday, July 5—8:46 a.m.

Monday morning hit Luke like a steel-tipped boot to the gonads. If he had been awake, he was pretty sure it would have hurt like hell. He had first looked at the clock at 7:30 and couldn't figure out what he was doing up so early or why his heart raced so badly. Then he saw the kid cocooned on the floor at the foot of his bed, and his brain went numb. The hangover from what had transpired the day before shot through him like a nauseous nightmare. He tried rolling over a thousand times, but all it did was wrinkle his face. He tried taking a couple bongloads, but that only made him more angst out.

When he finally rolled out of bed, Luke could see the kid still snoozing, so he left him there. No need to add early-morning babysitting responsibilities to an already overloaded schedule. Now he was practically sleepwalking into the kitchen, and it wasn't even nine o'clock yet. His dad had left for work about 8:30, catching the bus from Cherokee Road and De Los Amigos on his way to the winery. His stepmother left in the family car about ten minutes later, so he knew the coast would be clear for a while.

The events of yesterday had surged through his mind like sewer water and kept him up all night. It was as if he were living in a dream, and he kept thinking that when he awoke, it would be over, the kid would be gone, and he would be out doing yard work, taking bongloads, and be free of this constant nagging in the back of his brain. Now that he was awake, the only concrete reality Luke could put a finger on was that he had yard work to do. He had already paged Youngblood half a dozen times and couldn't wait to set up a time to get the kid out of here. If he had a car, he would have been tempted to drive the kid home right this very minute. But he had no car, and "ifs" weren't going to get him or the kid anywhere—and he knew that if he didn't get the kid out of the house fast, the place was going to blow like an inferno when his father got home.

He called his buddy Vegas to see what he was up to, and of course, his answer was what it always was. "Nothing." Luke then told Vegas what was what. "Dude, you wouldn't believe what Mickey Youngblood did. He kidnapped this kid because of a drug debt, and he left him over at my place." Luke thought he heard Vegas yawn. "You know, it's very stressful taking care of a hostage at home when your father and stepmother are hanging around." Vegas yawned again and sounded as if he were still asleep. He didn't seem very sympathetic to Luke's plight. Luke told him to get his ass over here, because there was work to be done.

"You still owe me money, dude."

A few minutes later, Luke was sitting at the kitchen table working on his second cup of coffee and like sixteenth cigarette, when the phone rang, causing him to nearly jump out of his Porn Rat boxers. He was ready to chastise Mickey for waiting so long to call him back, but it was his dad, telling him, "I don't want any partying at the house today, Luke. I expect you to get your work done. And I expect your friend to go home."

Fuck you. Luke listened to that nonsense for about a minute and hung up. What the fuck was his dad's problem? Luke wasn't in the mood to party; this was work, motherfucker. Work at trying to get rid of a hostage before he got busted for something bad. He wanted to explain it to Fritz last night, but his father was on his high horse, and there was no communication or understanding between the two of them. There rarely ever was.

Luke was on his third cup of coffee by the time he started the yard work. Vegas showed up about twenty minutes later, and he immediately disrupted Luke's train of thought by talking *mucho caca* about how he was going to kick Luke's ass in Terrorist Catcher. It made Luke want to gag. First of all, he didn't have time to play—there was work to be done. Secondly, he owned Vegas in Terrorist Catcher—Vegas having won like once in a thousand games, and that was only because Luke had been too drunk, or too stoned, or a combination of the two to be able to see, let alone play the stupid-assed video game. Luke would reveal all the codes, visit the Secret Stargate, unlock the Air Defense Simulator, and blow everything to blood and guts. Luke was the true Terrorist Catcher; Vegas was nothing more than a national security wannabe, and Luke was about to tell him this but felt he needed to get the trenches dug for the fall tomato plants first.

The intense sun beat down like a nuclear furnace. Luke didn't remember it ever being this hot in San Floripez before. The summers were always intense in the Valley, but not out here at his dad's. This summer was different, though. Every day seemed to grow hotter than the one before, which was great for the plants, but the heat sucked the energy and the will to work out of Luke. He was digging holes two feet apart in rows four feet wide, which he would soon fill with green tomato plants. As he bent down to clip the bands off the stakes, he gazed over at Vegas, who was sitting on a railroad tie staring absentmindedly off into the banana and mango grove.

Vegas Parsons was rail thin, with frizzed-out hair and long, athletic legs. Over-sized gym shorts hung down to the middle of his skinny calves; an oversized gray athletic T-shirt and black tennis shoes rounded out the ensemble.

"So what's up, dude?" Luke asked, spying through the halo of blazing sunlight that made Vegas look like a teenaged Jesus.

Vegas looked up at him with a glazed look, and Luke just laughed. His mouth tasted like cotton, and he knew he either needed to get something to drink or light up a joint. So he lit up a joint. And he said, "Dude, there's another shovel over there if you feel like helping."

Vegas acted like he didn't hear this as Luke handed him the joint. "Nah, I'm cool."

That was Vegas being Vegas. Come over, watch Luke work his ass off, smoke all of his dope, and never offer to lift a finger. Luke was determined to break him of the habit. "So dude, how much you owe me?"

Vegas had started to hit the joint, but stopped. "Yeah, I don't know, dude, I forget."

Luke stabbed the shovel into the the dry soil and leaned against it. "I think it's like up to eleven hundred bucks, if I'm not mistaken."

"No way, dude."

"Yeah, way."

Vegas shook his head vehemently. "Couldn't be."

"I'm telling you, man …" Luke gestured for Vegas to hit the joint. "You need to pay me or something."

Vegas wore the gloomy look usually reserved for funerals, as he hit the joint and passed it back to Luke. The problem with Vegas was that he was a pothead who always needed smoke but never had money since he hardly made anything work-ing for his mom, who was an interior decorator. So Vegas would get Luke to front some to his high school buddies, then pinch some off the top for himself. This way Vegas could keep smoking without ever having to pay for it. Unfortunately,

Vegas' little faggot high school buddies weren't paying Luke back, so the debt fell squarely back onto his shoulders.

Vegas opened his palms to the sky as if the gesture should explain everything. "I don't have it, dude—I'm broke."

Toward the end of May, they had suffered through the same problem. Vegas had owed Luke nearly a thousand dollars then, and he played the broken record of saying he didn't have it. Luke knew Vegas had a pair of DJ turntables and sound system and suggested that he just pawn them off. Vegas nearly came to tears. He told Luke he didn't want to do that, but he really didn't have any other way to pay him back. He called a few pawnshops and music shops, and the best he could come up with was seven hundred dollars for the whole set. That would have still left him nearly three hundred dollars short. Luke didn't want to see Vegas cry like a little bitch, so he told him to give him the turntables and they'd be even, which is what Vegas eventually did. But now, the debt was back up again, to eleven hundred dollars, and Vegas still didn't have any money but was loaded with lame-assed excuses. It was a broken record that Luke was tired of hearing.

"Dude, I need my money," he said, as he started digging. "I've got to get Mickey Youngblood paid off."

Vegas put his hand over his eyes, shading them from the yellow and white glare. "How much you owe him?"

"Two thousand dollars, man. And you know Youngblood. As soon as he brings his little ass over here, he's going to start ranting about his money. Trust me, dude, one thing you don't want to do is owe Mickey Youngblood money."

Vegas stood and slapped the dirt out of his gym shorts. A cloud of brown dust roiled in the air around him. "He's a pretty scary guy, isn't he?"

"Scary?" Luke stopped digging, and stared at his friend. "Fuck, man, that's not even the half of it. Mickey's not even the one I'm worried about."

Vegas sat back down. "Then who you worried about?"

Luke hesitated for a second, like he'd forgotten the question. Then he said, "His dad."

"His dad?"

"Yeah, man, I mean, fuck ... His dad's not like yours or mine, you know."

Vegas' face tilted with a puzzled look. "He's not?"

"No, dude. He's a fucking ..." Luke paused, eyes veering across the yard, making sure no one was listening. "He's a fucking animal, dude."

Vegas' eyes distended. "He is?"

Luke again searched the yard making sure no one was within earshot. "Look, if I tell you something, you can't tell anybody, okay." Vegas nodded. "I mean, if anybody finds out I told you this, we could both fucking get it."

"Get what, dude?"

Luke drew his hand from one ear across his neck to the other ear in a slitting motion. "He's in the underworld, dude. He's got like connections from New Jersey and shit. And from what I've heard ..." Luke pulled in closer. "He's like left bodies in ditches and shit."

Vegas swallowed uncomfortably, stood, and cricked his neck in a circle.

"Now you can't say anything, Vegas. I mean, you say something, and we both could end up pushing up daisies, okay?"

Vegas bent over and reached his hands down to his toes, taking in a long deep breath while stretching his hamstrings. "I'm not going to say anything."

"Good." Luke considered relighting the joint in his hand but decided to wait and shoved it in his pocket. "So dude, I need my money."

Vegas stood erect. "I don't have your money, Luke, I told you that."

"You owe me, dude." Luke stabbed the shovel into the dirt, nearly slicing off Vegas' toes. "I could use some help finishing this."

Vegas just stood there gazing blankly at the shovel by his feet, his mouth moving like a trout's out of water, with no words coming out.

"Mickey's coming over later, and he's going to want his money." Luke tried meeting Vegas' empty glare. "Dude, are you listening to me?"

"Yeah, I'm listening, man, I'm listening."

"Dude, Youngblood's unbelievable," Luke said. "Acts like a whiney little bitch whenever he doesn't get his way. And you know what, I don't want to hear it. Look, I took a chance with your boys, and they fucking let you down. So now, you owe me. And I need you to help me finish this shit up. So I can go back inside. And figure out how the fuck I'm going to pay him back." He held the shovel out for Vegas to grab. "Here, Vegas. I need some help. Trust me, dude; it's in both of our best interests."

Vegas didn't look like he trusted Luke at all. He just stood there, as if evaluating the consequences of Luke's request. Luke flipped his wrist, gesturing for Vegas to take the shovel, but Vegas didn't get it. Luke was getting very bent when he heard ...

"I'll help you."

They both turned around to see Bobby Leblanc standing there, barefoot, in his jeans and T-shirt, hair standing on end. His eyes looked puffy. And a big grin rode the bottom half of his face.

Luke introduced Vegas to Bobby. After introductions, Bobby turned to Luke. "So where do you want me to start?"

Luke's glance swung from Vegas back to Bobby. Damn, he liked this kid's attitude. He explained to Bobby what needed to be done, and in no time, the work was flowing smoother than gin over ice. They finished planting the tomatoes in about a third the time it would have taken Luke to do it on his own. Bobby worked hard and worked up a tremendous sweat. They laughed and told jokes, and the kid really enjoyed his time in the sun, the lush vegetation, and the fresh ocean air, while Vegas just sat like a bump on a log and watched.

Luke and Bobby knocked off almost half of his old man's To Do list by early afternoon. They soaked and fertilized all the hanging baskets by mixing water-soluble fertilizer into the water. They divided the summer perennials, including the daffodils, irises, and daylilies. They replanted the best clumps, and Luke chucked the damaged ones. They watered all the large-leaved plants, including the chrysanthemums and hydrangeas. Luke and Bobby were having so much fun and laughing so hard, like a couple little bitches in heat, that Vegas even got off his lazy ass to join the fun.

"So, dude, what can I do?"

Luke thought he might die from toxic shock. He scanned the yard, and he couldn't believe how much work they'd completed already. Even if he went the next week without getting anything else done, his old man would think he was ahead of the game. Luke wiped the sweat from his brow with his sleeve, and he could tell by the position of the overhead sun that it was getting late. It was time to give Youngblood another holler. The dude still hadn't called him back, and he wondered how long it was going to take to find Rick Leblanc.

He set the hose down and walked to the side of the house, where he turned it off. When he saw that no one was looking, he disappeared behind the purple hydrangea bush and then took off running around to the back. When he reached the sandstone path by the prehistoric-looking ferns, he slowed his gait. Then he raced up the wooden stairs, before sneaking through the back door and into the house. He then walked briskly through the hallway, and took a right into the kitchen, where he fell behind the orange curtains, and panted heavily.

He leaned up and peered over the window sill and could see Bobby and Vegas exhibiting great teamwork while transplanting his father's iris beds. Luke felt tremendous parental pride and thought it would have been so terribly uncool of him to deflate his new helpers' enthusiasm. So he just left them alone, allowing them to do their work, and ducked under the curtains. He then sprinted upstairs to climb in Mickey Youngblood's ass about picking the kid up.

Chapter Thirteen

Monday—2:02 p.m.

Rosy Kinski lived with her dad, stepmom, and brother in one of the nicest parts of San Floripez, called the Upper Mesa. The highlight of each of her summer days was when she got to go over and visit her buddies in Lost Valley. Luke Ridnaur's parents had a neat place, and Luke and Vegas Parsons always made her feel like one of the boys when she visited. They weren't like other guys, who just liked to act macho, stare at her breasts, and swear a lot. Vegas and Luke were a couple of decent guys who just liked to party and have fun, like any seventeen-year-old party girl's dream. Even when her friend Cheri Merced came along, the two of them knew they would be treated with the respect they deserved.

Today, it was no surprise when she got there and saw Luke had been sweating it out in the yard. Since they had been hanging out this summer, he'd been pretty much doing the same thing every day, working in the yard, smoking pot, and drinking beer. It was a ritual that she'd come to expect from him.

They had originally met last year, but they didn't start hanging out until this past May. During their summertime together, Rosy had grown to appreciate Luke's natural ebullience and the high energy that was the initial spark for their friendship. She came to know Luke as an intelligent, witty, warm, and very caring individual. He loved to talk about his family, especially his sister Zoe and his two-year-old niece Sierra. He enjoyed the responsibilities of playing uncle, and he was by his sister's side at the hospital when Sierra was born. He loved helping her take care of his little niece whenever his sister asked him to. He also spent a lot of time helping Zoe and her husband Fidel Chavarrias set up their business, their records and files, and he assisted them in their shop so they could spend more time with the baby. It was through those conversations that Rosy learned how loyal and trusting Luke could be. He also had a passion for art, a talent she often encouraged him to develop whenever he decided to go back to school.

There was something about Luke—as he hunched over in his knee-length baggy shorts and dug in the garden, sweat glistening off his long tanned body— that she liked very much. Even though she wasn't interested in him physically— he really wasn't her type—she loved to watch his lean muscles flex and crunch as he crouched over to transplant another plant or to dig holes for new fruit trees. She thought his shaved head was totally sexy.

Since Luke's brother-in-law Fidel opened his tattoo shop, called the Bloody Sword and located in downtown San Floripez—a place she thought was cool but didn't frequent because she didn't approve of the Nazi and White Supremacist paraphernalia they displayed—Luke had become a walking billboard covered in tatts. Cobras adorned both arms. His last name spilled across his belly, and he had a skull on his right leg. He was a simulation of ripped skin with tribal carvings wrapped around the other.

Looking all wide-eyed and amped out, Luke let her in the front door when she arrived, then disappeared just as quickly up the stairs, telling her he had to go make another phone call. When she walked into the living room, Rosy was surprised to find Vegas playing video games with another very handsome young male, whom Vegas introduced.

"This is Luke's friend, Bobby, from the Valley."

Bobby was tall and lean, and he had a curly shock of jet black hair and bedroom eyes that made her heart giggle. She sat on the couch and watched them scream and duck and work their little joy sticks just like boys who play video games like to do. When they were done, the body language of hunched shoulders and low groans from Vegas, and the huge smile and cock-of-the-walk strut from Bobby, told her all she needed to know about winners and losers.

They then went outside onto the patio to smoke cigarettes, and Rosy was immediately impressed by Bobby's strong demeanor. He was nicely dressed in denim pants, white tennis shoes, and a T-shirt with black sleeves and a teal-colored body, which she thought looked a lot like Luke's.

"Hi, how are you? I'm Rosy."

When she stuck her hand out, she could feel her toes turn inward like a pigeon's. Bobby took her hand and held it firmly yet gently, and Rosy cooed at the way he knew how to treat a woman. Then she tipped her head slightly, looked up at him from under her eyebrows, and she thought of Julia Roberts looking at Richard Gere with her famous come-hither look in that old movie she once watched with her stepmother.

When they talked, Rosy felt totally at ease. She told him she was seventeen. He told her he was sixteen, a figure he would later admit was actually fifteen. His voice was soft and confident. And his stories about skateboarding and karate and music cracked her up. Then, out of the blue, Bobby admitted that he was addicted to tranquilizers, and it made her sad to see such a young kid get so screwed up so early in his life. But he didn't seem concerned about it in the least.

She could hear thumping coming down the stairs, and a moment later, Luke scurried out onto the patio carrying an ice-cold six-pack of brewskis. He popped the tops, passed them out, and they all chugged away. She could sense the bubbly freshness of the new day when Luke lit up a joint and passed it to her. She noticed his perpetual smile, but he looked weary and tired, as if he hadn't slept in a month.

When she passed the joint over to Bobby, he looked up at Luke. "Dude, I'm hungry. Can I get something to eat?"

"I'll go with you," Luke said.

Bobby got up and handed Vegas the joint. As Luke and Bobby walked into the house, Rosy could hear Luke saying, "Dude, grab whatever you want out of the kitchen, but you can't use the telephone."

That was when Rosy felt the first jolt in her chest. She didn't understand what Luke had meant, but it really sounded strange. Can't use the telephone? She looked over at Vegas as he passed her the joint, but he avoided her gaze. She started to ask him what was up with the phone statement but decided against it. She didn't want to start something that didn't exist. Luke was one of the most generous guys she had ever known, the kind of guy who would literally give you the shirt off his back, which Bobby could attest to at this very moment. So whatever was going on, she was sure there was a logical explanation for it. She just couldn't figure out what it might be.

They finished the joint and kicked it back in the intense sun. It was starting to roast, and Rosy found herself sweating like a dog in a Chinese restaurant. She removed her long-sleeved shirt and felt better immediately. She was now relaxed and ready to get some sun on her freckled, white shoulders, when she saw Luke sprint out the sliding glass door as if his hair were on fire. "All right, let's get out of here," he said, panting.

"Excuse me." Rosy sat up, trying to figure out why Luke was so out of breath. "I just got comfortable."

"Yeah, well, maybe we could all get comfortable over at your house." Luke clapped his hands together.

"My house?" She saw Bobby standing by the door and lobbed him a quick smile. "Why would we go to my house? I just got here."

Luke smiled as if he had just swallowed the cat. "Because my stepmom might be home any second. And I'm not supposed to have parties here anymore. So what do you say, Rosy?"

Rosy knew Luke had been having problems with his stepmother. He had had them for the ten years he had known her. Luke's stepmother was a religious woman, who was active with Rosemary Chapel, played guitar in church, and sang hymns on a religious radio program. She was also always on Luke's father's back about Luke partying all the time and not working or going to school. But Rosy didn't ever remember the woman coming home during the middle of the day to check up on him. It always seemed just the opposite, as if she were trying to get away from him.

"Fine," she said, getting up and putting her shirt back on. "Let's go."

Luke turned to Bobby. "And I want you to help me clean up the house." He said it in an uncharacteristically bossy tone, then pivoted and rushed back inside, where he opened the downstairs closet. Rosy, Bobby, and Vegas followed behind.

Luke pulled the vacuum cleaner out, and turned to Bobby. "I want you to start by vacuuming everything, including the stairs. I don't want anything missed. And when you're done, I want you to clean all the ashtrays, dump all the beer bottles, and dust the table off. Understand?"

"Aye-aye, captain." Bobby said it while beginning a salute that was quickly aborted when Luke jammed the vacuum cleaner handle into his ribs.

*   *   *   *

The ride over to Rosy's house had been solemn and quiet. When they arrived, Luke and Vegas headed straight into the living room and flicked on the TV, while Bobby just sort of floated around in a wide-eyed daze, drinking in the luxuriant surroundings. Her place was immense, and Bobby seemed particularly interested in the living room view of the treetop forest of California oaks.

"This place is incredible, Rosy."

She smiled and took his arm into the curve of hers. Then she walked him upstairs and out onto the deck, which had the greatest view of all, including a full frontal shot of the Pacific. "We can see coyotes, rabbits, hawks, deer, and about any other kinds of animals you can think of."

He turned and smiled at her. "How 'bout bears?"

She flashed her pearly whites. "No bears."

She then showed off two exquisitely decorated bedrooms, before taking him back downstairs and showing off hers.

A huge California king-size four-poster bed centered Rosy's bedroom. It was topped by a cream-colored canopy. A white and pink lace comforter sat atop the bed. Rows of collectable teddy bears of all shapes and sizes lined one shelved wall. Rare collector dolls lined the other.

Bobby's expression said he had never seen a room quite like hers before. She pointed out her window through the dense forest of trees. "Down through there, although you can't quite see it, is the historic Old Mission. And over to the left ..." She guided his gaze with her hand. "Is downtown San Floripez."

Bobby nodded as if impressed by the splendidness of his surroundings. When they went back down into the living room, Vegas was sitting on the overstuffed couch, his arms folded across his chest. A wide grin sat across his face, and his eyes were slanted and red. He was watching cartoons on TV without any sound. Rosy glanced around the room but didn't see anyone else. "Where's Luke?"

Vegas barely shrugged. Rosy excused herself from Bobby and went into the kitchen. She wore a concerned look as she surveyed the bathrooms, the den, the upstairs bedrooms, and the outside decks, before walking back into the living room, where she stood with her hands on her hips. "I can't believe it."

Bobby was now seated on the couch next to Vegas. He looked up at her with stoned and red eyes. "What?"

"He's gone."

Bobby glanced around the room as if he had missed someone. "Who is?"

"Luke. He left without even saying good-bye. What a shit-turd."

Bobby laughed, and stood up from the couch. "I'm sure he didn't go far. Can I use your bathroom?"

"Of course you can. I don't know what that's all about, but you don't ever have to ask for permission to use the bathroom, okay?"

Bobby nodded with a smile and headed into the bathroom. Rosy looked over at Vegas who looked like he was asleep. She stepped over to the couch and tapped him on the knee. "Hey, stoner-boy, wake up." Vegas' eyes slid open, barely. "Let's talk."

He pulled himself up on his hands, and gazed at her groggily. She grabbed his arm and yanked him off the sofa. She then dragged him into her bedroom.

"Hey, what're you doing?" Vegas protested as she closed the door behind him. "What's going on?"

Rosy took a seat on her bed. "I was going to ask you the same thing."

Vegas looked like someone had poured sleeping dust into his eyes. "What?"

She tapped the space on the bed next to her for him to sit down. He shook his head *no*, and she asked, "What's going on with Bobby?"

"What's going on with Bobby?"

"I asked you first."

Vegas took a deep breath and exhaled. He surveyed the room like someone looking for a place to hide. "Uhm, what do you mean?"

Rosy's happy-go-lucky smile disappeared. "Vegas, try not to be an idiot for a change, okay?"

"I'm not—"

"Yes, you are. Why was Luke bossing Bobby around like that?"

Vegas shook his head and decided to take the seat next to her. "Like what?"

"You saw him at his house. Why was he telling Bobby what to do? You know, with the vacuuming and the yard work and all that stuff. What's going on?"

Vegas stood up from the bed. "I don't know. Maybe he needed some help."

Rosy grabbed his arm and pulled him back down. "Vegas!"

"What?"

She took a brusque breath. "Why did Luke tell Bobby he couldn't use the phone?"

"He did?"

"Vegas! What are you hiding?"

"Nothing."

"Then tell me."

"I don't know nothing." His hands fidgeted in his pockets, and he kept avoiding her gaze, as if he were trying to conceal something. With no question pending, he stood and started to leave.

Rosy leapt off the bed. "Vegas, come back here."

"What?" He pivoted. "I'm going to the bathroom."

"You'll go to the bathroom when I'm finished with you." She stepped over and grabbed him by the shirt. She then walked him back over to the bed and sat him back down. She hovered over him, her hands on her hips, like a mother scolding a child. "Vegas Parsons, I know you're hiding something. Now what is it?"

"I'm not," he whined.

"I know you are. Look at you—you can't even look me straight in the eye." His head tilted up, but he would not meet her gaze. "See ..." She reached down and lifted his chin with her hand. "Vegas ... look at me."

Although his face was slanted upward, his eyes peered straight ahead, at her chest.

She tapped the underside of his chin. "I'm up here, Vegas." Finally, his eyes met hers. "What's going on here?" He turned away again, his mouth clenched in torment. "Just tell me," she said. "I'm not going to hurt you."

"All right." He wriggled his chin out of her grasp. After a deep sigh, he said, "Promise you won't tell anyone."

"What, Vegas?" Her tone was filled with impatience and empathy.

"Yesterday, Luke, and ... and Mickey Youngblood, and a ... and a couple others went to the Valley. And were looking for Bobby's older brother, right. But ... but they couldn't find him. So ... so they found Bobby and threw him in the van. And then they brought him up to San Floripez." There, he got it out of his system. And he just sat there, his eyes bulging, like someone had just choked the words right out of him.

Before Rosy could respond to what she had just heard, the phone rang. She tried to ignore it, feeling a wave of upset flooding through her veins, and it took a minute of breathing deeply just to keep from crying. Then the words tumbled out of her mouth before she even realized she had said them.

"You mean he was kidnapped?"

Chapter Fourteen

Monday—3:54 p.m.

If Rosy ever needed someone to talk to, now was the time. Even Cheri Merced's dumb blonde routine would be a welcomed relief from the ice glacier chill that swept through her. When she had finished with Vegas and answered the phone, Cheri told her she couldn't find anyone over at Luke's, so she called and found Rosy.

"You got to come over right now," Rosy told her, hanging up without giving Cheri a chance to respond. It all seemed totally surreal, as she thought about what Vegas had told her. If anything, Bobby Leblanc acted like the poster child for the *un-kidnapped*. He had been free to walk around and do pretty much whatever he wanted both at her house and at Luke's. It's not as if she were an expert at kidnappings or anything like that, but they had been talking, smoking cigarettes and pot, drinking beer, and watching TV, and nobody had been particularly tense about anything. It didn't seem anything at all like the kidnappings she had seen on TV or in the movies, although Luke had been acting all nervous and jittery when they were over at his house.

Now they were out on the deck outside her living room smoking cigarettes. She studied Bobby and Vegas, who were talking their boy talk—discussing kick flips and half pipes—and it all sounded like pretty boring stuff to her. But not to them. They were just two little boys striving to be men, and that's all they were doing. So where was the problem? This kid was like every other teen she knew, so it pained her deeply when she stared at the beauty of the words he spoke. It was like slow motion, his full lips bearing the sweetest of smiles and those heavenly brown eyes, and it all made her want to cry just to imagine that he wasn't free to just get up and leave if he wanted to.

When Cheri showed up a half hour later, she sat across the table from Rosy and seemed oblivious to the trauma Rosy felt. Cheri started talking to Bobby and smoking, and he was practically telling her his life story. When he stood up, he asked Rosy if he could use her bathroom. She glared at him like she wanted to spank him.

"Okay, all right—I'm going." He smiled at her and walked into the house.

When he disappeared, Rosy leaned over the table and said, "He's been kidnapped."

Cheri flashed that dumb blonde smile that Rosy always wanted to slap off her face. "What do you mean?"

Rosy frowned for emphasis. "He's been kidnapped."

Cheri pressed two fingers to her temples. "Luke?"

"No," Rosy said impatiently, "Bobby. They picked him up in the Valley and brought him here to San Floripez."

Cheri looked around, more confused than usual. "Who did?"

"Luke and Mickey Youngblood."

Cheri pulled a strand of blonde hair out of her face, and tucked it behind her ear. She didn't look fazed in the least.

"Anyone got any rubbing alcohol?"

Rosy peeked up to see Bobby standing in the doorway, proudly displaying the crimson scrapes and scabs that ran the length of his arm, and she smiled to herself, thinking she had the perfect medicine for what ailed her new friend.

*   *   *   *

"I never really had a chance to get it cleaned up yesterday," Bobby Leblanc said. "I ripped it on the ground when they tackled me." He stood at the pink sink in Rosy's pink bathroom while Rosy rubbed a cotton ball soaked with alcohol across his arm.

Cheri Merced closely monitored the operation from behind them. "Why did they do that?"

Bobby grimaced from the sting. "They were looking for my brother. And I guess I just happened to be walking down the street at the wrong time."

Rosy tossed the cotton ball into the trashcan and pulled another one out of the plastic bag. "As I understand it, they were looking for your brother because he owed Mickey Youngblood money."

A flush of crimson ran through Bobby's face. "Yeah, I guess he busted out his windows or something."

"Aren't you afraid?" Cheri asked.

Bobby shook his head. "Not anymore. I was for a little bit when they first picked me up. But you know what? Now I think everything's going to be okay."

He really felt it was. Even though he hadn't seen a lot of his brother lately, Bobby knew that once Youngblood made contact with him and told Rick about the situation, he would get everything straightened out.

Rosy gently blew on his arm, helping to take the sting out of his burn. "Are you close with your brother?"

It was such a complicated question Bobby didn't know how to begin to answer it. "Yes and no," he said ambivalently. "I mean I love my brother about as much as you can love anyone. I just don't know him."

Even though, in his own inimitable style, Rick Leblanc had been the one to introduce Bobby to the world of sex, drugs, and the Valley party scene, he had worked hard to keep his little brother from following in his dangerous footsteps. This, of course, was greatly influenced by Bobby's parents. Sharon and Max Leblanc had spent Bobby's lifetime trying to keep him away from his half brother. For all intents and purposes, they had tried to put an end to the relationship before it ever started. Seeing what Rick could do and what he had done, they desperately wanted to remove Bobby from that reality.

Bobby couldn't ever remember his parents allowing his half brother to be around him when he was a baby. Ever. And when he was growing up, Bobby's mother would poison his mind regarding his half brother every chance she got. She would tell him—with contempt in her voice—how she would never allow Bobby to be like Rick. How, from the time he was born, Rick had cried and screamed and did whatever he could to become the center of things. She said even when Rick got in trouble, it was a way of drawing attention to himself.

When Rick got older and moved in with them, Bobby's mother made sure to schedule all their meals and activities at different times and different places, so the brothers' paths would never cross. In his photo album collection, Bobby had millions of photographs of every conceivable combination of family members, except for he and Rick. They had zero photos together—none—and Bobby never understood why. Sure, his half brother was a badass who'd generated more than his share of trouble. But he could also be kind and funny, and Bobby had wanted desperately to be a part of that.

Rick couldn't help the fact that he was one of the most infamous characters ever to step out of the Valley; it was just a matter of circumstances. Even though Bobby's parents told him he wasn't cut out of the same mold, Bobby still wanted to be involved. He wanted to have a relationship with Rick's notoriety. "I just want you to let me hang out with my brother," he would tell them. "I just want to be able to hang out with him."

For his part, Rick always acted as if it were no big deal either way. He had his own life, albeit a dangerous one, and he wasn't really thrilled with the idea of having a little tagalong. Most of the time he acted as if he didn't even care whether they had a relationship or not. He had been brought up not to care about things like that, and so he didn't.

To Bobby it was like, okay, if I can just convince my parents to let me hang out with my brother, I'm going to be able to do so many more things. Because when he was with Rick, they could go out and party. Rick allowed Bobby to be Bobby, not just some facsimile of Sharon and Max Leblanc's shortsighted visions.

The bottom line was Bobby's parents would not allow Bobby and Rick to bond on any level at any time. They were never allowed to feel like brothers—more like distant cousins who saw each other every few years at family weddings and funerals. Which was why, as far as Bobby was concerned, Rick acted out as he did. Like the time he showed up drunk off his ass at Bobby's thirteenth birthday party. Rick, with his shaved head and thick biker goatee, showed up driving a low rider convertible, insisting that he should drive Bobby home from the bowling alley, while Bobby's parents went apoplectic. Bobby just thought it was cool.

And what was so weird about the whole family situation was that the story was completely different for Bobby's half sister. Lisa, who was four years older than Rick, was allowed to be in the house, to play and bond with Bobby, to do basically whatever she wanted, whenever she wanted to do it. She had always told Bobby that she wasn't sure if it was due to his maturity or her immaturity, but whatever it was, she felt very close to him. Although their age difference had been nine years, in a lot of ways, it seemed like only two.

Even when she was a teenager, Lisa had always seemed proud to introduce Bobby to her friends. They had never fought or argued, leaving that for Rick and their parents. They spent a lot of time together, laughing and telling jokes. She used to pick him up from religious classes or karate, and she babysat him whenever the need arose. They would watch movies or play video games, and Bobby used to always end up on top. She would confide in her baby half brother her deepest secrets and had often asked him for advice. Bobby enjoyed her company very much and felt as if they had a unique understanding of each other.

But being a Leblanc, she had many issues of her own, and she often battled with Bobby's mother, her stepmom. They had screaming matches; doors would slam, tears would fall, and these scenes would often end with Lisa running out of the house, vowing never to return, only to fall back in line a few days later.

Rick wasn't like that. He had had many a battle with their father, but when the shit really hit the fan, he would just take off and disappear. He'd be gone for months on end, living with his girlfriends or their parents, dealing drugs, kicking people's asses, and whatever else he did that Bobby didn't even want to know about. But as far as Bobby knew, his brother never once bad-mouthed Bobby's mother to her face. And that was why Rick got back into Bobby's life in the first place; his parents feared Bobby was turning into the monster that everyone had predicted he would become, but without his brother's help.

What Bobby's parents never realized was that his troubles had less to do with Rick's past than from Bobby's own anger about the prison they had locked him into. He resented the fact that his parents didn't allow him to live his own life, only the life they planned for him. Whenever he wanted to go out, his mom would always want to know where he was going. She'd continually question him about the who, where, and when of his social life, and it really made him mad.

He continued to rebel against his parents' display of authority, and he had no problem exhibiting his lack of respect for his mother. He'd fight with and yell at her and call her horrible names. He started smoking pot regularly and got into fights at school. Early on in his sophomore year, he got thrown out of Valley High School for sexually harassing a football cheerleader.

After he switched high schools, things only got worse. At Bentworth High, he was arrested for possessing pot on school grounds. His parents continued to battle his attitude, and the more they did, the more agitated and disrespectful he became toward them. He treated everything they did as if it were a big joke. He was sarcastic about everything, and trouble continued to find him; each ensuing act escalated in volition as well as consequences.

Bobby's relationship with his mother soon hit rock bottom. They had become two immutable objects—like frigates in the open sea—facing each other's paths yet failing to yield to the other's right of way—to allow the other to pass into calmer seas. Dr. Seuss had called them *Zacks*. Bobby's mom called it outright rebellion. But that all changed when Rick had finally been allowed back into Bobby's life, because he threatened to beat the disrespect out of Bobby if it didn't.

Bobby looked up to his half brother and listened closely the day Rick told him, "You know what? I don't agree with everything your mom does either, but she's your mom. And she does a lot for you, and you have got to respect her for it. And if you want to hang out with me, or if you want to be my friend, you got to know that I would never disrespect my mom. I would never disrespect my elders. You know, if someone disrespects you, and they're your peer, then you've got to handle it like a man, or whatever. But when it comes to your mom, you're lucky to have a mom."

After that, Rick started hanging out with Bobby more. In turn, Bobby started showing more respect for everybody; more so than ever before. He soon started working for his father, who would drive him down to the furniture store three or four days a week, and he would take the bus home after work. Bobby developed a knack for the work and actually started to enjoy the responsibilities. Where Rick had problems staying attentive and remaining at his station, always wandering all over the store, Bobby would stay in his seat, keep an eye on his job, and do it right. He followed directions well, and both parents took it as a good sign that his rebellious stage might have been fading. Bobby started having good talks with them, but he also struggled to choose what kind of lifestyle he wanted to live.

When he wasn't at work, Bobby tended to put his mind to things that got him into trouble. He had moved away from being the ideal, goal-oriented kid he had once been to become a very confused teenager, just as his brother had always been.

When Rosy finished cleaning his wounds, she threw the cotton ball into the trashcan under the sink. She grabbed a towel off the rack and began to gently dry his arm. Bobby had to step back, because she was leaning against him so hard she had him pinned against the sink. "You know, you don't have to stay here," she said, nearly crushing him with her generous chest.

Bobby didn't believe it was an accident. "Thank you."

"I'm serious." Rosy turned and grabbed the healing salve out of the drawer. She started applying it to his arm in slow, rhythmic movements, and Bobby couldn't tell who was enjoying it more. "You know you can go in there and use that phone anytime you want," she said.

"Really?" Bobby blinked his surprise. As he met her gaze, he noticed how green her eyes were.

She rubbed his arm slowly with the healing salve, but none of it seemed to get near the wounds. It didn't matter. It was one of those rare moments where time stood still, and Bobby found himself momentarily speechless. There was something about this woman—this girl—who stood in front of him offering Bobby the door to his freedom. She was very affectionate, and it was obvious that she liked him. He liked her too, just probably in a different way.

"I don't want you to be stolen, Bobby," Rosy said emotionally. "I don't care what your brother did. I want you home where you belong."

His eyes drew away from her as he took in the whole picture, breathing in everything about her. She had a truly pretty face and a rack that wouldn't quit, but unfortunately, she wasn't the type he usually fell for. Bobby had always gone for the skinny supermodel look, never having done it with a dumpy chick, except for the one time he got really wasted at a party and lost his virginity to some chick twice his age and three times his size. He never told anybody about that experience, and he knew this was no time to repeat it. If he was going to be fucking anybody around here, it was going to be the pale blonde who watched over them both hungrily.

He shook his head and thought again about what Rosy had just said. She was right, of course. He did belong at home. He had been gone for over twenty-four hours, and he knew his parents had to be dying right about now. His mother had probably called everyone she knew that he knew, and no one would have been able to give her the answers she sought. Since he hadn't spoken to a soul since he got picked up, no one knew where he was right now. He had a history of running away from the heat at home, and they probably suspected he had gone to his brother's.

Last summer, he had taken off under similar circumstances, and he had stayed with Rick and his girlfriend without telling his parents. At the time, they knew he was safe because Rick had called them right away. "Just leave it alone," Rick had told his father, "I'll take care of it." That meant he would keep Bobby overnight and bring him home the next day.

In January, Bobby disappeared a second time, this time after an argument with his folks about wanting to go out to visit his half brother, who by that time was living with a cousin at the beach. Bobby went anyway and came home first thing the next day. Again, Rick had called and told his parents where the kid was.

But now, there was no one to call. Even though Bobby's parents must have been going crazy, there was really nothing he could do about it. He was afraid of what might happen if he broke his vow to Mickey and Luke about not using the phone. He knew that if he expected Youngblood to do what he said he was going to do, then Bobby also had to be true to his word. He feared that something might happen to him if he didn't, and he harbored concerns of what might happen to his brother or his parents. That's why he had to bite the bullet and hang out for a while.

"I appreciate it," he told Rosy, "but they're out looking for my brother right now. And I don't want anything to happen to him. Mickey was pretty upset about all this. I just want to do what's right so nobody gets hurt. As long as my brother's okay, I'm okay. And I'll go along with it."

Rosy's smile said she understood. But the way she continued to ogle Bobby made him slightly nervous. "If I can do this for my brother," he said, pulling away from her gaze, "I will. But he's going to have to learn to deal with his own problems from now on."

Chapter Fifteen

Monday—4:00 p.m.

Luke was so hungry he could eat the ass out of a dead skunk. He was so stressed out that he couldn't remember the last time he had had a solid meal. That's why he was more than agreeable when Mickey suggested they go grab a bite to eat.

He had phoned Youngblood just before leaving Rosy's house and made arrangements to get picked up down the street from the mission. Youngblood had said he needed to talk, and Mickey and his girlfriend Nicole Babbette picked Luke up in her little red Beemer, and that's when he suggested lunch. Luke still felt the agitation over Mickey's insistence that he clear out his house. It had been a hassle getting the gang loaded up and into Rosy's car, and Rosy had acted more than a little bent when he hustled her and everyone over to her place. Luke knew she'd want to know what he was up to, and it concerned him that she had talked so much with the kid this afternoon. He didn't know what Bobby had told her, but whatever it was, Luke wasn't quite ready to deal with her yet, so he snuck out without speaking to her.

Luke needed to know what Youngblood's status with Rick Leblanc was before he could talk to anybody intelligently about anything. Besides, getting them all out of his house was a blessing since his old man and stepmother were once again on the warpath. With no kid at his house, Luke would be able to at least deal with his dad, even though he knew there was going to be a battle. But at least the kid wouldn't be in the middle of it.

They had eaten at the beachfront Beachcomber Café back on Memorial Day and had a great time doing it. The food was plentiful, and they downed so many beers that Luke almost had to be helped out to the car. Youngblood's girlfriend sat at one end of the wooden table and picked at her shrimp salad. She was a sexy little trick who was even smaller than Youngblood—as if that were possible—and she wore blue jeans, white-heeled shoes, and a bare midriff. Luke had to concentrate on not staring at the diamond stud peeking out from her belly button.

Youngblood had followed Luke's lead and ordered the double Ortega chili cheeseburger with crispy fries. Youngblood's burger sat mostly uneaten, while Luke inhaled his with hungry fantasies of more. The air was still on the patio, and the sun stood in just the right position over the Pacific to avoid the blue and white umbrellas and laser beam the back of Luke's neck. But he didn't care. The ice-cold beer knocked off any discomfort the intense heat might have caused.

Luke licked the grease from his fingertips and was now hawk-eyeing Youngblood's uneaten burger. Youngblood seemed to notice, because he tossed the plate like a flying disc over to Luke, who attacked Youngblood's food like a famished buzzard on road kill. When Youngblood had first picked him up, Luke asked if they could run by his house so he could get Youngblood his money. "Don't worry about it," Youngblood had told him, and Luke thought he might die a happy man right then and there. He couldn't ever remember Youngblood telling him—or anyone else, for that matter—not to worry about a debt. He wondered if his friend was sick.

Now, as Luke finished his brew and ordered a second from the cute little waitress with an ass sharp enough to cut diamonds, he could think of only one thing: making sure Bobby Leblanc got home safely. "So, Mickey, what happened when you tried the kid's brother?"

Luke thought he detected Youngblood's mouth twitch, but other than that, his poker face remained. Youngblood could have been staring straight at Luke, or the ocean, or anything or nothing, but Luke couldn't tell for sure because of Youngblood's mirrored aviator sunglasses. Youngblood looked as if he was finally about to say something, but the waitress came back with another round of drinks. They waited another minute for her to clear out, and then Luke asked it again. "So what'd you find out?"

Luke guzzled his beer, as he watched Youngblood's hands clench into a steeple in front of him. Mickey then said, "Nothing."

Luke gagged on this response and nearly swallowed his lime. He hacked it up and spit it out, and the lime skidded across the table and onto the floor. "What do you mean, *nothing*, Mickey? I don't understand. What's going on?"

"Relaaax," Youngblood said, irritably.

Luke leaned in further, and lowered his voice. "What do you mean, relax, Mickey? Did you get ahold of him or not?"

Mickey shook his head. "Not."

Luke's body fell limp, and he could feel the weight of his entire chest collapse inwards. He took a deep breath, and pushed his chair in even closer to the table. "What happened?"

Youngblood frowned. "What do you mean, what happened?"

"Why didn't you talk to him?"

It was Youngblood's turn to be even cooler now. "Look," he said, slowly wiping his napkin across his mouth like some English squire at a country picnic, "it was too much of a risk to call him."

"What do you mean?"

"If you'd shut up. I'd tell you."

Luke nervously cupped his hands to the backs of his ears. "But Mickey, you were going to go and find him, not just call him."

"Look," Youngblood said, cricking the tension out of his neck, "while you were paging me fifty thousand times last night—"

"None of which you bothered to return."

"Are you going to shut up, or are you going to listen?" Luke sighed deeply and shut up. Youngblood glanced over to Babbette then back to Luke and said, "I didn't call you back because I didn't have anything new to tell you."

Luke nodded and frowned.

"I was so fucked up, man, I'm telling you … But I thought about calling him all night. Then I thought—what the fuck am I doing? Am I out of my fucking mind? I can't call Rick Leblanc."

Luke groaned. "But you were supposed to go and find him, Mickey. That's what the agreement was." Luke turned away agitatedly and glanced right into the sun, causing his eyes to nearly melt. He turned back and blinked at the fireballs exploding across Youngblood's face.

"Hear me out," Youngblood said. "We got a real dilemma here, okay? Remember when his mom paged him like a thousand times?"

"Ah, Mickey. We talked about that."

"I know, man, but what the fuck do you think she's gonna do?"

Luke threw up his hands. "I give up, what?"

"She's **going to call the cops. She's a fucking loon, man. She's got some fuck**ing **emotional problem that I guess runs in the kid's family.**"

"Oh, I see, now you're a fucking psychologist." Luke held his fork in one hand, the knife in the other, and he looked as if he wanted to stab something. "Mickey, the kid's not going to tell her what happened. He already told me that. He's got issues with his parents. That's why he was out there in the first place."

"Yeah, yeah, yeah, I know what the kid said. But it's his mother we're talking about. You think she's gonna just sit still after the kid's been gone for two days?"

Luke shook his head in disgust. He sucked in a deep breath and tried to calm his racing heart. Youngblood leaned in closer. "If I talk to his brother, and we don't get things resolved, he's going to know I'm involved in this."

Luke started to say, "Tough fucking shit," but he didn't. Instead, he said, "Mickey, we've got to do something."

Luke's eyes wandered onto the Pacific as he tried to regain his composure. When he turned back, he spotted Youngblood's untouched beer, and grabbed it. When he finished the entire beer, he belched into his fist loud enough to wake up the chef.

"Impressive," Babbette said disgustedly, leaning away from the table, acting so cool in her dark shades, just like her beau.

"I don't know what you're going to do, Mickey," Luke said, "but you can't leave the kid with me."

"I know," Youngblood said thoughtfully, "I know."

Luke peered furiously at his friend. He wanted to tell Mickey that he was a fucking asshole for having gotten them both into this situation. That whatever problems Mickey was facing were his problems, not Luke's. But that wasn't the truth, not so long as Bobby Leblanc was under Luke's supervision. That's why he had to be cool, try to resolve this thing, and get the kid out of his care.

"So if you're not going to contact Leblanc, then what are you going to do?"

Youngblood smiled as if the answer waited on the tip of his tongue. "You know, I was thinking about that money you owe me."

"Ah, Mickey," Luke said in a high, whiny voice, "I told you I don't have it with me. We got to go to my house and get it."

"I know," Youngblood said dismissively. "But I was thinking that maybe you should just keep it."

"What?" Luke said it way too loudly. He cleared his throat and looked around, but no one was paying them any attention. He turned back to Youngblood. "What are you talking about, Mickey?"

"For taking care of the kid, I mean."

Youngblood looked sincere, but Luke really had no idea what he was talking about. "I appreciate that, Mick. But the agreement was that we'd take two hundred and fifty bucks off for last night. So I still owe you seventeen fifty. And I intend on paying you back."

"I know," Youngblood said, waving his hand. "But that's what I'm saying. I think you should keep it."

The right side of Luke's brow wrinkled. He felt totally lost. He leaned back and signaled for the waitress to bring another beer. Maybe it was the heat, or he was still dreaming or something, but Luke was pretty sure he didn't just hear what he thought he had just heard. "Mickey, you're not making any sense."

"Hear me out," Youngblood said. "We got a problem, right?"

Luke sat up straight in his chair. "Mickey, you were supposed to get ahold of his brother. And then you were going to take the kid home. That was the plan. Where's the problem in that?"

"Well, I couldn't get ahold of his brother."

"You didn't even try."

"I know, I admit that." Youngblood smacked his palm on the table. "There's nothing I can do about it now. I told you, I'm not going to call the guy and give my hand away."

"Then what are we going to do?" Luke sounded panicked. "I can't just hold onto him forever."

"That's what I'm saying."

Luke shook his head violently. "Mickey, I'm sorry. I just don't understand. What are you saying?"

Youngblood pulled his seat closer to the table and removed his sunglasses. His thumb and forefinger pinched the red marks on the bridge of his nose as his stone green eyes burned a hole in Luke's forehead. "If his parents go to the police, we're going to have some problems. You are gonna have some problems. That's why I think you should keep the money."

Luke wagged his head like a dog shaking a rat. "What are you talking about, Mick? What kind of problems am I going to have? I'm not following you. Why are you telling me to keep the money? I'm not keeping him at my house, if that's what you're getting at."

"That's not what I'm saying."

Luke put his hand over his chest. "Well, then what are you saying, Mickey? Please, I'm just a little too uptight to play games. What *are* you trying to say?"

Youngblood leaned his head in even closer. "I want you to keep the money as payment."

"As payment?" Luke looked perplexed. He grabbed the beer bottle and upturned it, allowing the last of the suds to stream onto his tongue. "Payment for what, Mickey?"

"For killing the kid."

Time stood silently still as a sheet of chalky white spilled across Luke's face. A barely audible gasp escaped from his lips. And then he coughed, and choked, and sprayed Youngblood and Babbette with beer and spit. Luke quickly regained his breath, but nearly gagged on the icepick in his throat.

"You can't be serious, Mickey."

Youngblood removed his glasses and wiped them with his napkin. "I've never been more serious in my life."

Luke felt the panic coagulating in his chest. His legs went numb, and he was afraid he might be paralyzed. "Dude, no way." He said it way too loudly. He quickly glanced around the patio—his head swirling in the clouds—and then leaned in closer while talking softer. "Dude, no way. The kid's lived with me for the last two days. He's a good fucking kid. There's no way I'm going to hurt him. Not a chance. I mean I may be a fucking idiot when it comes to some things. But that's where I draw the line, okay. My line may be real low, Mickey ..." His hand lowering to about a foot off the floor. "But murder is where I draw it. The kid needs to go home."

"You're right," Youngblood said without hesitation. "You're absolutely right." And Mickey was smiling again. And his mirrored sunglasses were back on, and he leaned back and turned to Babbette, who was also smiling. And they sat there acting like it was all just a big fucking joke, which allowed Luke to breathe again.

"You're right," Youngblood repeated assuredly. "I agree with you one hundred percent. We need to send the kid home. But you need to hold onto him until we do."

Chapter Sixteen

Monday—8:42 p.m.

Fritz Ridnaur had sex on his mind, and why wouldn't he? When he drank, it became an obsession. It had been that way ever since he was a kid. For some reason booze made him hornier than a teenager on Ecstasy. That's why he loved the happy hour at Cousins Steakhouse. It was Monday evening, and after a long day at the office, he liked to reward himself by catching the bus to the Flores Shopping Center, where he'd walk up the thirty or so steps and begin his "night job." He felt it his obligation to punch in the clock to social experimentation. He loved the idea of analyzing the relationships between different drink specials and their equally exciting counterparts: free hors d'oeuvres.

There was nothing like combining the little hand-rolled tacos or chips and salsa with a couple Mexican beers and shots of tequila. If they were serving the finger-licking, spicy Buffalo wings—his personal favorite—no problem. Two shots of vodka and a couple German beers, and he'd be good to go. Hotdogs? Love 'em, especially with Australian lager and little southern comfort. The list could go on and on, and many nights it did. But tonight was slow, and the vegetables didn't have their usual pizzazz, and they were an ill mix with the dry potato skins anyway. The bartender told him she was out of his favorite single malt scotch, and if that wasn't enough to ruin a man's night, his wife, who had just joined him, was on his ass again.

At first he thought it might be the potato skins. "I'll order extra sour cream if you need it," he told her. But she just shook her head indignantly. He figured that either Milsty was sick, or she had female issues, and either way, he wasn't going to let it spoil his evening.

Fritz loved Cousins for its fine gastrointestinal fare, but it was the delicious talent of all shapes and sizes that strolled the floor that kept him coming back for more. There were the college-age girls who loved playing the sophisticated dress up games to impress the wealthy white-collar wolves. There were the cute little waitresses who traipsed around wearing practically nothing. He loved guessing whether or not they shaved under those sexy little skirts. He fantasized as to the shapes they carved their sweet little love patches into. He loved the porky bartender and the way her left eye glinted when she poured him his favorite drink. He loved the old hag seated alone at the end of the bar, and the way she would turn away every time he looked at her. The truth was, and Fritz hated to admit this, he loved and wanted to bang basically every female on two legs—other than his wife.

Every time he looked at Milsty, with her doughy body and saggy bloodhound face, he had to wash it down with another shot of happy-hour tequila. It was weird the way life went on, how people tended to lose their youthful appearances. It wasn't as if Fritz were any kind of athlete when he was a kid, but at least he had some natural shape to him that hadn't all turned to starch. None of the young hotties he knew wanted a flabby midforties, out-of-shape guy. They all wanted the hot, young beefcake with muscles for brains and rips up to their foreheads. So guys like Fritz Ridnaur got stuck with women like Milsty. Yeah, right, life was fair. That's why they made places like Cousins.

Fritz finished off his scotch on the rocks and looked around for his waitress. When he caught her attention, he circled his finger in the air, and she nodded. Another round was on its way. As he waited for his drink, avoiding his wife's glare, Fritz couldn't help but thinking how ironic life was sometimes. His sex life at home might be stuck in neutral, but he still vibrated from the excitement of his day at work. As head winemaker at Red Satin Wines, it was Fritz's job to oversee all winemaking responsibilities at the two hundred-acre valley-floor vineyard. He loved nothing more in the entire universe than to bury himself in a good day's work, which often included breeding some of the world's most exotic grapes.

On the rarest of occasions, there would appear a special vine or cutting or seedling that would provide him with the opportunity to observe nature at its core, to coexist with the mother of creation, and nurture one of God's greatest living wonders. Today, Fritz had caught himself in the act of one of the most exciting pollination cycles of his life: a union between the Spanish *Vinifera* and the wild grape, *Vitis girdiana*.

Since Fritz's Red Satin grape was not hermaphroditic, he knew he would need to pollinate it from other plants. When the Red Satin grape was ready for sex,

Fritz would take great care in applying each and every step of the pollination cycle to every flower on each chosen cluster. He would follow to a T his guiding principle in preparing his female flowers. Under no circumstances could he, or would he, allow his flowers to accidentally pollinate before the application of pollen from his selected male parent.

Today, when he had raised the sterilized paintbrush to his flowers, the herbal pungency of the grapevine tore at his olfactory senses. Fritz trembled when his hand guided the pollen-laden bristles of the paintbrush across the stigmas of his emasculated clusters. Which was pretty much how he felt when the cute little waitress brought their next round of drinks. He watched her bend over to set the glasses on the table, her soggy pillows overflowing the white ruffles of her skimpy outfit, and when she turned and walked away, he almost moistened himself.

"When are you going to find out what Luke's doing with that little boy?"

The question was Milsty's, and it temporarily knocked Fritz off balance, causing him to spill his drink down the front of his shirt and trousers. "Goddammit," he slurred as he wiped the booze off his pants with a tomato-stained napkin. He was tired of his wife's complaining about his son. She'd been on his ass pretty much nonstop ever since Luke moved back in the last time, and now she was carrying on about his doing unsavory things with teenaged boys. First, it was Luke's friend Vegas, who spent the night fairly regularly, and now it was this new kid who almost looked too young for even Michael Jackson.

Fritz really didn't see a connection, but he hadn't thought about it seriously due to his concern of what the waitress might look like naked. He really thought Milsty was off base on this one, and he didn't believe his son was fucking little boys. Teenage boys have an inherent need to get to know each other. They play Little League, have sleepovers, and try on each other's jockstraps. It didn't mean they were having sex with each other. It meant they were bonding. But try telling that to his wife.

One of Milsty's biggest problems was that she had always enjoyed her privacy, but she enjoyed sharing it with Fritz and no one else. This left Luke spinning around in a sort of unwanted purgatory. Milsty had been raised as an only child, so she was used to spending her time alone. She had never been married before, but in meeting Fritz, she had opened herself up to a whole new world of sophistication and excitement. Yet she failed to understand that sharing meant not only partaking in other people's pleasures, but also their pains, which included their children.

"What do you want me to do?" Fritz asked.

He knew what the answer was, but he wanted to put it back into her court just the same. If it were up to Milsty, Fritz would send Luke to a boot camp where he would work long hours by day, sleep short hours by night, and be out of their lives forever. Fritz had no intention of doing that, of course, but he knew he would have to do something. Luke was starting to get on everybody's nerves, and the pot dealing was making them both skittish. If Luke got popped, Fritz and Milsty could lose everything. Besides, he owed it to the kid's mother (sounds better than calling her his ex-wife) to try to help get him employed and straightened out, which was exactly what he was going to do. Right after he had another drink. Just one more short little double on the rocks, and Fritz'd be fit to roll back home to have that talk with his boy.

"I'm going to talk to him tonight," he said, trying to flag the waitress down for another peek and drink. "How does that sound?"

"Fine," Milsty said, polishing off the last of her third chardonnay, "as long as he doesn't have that little boy spend the night again."

*   *   *   *

Rosy Kinski felt desperate in the worst kind of way. She sat downstairs at the dining room table needing to speak with her father, which was pretty much of a joke since her stepmother, with whom she really wasn't on speaking terms again, seemed to be in the way—again. Oh, sure, they spoke, the way two people involved in an automobile accident talked, exchanging pertinent information but not really saying anything with any depth. They lived in the same house, but the communication wasn't really there, because they avoided each other like lepers. It had been that way ever since they had known each other.

Rosy's stepmom was one of those high-heeled, slickered-down family therapists who had known what she wanted early on in life and took it, even if it belonged to someone else. She was very much into the prestige of the title, the fine suits, the power lunches, and she looked down her nose at the nonprofessionals surrounding her, which always included Rosy. When the woman was around the house, her favorite pastime was getting on her stepdaughter about growing up and getting a job.

It was a great idea, but the fact was that Rosy wasn't ready to grow up yet or get a job. She was still working out what it was to be a teen, and until she figured it out, she didn't want to waste her youth on some meaningless job. How many people had made that mistake and lived to regret it?

Besides, that was easy for stepmom to say. Her stepmother was nothing more than a little Miss Overachiever who got lucky and met wealthy husband number two—Rosy's father—who paid for her to attend graduate school, and she now acted like Mrs. Bigshot Headshrink, who thought her shit didn't stink. Her stepmother didn't really get her own act together until later in life, and if that's what it was going to take for Rosy to get it together, then fine, that's just the way it was. If her stepmother had better things to do than try to understand her stepdaughter, then that was okay too. She couldn't blame her stepmother, because half the time, Rosy didn't even understand herself.

Her father, on the other hand, liked to play the invisible man. He was a bigtime criminal defense lawyer whose time given to his only daughter was about as scarce as the fragments of hair on his head. They rarely talked father-to-daughter, but when they did, Rosy could see his mind working as if she were a client's file, and then he would try to solve her problems as if all she needed was a little criminal defense advice. But that was okay, too, because he was a guy, and what did guys know about seventeen-year-old girl problems anyway?

As far as Rosy was concerned, what was important was the fact that William Kinski knew everything there was to know about criminal law, and that's why she needed more than anything to sidestep her way-too-busy stepmother and talk to her way-too-busy father about the serious legal issues that threatened her. Rosy had been deeply troubled by the unfolding of the day's events, and she wasn't sure what she was going to do about it.

She was still mad at the way Luke had bossed Bobby Leblanc around. Bobby was a sweet, good-looking kid, who had gotten himself caught in a terrible bind, and Luke should have been more sensitive to the situation. Mickey Youngblood, she could understand. The guy was an arrogant little prick who thought he could boss everybody around, and considering the clowns he hung out with, she understood why.

It had agitated her to no end this afternoon when they went back to Luke's parents' house and she saw Youngblood—with his little fake miniature Barbie doll girlfriend—there with Luke in the living room. As soon as they walked in the door, she could see Bobby trembling. She had read the fear in his eyes, the way he averted Youngblood's gaze from the living room, and the way he had just walked straight upstairs to Luke's bedroom without saying anything to anyone.

Then she had to go into the living room as if it were some grand social event. Cheri led off with her dumb blonde routine, introducing herself to the crazy little Babbette chick, telling Rosy later, "Very lovely, but a little unreal." Like, no shit, Sherlock. Rosy was surprised Cheri even had the insight to notice. Of course, the woman was unreal. Her whole physical makeup looked like it was made from one of those cheap plastic molds. The dark skin. The shoulder-length hair. The manicured toenails. The French manicured fingernails with the white tips. The tight jeans. The white-heeled shoes. The tight little shirt with the bare midriff. The belly button sticking out for all the world to lick.

All of that was fine, though, really. None of it bothered Rosy in the least. It was the typical look of a Valley girl with rich parents, and she understood that. What bothered her most—and she wasn't really sure at first, but had been thinking about it all afternoon—was the tiny petite body centered by those huge silicone globes. *Those* were unreal. They were gargantuan. And she would just sit there, with her little tight top and high squeaky voice, bouncing around on Youngblood's lap, calling him "Mick," and acting as if she were the center of the whole goddamned universe.

If that wasn't bad enough, Rosy then had to listen to all the nonsense Luke and Mickey were talking. Everyone was smoking pot, and Youngblood was bragging about the big plans he had this evening with the little trollop on his lap, while Bobby was upstairs waiting for somebody to decide what they were going to do with him. And Youngblood was treating it all like it was just a big joke.

"I think we'll just go ahead and stay here in San Floripez tonight."

"What about the kid?" Luke asked nervously.

Youngblood said, "What about him?" And the little trollop laughed it up. Luke wasn't laughing. "We could just tie him up," Youngblood continued, "throw him in the trunk, and stay at the hotel."

The fake Barbie doll acted as if that were the funniest thing her little mind had ever heard, and she let out this high-pitched wail of a laugh that made Rosy want to rip off her white stilettos and shove them through the chick's eye sockets.

Luke looked at Youngblood with this dead serious gaze and asked, "What hotel?"

"I don't know," Youngblood said. "We were thinking of maybe the Paradise Hotel or the Flexion Resort."

Nobody was laughing then, and Luke started pacing around the living room as if he were really trying to figure this thing out. "Well, we need to do something. I got to get the kid out of my house."

That was when Vegas walked in, sat down, and took a bongload, and Youngblood just sort of snapped. He pushed the midget off his lap and told Luke, "I need to talk to you."

They walked outside, but Rosy could still hear Youngblood's mean voice. "What the fuck are all these people doing around here anyway?"

"These are the people I party with," Luke tried to explain. "These are my friends. They're always here."

"Yeah, well you're fucking things up. You shouldn't have so many people over. At least not while the kid's here."

And then Luke just kept repeating how Youngblood needed to get the kid out of there.

"I will pick him up later," Youngblood told him, "so stop worrying about it."

Then they were gone. The little hood took his fake little Barbie doll and left. And everybody breathed a sigh of relief. Bobby came back down, and they all partied, but Rosy was still pissed as hell at the way that arrogant little brat Youngblood just sat there as if he were God, and it was his job to contemplate Bobby's future. And then the doorbell rang.

It was another one of Luke's thug-buddies, Jaime Gabrial, showing up with his wife and eighteen-month-old baby, acting as if it were family day at the zoo, with Bobby being the center attraction. When Luke answered the door, Gabrial told him, "My wife has never seen anyone, you know, kidnapped before. She just wanted to …" So Luke walked them into the living room, where they witnessed the four juveniles through a thick cloud of cigarette and pot smoke, and the baby coughed, and Gabrial figured maybe a day at the zoo was not in his child's best interests.

After everyone left, Rosy just sat there, gazing at the dumb expression on Cheri's face. The girl was very sweet and cute and perky, but light on intelligence quotient. Rosy never could understand why the cute ones like Cheri generally had no brains, while the smart chicks like Rosy—who was about as smart as any seventeen-year-old chick she had ever met, which was what basically everybody else told her as well—got stuck with the dumpy bodies and the less-than-average looks. Cheri got to have the crush on Luke, and Luke had a crush on Cheri, while Rosy got to go home and masturbate in her bathroom. And it just wasn't fair. To make matters worse, Rosy could now feel heart murmurs of her own developing for Bobby.

It was strange, too. He was such a good-looking kid, a little young and gangly maybe, but smart and tough, and he had the kind of smile that made you want to tear another girl's heart out. But he was about as likely to notice Rosy as Brad Pitt was to notice Roseanne Barr. It just wasn't going to happen. And she knew it. But Bobby's silent rejection of her amorous desires did not earn him the death penalty, although there were those who might think otherwise. And that's what she was afraid might happen if she didn't speak to her father right away.

When Tia Kinski finally made her appearance downstairs, her eyes were wide, and she walked with this sort of rabid buzz like she was gliding atop some sort of an electrical current. She wore a blue and white Japanese silk robe that flattered long, tanned legs and a body that Rosy wanted to saw off at the waist.

Rosy got up and followed Tia into the kitchen, and watched her open the refrigerator door. "I need to speak with my dad. Is he coming down?"

Her stepmother said something like, "That's nice," shut the refrigerator door, and walked out of the kitchen.

Rosy chased her into the dining room, and said, "Tia, I'm serious—it's important. I've got a serious legal matter I need to discuss with my father."

Her stepmom stopped, and turned around; her eyes exploding like stars. "Honey, it's my birthday tonight. And your father and I are celebrating it. And I really need you to leave us alone."

"But—"

Her stepmother shook her head and put a finger to Rosy's lips, effectively silencing her. She winked at her stepdaughter and then turned and shook her head and walked back up the stairs without saying another word.

When Rosy got back into the kitchen she realized what was going on. While she was downstairs sweating her ass off about her and her friends' legal predicament, and her insides were being eaten by the malevolent bug of guilt, and she was trying to figure out how to save Bobby Leblanc's life, her stepmother and father were upstairs doing Ecstasy and fucking their brains out, and it was really starting to piss her off.

*   *   *   *

No matter how many bongloads he took, Luke could not calm down. He wasn't sure he ever would. His lunch and subsequent conversation with Mickey Youngblood had been as unnerving as a nuclear explosion on a chicken ranch. He couldn't believe the situation he had gotten himself into, and he had no idea how to get out of it. He scrounged through the refrigerator, looking for something to eat. Bobby was toast upstairs, vegging in front of the TV, and Luke knew he could probably just slap two pieces of white bread together and they'd both be happy, but that really wasn't the point. The point was that he had a big decision to make on what to do with the kid, and he really felt as if he had to talk to someone about it. He thought about talking to the police, but all they would do once they heard his story would be to slap the cuffs on him and lock him away. So he decided that option wasn't in his best interests.

He thought about letting Bobby call his folks to kind of discuss the situation with them. But then reality slapped the back of his head like a falling piano.

He wanted to talk to his sister and came real close to calling her, but he was scared to death about involving Zoe. She'd become his accomplice if she knew what was going on and didn't notify the police. The last thing he wanted to do was drag his family into his mess any more than he already had, and that's when he made the decision. He couldn't talk to anybody about this.

Youngblood had seemed to calm down when he left this afternoon, and he hadn't said anything else about offing the kid, so Luke was hoping—praying really—that Mickey had put that option to rest for good. Even if he did, that still didn't solve the issue of what they were going to do with the kid. Luke had suggested that Youngblood just take Bobby back to Mickey's house and wait it out until Rick Leblanc came by, but Mickey didn't like that idea very much. His mouth became all distorted, and he told Luke that it was one of the dumbest ideas he had ever heard. And he called Luke a fucking idiot for even thinking about it. Luke thanked him very much and agreed that was probably not the best way to go.

He found some cheddar cheese and slapped it between two tortillas and tossed them on the burner to melt. As he flipped over the tortilla, he fingered through the yellow pages trying to find a lawyer with a kind face who looked as if he might want to talk to Luke about his dilemma. Unfortunately, none of the lawyers had kind faces, and even if they did, who would want to take the advice of a lawyer with a kind face? People didn't become good lawyers by being kind; they became successful at law by being ruthless and wearing scowls to the office. Besides, any lawyer worth his weight would charge Luke an arm and a leg, and maybe another arm to tender the best legal advice.

He even thought about talking to Rosy about going and talking to her father, but Mr. Kinski too was a lawyer who would want a lot of money to talk, and he just didn't have it. Luke spent too much time on the yellow pages and burned the tortillas beyond recognition. When he slapped at the fiery mess, he nearly melted his fingerprints off. *Fuck this noise.* He wasn't hungry anyway. Besides, if he smoked enough pot and got enough beers in him, he could scarf down a burning bottle of bleach and never know the difference.

The sniggle of indecision infected his better judgment. The more he thought about it, the more Luke realized he needed to talk to someone—just to go over the basics, to figure out how to get the kid home without pissing off Mickey, and without getting himself into trouble. He thought about calling his mom, and he knew she'd just be thrilled to hear from him about his little legal problem—not.

"Oh, yeah, hi, Mom, I uh, you know, need some help figuring out what to do with this hostage I've been hanging onto for the last couple days." She'd suck right through the emotional matrix she experienced every time Luke's father had given her similar bullshit stories when they were still together.

His mother and stepfather Chris had worked hard through the years to bring structure, consistency, and love into Luke's life, and it would destroy Luke's mom to hear about what her only son had gotten himself into. The last time Luke visited his mom, she told him that she could actually see signs of his maturing toward young adulthood. She said that she appreciated the way he loved and cared for and acted like a big brother to his stepbrother Bryan, who idolized Luke immensely. She acknowledged that thirteen was a tough age for any young person to lose their family, but it had been especially difficult for Luke. He had been a sweet, loving, and considerate kid, who possessed a wide-eyed, youthful bluster filled with the kind of happy-go-lucky exuberance common in most young male teenagers, yet he continued to turn his father's pain into his own, she had said. Any emotional gains Luke would make when he was with his mother would be quickly sabotaged by his father, who would not allow either one of his children to bond to their new family on any level, at any expense. Any consistency Luke developed in school or work would sooner or later be trumped by Fritz's philosophy that "life sucks, so why bother growing up?"

This all resulted in Luke and his sister growing up with the feeling that they never had a place they could truly call home. Luke attributed it less to the divorce than it being a natural byproduct of his father's selfish, childlike behavior. But the more he thought about it now, the more he believed that his father might actually be the best person to talk to under these particular circumstances.

They had severe communication problems, no question about it. And Luke felt he had grown up never having had a legitimate father figure to guide him from childhood into adulthood, which caused him to remain an angry child, just like his father. Yet he believed, deep down in his heart, that his old man still cared about his well-being. He knew his father wouldn't freak out the way his mom would, or just run to the phone and call the cops on Luke when he told him what an asshole he had been. Fritz might get pissed, or throw a childish tantrum, but he wouldn't hurt his own son, at least not intentionally. And if everything turned out the way Luke hoped, his old man would be reasonable in helping him figure out how to get the kid home without everyone ending up in prison. As he threw another tortilla on the burner and piled it high with Jalapeno Jack, for the first time in his life, Luke actually felt as if he were kinda looking forward to his father coming home.

Chapter Seventeen

Monday—11:01 p.m.

Rosy was still waiting at the kitchen table when her father finally came downstairs fifty minutes later. She had gambled that he would play her stepmother's knight in shining armor and eventually bring the dinner dishes and the champagne glasses down to leave them in the kitchen for the housekeeper, and that's when she would pin him down and talk to him. Rosy's gamble, thus far, had paid off handsomely.

When he strode down the stairs, William Kinski wore what Rosy imagined to be a warm postcoital glow, and it made her want to gag. Sex bored her. Not that Rosy had ever actually tried it or anything. But from what her friends had told her, and from her own limited experiences, and from what she had seen in the movies and DVDs she had found in her father's closet, she really couldn't imagine ever getting tangled up like that with any guy unless she really loved him. She had never met that guy.

Besides, just thinking about her dad and stepmom doing the twisted pretzel was enough to make Rosy want to remain abstinent for the rest of her life. The touching and groping and making out never did anything for her, so she couldn't imagine her parents getting worked up over it either. But there was her father, seemingly glowing and donning a tired, yet blissful smile that Rosy wanted to slap off her stepmother's face.

"What's going on, kiddo?" William Kinski asked, kissing the top of Rosy's head.

Kiddo? "Dad, I'm really upset. And I need to talk to you."

"Can it wait until the morning, darling?" William Kinski said, setting the tray down. "I'm really exhausted."

No, it can't wait until morning, you lazy man. And if you didn't spend all night doing drugs and fucking your self-possessed slut of a wife, you'd have time to talk to me, your only daughter, was what Rosy thought. What she said was, "No, Dad, I'm really stressed out, and I need to talk to you now."

"Okay," her father said, and he sat down at the table and smiled sincerely.

Rosy was taken aback. She had her father alone, which was no small miracle. She had halfway expected her stepmother to come traipsing down the stairs at the last second and ruin everything. Which was her usual MO. But when that didn't happen, Rosy decided to take advantage of the situation while she could. "I've got these friends, okay."

"Okay ..."

"And, uhm, okay, so these people, they picked up this kid—"

"Rosy?"

There it was—her father was tired of the conversation already. Fifteen seconds, and he was out. "Yes, Dad?"

Her father surprised her again. "These people? This kid? Can you tell me who we're talking about?"

"No, Dad, I can't."

"Why not?"

Rosy slapped both hands on the table. "Dad ...? Because. I just can't."

William Kinski arched his head back across his compact shoulders. "Why not?"

"Will you quit being such a lawyer for a second and just listen?"

"I thought you wanted a lawyer."

"No, Dad. I just want you to listen. Like you're my dad."

"I am your dad."

"I know. So listen."

He interlocked his fingers and set them on the table in front of him. "Okay, I'm listening."

Rosy was again taken aback by her father's kicked-back attitude. *Maybe he should get laid more often.* She could see that the train of opportunity had arrived, and she was determined not to miss it. So she went ahead and told her father everything. She didn't use real names. But she explained what had happened with the kidnapping, about her friends partying with the kid, and about the kid staying at another friend's house. She didn't tell her father that she had had the kid over that afternoon, but she gave him pretty much every other gory detail.

Her father's cocky smile faded. He tugged at the white terry cloth robe that covered the billowing gray fur from his chest. "That's very serious—what you just told me."

"I know, Dad. I just don't know what to do."

"Let me see if I've got this right. You're saying everyone involved in this is kids?"

"Pretty much, yeah."

"What does that mean, 'pretty much?'"

"Well, they weren't all under eighteen, if that's what you're asking."

Her father nodded thoughtfully. "Even if they were all under eighteen, they could still be in trouble. You understand that, don't you?"

Rosy placed a shaky hand over her rapidly beating heart. "Even the kids?"

"Everyone."

Rosy's heart sank into her stomach. "Will they all go to prison?"

"Let's go back a second—okay, honey?" William Kinski shifted his position, sitting up in his chair and adjusting the package between his legs. He then tucked himself back into his chair, and slid it back under the table. "You said they were all partying the whole time, right?"

"Yeah, like for two days."

"And the kid was free to walk around?"

"Yes. Someone—one of the girls he was with—even told him he could go use the phone and call his mom."

William Kinski's slanted eyes widened. "And what did he say?"

"He said no. He didn't want to mess things up for his brother. Dad, that girl even told him he could walk out that door. And he didn't do it." Rosy pointed to the front door, and her father turned to see what she was pointing at. She quickly dropped her hand back to her side.

There was a long delay as Rosy's father's contemplative eyes washed over her. "So you say he was free to leave?"

"For a while, yes. But then, when the kidnappers were around, he was just going along with it. But the guy who was watching him promised he'd let him go also."

"Did he?"

Rosy peered at her father as if confused.

"Did he let him go, I mean."

"I don't know. But he was supposed to do it tonight."

William Kinski let out a sigh and leaned back in his chair. "I've never heard of anything like this before."

"I know, me too."

"If he was free to leave," William Kinski said, "it doesn't even sound like a kidnapping to me."

Rosy's palms pounded the table. "I knew it. That's what I was saying. So what should I do?"

"As far as you know, the kid's already gone home, right?"

Rosy nodded frantically. "Yes. As far as I know."

The erupting smile on William Kinski's face said he had reached his decision. He stretched his large, calloused hand across the table and took Rosy's hand. He stared at his daughter gravely, and she jerked her hand away. "Rosy, I need you to tell me the truth." She nodded cautiously, and he said, "You didn't have anything to do with this, did you?"

Rosy's head jerked back. And her mouth burst open. And her lips started trembling, and she looked like she was about to erupt in tears. "Of course not, Dad."

"Good." Her father stood abruptly and then patted his daughter's head. "Good night, sweetheart." He then pivoted to leave.

"Daaad!"

William Kinski turned back to face his daughter. "What?"

"What should I do? I mean—what should my friends do?"

William Kinski tilted his head. "I told you. They should go to the police."

Rosy's mouth wrenched. "No, you didn't. You said that it didn't seem that serious."

"You asked me what I would do. And that's what I would do."

"Go to the police?!"

William Kinski smiled; obviously pleased with himself. "That's right, darling. May I go now?" Rosy glared at her father as he leaned over and kissed her on the forehead. "Good night."

And he was gone, upstairs to sleep off the Ecstasy and the sex, while Rosy got to stay downstairs and sweat through the night. *Nice help, Dad.* She still didn't know what to do. One minute he's telling her there's nothing to worry about; the next he's telling her to go to the police. She wondered if she had blown the whole thing by not telling him about her own involvement. That the kid sat right here, at this very table. That it was Rosy who had told Bobby Leblanc he could use the telephone. That he could walk out and leave forever if he wanted to. She thought about going upstairs and telling her father the whole truth but quickly decided against it.

Although her father had thought it was serious, he didn't appear overly concerned. He hardly batted an eye when Rosy told him what had happened. Maybe it was the drugs, or maybe it was just sheer apathy—or maybe it was because her father was tired—but the message appeared unmistakable nonetheless. It wasn't that big of a deal. Her father also confirmed the very point that Rosy had stressed about the whole time: it wasn't really a kidnapping. Bobby had been free to leave. He had been free to walk around; he could have walked right out her door and disappeared down the street, and nobody would have done anything about it. Bobby Leblanc had his chance to go home. But he didn't. What else could she do? Besides, Luke was one of the sweetest guys in the world, and he wouldn't hurt anyone. Even Vegas and Cheri had both assured her. Bobby was going home. Tonight. So why should she get involved in something that no one else was even remotely concerned about?

$$* \qquad * \qquad * \qquad *$$

Luke fought the urge to hurl for allowing Youngblood to badger him into agreeing to keep the kid for another night for another two fifty off his debt. He tried smoking himself into oblivion, but there was only so much his lungs could take. When he finished his five-minute coughing spasm, which nearly collapsed his esophagus, he fell back onto his bed and almost shed tears. Bobby was kicked back on the mattress watching cartoons, while Luke writhed in exhaustion. After what seemed like an eternity of vibrating to the stress that percolated throughout his system, miraculously, he fell asleep. Fifteen minutes later, the thrum of the garage door opening awakened him. Luke could hear the drunken slur of his father's and stepmother's voices slithering up the stairs as they walked into the kitchen below. They had done their grocery shopping and were now putting everything away.

It was a family routine for his parents to go to Cutter's to shop on Monday nights after dinner and drinks. They would snipe at each other while unloading the groceries before she would shuffle up the stairs and off to bed, more times than not, in tears. His father would have one more nightcap—usually a scotch— to top off the night and sit in front of the TV before passing out. It was at this stage that Luke would talk to him. Just feel him out a little before he had that last drink. Before his father's mind completely glazed over, where he wouldn't be able to understand a word Luke said, let alone gather a cohesive thought to talk intelligently about his son's dilemma.

Twenty minutes later, the sound of creaking stairs alerted his attention to the hallway outside his door. Luke imagined his stepmom, drunk as an Irishman in a distillery, grasping the handrails with two hands, huffing heavily and dragging her flaccid self up the stairs.

He sat up on the bed and flagged Bobby's attention. "I want you to stay here, okay? And whatever you do, keep the door closed while I'm gone."

Bobby nodded sleepily without taking his eyes off the smart-assed rabbit with the carrot on TV. He looked stoned out of his mind, but he understood the score with Luke's predicament.

Luke knew he needed to move fast. He needed to get downstairs before his old man came up and saw Bobby before Luke had a chance to tell him why the kid was still there. He pushed over to the door and pressed his ear against it, listening for any signs of life. There were none. So he yanked the door open, and nearly soiled himself.

Outside his door, stood his father, propped against the doorjamb, leaning against one arm for support, swaying badly. When Luke started to ask him what was going on, Fritz stiffened as if he'd been awakened from a siesta. He blinked and gawked at Luke. They started to speak at once and couldn't understand a word the other one said. Then they both waited for the other to speak, but no one said anything.

Finally, his father put up a wobbly hand and said. "Luke, we need to talk."

"I know," Luke agreed anxiously, "I need to talk to you too."

So far so good. They had exchanged opening salutations, and nobody had flown off the deep end—yet. Luke quickly stepped out into the hallway and tried pulling the door shut behind him, but his father wouldn't let him. He just stood there like dead weight, his doughy body blocking the doorway, red eyes snooping around Luke's room.

Luke stepped back to block his father's view. He tried shutting the door but accidentally slammed his father's head against the doorjamb. Fritz didn't even flinch. He just bowed his head foreward and pushed the door back open. And then he tried desperately to focus on what was lying in the middle of Luke's bedroom floor. He turned to Luke unsteadily. "Thought we agreed you were going to send the kid home."

"That's what I need to talk to you about, Dad." Luke latched a hand around his father's wrist and again tried to pull him out into the hallway, but the guy was an anchor. "Can we please go downstairs? I need to talk to you about what's going on."

"There's really nothing to talk about, Luke. I'm terribly disappointed in you. We agreed you were going to stop doing this."

Luke's head bowed impatiently. "Doing what, Dad?"

Fritz leaned back against the wall for balance. Peering at his son from beneath carpet brows, he said, "We just talked about you not having anyone sleep over during weeknights. We talked about you taking more responsibility. I asked you specifically to send the kid home. And you said you would."

"Dad, that's what I need to talk to you about. You have no idea how bad I want to send the kid home."

Fritz cut him off with an open palm. "We have rules and regulations just like everyone else does, Luke. And I think it's time for you start following them. We're trying to have patience with you. But sometimes you make it very difficult. You've got to stop all the partying … I'm serious. I think it's really affecting your health. And the way you think."

Luke's watery eyes traced the road map of broken blood vessels traversing his father's swollen and saggy face. "You're one to talk, Dad. Have you looked in the mirror recently?"

"We're not talking about me, son. We're talking about you."

"Don't be such a hypocrite, Dad."

"Please don't use that kind of language around me, Luke. It's very disrespectful. I want you to send the boy home. Do his parents know where he is? Maybe we should give them a call."

Luke's chest heaved as he glanced back to check on Bobby. "Can we please go downstairs, Dad? So we can talk in private."

Fritz searched his son's face. "There's nothing to talk about, Luke. Milsty wants the boy to go home. And so do I. You need to take more responsibility."

"Why don't you take some responsibility and try listening to me, Dad? I have something very important I want to tell you."

"Why don't you listen to what I have to say first?"

"I am, Dad. But what I've got to say is much more important than what you have to say—trust me."

"That's what I'm trying to do, Luke. But trust is something you have to earn. And frankly, son, you haven't done the things we've asked you to do. It's very difficult to trust you about anything."

"Dad!"

"Luke. We all have to grow up some day. And I know it's not always easy. Life is very difficult sometimes. But that's why we have family. Milsty and I love you very much. We only want what's best for you. But you have to prove to me that you're capable of making the right decisions. Partying all the time, and dealing drugs, and having little boys spend the night are not the right decisions. They're just not."

Luke slammed his head against the wall. "Dad, will you please listen to me? The kid's not here to party. He's here because ..." He sucked in deeply, and exhaled, "I need some help, Dad."

Fritz put a trembling hand on his son's shoulder. "I'm here to help you, Luke. But you have to help me help you first, okay?"

Luke's heart capsized as his knees bent, and he slid down the wall until his butt slammed onto the floor with a thud. With a fissure in his voice, he said, "Dad, if you'd shut up just for a second. Maybe I could get a word in edgewise."

Fritz's hand fluttered to his mouth. "There's no reason to speak to me like that, Luke."

"Jeez Louise, Dad." Luke screamed into starfish hands. "You come up here, jacking your jaw. And you don't listen to anything I got to say. What the hell's the matter with you? You act like I can't think for myself. I've got some fucking issues to deal with, okay? I'm really stressed out. And I need someone to talk to."

Luke's fingers slid away from his face. He glared at his father. And his father's head kept jerking back while the anger in Luke's voice grew meaner. Luke was yelling, and spit was flying, and his father was at the brunt end of it all. Then Luke heard the sound of a door sliding behind him, and he turned to see Bobby stepping outside onto the balcony trying to escape the ugliness of domestic battle. Luke's eyes squeezed shut and then opened when he turned to his father. Softly, he said, "Dad ...?"

Fritz's right eye opened. "Where's the boy?"

"He went outside."

Luke's father nodded and spotted Bobby sitting forlornly on the balcony. Fritz's joyless eyes then shifted back to his son. "Now what was it you wanted to talk about?"

Luke could see his father was in no condition to understand the questions he needed to ask. Fritz was so fucked up and so far off base, there was no singular point of common ground for them to communicate from. There never had been. The bottom line was his father thought Luke was a fuck up. He knew his son had grown up with learning disabilities, and he figured Luke had no shot at learning a simple fucking lesson. Fritz had told him countless times to stop dealing drugs with Mickey Youngblood. He had practically begged Luke to get away from the guy, to move on with his own life, to become a productive citizen, but Luke had refused. And look where it had gotten him.

Luke was a fuck up; there was no question about it. He had been fucking up his entire life, but he had fucked up this time like never before. And he was afraid that if he bothered telling his father the truth of why the kid was really there, his father would just throw up in his hands and toss Luke out on his ass. If Luke told Fritz the truth of how he had let Mickey Youngblood bully him into this untenable situation, his father would probably disown him. Or worse, he'd call the cops, and Luke just couldn't allow that to happen.

He needed his father right now. But by the same token, he needed someone who was alert enough to be able to offer support. Someone who could help Luke make the important decision of what to do with Bobby Leblanc. Luke needed someone who could understand that he didn't mean to fuck things up, they just sort of happened that way. And Fritz was not that person. He had never been that person, and he probably never would be.

Which was why Luke's head exploded with depression as he slid back up the wall on two trembling legs. With a chink in his heart, he said, "Forget it, Dad, okay? Just go to bed, and leave me alone." He pushed past his father into his room and slammed the door shut.

Chapter Eighteen

Monday—Midnight

Bart Pray's mind loved to play dirty rotten tricks on him. Like for instance, he had just finished scrubbing the wall in Mickey Youngblood's living room—the one John Barbados had plastered his head against when he came home yesterday—scrubbing away all the grease and grime, when a wild hair climbed up his ass, causing Bart to go crazy and attack all the marks on all the walls and all the baseboards in Mickey's entire house. He scrubbed and ground his fingertips into the plaster until the place was spotless and his knuckles were raw.

Then he noticed a sparkle in the carpet. He bent down on one knee, and found a sliver of glass from the broken windows. He knew Mickey would have a shit fit if he stepped on it. So he got up and grabbed the vacuum cleaner out of the closet and vacuumed the entire house for the third time today, the thirteenth time in the past week. Then he wiped the perspiration from his forehead and hoped he had finally gotten it right.

But he was now back on his hands and knees, checking out every angle and shadow, making sure nothing else could be found anywhere near Mickey's beige carpet, because he wanted Mickey to be happy with him. Mickey had checked in earlier in the day, making sure everything was okay, but he didn't say a word about when or if he'd be back. Bart needed to see Mickey, because he wanted to straighten out the debt situation with him once and for all. He needed to free himself from the burden of being Mickey's slave boy. This would allow Bart to put his energies into helping his mother out of her bad situation, so he could then turn his attention to himself.

Cyndy Pray should have played the lead in *One Flew Over the Cuckoo's Nest*. By the time she was sixteen, Bart's mother had been diagnosed as manic-depressive. She suffered from bouts of abusing both alcohol (she was a binge drinker) and cocaine and had continued to this day to engage in outrageous behavior and violent outbursts. Due to her financial limitations, she had been without her medications for over a year. Bart understood that he had inherited much of his mother's wackiness. After all, why else would he live the way he did? Who in their right mind would climb on their hands and knees in the middle of the night, in a completely empty house, skinning his knuckles to the bone from scrubbing someone else's baseboards? Nobody that he knew. And who would possibly take the kind of abuse he continually fielded from Mickey Youngblood without either getting away from the guy or doing something to stop it? Only one person he knew.

Oh, sure, Bart had tried getting away from Mickey before, just as he had tried getting away from his own family, but in both instances, it never lasted very long. He'd always end up returning, resubjecting himself to the risks he'd run away from in the first place. Surely, Bart's was a sickness, just as his mother was sick, but in terms of genetic predisposition, the sickness had preceded them both.

Bart's maternal grandmother was also manic-depressive, and an obsessive-compulsive neurotic. His maternal grandfather had suffered from both manic and depressive episodes most of his life. Bart's grandfather had been suicidal from the time he was a child, and he had taken several medications on and off throughout his life. He would become so depressed that he couldn't speak for weeks on end, a silence which always promised cheery times when Bart would stay over, which was often, both when growing up and now.

Bart's father was just plain violent. Jack Pray had grown up with an alcoholic father who beat him severely and regularly, and as a result, Bart's father was verbally and physically abusive to his own family. Bart grew up believing his father's favorite line to be, "Fuck you, you worthless piece of shit," and he believed him. His father had a hair-trigger temper and flew off the handle with the slightest provocation.

Of course, this didn't deter Bart's wacky mother any, because she married him as soon as she turned nineteen. At the wedding, she had been pregnant with her first child—Bart's sister Jenny—knowing all along that Bart's future father was not his future sister's biological father. Cyndy's mother was the only other person who knew this, and they kept it between themselves out of fear of what Jack might do if he ever found out the truth.

Bart's mom was twenty-one when Bart was delivered fourteen days early, weighing in at eight pounds three ounces. And it was only a matter of time before Bart began suffering from the same dysfunctions that plagued his family. When he was five months old, his mother carried him through a home improvement store where she tripped over a piece of fishing line that had been strung across the aisle and dropped Bart on his head. She rushed him to the Oasis Medical Center, where he was diagnosed with a skull fracture. Several months later, Bart suffered from a severe ear infection, and rather than taking him to the doctor, his mother felt a day of sunshine at the beach would suffice. That night, however, Bart suffered from a high fever and spiraled into convulsions. He turned a bright purple-blue. She finally called 911, and an ambulance rushed him to the hospital, where he survived, but barely.

Meanwhile, his father had become a master at classic passive-aggressive behavior around the house. After beating the shit out of Bart's mother, his father would always ask, "What happened?" as if he had missed the attacks due to his blacking out. Bart's father assaulted his mom so often that she continuously sported facial bruises and black eyes. She became a learned expert at applying makeup to cover perpetual facial discoloration. When Bart's father got bored with venting on the wife and kids, he liked to turn his anger on the family dogs. He made a habit of kicking the hell out of them and then suddenly petting and showering them with love. The beatings occurred weekly, with Bart and the kids seeing and hearing everything. They would become upset and scream, and Dad would then redirect his anger toward them.

Jack Pray simply could not tolerate the sound of a crying child.

The crying and begging made him violent. It caused him to yell at his kids viciously, telling them how fucking worthless they were, and then beat the hell out of anyone who so much as whimpered. He always promised Bart that if he really wanted something to cry about, he would be more than happy to give it to him—and he did.

It depressed Bart greatly when his father beat him and other family members. His dad would then try to blow it off, calming himself down by drinking excessively and smoking pot, always in front of the kids. But the damage had already been done. The trauma had set in. And Bart became desensitized to the violence that had become a nonstop ritual in his house.

His mother desperately wanted to take the kids away, but she feared what his father would do if she ever divorced him. Besides, where would she go? She was too emotionally disturbed to live at her parents' house. She wasn't working, and she had no job skills or money. She was living a dead-end life with seemingly no hope for escape. Bart understood his mother did the best she could under impossible circumstances. She was a stay-at-home mom who simply did not have the emotional equilibrium to properly care for her children through the storm of violence and anger that constantly whorled around them. She begged Bart's father to go with her for counseling, to see if they could resolve the emotional and physical abuse issues, but he refused.

Instead, he got his father to hire him an attorney, and he filed for divorce. He told his wife, "You're not taking the kids, so you might as well get out now before I run your ass over with the car."

With no money to fight and a fear of what her husband might do if she did, after ten years of brutish marriage, Cyndy Pray walked away from the violence, the emotional abuse, and her three crying children. Taking nothing more than the clothes on her back, Bart's mother went to live with friends. The move devastated her as much as her children. They were all scared to death at the prospect of living alone with their father.

Toward the latter stages of their marriage, Bart's mother had done well to stay away from drugs and alcohol. For the first time in her life, she had made it a point not to party in front of the kids. But that lasted for only a short time. After the divorce, she fell back off the wagon and began drinking and freebasing excessively. She still didn't do it in front of the kids, but she was so psychologically beat up that she wasn't able to take care of them either. The slightest provocation from any of them would launch her into a violent rage. She too had become a danger to her own children's well-being.

Bart's father, in the meantime, had begun dating Kitty Ambrose, an overeating, domineering woman with control problems and her own set of issues with the inside of an alcohol bottle. Five months later, Bart's family size had doubled. That's when his father married Ambrose, who already had a dispirited brood of her own: Seth, who was three, and Christian, who was four. A year after that, they added a newborn they named Jimmy to what had already become one huge and violently unhappy family.

Stepmom picked up right where Bart's father had left off with his kids. She verbally assaulted and demoralized them at every opportunity. She constantly called Bart "stupid" and a "pig." For his part, Bart's dad just stayed away as much as possible. He liked to stay out late drinking, then stumble home drunk off his ass. **Before he could pull his stinky work boots off, Kitty would start bending his ear about the horrible atrocities committed by his worthless children during the day.**

When the complaints were about the boys, he'd just walk in and smack 'em, whether they were asleep or not. When they were about Jenny, he would sneak into her room and start beating her legs with a wooden yard mark. She would stifle her cries and pretend to be asleep, hoping he would eventually stop and leave her alone.

Besides observing the damage being done to his natural siblings, Bart often witnessed Kitty viciously shake his half brother Jimmy when he wouldn't stop crying. It broke Bart's heart to see his little brother suffer through her violence. It caused Bart to take more responsibility upon himself, to play caretaker for Jenny and Shawn. He figured his father, and Kitty in particular, were going to blame him for things his siblings did anyway, so why not minimize the beatings that went around by taking all the blame upon himself? So he did. And so did they.

The older Bart and his siblings got, the more severe the beatings became. Shawn and Jenny were beaten so often and so badly (particularly by Kitty) that they both moved out at their first opportunities.

Due to her eating and drinking binges, Kitty put on over a hundred pounds after her wedding to Bart's father, which made her an even more miserable human being than before. She was now pounding more booze than ever, and she exhibited some terribly bizarre and destructive behavior toward her stepchildren. She liked to padlock the refrigerator and turn off the water main during the day so Bart couldn't eat, shower, or do his laundry without her explicit approval. This made it impossible for Bart to feel "at home" even when he was at home.

By the age of fifteen, Bart was drinking alcohol and smoking pot regularly. He drank to get drunk, to forget about his wretched life, and to pass out if he could. He started spending more time at his grandparents' house, especially with his grandmother. He didn't see his grandfather much, because the old man was usually bedridden with severe depression, but his mom would come over, and the three of them would socialize as often as possible. His grandparents' house became a sort of "home away from home" for Bart. There, he would be fed, clothed, and supervised, if not nurtured. He was there almost every day. Unfortunately, his mother still had a serious substance abuse problem, and since she was making every effort not to be around Bart when she was wasted, she was not around very often.

But that Christmas, Bart, Shawn, and Jenny all gathered at Grandma's house, with the grand expectation of spending Christmas with their mother. It would be the first time since the divorce that they had all been together. With Bart's father out of the picture, it promised to be fun for everyone. As the hours passed, and the day grew late, Bart's mom still hadn't shown up. And the kids began to worry. What they didn't realize was that their mother had stayed up all night freebasing and would be far too wasted on Christmas day to spend any time with her kids. Instead of spending the day opening gifts and playing games with her children, celebrating family and the spirit of the season, she would lie in bed in total darkness, trying desperately to control the race of her heartbeat.

Bart Pray too tried to control the pace of his heartbeat, as he climbed to his feet in Mickey's living room. He could feel the blimp of anxiety swelling inside of him, again. He really had no idea whether he'd turn out like his mother or not, but he'd read tons of literature on the subject, and he tried desperately to comprehend his situation. He understood the significance of genetic predisposition for later development of depression and drug abuse, and he considered himself the perfect specimen for such a concept.

As Bart understood it, the genetic and psychosocial factors he'd faced while growing up—the disturbed, chaotic, verbally and physically abusive family, combined with the psychological abandonment by his mother and father—led him to his path of severe depression and anxiety. This in turn caused him to fail in school, which led to his alcohol and drug abuse. "Anxiety assuaged on the street by excessive amounts of alcohol and drugs to alleviate psychosocial pain and alienation" was what he liked to call it.

The reality of these "life circumstances" led Bart to a profound dependency on the goodwill of others, particularly those he saw as authority figures. As a result, he had spent a lifetime seeking recognition from others.

Bart didn't care so much about himself, because he never felt as if he belonged anywhere or to anyone. Through the violence and neglect of his family life, Bart had never lived anywhere long enough or peaceably enough to call home. This caused him to develop a strong dependence upon his grandparents, especially his grandmother. She was the only member of his entire family who could function with any semblance of normalcy, and she tried, as best as she could, to help take care of and provide him with a loving home environment. Unfortunately, Bart's condition also fueled his bizarre dependence/relationship with Mickey Youngblood. And he was still trying to figure a way out of that.

Chapter Nineteen

Day Three
Tuesday, July 6—2:17 p.m.

It boiled in Lost Hills when Rosy Kinski found herself crying hysterically. She was in one of her adolescent emotional moods while walking to the park with Cheri and Vegas. They had just left Luke's house, where Rosy had gone ballistic.

The day had started off like any other summer day. Rosy had arrived at Luke's at the normal time, and the usual suspects were there. Luke wore his usual summer uniform of blue jeans, white tennis shoes with black trim, and a collared shirt. He said "Hi" and then ran upstairs like a chicken with its head cut off, which was sort of his MO. Rosy then walked into the living room and found Vegas and Cheri on the couch, accompanied by a very strange silence. When she looked around to see what was going on, they both avoided making eye contact with her, and then they got up and left the room without saying anything. Rosy could tell something was going on, and she wanted to know what it was. When she set her things down, she gazed outside, and her hair almost stood on end.

Bobby Leblanc was still there. Luke hadn't sent him home as he said he would, and everyone had conspired to keep it from her. Rosy immediately burst into tears, which was her usual MO. It wasn't as though the kid was hurt or anything, he was just sitting out on the patio smoking a cigarette. But it pained her tremendously to see him there. She loved the kid's looks very much, but she didn't love the looks of his still being stolen and away from his parents. It wasn't supposed to be that way. Mickey Youngblood was a loon, and Luke knew it. Why hadn't he let the kid go home? And why was he acting so stressed out? He was usually so easy going, but Rosy didn't know what was wrong with him.

When Luke flew back down the stairs a couple minutes later, she asked, "Can I speak with you for a moment?"

"Not now, Rosy," he said, all out of breath. "I'm waiting for a call from Youngblood."

Rosy didn't like the sound of that either. And she didn't understand what one had to do with the other. So she went outside to talk to Bobby. She drew the glass door closed behind her, and they were alone. "How you doing?"

He smiled up at her pleasantly. "Everything's okay."

His jeans were rolled up above his knees, and he was just kicking back enjoying the sun. His eyes were bloodshot, and she could tell he was stoned. What she didn't believe was that he was okay. Rosy wanted Bobby to go home where he belonged, and she wanted to see it now. But he didn't look or act the slightest bit concerned, and she really didn't know what to do about it. As the conflicting emotions tumbled inside of her, she looked around for a tissue. She excused herself and climbed back inside before bursting into tears again. When Cheri and Vegas came over to see if she was okay, she asked them to take a walk with her, which is what they were doing now.

Lost Hills Park was a vast green landscape covered with elegant rolling hills and shaded by enormous, historic trees. It was located just a couple blocks down from Luke's parents' house. When they arrived, Rosy pointed to a bench underneath a grove of trees and found a seat. It had to be at least ninety-five in the shade as she looked up with big red eyes at Vegas and repeated her question. "What's going on, Vegas?"

The sun washed scornfully over half of Vegas' face, the other half remaining in silhouette, and he looked very uncomfortable wearing it. His eyes were gripped by something in the grass by his feet as he wiped the moisture dripping from his chin with his shoulder.

"Vegas? What's going on?" she repeated.

Vegas scratched his shoe across the dirt beneath the bench and acted as if he didn't understand the question.

"Why didn't you guys let Bobby go?" she asked.

Vegas' chest rose and fell with heavy breath as he tried to blink the sweat out of his eyes.

Rosy glanced over at Cheri and then back to Vegas. "What are you planning on doing with him? Are you going to kill him?"

Vegas' eyes burst open as his mouth filled with a calculated response. "Oh, no—of course not."

"Then what's the story?"

Vegas refused to meet her glare. "Well, uhm, that's what they were going to do."

"That's what who was going to do?"

Vegas' other foot dug into the grass. "Uhm, you can't say anything, okay?"

"Vegas!"

"Okay, okay." His eyes darted up to her at last. "Uhm, well, you see Luke was offered like two thousand dollars by Mickey Youngblood."

"For what?"

Vegas swallowed hard. "To kill Bobby."

"Oh, shit." Rosy let out a resounding groan, and her entire body fell limp. Her arms wrapped around her stomach; feeling for blood from the gut shot.

"But ... but he turned the offer down," Vegas continued in a panicked voice. "Luke told him, 'I can't do that. I—I'm not going to do that.'"

It was out there now. Rosy's worst fear had come to life, and it was sitting right there on its rear legs, bearing fangs, ready to jump up and bite her head off. She was shocked and appalled by her friend's casualness. "So what're you going to do?"

"We're all trapped in this," Vegas said. "But we're not going to hurt Bobby. We're just ... we're just waiting to hear from Youngblood before deciding what to do."

Rosy took in several deep breaths as her eyes surveyed the park. It was so hot that no one else was even out. "Look, we're all in this over our heads," she said. "Maybe we need to tell somebody. The truth is, I don't know how much longer I can go on like this."

"You can't say anything, Rosy."

"Why not?"

"Because Mickey Youngblood could go to jail."

"So what!" she yelled. "He should go to jail for what he did."

"Look, Rosy, I'm as worried about this as you are. But I feel ... I feel totally helpless. I really don't know what we should do."

"That's why we need to talk to somebody."

"No," Vegas cried. "You can't say anything. Because if you do Luke could be in real trouble. We could all end up dead. Youngblood's crazy, you know. Just, just act like you don't know anything. Like you're not involved. And ... and don't worry about it."

The last thing Rosy Kinski was going to do was not worry about it. She was damned worried, damned upset, terribly confused, and the river of tears started flowing again.

"This is a very serious matter."

Cheri took a seat next to her friend and offered a comforting hand on her back, but Rosy pulled away coldly. Cheri smiled up at Vegas, who shook his head as though all this talk were nonsense.

Rosy noticed the mutually exchanged look. "I'm not kidding, guys. You've got to take this more seriously."

"It's not that big of a deal," Vegas said.

"He's going to be okay," Cheri agreed. "Luke won't hurt him. You know that."

Rosy looked at her with tear-stained eyes. "It's not Luke that I'm worried about."

"You're making way too much out of this, Rosy," Vegas said. "We should just go back and not worry about it. It's not our problem."

"The hell it's not. We have no idea what Youngblood has planned for Bobby. He's already offered Luke money to kill him. And we have no idea what he's going to do next, do we?"

Vegas put his hands out trying to slow things down. "Rosy, please don't be like that. Everything's going to be fine. They're probably on the phone right now making plans for him to go home." Vegas winced at the intense orb cracking through the trees like an interrogation lamp. "Come on, it's getting hot. Let's get out of here."

"You guys go back," Rosy said solemnly. "I've never been in this situation before. I'm far too upset to go back right now."

She was far too upset to go anywhere right now. What she needed to do was stay in the park, be left alone, and calm herself down. Once she did that, and her head was clear, maybe she would be able to think clearly enough to figure out what to do.

"Go ahead, and I'll join you later," she said.

Her two friends lobbed her concerned smiles as they left and headed back to Luke's.

*   *   *   *

Nicole Babbette loved it when it was hot. She loved slipping into her string top bra and string tie thong, and she loved watching the men's eyes melt by the pool. She also loved dressing in practically nothing and just walking down the street and watching little boys' jaws drop, all wishing they could have her but knowing in their little heart of hearts that they never stood a chance. She loved that.

She also loved teasing older men, working them into a hormonal rage where they'd just stand there, slack-jawed and drooling, promising her the world, but getting only what she wanted to give in return. She owned men; they did not own her. And today, being her twenty-first birthday, Babbette felt as if she owned the world. Her parents had just left town, and she was thrilled to see them go. The house would be hers, and there'd be no stopping her once her birthday shopping spree began. She thrilled at the idea of going out and buying all the best clothes in town. She would need a new bottle of French perfume, another very expensive handbag, and several new pairs of shoes. She was feeling totally sexy about her shopping prospects, until the grouch came over and nearly ruined everything.

She had seen Mickey Youngblood in one of his funks before, but never like the one he walked in with today. It had actually been for the last couple days, where he would just mope around and hardly even look at her. And she was getting sick of it. There she was, sexy as a centerfold, hot to trot, ready to tease and please, and he acted as if he were a monk. Then he started cussing about how hot it was, and how he had more important things to do than take her shopping for her fucking birthday, and Nicole was stunned.

What could possibly be more important than her? She tried to get him to take some bongloads to calm his little uptight ass down, but all he did was yell, "I need to fucking be able to think straight, okay?"

It had never stopped him before, and she asked him if he was sick or something. He said something about being sick of her fucking attitude, and she was ready to toss his ass out and call in the replacements.

"Fuck this noise," she told him, and she poured two amber beers. "I should've gone to the resort with my parents."

She slid one over to him, but he pushed the beer away. "Why? So you could go out and fuck someone for another tit job?"

She laughed and gulped the frosted glass, and half the beer spilled down her top and onto the floor. She then grabbed his mug and did the same thing. When she finished, she slammed the mug on the counter, wiped the dripping suds mustache from her mouth, smiled at Mickey, and said, "No, I'd fuck them for free."

*   *   *   *

"You know what that makes me want to do?" Nicole Babbette said twenty minutes later.

Youngblood flashed her a half-assed smile as they blew down Lopshire in her brand new Bavarian convertible. "No, baby, what does it make you want to do?" His hand lifted from her thigh up onto the radio dial, and spine-thumping rap music pounded the air. He was calmer now, but barely.

Before leaving her house, Babbette had finally convinced him to have a smoke, and it had been the right call. It calmed his ass down a lot, but he was still uptight as a motherfucker, which was a lot less uptight than before. When he mellowed, if that's what you should call it, so did she. After her two beers, Nicole then got real loose and told him she wanted to fuck. But the last thing Mickey Young-blood felt like doing right now was fucking, because when he really thought about it, he was already fucked. Reamed up the old kazoo with a twelve-inch molten spike.

He needed to get his mind clear enough to figure a way out. He knew some-thing was going to have to go down with the kid, but none of his options looked good. He had been trying all morning to discuss the situation with Babbette, but she couldn't give a shit. She was like all women: concerned about herself and what was next on the shopping list, and that's it. They had been out all morning, and she had already broken the piggy bank. There was the new purse, five hun-dred twenty-five dollars; the perfume, one hundred fifty dollars; the pass to the health spa, four hundred fifty dollars; the new bathing suit, one hundred thirty-nine dollars—as if she needed another one—and they still weren't finished. The bitch now needed shoes.

Babbette loved playing Imelda Marcos and already had a closet at home stacked with shoes. Big shoes, small shoes, open-toed shoes, leather shoes, plastic shoes, tennis shoes, formal shoes, high-heeled shoes, shoes for summer, shoes for winter, shoes for bedtime. The bitch had more fucking shoes than Florsheim, and now she needed another pair about as much as he needed another fucking hole in his head. She never got out of there without buying at least two or three pairs, each costing a small mint, and the bitch was going to break him.

But what really pissed him off was the fact that he was about to make the most important decision of his life, and she didn't give a fat rat's ass. That's why he **needed to talk to his lawyer. He needed someone to hash out his options with.** Someone who cared about what he cared about, who would show the tiniest sem-blance of interest in his problem. He had been trying to reach the pettifogger all morning, leaving about fifty messages, but the dickhead hadn't called him back yet. If Mickey didn't hear from him by the time he was done taking the bitch shopping, he would go over to his house and roust him.

All Mickey had wanted to do from the beginning was just scare the kid and then let him go. That's it. And that's what he still wanted to do. Christ, he liked Bobby Leblanc. Ink Stain used to bring him over all the time when they lived together. They'd party, and the kid would pull out his little stress weed, and they'd smoke it, and Bobby even worked out with them once. He was a good kid, and Mickey had had no intention of hurting him—at least not at first. He just wanted to deliver the message loud and clear to his fucking brother that he had better stop fucking with Mickey Youngblood. That's it. He just wanted the fucking asshole to back off, to leave him and his family alone, and to pay him the fuck back. Which was what Mickey was going to do until the kid's fucking mother went crazy with the pager. The woman was totally obsessed, and now Mickey knew where Rick had gotten it from. She paged the kid so goddamned much, Mickey was sure she'd go to the cops as soon as the kid walked through the front door.

So what was he going to do?

One thing he wouldn't do was call Rick Leblanc. Way too risky. If he somehow couldn't get ahold of the nutcase and left a message, it would surely tie him to the missing kid. Even if he talked to Rick, Leblanc would be totally suspicious of why he was calling and would probably try to meet him somewhere. Mickey doubted Leblanc would give him his money or agree to leave him and his family the fuck alone anyway, so what good would it do? There'd either be a big shootout, or Rick would have the cops there trying to set Mickey up, and he'd be fucked either way. He couldn't allow that to happen.

When he felt the sudden vibration at his side, Mickey yanked the pager off his belt. He was hoping it might be his lawyer, since he had left both his and Babbette's numbers, but upon glancing at the readout, he realized it was Luke, again. He wanted to shove the phone up Luke's ass. The clown had nothing better to do than call obsessively like every five minutes, and it was beginning to wear on Mickey. There was nothing new to tell the dude.

Mickey still felt confident that a cure to his problems would be found. Somehow, some way, Sheldon Barnes would find a way out of this mess. Barnes was a damned good lawyer and had done well for Mickey on other legal matters, including the insurance scandal caused by Rick Leblanc. Barnes had also practically made a living keeping Mickey's dad out on the streets and in business, and had at one time or another represented six of the eight siblings born into Dick Youngblood's family. If anybody could help, Sheldon Barnes could, if the shyster would ever bother calling him back.

While the bitch sitting next to him flipped through her magazine and filed her eight-inch nails, Mickey's head spun like a gyroscope. If it had been Rick Leblanc, everything would have been cool right now. He'd have plugged the motherfucker, and the world would've been a better place. But it wasn't Rick Leblanc; it was his fucking kid brother, and the only way to get to Leblanc would be through his kid brother. But Mickey couldn't be a fool about it. He had his own kin to think about.

Rick Leblanc had threatened Mickey's family. He had killed Mickey's dog, and then he had broken out all of Mickey's windows. Rick Leblanc had taken this whole pissing contest to the point of no return, and Mickey couldn't imagine what it would be like if the shoe were on the other foot. If it were Leblanc holding Mickey's little brother captive instead. Mickey would have gone ballistic. He would be figuring out a way to kill the animal right now. That's why he had to be really cool with what he did.

Mickey had his own family to protect.

Deep down in his heart, Mickey knew he should just take the kid home without looking back. But if he did that, he would lose whatever leverage he might have in finally getting the kid's pussy brother to come out to talk to him. There was no escaping it, neutralizing Rick Leblanc once and for all meant dealing with him head on, whether it be duking it out, shooting it out, or Leblanc just paying Mickey his money and promising to behave himself, which probably wasn't going to happen. That's why Mickey needed to keep the kid for a little while longer; to flush his brother out. All other options were incomprehensible.

A sharp acrid smell of acetone hijacked his thoughts. Mickey turned and saw the bitch painting her nails. "What the fuck's the matter with you?" he said. "Get rid of that shit."

She ignored him as she always did when he talked this way. So he reached over and ripped the bottle out of her lap and threw it out the window.

"Don't do that, you asshole," she yelled.

"I want to talk to you."

"What do you want?"

"I want you to fucking listen to me."

"I have been listening to you." In a mocking voice, she said, "'Oh, me, oh, my. I'm such an asshole. I never should have picked the kid up.' What do you want me to say? You're right, Mickey. You're an asshole! You never should have picked the kid up. You made a bad decision, and you have no one else to blame but yourself. Not me. I didn't do anything. But no, you're going to take your bad mood out on me."

He reached over and clamped down on her thigh, tightly, trying to shut her ass up.

Her eyes detonated with red, as she squealed, "Let go of me."

He squeezed tighter, digging his fingers into her crotch. "I thought you like it when I do this."

She latched onto his wrist and dug her nails into his skin, but his grip was vice like. "I like it when a real man touches me there, if that's what you mean."

His grip went limp. "What the fuck is that supposed to mean?"

"It means that all you ever think about, Mickey, is yourself. You don't care about me. It's my birthday, and you haven't thought about me for a second."

He wanted to bitchslap her. "What the fuck are you talking about? I just spent a thousand bucks on you."

"So?"

"So you're a fucking ungrateful cunt."

"And you're a fucking asshole who can't even get it up."

His hand slid from her crotch to the stick. He started to downshift for the approaching yellow light, but thought, *Fuck it,* and accelerated through. "I've been under a little stress, lately, okay?"

"No, it's not okay. If I wanted a eunuch, I'd go to Greece."

"What's that supposed to mean?"

"It means you're not a man, Mickey. You're a fucking pussy who's afraid of his own shadow." She was mocking him again. "Ooh, Rick Leblanc hurt me. Fuck Rick Leblanc!"

He scowled at her viciously. "I thought you already did."

She smiled provocatively. "Maybe I should have."

"Just like you fucked everyone else, right?"

"Maybe." Her arms folded across her zeppelin chest. "At least Rick would know how to fuck me. I'm sure he doesn't have a problem getting it up, like some fags ..."

She was about to finish with "I know," but was so stunned by Mickey's backhand across her mouth, that she never got the words out.

Didn't stop her from acting though. As she twisted agitatedly in her seat, she raised her fist and coldcocked Mickey across his right eye hard. Mickey's head jerked sideways violently, and his whole body careened into the door, causing the car to swerve into the next lane and nearly cut off the truck behind them.

Mickey straightened the wheel while rubbing the sting out of his face. He glanced in the rearview mirror and didn't notice any blood. But he did notice the red rage building in his eyes. He corkscrewed in his seat—his arm cocked and ready to lay the bitch out—when his mind took a full 360-degree turn upon noticing his gun in her hand, pointed straight at him. At that exact moment, Mickey could hear the stupid Madonna song blasting from Babbette's cell phone in her purse, informing him that his lawyer had finally bothered to call his ass back, and the ambulance chaser's timing couldn't have been worse.

Chapter Twenty

Tuesday—2:57 p.m.

Rosy arrived back at Luke's doorstep twenty minutes later, still visibly upset. The skin around her eyes was swollen and red. A ball of wet tissue filled her hand.

Bobby, Cheri, Vegas, and Luke were all kicking it back in the living room talking. When Luke saw Rosy walk through the front door, he got up, and strolled over. He cranked his arm around her shoulder and said. "You look like you've been crying."

She sniffled. "Yeah, I have been."

He pressed his chin into the side of her head sympathetically. "Why?"

"Because I don't know what you're going to do with Bobby." Her lips and hands trembled. "I don't want you to hurt him. He's not supposed to be here. He should go home. He should be home."

Luke's stomach churned as his head lifted. *What the fuck is this all about?* He wasn't sure what all Rosy knew, but whatever it was, it was too much. And he hadn't told her anything. He backed away and planted his hands on his hips. "Oh, I see. Now everyone knows." His head circled the room, and when he spotted Vegas, he shot him a look that he hoped would kill him. Vegas turned his head away like a dog in trouble.

"Keep your fucking mouth shut, Vegas, okay?"

Vegas looked like someone rapidly sinking in quicksand. On the living room couch, Bobby leaned over to Cheri. "Why is Rosy crying?"

A compassionate smile played across her cherry red lips. "Because she's extremely concerned about you."

"Why?"

"I don't know."

He got up, sidestepped an agitated Luke, and marched over to Rosy. His finger tenderly wiped a tear from her cheek. He then wiped it on his pants. "Are you worried about me?"

"Yes," she said, a fresh torrent ready to unleash.

"You don't have to worry about me," he said, hand reaching under her chin, tilting it up. "I'm going to be fine."

Rosy inhaled deeply, her eyes glistening to his every word. When he leaned in closer, her eyes drew closed, and her lips rose with anticipation. When nothing happened, she opened them and realized Bobby hadn't kissed her at all. His back was to her, and he was walking back into the living room, while everyone else stared at her like she was a bug.

"You have to let him go," she said, shooting daggers across the room at Luke. "You have to take him home like you said you were."

"I know," Luke said, pacing across the dark mahogany floor like a caged tiger. "I'll take him home. I just can't do it right now."

"Why not?" Rosy cried.

Luke's eyes darted over to Bobby. "Because!"

"Because why?" she asked.

"Because I don't want the cops coming to my door tomorrow, you know." Luke stopped pacing right in front of the couch, and faced Bobby dead on. "You're not going to say anything, right?"

"No," Bobby said laughing. "Look at me. I'm not doing anything. I'm going along with it. I'm not going to tell anybody anything. You guys have been nice to me."

"Are you sure?"

"Yeah," Bobby said, "I'm sure."

Luke pivoted and moved back to Rosy. He put his hands on her shoulders and looked her straight in the eyes. "I swear to you on my mother's life that I'm going to take Bobby home. I swear, so you don't have to worry about it anymore, okay? I will give Bobby fifty bucks to get on a train tonight and go home. I just ... I will wash my hands of it. I just better not have the police at my door tomorrow." He twisted around, and **gazed pointedly at Bobby.**

Bobby flashed him a **toothy smile.** "I promise you won't."

Everyone now looked over at Rosy to see if she was satisfied. She wiped a fresh flow from her eyes and looked chagrined. A compromising smile slowly filled her face. Her mouth swelled with questions that she wanted to ask Luke about Youngblood's offer to kill Bobby. But she didn't want to upset anyone anymore. She didn't want to be upset herself anymore. All she wanted was for Bobby

Leblanc to go home, and Luke had promised to do that. He had sworn upon his mother's life to make sure Bobby Leblanc got home safely, and that was good enough for her.

✳   ✳   ✳   ✳

When Sheldon Barnes opened the front door to his home, Mickey Youngblood marched right past him, face down, without saying hello or even acknowledging that the lawyer was alive. Nicole Babbette did the same thing, with a giant red welt across the side of her face. On her way by, Barnes heard her yell to Mickey, "Hey, asshole, when are we going to eat?"

Barnes closed the door and followed them inside. In the living room, he saw Youngblood nervously chomping on a cigarette, about to light it.

"Why don't we go outside on the patio and talk," Barnes suggested.

Youngblood nodded anxiously. Barnes noticed his right eye was also red and swollen, as if someone had punched him. Barnes opened the sliding glass door and herded the two outside.

Sheldon Barnes was a large man with a salt-and-pepper beard, kindly blue eyes, and a sixties ponytail. He was a sole practitioner at the firm of Barnes and Associates, where Sheldon had worked until his bout with skin cancer last year. When the cancer was discovered, he moved his practice to his home in the hills overlooking Mineral Valley. He battled hard, and by the time the cancer went into remission, he had decided to remain at home where the benefits were greatest, the stress the least.

Youngblood and Babbette were playing chimney around the glass table, when Barnes tossed a ceramic ashtray between the two and took a seat in the shade, opposite them, facing away from the sun. Since moving his practice to his home, Barnes had learned to judge the shadows that fell across the southern side of his house. He knew precisely how long he could stay outside on any given day. Since his battle with melanoma, he wouldn't even entertain the idea of getting one iota of sun. But cigarettes were another story. Barnes was a longtime smoker who quaked with the urge to return. He lusted after Youngblood's cigarette but fought hard against asking for one.

He could sense from the way his two guests were looking away from each other that they were both tense. Barnes watched her smile at her mouthy reflection in the sliding glass door, while Mickey stared off into the distance, his foot nervously tapping an indentation into the side of the table. Barnes figured the red marks on their faces may have accounted for some of the tensity they shared, and he tried to find out about the rest. "So how's your dad doing?"

Youngblood grunted something unintelligible without looking over.

Barnes nodded agreeably, deciding to attack it from another angle. "How about your mom?"

Youngblood tossed him a preoccupied nod.

Barnes gazed over at Babbette and decided to throw a curveball. "How's business, Mickey?" Out of the corner of his eye, Barnes could see Mickey blinking, and he knew he had his attention.

Sheldon Barnes had represented Mickey Youngblood's father regarding various legal and quasi-legal business matters for the better part of the last two decades. Dick Youngblood had almost single handedly kept the Valley green with top-quality bud and had always worked hard at not only staying ahead of the competition, but also the authorities. Whenever they got close, Barnes would move in to keep the wolves at bay. He knew that Mickey had moved in too, aggressively attempting to take over the family business, but it didn't seem as if that's what he was there to talk about.

Barnes frowned when Youngblood flipped his cigarette into the pool. "So what's the penalty for kidnapping?" Youngblood asked.

Barnes smiled; the question seemed odd, and it caught him totally off guard. "There are different kinds of kidnapping with different kinds of penalties." Barnes turned his left palm sunny-side up. "Maybe you might want to explain the circumstances you're talking about."

Youngblood glowered off into the distant mountains, unable or unwilling to face his lawyer. "Yeah, okay, so these friends of mine picked up the brother of some guy who destroyed this one dude's house. So how much time would they be looking at?"

Youngblood looked like his breathing was labored, and Barnes stopped him with a wave of the hand. "Slow down, Mickey, I don't understand what you're saying. They picked him up because he destroyed someone's house?"

Youngblood balled his tongue under his lower lip. "His brother did."

Barnes shook his head. "That doesn't make any sense."

Youngblood finally turned to face him. "Okay, look—this guy owed this other guy money, right? And then, on top of owing the guy money, he did a lot of other bullshit, right?" Barnes nodded. "And then he goes and breaks the guy's windows out of his house." Youngblood stared at his lawyer as if that should have explained it all.

Barnes' face twisted into a morass of confusion. "So the guy who was owed the money also had his house vandalized. And then he kidnapped the other guy's brother? Is that what you're saying?"

"Exactly." Youngblood bobbed his head and then relaxed into his chair.

Barnes brushed meaty fingers through his beard. "So why did they kidnap his brother?"

"To hold him until his brother paid off the debt that he owed him. And for the windows that he broke. And also because he threatened his family."

Barnes' hands splayed out as if he were surrendering. "Wait, wait, wait … He threatened his family?"

Youngblood bounced his head aggressively as he sat up in his chair. "That's right. And then they held onto the kid for a couple days. You know, partying and drinking with him, hoping his brother would finally pay him off."

"And so what happened?"

Youngblood spit on the ground next to his chair. "They couldn't find his fucking brother, and … And now they still have the fucking kid and want to send him home."

"Shit, Mickey." Barnes shifted uncomfortably in his seat. "This isn't your typical kidnapping case. You realize that, don't you?"

"Yeah, no shit."

The lawyer shifted in his seat and watched Youngblood grab the back of his own head, and dig his nails deeply into his skull. "Let me see if I got this straight, Mickey. On the one hand, you said this guy owes this other guy money. He then threatened him?"

"And broke out all his windows."

Barnes' black and silver brows rose in unison. "He broke out his windows after he threatened him?"

"Yes!—well, no." Youngblood shifted impatiently. "He broke out his windows. And then he threatened to shoot his family."

"You're kidding."

"No, I'm not fucking kidding. That's why we got a problem here."

Barnes tugged on his earlobe. "Shit, Mickey, it just doesn't make any sense. There's no real definitive answer from what I'm hearing."

Youngblood squinted up at his lawyer. "What do you mean?"

"I mean that … Well, let me ask you this. You said that your friend had the kid for a couple days, right?" Youngblood grunted in the affirmative. "And everyone was partying and drinking?"

Youngblood gazed vacantly at the pool, and then back up at Barnes. "Look, from what I understand, they had these other kids his age going in and out all the time partying with the kid. I mean it wasn't like he was tied up in a closet or anything. He was free to walk around … and smoke dope. And that was pretty much it."

"So he was free to walk around?"

"Yes. He was totally free to do whatever the fuck he wanted."

"But he couldn't leave?"

Youngblood's eyes filled with red. "No, he wasn't free to fucking leave."

Barnes leaned back in his seat thoughtfully, stroking the length of his salt-and-pepper whiskers. He suddenly jerked upright in his chair, his eyes lighting up like a lighthouse at the edge of a cliff on a stormy night. "Shit, Mickey!"

"What?"

"Your friends are looking at potentially two different kinds of kidnapping here."

Youngblood gazed at him desolately. "Yeah, okay."

"First, there's the standard type of kidnapping—where someone kidnaps someone else with no other motivation other than to kidnap him. That carries a maximum of nine years in prison."

"Shit," Youngblood said, letting out a heavy groan. His chin dug into his chest, as Babbette twirled in her seat and slapped the side of his head like a coconut. "See! Don't worry about it. You could do that standing on your head. What are you crying about?"

Youngblood turned and raised his fist like he wanted to launch her. Babbette flinched in retreat. But instead of smacking her, Mickey patted his hand to his swollen eye and rubbed it. Then he glanced back at Barnes.

"And what's the other kind?"

"The other kind is aggravated kidnapping. That's where they hold the victim for ransom or extortion."

Youngblood winced with grave recognition. "Yeah, okay, that's probably what we're looking at. What's the story with that?"

"Well let me see if I got this straight." Barnes shifted uncomfortably. "You said your friends kidnapped the kid in order to get his brother to pay for the debt and broken windows, right?"

"Correct."

Barnes sagged in his chair. "Shit, Mickey."

Mickey's shoulders slouched with concern. "Shit what?"

Barnes glared at him intensely. "They're fucked! That's what."

Mickey's nervous eyes skidded from Babbette back over to Barnes. "Who's fucked?"

Barnes pulled up his chair. Crossing his right leg over his left knee, he said, "Your friends are fucked, Mickey. If they were doing this for ransom, they're looking at life in prison."

The words hung out there interminably. And Barnes thought he could hear a slight gasp escape Mickey's lips. Mickey looked like he wanted to speak, but he couldn't. He swallowed hard and then peered up at his lawyer with wetness building in his eyes.

In an unmanly voice, Mickey asked, "All of them?" He cleared his throat. "I mean are we talking about the guy who held him? Or the guys who picked him up, or what?"

Barnes clasped his hands together on the table in front of him and swung his body around to face Mickey. "When you're talking about ransom, Mickey. Each participant in the kidnapping, no matter what their involvement, is looking at a life sentence."

Mickey fell slack-shouldered into the back of his chair, and Barnes could definitely hear the sound of a ball deflating.

"But there's a chance for parole, right?" Babbette interjected, displaying the proud pose of a peacock who had just solved all the world's problems.

"Sure, there's a chance for parole," Barnes said. "But they're each looking at life sentences. Shit, Mickey, your friends' lives are over. They might as well dig a ditch and bury the kid right now."

Youngblood scowled in grim silence, and then he leaned back and kicked the table violently. The ashtray went flying, and the table rattled and spun like a top on two legs. Barnes reacted quickly for a big man. He jerked one hand up to grab the table, while stretching the other hand toward the airborne ashtray. He looked like a first basemen digging for a wide throw in the dirt. Ashes were flying everywhere. And the table was broken in half in Barnes' hand, with Barnes sprawled out, yelling, "Calm down, Mickey. What're you doing?"

Youngblood didn't calm down, as his mouth twisted into a violent knot. "You gotta be fucking kidding me!"

"I wish I was, Mickey. But you gotta calm down. And tell me exactly what happened."

Mickey's chest rose and sank rapidly, while his breathing strained in short, depleted gasps. His neck and face roiled from red to pale. And he didn't look calm at all. He looked extremely agitated, even more so than when he had arrived.

Barnes watched as Mickey tried to light up another cigarette with trembling hands. And then a look of stark realization seized the esquire's face. He leaned over anxiously and asked, "Mickey, did you have anything to do with the kidnapping?"

"My life is fucking ruined," Youngblood cried, as he sprang up from the table and angrily flicked his cigarette into the pink camellias that ran along the side of the house.

"Mickey, please sit down," the lawyer appealed. "And let's talk about this."

But Youngblood didn't sit down, choosing instead to ignore his lawyer's advice and take off down the back steps.

"Mickey," Barnes yelled, jumping up from his seat, "please come back here and talk to me!"

Youngblood acted like a deaf man on a mission, as he sprinted toward the back yard gate. Babbette got up from her chair and gave chase, and Barnes followed her.

Sheldon Barnes had associated with the Youngbloods long enough to know they were a family of out-of-control hotheads, and there was no telling what they might do when their emotions got the best of them. That's why he had to get Mickey back, to sit him down and try to calm him down. When Mickey had gotten up, he had possessed the look of a man who was hiding something. Barnes had been a criminal defense lawyer long enough to know when he was being lied to. Maybe there was a scintilla of truth to what Mickey had told him, but Barnes was willing to bet the house on the fact that Youngblood hadn't even told him the most damning part. That's why the lawyer needed to sit his client down so he could talk to him. He needed to calm Mickey down and make sure he didn't do anything irrational.

On many occasions, Barnes had gone through the same type of thing with Dick Youngblood. Mickey had to understand that no matter how bad things looked, or what the state of the evidence seemed like, there was always a way around it. They just had to look at the facts and see what they really added up to. But Barnes wouldn't be able to do that until he got Mickey calmed down and thinking rationally.

He sprinted down the stairs after him. Unfortunately, it was a bad time in the afternoon, and Barnes' backyard was drenched in sun, so he stopped. His hand flew up to protect his face, but he knew he was fucked. Sheldon Barnes could not go all the way down the steps, because he could not take the chance of exposing himself to the sunlight. That's why he stood there, unable to continue his chase.

With his hand shielding the brightness, Barnes yelled, "Mickey, please come back here so we can talk about this. There are things we can do. But we can't do them unless you tell me what happened."

But it was too late. Mickey Youngblood acted like a man possessed, one whose mind had been made up. He slung open the gate and sprinted out of the yard in the direction of his car.

At the exact moment Nicole Babbette reached the gate, it flung back and bashed her so hard, it nearly tore her arm off. Her body spun forcefully in a circle, as her shirt snagged on the post, and she almost fell on her back. She caught herself at the last second by slapping her hand against the fence and pulling herself up. Upon regaining her balance, she let out a high-pitched scream. "Shit!" Her hand shook manically through the air, and she yelled over the fence, "You broke my fingernail, you fucking asshole!"

Chapter Twenty-One

Tuesday—6:15 p.m.

Vegas Parsons had a secret. It ballooned in his chest, as if filling him with helium, just waiting to fly out. It had come out a little bit already—well, make that a lot—when he had his little talk with Rosy. And for the moment, he felt better about it, having relieved himself of the tremendous burden. But now, he could feel it right there building again, squeezing through his ribcage, dying to stick its ugly little head out there for everyone else to see.

He was riding the NTD bus with one of his best friends, Peter Melonking, and Vegas wanted to tell him everything he knew. But he knew he couldn't do that. It wasn't as if he'd kept his mouth shut about it up to this point, but now he had to be careful with everything he said. Luke had told him as much in a very angry and uncompromising tone, and Vegas didn't like that very much. He liked it much better when he could just blab his mouth and add whatever spin he wanted to whatever story he happened to be telling at the time.

He was glad Bobby Leblanc was going home, that much he knew for sure. The sooner the guy got back home, the better, so long as none of it came back to Vegas. It was all still kind of weird, though, with Luke saying he was going to take Bobby home, but having to wait until he spoke with Mickey Youngblood. Rosy had been right about that. Who knew what Youngblood was going to do? Vegas certainly didn't. And neither did Luke, who'd been totally uptight about the whole thing from the very beginning. But none of that was of concern right now.

Right now, Vegas' only concern was getting some pot.

He looked out the window and thought it was so cool that he could take this electric bus anywhere he wanted, and nobody would know where he was. His parents would be working, and he could be riding from the historic downtown shopping center, through the narrow tile-paved streets that were too small for the traditional diesel buses, and he could just disappear, be anyone he wanted to be, and no one would notice the difference. They could look at him and wonder what he was up to, but no one would know he was on his way to score herb.

When he was at Luke's, Luke had asked him if he would go get some pot. This amazed Vegas, because Luke always had pot, and if he didn't, there was always someone close to him to whom he had sold who did. But not this time. Everybody was dry. They'd even finished all the smoke Bobby had, so that's why Vegas told Luke he would see what he could do. He called up his buddy Peter and asked if he wanted to go to downtown San Floripez to party and hang out. Vegas knew Peter loved to party and hang out, and Peter said he was all into it. Vegas then asked, "Oh, Peter, by the way, nobody's got any weed. Can you score some?" Peter said he could.

Luke had come up with the brilliant idea of taking the party down to the San Floripez Inn, to have a kind of "going home" party for Bobby. He told Vegas that his old man had even given him the money to get the gang out of the house and take them down to a hotel so Luke's stepmother wouldn't have a cardiac arrest. Everybody was thrilled to see Bobby was going home, and even Rosy, with her big dramatic crying eyes, looked happy.

Vegas felt pretty sure his mom wouldn't have approved of her seventeen-year-old son going to a hotel to party, so when she came to pick them up, he had her drop them off at the Frank's Market parking lot right next to the hotel. He told her they were going to shop for skateboards, and she fell for it. At the hotel, Luke gave Vegas money for the pot, and he took off. He saw the NTD approaching right away and sprinted across Andrade to pick it up. The bus sped up Andrade and over to County Street, and he was out of there. He then marched a block up from the transit center to the corner where the Thai Times stood, and that's where he met Peter.

They hiked a couple blocks past Gibson's Market to where Peter's friend lived. They had each put up fifty dollars, and they bought a quarter ounce. After they left, Vegas told Peter he needed to stop by his house to pick up something. His father had an old bottle of southern mash collecting dust at the bar, and Vegas figured they could use it for the party. He would take it back to the hotel and tell Luke that he had an older friend buy it for him. That way Vegas could pocket the entire twenty spot Luke had given him for the alcohol. When they got over to Vegas' house, he got the booze out of the liquor cabinet and pinched the choicest bud out of the bag of pot when Peter went into the head. *Sweet.*

Vegas had it totally wired as the middleman between buyer and seller. People were always coming to him wanting to buy pot, because he knew the people who sold it. As far as he was concerned it was a business deal, and the pinched bud that he took off the top was his finder's fee. It was what he used most of the time to support his own habit. Sure, he was a little opportunistic, but he loved that part of the game. He loved being free to do what he wanted. So what if he'd been arrested four times in the past year for pot-related infractions? Who cared that he had been expelled from school, been caught violating curfew, and had stolen small amounts of money from his mother? Those were the costs of being free. He loved his mother and father dearly, but they didn't understand how tough it was being a teenager these days. And as far as Vegas was concerned, the less they knew, the better.

That's why they would never know that for the past year he had been experimenting with heavy drugs like cocaine and Ecstasy, although he had had a really bad experience with the cocaine, and decided he would never use it again. But that didn't stop him from experimenting with pills or mushrooms or his need to smoke the magical weed. It was only last month that he was pulled over while driving with several of his buddies who were drunk. Vegas had pot on him at the time, but he'd been able to charm his way around any suspicions of his wrongdoing. The cops never even tried to search him. No harm, no foul, and his parents never found out about it, so they had nothing to get worked up over.

His mother was sweet but very naïve. She trusted Vegas deeply, and that was probably her biggest fault. She was an honest woman who approached life as if everyone she met could or would want to be as honest as she was. But the truth was that kids could not always be honest with their parents. Most of the time, parents wanted what was best for their kids, but their own problems prevented them from understanding what their kids were going through. Times were much more difficult for teens growing up today than they were when Vegas' mother was his age. She was never athletic, so she had no idea of the pressures behind trying to be a topnotch athlete. The pressures were huge, and the parents always put their emphasis on the wrong things. Sports should be about the act of competition, the ability for the kids to see if they could drive beyond their limits, testing themselves against others their same ages.

Instead, the parents' emphasis was always on winning. Or making sure their kid was the star, or making sure the coach played their kids more than the others. Vegas realized that the pressures from succeeding in soccer far outweighed the pleasures he derived from playing it. It had gone from his going out onto the playing field to have fun, to going out there and trying to be the best so he could get a scholarship and please his parents.

Fuck that.

That's why Vegas started smoking pot. It allowed him to forget those pressures. Since he had to hide in the closet due to his smoking, the only ones who understood his plight were fellow teens. They were the ones who smoked pot to escape the pressures that their parents and society placed on them to be the very best they could be, not according to the kids' standards, but according to those of their parents and society. *Fuck that too.*

What did society know about the psychological pressures Vegas faced? Neither society nor his parents had any idea that he had developed a tolerance for pot over time, nor would they know how to deal with it if they did. Vegas needed more pot than ever to get high. He was smoking several times a day just to catch up with the first high of the morning. And it was taking more and more to even accomplish that. Vegas wasn't rich, and he worked a poor-paying job that required him to be creative in his efforts to have enough dough to buy enough pot to smooth out his stress-filled existence.

Although scientific research was still undecided as to whether people could develop physical addictions to pot, there was no question Vegas was psychologically dependent upon the stuff. To be more precise, he was addicted to the release from the outside pressures of his parents and society that the pot provided him. In fact, after Vegas completed the substance abuse counseling and education program as part of his informal probation, he made no attempt whatsoever to stop smoking pot. He started again as soon as he could afford to buy more, and the lying to his parents had continued to this very day. As far as he was concerned, it was a form of damage control for both him and his parents.

That's why he told his mom they were going downtown to a skateboard shop before going to a swim party at a friend's house. She simply would not have understood why they had to go to a hotel. Because there was nowhere else for teens who needed to smoke pot to smoke it, that's why. The adults had taken away all the best spots. Which was what Vegas was thinking about when he realized he couldn't hold back any longer and had to tell Peter about the kidnapping party they were on their way to at the San Floripez Inn.

*   *   *   *

Nestled on a hillside overlooking Crystal Valley's dramatic coastline stood one of the world's most exclusive retreats. The Clemente Spa and Inn, situated thirteen hundred feet above the Pacific Ocean, provided a luxuriously rustic backdrop for conducting business, as well as a serene romantic setting to help kick-start dying relationships.

Dick Youngblood loved working from the freestanding cottages with the over-sized rooms and the wood-burning fireplaces. He enjoyed kicking back with a light beer or a doobie in the private on deck hot tub, which opened up to the glow of moonlight and a spectacle of stars. Here, he could sit back comfortably and be the schemer of dreams, dreams of where he had been, dreams of where he was going.

This was Dick's third business trip and honeymoon getaway with his high-school-sweetheart-turned-wife of twenty-two years. This was also Dick's third stop on his whirlwind three-city business tour that had begun in the Bay Area with a midpoint stop in wine country, where he and his bride had cooked with the wine grapes in the intense northern valley heat, before cooling down with three days of misty coastal paradise.

He had made his monthly trip to his supplier, some Native American chieftain of something or another up near Klamath Falls, just last week, and he had returned to the Valley with forty fresh pounds to unload. He met his connection when Kathy went out to get her facial at the Selysian Spa, with everything running smooth as a baby's ass in between. He had opened the blue duffel bag loaded with pillow-sized plastic bags filled with the finest bud this side of the border. His buyer had been pleased, as the others had all been, and he delivered his pleasure in the form of a manila envelope filled with U.S. currency. It was a deal gone perfectly smooth, and Dick even threw in the duffel bag as a bonus. He had made over five thousand dollars profit on the deal, which added to the fifteen thousand he had made on his other three deals, and he was whistling to the sweet tune of twenty thousand dollars profit (and a vacation) for two weeks' work. Not bad for a high school dropout.

He drained the last of his light beer and decided it was time to head inside. The fog had started to move in, and he could hear the roar of the waves crashing on the rocks thirteen hundred feet below. The air was crisp and tasted of salt. His head was light, and he felt as if he were on top of the world, and why shouldn't he be? He was in love again, and this time he was determined to make things work out. Kathy had been by his side through thick and thin going on two and a half decades now. Although they had been through more than their share of battles, Dick was grateful to have her in his life still. She was a tremendous mother, and she had been a tremendous wife and lover. They had had their share of differences, but then—who hadn't?

When he hopped out of the whirlpool bath, Dick realized he had left his towel inside. The wind had picked up, and goose flesh dotted his arms and legs. He tip-toed across the redwood deck and wondered if Kathy was back yet. When he opened the French doors, he could see her passed out on the bed. She had had a full day of facials, pedicures, and bodywork that had obviously worn her out. She wore nothing more than a black pareo around her waist, and she looked damn good wearing it. Dick thought she looked even better than she had the day they first met at St. Mary's High School.

There she was, this hot, petite, blonde rebel in her own right, and together they had taken his "nobody's going to fuck with me" attitude to new extremes. She didn't like to party as much as he did, but she wasn't afraid to mix it up either, and their passion between fucking and fighting attained epic proportions. In the eleventh grade, Dick reached the conclusion that a steady girlfriend, high school, alcohol, and pot dealing were not the best of mixes, so he dropped out of school to concentrate on the other three. The following year, he decided to marry Kathy, and within a year after that, a third party would join them, someone Dick would be able to pass his accumulated talents and wisdom to: their firstborn child, Mickey.

He went inside, closed the French doors behind him, and snapped out of his reverie the second he heard the vibrating sound of his pager. He stood there, debating whether to crawl up next to his wife and spoon her or to take a potential business call. If it were someone he was going to have to speak to, he would need to drive down the coast to return the call. From many years of experience, Dick knew that you never made business calls that could be traced back to you. Never.

But Dick wasn't really in the mood to drive down the coast, and he and his wife had dinner reservations in less than an hour. What he wanted to do was ignore the annoying sound and fulfill his lustful desires with his wife. That's what he wanted to do. But the pager wouldn't stop buzzing. Concerned that it might be one of his kids, he grabbed his pants off the couch and checked to see who it was.

When he reviewed the numbers, he couldn't believe it. There were fifteen calls within the last hour alone. One was from his brother, with all the others coming from his lawyer. What the hell did *he* want? Dick wondered if he was under investigation again. Or if he had been indicted? Was there an arrest warrant out for him that he didn't know about? Had the guy he had just sold to actually been a narc? But if that was the case, why didn't they just arrest Dick right then and there on the spot? Why would they have contacted his lawyer when they could have slapped the cuffs on him with no legal technicality to worry about? No reason Dick could think of. And then he thought about his kids.

His second thought was to call the Hermses to see how his youngest kid Rudy was doing. But why? The kid was an angel who never got into trouble, and even if he did, Janet Hermses would have called Kathy and told her about it.

All the trouble in the family generally gravitated toward his number one son, Mickey. Dick cringed as he thought about what Mickey might have done now. They had been having a major disagreement ever since Dick caught his kid trying to circumvent him in his dealing hierarchy, cutting Dick out as the middleman. When Dick found this out from his connection in Oregon, he vehemently showed the kid what was what, and that had pretty much been the end of it. By reconnecting with his connections and straightening them out as to whom they were dealing with, order had been restored. Of course, Mickey had had a hard time calming down about it. But he got over it, or so Dick thought. Now, he wasn't so sure.

Chapter Twenty-Two

Tuesday—5:27 p.m.

Half an hour later, Dick Youngblood stood on the side of Highway 7 freezing his ass off. He had driven the three miles up the coast to a roadside pay phone at a small market gas station, and his drive took ten minutes longer than he had anticipated. The fog had socked in, and he had difficulty seeing the lines on the road. When he arrived, he called his lawyer three times, getting nothing but the voice mail on his cell each time. He now glared at the solitary roadside pay phone, and willed it to ring. His hands were shoved deep into his pockets, and he was shivering from the cold wind that whipped in off the coast. He was pissed that he had forgotten his windbreaker at the hotel. He was pissed about a lot of things.

That's what happened when you grew up just one of many rats in a maze. It seemed like ever since he was a kid, the only emotion Dick Youngblood ever understood was anger. He blamed it on the fact he was born the fifth of eight children in nine years. With three brothers ahead of him, and two behind him, Dick had always felt as if he were stuck in the middle of a family going nowhere, and he resented it tremendously.

While growing up, he had battled his brothers to get out of bed in the mornings, the survivor having first dibs to the only bathroom, the others having to bounce around in the hallway, exercising tremendous bladder control, or popping outside and watering the neighbor's hydrangeas. Dick battled at the dinner table for the scraps that trickled down before the dog got them. He battled for lunch money, battled for new shoes, battled for practically everything he ever got, and by the time he was old enough to appreciate what he was doing in life, his parents had nothing left for him. They were dried up as a desert creek.

It was after 5:30 when he heard the phone ring, and Dick felt like a snowman shivering in the coastal drizzle, when he picked it up.

"So what's the emergency?" he asked, trying to sound light.

"Hey, Dick," Sheldon Barnes said in a strained voice.

"What's up, Shelly?" Dick rubbed his arms in an effort to stay warm. "Who's after me now?"

There was a long pause before Barnes said, "It's Mickey."

The grinding gears of a passing eighteen-wheeler grated on Dick's spine as it blew down the highway behind him. He waited for it to pass before continuing. "What did you say about Mickey?"

"I said I shouldn't be discussing this over the phone with you."

"Okay," Dick said, puzzled.

"Let's just say there's been a kidnapping, and it doesn't look very good."

"Oh, fuck." Dick could feel his heart sink with the sun he hadn't seen since his arrival in Crystal Valley. His number one son was in trouble. And his first reaction was to want to reach out and grab Mickey by the neck, to shake him good, and ask him, "What have you done?" He then wanted to ask the same question of himself. *What have I done?*

In Dick Youngblood's skewed vision of reality, he had tried to give his first son everything Dick had been denied in his own life. While Mickey's mother worked a real job, Dick had taken the responsibility of caring for the kid, and had done so with great pride, while living a life to be envied. He had worked as a greens man cruising the Valley city golf course, where he got paid for smoking pot, golfing in the afternoons, and unloading his merchandise under the cover of darkness.

When Mickey was two years old, Dick handed him his first set of golf clubs. He took an old set someone had left at the golf course, and he hacked them off in the garage before refitting them with smaller grips. The child took to the game immediately and developed a solid knack for hitting the ball before he turned three years old. That was about the time Dick got Mickey started in baseball, by throwing tennis balls into the air so he could catch them. Then Dick moved to a **tennis racket, hitting them higher and higher, and by the time Mickey was four,** the kid could catch high-spiraling pop ups.

Nobody else's four-year-old could do that.

Of course, every now and then one would miss Mickey's glove and crack him in the mouth. Little Mickey would run screaming to his mom, blood gushing down his face and neck, and Dick would run after his kid telling him to "quit being such a pussy." Kathy would come out, raging at Dick that the kid was only four years old, and he wasn't ready yet to be a major leaguer. Dick would just brush her off by telling her, "Don't worry about it." And that had become his signature line. If there was one thing that was consistent with Dick Youngblood, it was the fact that he didn't worry about it. But now, his confidence appeared on the verge of cracking.

"And *you know who* is involved?" he said into the phone.

"I think so," Barnes said. "He came to meet with me this afternoon. But he got so upset, he took off before I could really find out what was going on. I've been paging him every five minutes since he left. But he hasn't returned any of my calls."

Dick grabbed the collar of his shirt and pulled it tighter around his neck. "So what did he tell you?"

"I really don't think we should discuss it over the phone."

Dick racked the phone off his forehead, trying to figure out what was going on. Mickey had gotten himself into some kind of trouble involving a kidnapping of some sort, and Sheldon was calling him for help. He was being very smart about not mentioning too much over the phone just in case he was being wiretapped. Even if it was as serious as it sounded, Dick wasn't sure what he could do about it from way up here anyway. He was seven hours away from doing anyone any good about anything.

"So you're telling me things are pretty serious down there, huh?"

"Dead serious, Dick," Barnes said. "We need to get ahold of him, now."

Dick turned his back to the drizzle. "I'll tell you what. I'm going to come down later tonight so we can discuss what's going on."

"I think that'll be too late," Barnes said. "We're going to need to act before then. He was really agitated when he left here, Dick. We need to sit him down and talk to him. I'm afraid of what might happen to the kid."

Dick made a sandpaper sound as he scratched the two-day growth under his chin. "What kid?"

"He didn't tell me who it was. But he said a friend of his kidnapped the brother of someone who still owed him money."

"Oh, shit." None of this was making any sense, but it was stressing Dick out badly. He needed to know more. "I'm not following you, Shell. What does this have to do with *what's his name* if it was a friend who did the kidnapping?"

Dick could hear what he believed to be a long sigh coming from the other end of the line. "I don't think he was talking about someone else, Dick. I think he was talking hypothetically about himself as the one who kidnapped the kid."

"Oh, fuck." Dick was floored by the severity of what he had just heard. His chest constricted, and his head felt like it had been stepped on and flattened.

"See if you can get ahold of him, Dick. Like I said, he's not returning my calls. We need to sit him down and find out what's going on. He was pretty upset when he left my place. Have him call me immediately. I'll see you when you get back."

When Dick hung up, a sharp pain of guilt blasted through him like a frozen wind. He shuddered and couldn't help but feel responsible for what might have happened. He had committed many errors as a parent, but the biggest had been teaching his eldest son the drug business.

At the time, it had been an honest delusion committed with the best of intentions. Dick had no idea he was creating a monster. He had moved the family to Butte when Mickey was fifteen, and then he caught the kid dealing coke at school. Mickey had had a good source and made lots of money at it, and it pissed Dick off beyond belief. Remorse set in quickly, however, when Dick, with a lot of encouragement from his wife, took the responsibility for getting his kid involved.

Since he had set the not-so-great example of drug dealing in the first place, Dick set out to teach Mickey how to stay out of trouble. It was what any decent father would have done. If you're a plumber, you teach your kid how to clean shit out of pipes. If you're a lawyer, you do pretty much the same thing. But if you're a drug dealer, you teach your kid how to avoid the long arm of Johnny Law. The key was to teach them how to do it right.

Dick understood the quickest ticket to a life behind bars was to sell chemicals like cocaine. With mandatory sentences, conspiracy laws, and the hard-line approach government legislatures and judges had taken against drug dealing, Mickey was looking at heavy time if he ever got caught.

Cocaine was being processed cheaper than ever, and it was available all over the streets. The laws had been rewritten to catch those of color, so the mules, the street corner vendors, and all the niggers and spics caught with a little crack here or a little powder there could be corralled and fed into the slave population of the newly privatized American prison system. Dick didn't really give a shit about the darkies buried behind gray walls, stamping license plates and selling travel packages, but he damn well wanted to make sure his own kid didn't get caught up in any of that. Mickey was too white, too soft. He would be lost in the system, and it was up to Dick to make sure that didn't happen. It was one of the parental responsibilities he took very seriously.

Mickey may have acted tough, but Dick knew he was just a kid at heart. So he sat him down and had a heart-to-heart about the finer nuances of drug dealing. The first thing he told his boy was, "You only sell pot." The sentences were much more lenient, and you could always get out on bail in a pot case so you could help defend yourself against the unjustice system. You never kept it on you or at your house. You never discussed sales over the phone. You always fronted it, dirtying the hands of those down the line who wouldn't snitch you out without implicating themselves first. And then it was their word against yours anyway. Dick had discussed all the basics with his kid, and when they were finished, he felt as if Mickey knew what he needed to know to become a successful businessman. The problem was, none of Dick's lessons included Kidnapping 101.

Dick Youngblood had mastered many shady techniques in his life, but abduction was not one of them. Neither was accepting personal responsibility for anything he did. That's why he started drinking at the age of thirteen. Because he believed alcohol gave him bravery. If Dick were going to maintain his mercenary "me against the world" attitude, he needed to be brave to survive it. It was the same hard attitude he took to school and battled his teachers with and later got thrown in jail for. It was the same attitude he fought his parents with and carried into adulthood. And it was the same attitude his son had inherited from him.

Dick drained more coinage into the machine. His buddy picked up on the second ring. Denver Mattson was an old-time pork-eater who had caught on with the old boys back in Jersey before moving his game to Las Vegas. They had first met after Mattson planted his books in the Valley back in the midseventies. Mattson had always been easy money for Dick, who had practically made a living off the guy. They eventually became great friends, Mattson at one time going into business with Dick selling herb. When Mickey was born, Mattson was there as his godfather. On his eighteenth birthday, Mattson gave Mickey his first gun.

Dick told his bookie about the muted conversation with his lawyer.

"Jesus Christ, no wonder," Mattson said with aggravation.

"What?" Dick asked.

"Mickey borrowed my van a couple days ago so he could use it to help him move." Mattson paused as if waiting for Dick to say something. When he didn't, Mattson continued. "A couple buddies of his dropped it off on Sunday. Apparently somebody shot a goddamned hole through the ceiling big enough to stick my ass through."

Dick almost gagged on the image. "Had to be a damn big hole."

"Very funny," Mattson growled. Dick didn't detect any humor in his voice. "Anyway," Mattson continued, "it sounds like Mickey fucked up big time this time."

Dick didn't want to talk about it over the phone, but until he got back, he knew he was going to need some help. "I can't talk about it now, if you know what I mean. But I was hoping you wouldn't mind going over and meeting with Sheldon Barnes for me. Maybe find out the details of what's going on."

"What's Barnes got to do with it?"

"He's the one who told me what's going on. Maybe you could also try to get ahold of Mickey for me. Sit him down until I get back. That kind of thing."

"No problem," Mattson slurred, and Dick wondered how much his friend had been drinking tonight.

Chapter Twenty-Three

Bobby Leblanc was finally going home, and Luke couldn't have been happier about it. He felt the smile bubbling beneath the surface of his skin, wanting to break out onto his face, and it probably would have, if it weren't for the meat grinder in his stomach that churned everything into hamburger. The grinding intensified when Vegas' mom had picked them up to drive them to the San Floripez Inn.

California Parsons reminded Luke of a sixties flower child who never grew into adulthood. She still looked young enough to be Vegas' sister, and if she didn't have that annoyingly bubbly personality, Luke would have considered her MILF material. But she did have the bubbly personality of an earth mother and an inquisitive nature to match, and she annoyed the hell out of Luke on the drive over with her battery of questions to Bobby about his family. It was as if she had zeroed in on the situation and was trying to pry the gritty details out of the kid. "So where are you from?" "Where are your parents?" "Do they let you stay out often?"

Luke had to step in and stomp on her questions, becoming Bobby's mouth-piece and irritating just about everyone in the car. He breathed a happy sigh of relief when she dropped them off, afraid that he was going to have to bitchslap her for asking all the wrong questions. Things lightened up considerably when they reached the hotel. Vegas took off to score, while Luke, Bobby, and Cheri Merced—all sweating like city kids in a police lineup—traipsed into the lobby of the San Floripez Inn. Luke told Cheri and Bobby to go have seats by the fountain, hoping that no one would get a good look at the kid. Luke sweated it out through the check-in, trying his best to remain cool, and left cash for the deposit.

Since no one seemed to do anything strange or make any sudden movements, he figured everything would be okay. When the clerk asked him how many people would be staying, he glanced around, and said, "Just me." The clerk looked at Luke through one long eye but said nothing and gave him the form to sign. When Luke finished, Bobby and Cheri followed him up the stairwell. Luke intentionally avoided the elevator, not wanting to risk a conversation or spotting of the kid that he would later on regret. When they got up to room 215, Cheri said she needed to call Rosy, who had paged her on their way upstairs.

"Go ahead," Luke said and he picked up the television remote.

When Cheri got Rosy on the phone, Luke yanked the receiver from her hand and tossed the remote onto the bed. "When you coming down, chick?" he yelled, his voice sounding all hyper and nervous. "Yeah, you should come on down. It's going to be fun ... I told you, we're going to have a great time ... Come down, now. Yeah. We're at the San Floripez Inn—room 215. There's a party going down, bitch, and you're missing it."

*   *   *   *

"Then whose fucking fault is it?" Kathy Youngblood yelled, as she gripped the dashboard around another hair-raising turn. "Surely you're not blaming me!"

Dick Youngblood had never seen his wife so angry. She was seated in the passenger's seat of his collectible black and gold 1986 European luxury sedan, and she hadn't stopped yelling at him for the past hour. She had not taken the news well of her son's alleged legal troubles.

"It's nobody's fault," Dick kept saying, his gloved hands on the wheel around the dark, hairy curves of southbound Highway 7. "These things just happen sometimes."

"The hell they do." Her fist pounded the dashboard. "People don't just grow up to be big-time drug dealers. Especially white kids. They go to school and get college degrees. They become postmen or executives of major corporations. But, no—not my kid. He's got to follow his lazy-assed father into the drug business. After his brilliant fucking idea of turning his son into a professional ballplayer failed miserably."

Dick felt underappreciated. His wife wasn't giving him nearly the credit he deserved. Dick actually had two brilliant ideas in his life. The first was to become a wholesaler of fine bud, which he did, using his longtime coaching position at Valley Little League, a family-oriented club where most attending parents became close friends while rooting for their favorite children, as a cover. Yet, at the time, he had harbored no notion whatsoever of his son following in his footsteps.

That was where brilliant idea #2 came in. Dick wanted to turn Mickey into something Dick never was—a professional baseball player—to sort of make up for Dick's own failings as an athlete. Dick was an avid fan of the game, and he had turned Mickey onto it at a very young age. As the kid was growing up, Dick drilled him from dusk until dawn, hitting Mickey thousands of scorching grounders and mile-high pop ups, throwing him hundreds of hours of batting practice. Even Mickey's mom got into the act whenever she could, going to all of his games and most of his practices, flipping burgers and selling sodas at the Burger Shack.

For the little fart that he was, Mickey actually got pretty good. He worked hard and turned himself into an all-star pitcher and third baseman in his last year in Little League. Three years later, Dick blew it all by packing up his family and moving them to Montana to start a sports bar and restaurant with one of his former high school buddies, who also happened to be another of Mickey's godfathers. Mickey had just begun high school, and the move away removed him from his personal comfort zone. Mickey would never be the same ballplayer again. He looked like a little midget out in the field, totally lost, his hat tilted to the side gang-like, with that smirk on his face, mouthing off to everyone.

Dick's family never recovered from the move either since the restaurant business failed miserably, just as all of Dick's attempts at going straight had ended. Dick Youngblood knew how to perform one kind of business only, the kind that caught the attention of law enforcement officers and always created tension around the house.

A year later, Dick dragged his family back to the Valley, but by then it was too late for his kid's baseball career. Mickey had changed, and not necessarily for the better. He was partying heavily and dealing pot behind his mother's back. Dick would encounter no such problems during his smooth transition back to his familiar roles of Little League coach and large-scale pot trafficker. But the starch in his family had been all but washed out for good.

Mickey still played ball though, now as a sophomore at Valley High, where he played second base on the junior varsity team. He played with agility and focus, and his ability seemed to promise a strong season, but that all ended when he blew up at one of the school administrators and got thrown out of school. So much for his sophomore season. At the time, Mickey's mom screeched at Dick mercilessly for raising a kid who had no ability to control his temper whatsoever. And Dick just sorta bent over and accepted the blame without retort. His wife had little introspection as to her own involvement with raising the kid, so what good would the blame game have done anyway? She never accepted it, so why should he lay it?

At the time, Dick had many talks with Mickey about the need to grow up and take responsibility for his future. They discussed Mickey's potential career and the universities he might like to attend. Mickey told his father that he had always wanted to play for the Air Force Academy or Penn State.

Dick was determined to send his kid to the best school possible and had a friend, a former pro ballplayer, work with Mickey on refining his skills, hitting him pop ups and grounders by the thousands, working him hard so that he might one day get a scholarship to the school of his choice. Dick did everything humanly possible to enable his kid to succeed on the athletic field, but there were some things that you just couldn't control.

Mickey Youngblood had always been small for his age. The kid had been born the size of a puppy dog that fit in one hand. He was always the smallest in his class and whatever team he happened to be on. That's why Dick started getting up early in the mornings and feeding Mickey protein shakes with desiccated liver and tuna. And then he took him to work out at the gym at night. Size was something you could not teach. It was an old sports maxim, another bitter meal for Dick Youngblood to swallow in his battle with life for cutting him short: a son who had been cut even shorter.

Mickey transferred to Chaparral High as a junior and played on the varsity squad, a strong team that won the league championship. The gritty infielder rode the pine most of the season, but he caught the coach's eye as a pinch hitter and batted in several significant games. Mickey had an uncanny ability to get on base, and his coach had big plans for him the following year. But Mickey tore up his knee before the start of his senior season, and his career—along with his father's second brilliant idea—evaporated in a cloud of dust at second base.

"I am not lazy," Dick assured his wife. "I may not have done things the way you wanted, but you certainly never complained about what I was doing when you were spending my money."

"*Your* money?" She glared at him with beet red eyes. "Don't forget, I worked too, buster. I worked every day of my life. And I had two kids ... no, make that three kids to raise. I fixed them breakfast. I bathed them. I took them to school. I picked them up. I fixed them dinner. Sure, I didn't get the big cash payout. But nobody ever worried about the cops raiding a beautician's house. No one ever worried that the FBI had tapped my phone because I was doing too many hair colorings. Nobody ever stayed up late wondering if I would come home at night.

Or end up needing to be bailed out because I had sold shampoo to an undercover officer. No, while you were out living your little fantasies, I was raising you and those kids in a single-parent household."

"Well then …" Dick started to say she didn't do a very good job with any of them, but then he stopped. Why bother? That's not where he wanted to go. Instead, he shifted his focus to the road, appreciating his car's smooth handling. They were approaching eighty, and the car drove as if it was on glass, fast and powerful. There were those who criticized the 300E series for its plastic style, lighter components, and soft door slam, but not Dick. "Subtle class" was what he liked to call it.

"Well then, what?" she screamed.

He kneaded the knot in the back of his neck with arthritic fingers. "Well then, you answered your own question."

She sat there silently for a second, the only silent second of the trip. She gritted her teeth and gripped the dashboard with such ferocity, he was afraid she might rip it off the car with her bare hands. "I know you're not saying it's my fault that our son is going to prison."

"Will you stop?" He waved his gloved hand. "He's not going to prison, okay?"

"You said he kidnapped someone …" She clung desperately to the door handle while he took a hairpin curve at an unreasonably high rate of speed. When he straightened it out, she jumped back on him like a buzzard on roadkill. "A kid is what you said. He kidnapped a kid. And if he kidnapped a kid, he's going to prison."

"I said someone has been kidnapped. We're still not sure who did what to whom. That's what I need to find out."

Dick had paged Mickey eight times on the trip down the coast, but he hadn't heard back from him yet. He was also waiting to speak to Denver Mattson about his meeting with Barnes.

"Oh, that's just great," Kathy said. "He kidnaps a kid, and now what's he going to do with him, huh?"

"I don't know." Dick's ears were burning. He knew this to be one more fight he had no chance of winning. Women were funny that way. They were different from men. They usually expressed their emotions in painful, hurting ways. They withdrew, and pulled, and sucked the energy out of their men, while the guys just vented their anger and got it all out of their systems. That's why men were healthier than women. By being healthier, they were in turn stronger and better leaders. But his wife was different. She vented as badly as Dick did. She could usually outcuss and outyell him, and that's why, with her, he always had to take the opposite approach. There was simply no winning an argument with Kathy Youngblood when she was like this.

When Dick saw the blue and yellow light on the phone booth approaching, he decided to pull into the gas station. Anything to escape the psychological beating his wife was administering to him. He felt mentally and emotionally exhausted, which was amazing considering he had just been on a totally relaxing seven-day vacation until the nightmare call from Barnes. Dick hated to admit it, even to himself, but his wife was right. He had fucked up in his responsibilities as a father to his number one son. He had gotten angry with Mickey too many times. He had tried to make up for the lapses in his own life by making his son into something he really wasn't.

At one time, Mickey was actually a very sweet boy. All the kid wanted to do was be like other kids. But that was never good enough for Dick. His kid had to be something special. He had to be different than all the other kids. And that's why Dick's wife resented him so much. It's also why she refused to let him have anything to do with raising their second son, Rudy. She would not allow Dick to fuck him up as he had done with Mickey. One nightmare gangster son was enough for any household.

Dick's loafers crunched on the gravel as he worked his way toward the phone booth. It was cold and windy, just like his marital relations. He pulled the collar up on his black and orange baseball windbreaker. The coins dropped into the machine as he leaned against the squared hood covering the phone.

When Mickey's baseball career had died, in a way, so did Dick. He couldn't remember which one of them was more depressed about it. They had both been looking for a big season—something to attract the attention of college scouts—but it never materialized. Then Mickey lost his drive to play. It didn't help that he had found that little trollop of a girlfriend at Chaparral High—Nicole Babbette—who drank more alcohol and smoked more pot than any chick Dick had ever seen. The little slut led Mickey down the wrong avenue of drugs, alcohol, and debauchery that the dumb kid still seemed totally oblivious to.

Dick could feel an ice-cold draft blow straight up his ass when he glanced over at Kathy sleeping in the car. He liked her that way. Quiet. He shifted the phone to the other ear and heard the sound of someone picking up on the other end.

"Hey, what do you know, Denver? Talk to Barnes yet?"

"Yup." Denver Mattson sounded as if he'd been sleeping. Or drinking. "And it doesn't look good, Dick. Find your kid yet?"

Dick rubbed his hand through his thinning red and gray hair. "Not yet. I just paged him again. I'm hoping he'll call before I get back on the road."

"You need to get home."

"No shit. I'm trying." Dick hugged himself. "What'd you find out?"

There was a long pause before Mattson said, "Everything."

Dick leaned back against the phone booth, listening attentively as Mattson explained his meeting with the ponytailed lawyer. "… I was at his house less than ten minutes, when the reality of the situation hit me. When I found out what your kid did, I was floored. Then we discussed how to find him. Because no one knows where he is. Once we find Mickey, we can divert our energies toward finding the kid." Dick heard a muffled cough, and then his friend said, "So how long's it gonna take you to get back?"

"I'll be back in a few hours."

"All right. I'll fill you in on the rest when you get here."

Dick could feel the pressure building behind his eyes. "So what are we going to do, Denver?"

"I said we'll discuss it when you get here." Mattson sounded impatient. "But hurry your ass up. We ain't got all day."

Chapter Twenty-Four

Tuesday—7:06 p.m.

By the time Rosy Kinski arrived at room 215, the party was in full swing. Everybody was laughing and joking, and Luke acted more relaxed than he had all day. He was back to being his usual, jovial self, and Rosy told him that she was happy to see it. They had all been terribly stressed by the ordeal, but it was all about to come to an end.

Vegas' friend Peter Melonking had no problem fitting right in. He was just one of the boys, partying and smoking dope with Cheri and Vegas. Bobby sat back on the bed with a big old grin on his face and huge, red eyes, looking as if he weren't feeling much of anything. Luke played the happy bartender from the makeshift bar that he had set up on the desk next to the TV, and he mixed drinks for everyone. By 8:00 p.m., they were all out on the balcony smoking cigarettes and drinking, and nobody was feeling any pain. That was when Luke decided to make his move. On his way out the door, he told Rosy to answer the phone if it rang.

His first stop was half a block down County Street at the Painted Branch Liquor Store, where he picked up a bunch of cheap ninety-nine-cent cigars to make blunts out of. He then ran across the street to Gordos, where he picked up six double Gordos cheeseburger dinner specials with colas and fries well done. On his way back to the hotel, he stopped at the pay phone in front of Frank's Market and paged Mickey Youngblood three more times, leaving the hotel number. He needed Mickey to call him back so he could break the news to him. Luke needed to tell Youngblood that he was taking the matter out of his dirty little hands for good. He then picked up the bags and returned to the hotel and resumed his conversation with the whiskey bottle.

Everyone in room 215 scarfed down their cheeseburgers except for Cheri, who reminded Luke that she was a vegetarian. Luke never could figure out how vegetarians survived without eating hamburgers. It seemed so unnatural. Double Gordos cheeseburgers were the ultimate food, the ultimate energy picker-upper, and that's why he agreed to take Cheri's burger, giving her his fries in the exchange.

Cheri's burger tasted better than ever. When he finished, Luke found himself licking the reddish-brown grease off his fingertips, and the phone rang. Luke froze in mid lick. He then slowly enticed his tongue to move, while pulling his finger out of his mouth and staring at the phone as if it were radioactive waste. The party continued to swirl around him, except for Rosy—who also stood dead still—glaring at Luke as if *he* were radioactive waste. Her mouth swelled with words and she looked as if she wanted to know what he was waiting for.

Luke wanted to ask himself the same thing. It was the phone call he'd been waiting three days for, and it was time to make his move, yet he felt panic-stricken inside. He stood up and willed one foot and then the other to lead him across the room, and he picked up the receiver.

"Hey, Mick, what's up?" The silence on the other end grated on him heavily. "Hello …?" Luke listened intently, a million responses wading through his mind, when he finally turned around to Rosy and said, "He wants to speak to you."

Rosy's eyes shot wide with trepidation, as she took the phone and placed it next to her ear. "Hello?" Luke glared at her anxiously, as Rosy let out this egg-melting smile and said, "Oh, hi, Dad … Yeah. That was Luke … Right. That's right. And that problem we talked about? Well, it's not a problem anymore … Yeah. He's going home … That's right. Tonight. We're having a 'going home' party for him right now … Yeah! You too. Thanks, Dad. Good night …" And she hung up.

And Luke looked stunned. His hands slapped his hips, as he said, "You told your dad about Bobby?"

"Well, I didn't tell him names or anything, but yeah." Rosy sounded relieved as she pulled her hair back into a bun. But Luke just stood there glowering at her like he wanted to behead her. "I was worried, Luke, okay. Come on, I needed someone to talk to. But everything's okay, now, right? Bobby's going home, right? So there's nothing to worry about."

"Right," Luke said, his head floating into another galaxy. "Right."

He stepped over to the makeshift bar and poured himself a strong one. When he heard the front door creak open, he looked over and saw Vegas stroll in with two young girls in colorful bathing suits who couldn't have been more than fifteen years old. Luke couldn't believe it. He knew fifteen could get you twenty, and in his case, probably a lot more. Bobby was in the bathroom, and he would be out any minute, and Luke had to get the chicks out of there before they saw him.

"What the fuck are you doing, dude?" he screeched to Vegas. "Tell your friends to get lost before I lose you."

Vegas' lower lip began to quiver and he peered back at the young babes. "But I don't want to."

"Dude ...?" Luke pushed over and got right up in Vegas' face. From point-blank range, he said, "I wasn't asking you, dude. I was telling you. Now get the fucking chicks outta here."

And that's what Vegas did, reluctantly. He put his head down and herded the girls out the door, telling them, "We'll meet you down at the pool in about ten minutes."

After he closed the door, Vegas took a seat in the orange chair and sulked. When Bobby sauntered out of the bathroom forty seconds later, Vegas jumped back up. "Are you ready to go swimming?"

Bobby said, "Sure."

Vegas tossed him a bathing suit, and Bobby pivoted and headed back into the bathroom.

"Vegas, why don't you come over here for a second?" Luke said from his seat on the bed. He had pulled out the bag of pot and spilled it onto the side table. "Why don't you help me roll some blunts."

"Ah, dude," Vegas whined. "I want to go swimming. Those chicks are on fire. They'll be down there waiting for us."

"Sit down, Vegas," Luke said sternly. "I'm not fucking around."

Vegas looked as if he were about to whine louder, until Luke flashed him that look again, and Vegas plowed right down next to the bed and started rolling blunts. Luke then inhaled broadly, sat on the bed, and leaned his head back against the pillow. He raised his hands, and his fingers started massaging his temples. His eyes drew closed. And he listened to the party's thrum around him. He felt exhausted, and he dreamed about going to sleep and never waking up. *It is almost over*, his mind told him, and he tried to imagine how happy he could be once he washed his hands of the entire mess. When Luke told Mickey about his plan to let the kid go, he knew Mickey would react one of two ways. Either he would agree with Luke's decision, and that would be the end of it. Or he would throw a fit. And the latter seemed more Mickey's style.

Youngblood had originally told Luke that he didn't want to let the kid go before he had a chance to speak with his brother. But now that Mickey had pussed out on contacting Rick Leblanc, there was no reason to hold onto the kid anymore as a marker. Luke knew Mickey wouldn't be happy about it, but that's just the way it was going to be. Mickey would have to understand that Luke had finally made up his mind. His decision was final.

Besides, the last time they had spoken, Mickey's story had changed. He told Luke, "Settle down. I'm going to come up and get him. Just have him ready. We'll bring him back home." But then those plans changed as well. Mickey never showed up or sent anybody to pick the kid up, and Luke wasn't sure at this point whether he could even trust Mickey to do what he said he was going to do. Youngblood was crazed beyond belief. He had totally lost his ability to think this thing through rationally. That's why Luke was going to give the kid fifty bucks, walk him down to the train station, and send him to the Valley. Period. He had done it a million times himself, taking the train into the Valley to visit his mom, and he knew the routine by heart. That way Bobby was sure to make it. But Luke still felt an obligation to at least tell Youngblood, just to be sure.

When the phone rang suddenly, it took Luke five seconds of blinking just to gather his bearings. Then his eyes gorged open, and his heart nearly hammered through his chest. After the second ring, he nearly kicked Vegas in the head as he jumped off the bed. Before it rang a third time, he just about tore the phone out of the wall, and answered it. He stood there wheezing and listening until he realized it was Mickey. He told him to "Hold on" and tossed the phone on the bed, and ran over to the bathroom door. But it was locked. "Fuck!" He ran back to the phone on the bed, picked it up, and said, "Hold on a second, Mickey." He then pressed the mouthpiece against his chest, stretched his leg out, and kicked the bathroom door as loud as he could. "Dude, I need to get in there."

"Come on in," he heard Bobby's muted voice say.

Luke dropped the phone again on the bed, and tried the bathroom door handle, but it still wouldn't open. "I can't, dude, it's locked."

He then heard the sound of the door unlocking from the other side, and he opened it. Bobby stood in the middle of the bathroom wearing nothing more than Vegas' bright red bathing suit and stained white socks that looked as if they could stand on their own.

Luke walked in and closed the door. "Dude, why don't you let me have some privacy."

"Sure," Bobby said, and he bent down and grabbed his clothes off the floor. He then opened the door and walked out.

"And hang it up when I pick up," Luke said. He slammed the door shut behind him. When he picked the receiver up off the bathroom wall, he could hear the sound of the other phone hanging up. Luke was now alone, and he could finally breathe. He pulled the toilet cover down and took a seat. When he put the receiver to his ear, he was completely devoid of breath. "Hey, what's up, Mickey?"

"I was going to ask you the same fucking thing," Youngblood spat. "Christ, what're you doing over there? Having a fucking party?"

Luke's head shook rabidly. "No, of course not, Mickey."

"Still got the fucking kid, I hope?"

"Oh, yeah," Luke said, drawing in air, trying to find the right words to deflect Mickey's aggression. "You know, Mickey ... damn I'm glad you called." He swallowed again. "You know, I been thinking a lot about this." He stopped and sucked in through his nose when he heard what he thought to be a huge sigh coming from the other end. But when no words followed, Luke continued, "I been thinkin' a lot about what we talked about the other day. And you know what? I decided I'm going to send the kid home."

Dead silence greeted Luke's proclamation. He shifted uncomfortably on his throne, but his confidence grew when he heard no opposition arising from Youngblood. "It's time to do this, Mickey. I really feel things are going to work out better this way."

"What the fuck are you talking about?"

Luke flinched at Youngblood's predacious tone. "Look, Mickey, we can't hurt the kid, okay? I was thinking about what you said when we were down at the Beachcomber. And, I mean, we just can't hurt him. He's a sweet kid. He needs to get home to his parents. So I'm going to give him fifty bucks and send him home on the train."

There, he said it. It was all out there now. And Luke felt a million times better about it. He sat there, rocking back and forth uneasily, squirming on his seat, waiting for Youngblood to say something—anything—but the phone sat reticent in his hand. "Hello ...? Mickey, did you hear me?"

"Yeah, I heard you ... So if you're so fucking anxious to get rid of the kid, why didn't you let him go already?"

"Because I—I wanted to tell you first, Mickey."

"You know what we're looking at, don't you?"

Luke held the phone out in front of him, staring at it as if it were ablaze. Then he put it back to his ear, carefully. "What we're looking at?"

"What the sentence for this kind of kidnapping is?"

Youngblood's tone sounded angry and frightened, and Luke's heart shimmied up through his glottis. He couldn't understand what Mickey was talking about. Who cared what the sentence was? All Luke knew was that the kid had to get home. And he was about to tell Mickey this, when he heard a loud rap on the door. He covered the phone with his hand. "I'll be out in a minute." He put the phone back to his mouth, this time whispering, "What are you talking about, Mickey?"

"I'm talking about the kidnapping. Do you know what you're fucking looking at for your part?"

"What I'm looking at?" Luke's voice sounded panicked now. "Mickey, I'm not looking at anything. This isn't my deal, dude. This is your deal. All I did was hold the kid—for *you*."

"Motherfucker," Youngblood shouted, "you held a kidnapped kid at your house for three fucking days. You think you're just going to slide out of this unscathed?"

Luke swallowed hard, putting his hand over his chest. "Mickey, I didn't kidnap the kid. You did. You and John. It's your debt, not mine. If there's anybody looking at jail time, it should be you, not me."

"Who the fuck are you kidding, Luke? We're all involved in this together. You especially. You drove the van that picked the kid up. You kept him at your house for three days."

"Because you asked me too," Luke cried.

"You could have let him go anytime," Youngblood cried back.

"But you wouldn't let me." Luke rose and started pacing the small tiled floor.

"I wasn't even there, Luke. He was your responsibility, remember? You could've let the kid go anytime. But you didn't. I talked to my lawyer, and I'm telling you, dude … We're fucked."

Luke's deep groan reverberated off the shower walls. He rubbed his hand across his head, and he felt as if he were going to hyperventilate. "Okay, so, say I am involved in this—so what? Even though I fed the kid, gave him clothes, and treated him about as well as anyone could treat someone … All right, fine. What am I looking at?"

"Life."

The word floated out there for more than a minute, before Luke's hand rose, and he touched the numbness that had become his face. His heart had stopped beating, and his mind doubted the veracity of what it had just heard. But when Mickey repeated the words, the ugly reality of his situation sliced through Luke's spine like a sharpened scalpel. His eyes sat riveted on the phone, and his brain willed his mouth to say something in his defense—anything—but Luke felt so overcome by grief, he was temporarily mute. Paralyzed with fear.

Youngblood had no such problem. "If the kid goes to the police—we're dead."

"He said he won't," Luke said anemically.

"I know what he told you. But if he or his mother … or his fucking brother go to the police, we're all looking at spending the rest of our lives in prison."

Luke's whole body shriveled into itself. He desperately needed a drink. He desperately wanted to die. "Mickey, can I ask you something?"

"What?"

"Tell me, why would I be looking at life? What did I do?"

Youngblood laughed derisively. "You held onto the kid so his brother would pay me my money. That's kidnapping for ransom. Everybody involved in a kidnapping for ransom is looking at life in prison."

Luke sniffled, and he could feel the wetness building in his eyes.

"Even your parents could be looking at life just for having the kid over there."

The moisture began to drain down Luke's cheeks. He grabbed a tissue off the counter and wiped his nose. He tried to speak, but he literally could not get the words out of his mouth. He could taste the bile surging inside his stomach, and knew he was going to be sick. He leaned over the sink and tried to spit out the wretchedness. He glared up and into the mirror—at the bloodshot eyes—the profusely sweating, tear-stricken face that glared back at him.

"You still there?" the voice on the phone asked.

Luke cupped his hand under the faucet and filled it with water. He lapped it up thirstily. When he finished, he said weakly, "Yeah, I'm still here."

"We can get out of this, Luke. If we do it right." Youngblood's voice was now rising with certainty. "Get everybody out of there. And I'm coming down so we can take care of business. We'll take care of this, Luke. Don't sweat it. I'm not going to let anything happen to you. But whatever you do, don't let the kid out of your sight. I want him thinking we're taking him home to meet his brother. I'll call you before we come out. Just have him ready when I get there." And he hung up.

And Luke turned and vomited his life away into the sink.

Chapter Twenty-Five

Tuesday—10:22 p.m.

Luke stared at someone in the bathroom mirror whom he did not recognize. He knew he had barely survived his stay in jail on his DUI, so how could he possibly survive a life sentence for kidnapping? The answer was that he couldn't. Luke had about as much chance of surviving a life sentence in prison as he had of becoming the next president of the United States. None. Zilch, nil. No chance whatsoever. He was a dead man if he went to prison, and he knew it. But that didn't mean the kid had to be one as well.

There was no reason for it to have come down to this. Mickey could have done something long before, but he didn't. He could have called Rick Leblanc, gone over to see him, gone to his parents' house, anything. Instead, he did nothing but set Luke up. Luke felt as if he had been violated by Mickey. Manipulated and abused. Used up and then thrown away like a tampon. Youngblood had gotten himself into this situation, and then he had played Luke like a rat in a corner so he could get himself out scot-free.

First, he had convinced Luke to drive the van. How fucking stupid was Luke for falling for that trick? He should have just let Mickey go, been done with him, and gotten a ride back home on his own. But for some reason, like the total moron he was, Luke had felt sorry for Mickey. And then he agreed to keep the kid at his house. How stupid was that? Although his old man had been drunk as a fucking snake, Fritz's instincts had been correct when he asked Luke why the kid was there. Why hadn't Luke just told his dad the truth? If he had, it would have been all over by now. His father would have helped him figure something out, if for no other reason than to keep his own ass out of a sling.

There was another loud rap on the bathroom door, and Luke straightened up quickly. He could hear Rosy's voice outside. "Luke, are you okay?"

"Yeah. I'll be right out," he said. He could see himself sweating through his sweat, and it totally disgusted him. He grabbed a towel off the rack, used it to wipe his face and under his arms, and tossed it into the shower. Then he opened the door.

Rosy greeted him with an ear-to-ear grin, as her eyes surveyed him up and down, calculating the damage. "Was that him?"

The question temporarily caught Luke off guard. "Uhm, yeah. Yeah, it was."

Rosy continued to eyeball him, but Luke refused to meet her gaze. He just pushed past her without saying anything. The party still roiled outside, with everyone looking bleary-eyed and happy. Everyone except Rosy, who kept following Luke around and eyeing him with her way-too-concerned look. He just kept turning away, knowing there was nothing he could do about it now. He needed to think, to concentrate on what he was doing. Get his head around this crazy situation. So he grabbed a blunt off the table and went onto the balcony and smoked it.

Luke wanted no part of whatever Mickey was about to do. He just wanted to take the kid outside and send him on his way. Just wash his hands of the whole affair and see what happened. *Yeah, right. And watch the cops drag my ass out of bed first thing in the morning. So I'll never see the light of day outside a prison cell again.* On second thought, maybe he wouldn't do that. At least not at the moment. And not before he had the chance to talk to Mickey again. He had promised Mickey he'd hold onto the kid until he got there, but he didn't understand why he had agreed so easily. He knew what Mickey wanted to do. Was he just going to let him get away with murder? He couldn't do that, if for no other reason than he liked the kid. The kid was sweet and human, and he trusted Luke implicitly. And that was probably Bobby's biggest downfall.

But there was something else there too. Something deeper that Luke just wasn't seeing. What was it? It was like, why had he gone along with Mickey during all this nonsense from the very beginning? He liked Mickey, sure, but this was **going way above and beyond the normal course of friendship.**

Mickey Youngblood had been good to Luke; there was no question about that. He had treated him like a brother ever since they hooked up again after Luke's DUI. Mickey had Luke over to his house; he fed him and liquored him up and never seemed to ask for anything in return. Except, maybe, for the money that was owed to him. Was that what Mickey had expected from the beginning when he first told Luke what Rick Leblanc had done? That they were going to get rid of his kid brother? Luke sort of doubted it, since there was no way Mickey could have anticipated that Bobby would be on the street at that time to begin with. It was a stroke of pure, dumb luck that the kid would get into a fight with his parents, then run away at exactly the same time Luke, Mickey, and Barbados were on their way to fuck up his parents' house. There was no way Mickey could have anticipated that. No way.

Mickey had definitely gone over there looking to fuck Rick Leblanc up, but kidnapping was not in the blueprint. It was only when Mickey saw an angle, a way to squeeze the kid to get to his brother, that he decided to keep him. And it was only after Youngblood realized it would be unwise to get ahold of Rick Leblanc that he had decided to pawn the kid off onto Luke in the first place. But why had Luke accepted?

Because I don't want Mickey to get hurt, that's why.

It was the only logical excuse he could think of. Luke had been an on-again, off-again friend of the Youngblood family for the better part of a decade. They used to have him over to their house; the family had always treated him well, and Luke's dad used to hang out with Mickey's dad and party by the week. Both families had ties dating all the way back to Little League. And it was those feelings of that relationship, generated way back then, that caused Luke to try to protect Mickey now.

Little League was a time of innocence and big dreams. Kids played and imagined themselves growing up to one day be Big League ballplayers. They developed relationships during a time when the only important thing in life was winning or losing. They didn't have to work overtime or worry about paying the bills. They didn't worry about nuclear bombs or terrorists under their bed. They worried about being kids. And when those kids got older, they were only older in age, not necessarily in maturity. Growing up was not necessarily part of the equation. It was as if Luke had remained locked up in that youthful innocence, never seriously thinking about growing up. He hung out with Mickey and tried to carry on a relationship that was buried in childhood memories, yet which had probably died years earlier, and which now might cost Luke his freedom. Why?

Because Mickey has been good to me.

Youngblood was panicked with worry that the kid would go to the police, or that Rick Leblanc would find Mickey or his family and fuck them up. Rick Leblanc was a fucking animal who didn't know when to quit. He had left Mickey very little choice, and Luke could now see that clearly. He could feel the panic in Mickey's voice whenever he spoke about Leblanc. Although Luke never imagined saying it to Youngblood's face, Mickey seemed a little bit scared. As if he were over his head with this whole Leblanc thing and didn't know what to do about it.

So Luke came to the rescue. "Oh, sure, I'll keep the kid for two hundred and fifty dollars a day." What a moron he was for letting Mickey talk him into it. But now, it was Luke's turn. If Mickey could talk Luke into keeping the kid for two days, then Luke could certainly talk Mickey into taking the kid home. He knew Mickey didn't really want to hurt Bobby. That wasn't Mickey's way. Mickey Youngblood wasn't a killer; he was a pot dealer. He was the kind of guy who liked to act macho, carry guns, talk a lot of shit, and then have his boys back him up.

That's why Mickey always had so many people around him at all times. Sure, some of them leeched a little—like Barbados—who didn't sell and never seemed to do anything but eat and drink and smoke dope and bring his lazy-assed girl-friends around. He didn't really serve any function except to act as a crazy-assed motherfucker who was willing to stick his head through a wall, if that's what Mickey asked him to do. But they were all like that. Pray was Mickey's personal slave. Zit would eat an apple out of his own ass if Mickey asked him to. And there was a while there where even Rick Leblanc had fallen under Mickey's spell, before he took off on his own insane trip.

Luke had suffered from the same delusions. But one thing about him, he never lost sight of who he was in all this. Whenever Mickey stepped out of line, Luke told him about it. If Youngblood was wrong, Luke pointed it out, the way he did on Sunday when Mickey wanted the kid's ring. It was wrong; Luke had told Mickey as much, and he gave it back. The key was to make Mickey realize his mistakes without pissing him off. Mickey wanted to do the right thing most of the time; his ego just got in the way sometimes. And that was how Luke was going to appeal to him tonight. When Mickey came by, they were going to have a long talk. He was going to tell Mickey to have a smoke and mellow out. Maybe they'd have a drink and share a couple laughs. And then Mickey would lighten up, and they'd discuss their options. They didn't have to kill the kid. What they had to do was make sure he didn't finger them. They had to make it worth the kid's while to keep his mouth shut.

Luke felt a paralyzed simper scratch across his face. He reached up and touched it. And it felt good. *There is a way out of this*, he thought. The blunt in his hand had gone out, and he relit it. He took a huge drag off it. Everybody was still partying, and he passed the blunt over to Peter, who also took a huge drag. Luke was a good talker, and when he could get Mickey to sit down for a second, he could be a good listener. Tonight, he was going to have to be. Mickey had said he was going to call Luke back, and when he did, Luke would give him no choice but to listen. He was going to talk Mickey's ear off. He would scream and cry and stomp his feet, if that's what he had to do. Luke was going to make it so uncomfortable for Mickey that he would have no choice but to listen to him. Luke was going to tell Mickey Youngblood exactly what he was going to do, and Mickey was going to do it.

Why? Because Mickey didn't want to hurt Bobby Leblanc any more than Luke did. Because Mickey Youngblood had as big a heart as anyone, and Luke would help him scrub the tarnish away and allow Mickey's heart to shine.

Luke was feeling so good about things that he excused himself from the balcony, walked inside, and poured himself another drink. The burn felt like cold water on a blister. It made him feel so fantastic that he lit up a cigarette, took the biggest drag he'd ever taken off a cigarette, and was immediately overwhelmed by the head rush. He stumbled back out onto the balcony, tripped over Peter, and heard the telephone ring behind him. His head felt light as he tossed the butt over the balcony and sprinted back inside. He couldn't wait to talk to Mickey again, to convince him that it was in everyone's best interests just to let the kid go. Luke was excited for Bobby too. He would get to go home, and this was going to work out perfectly for everyone.

Luke picked up the phone on the second ring. "Hey, Mickey, where are you?" He felt out of breath, and his heart beat a million miles a minute as he listened intently to the extended silence from the other end. "Hello?" Luke said, smiling at Rosy's concerned look as she stepped in from the balcony. Luke pushed over to the other side of the bed. "Hello, Mickey?"

After the delay, a voice spoke, but it wasn't Youngblood's. "I'm lost. Tell me how to get there."

Luke felt his heart snap. He couldn't believe that Bart Pray was asking him for directions to the hotel. The last thing on earth Luke wanted to do was let Bart Pray know where he was. "Where's Mickey?" Luke asked in a panicked voice.

"It's Nicole's birthday," Pray said easily. "I think he took her out to dinner. He wanted me to come up and drop something off to you."

Luke was stunned silent. He couldn't breathe, and when he tried moving his lips, he couldn't speak.

Bart Pray had no such problem. "And make sure no one's there but you and the kid when I get there."

Chapter Twenty-Six

Tuesday—10:35 p.m.

The green sign on the side of the road said Barksdale, but Bart Pray had no idea where Barksdale was. He had no idea where he was. So he pulled over under the dim lights past the blue and white gas station and turned the engine off. He needed to collect himself and focus on what he had to do, because *it* was throbbing again. He could feel its slimy head pulsing down into the gorge of his mind. He could see the darkness hovering over him like a giant black snake ready to devour him. He hated that. He wanted to get better, but he knew that wouldn't happen until he had finished the job, and his debt was forgiven.

He'd gotten sucked deep into his subconscious and agonized on Mickey's living room floor for hours. Trying to figure out how to solve it all. The grinding whir of knowing that his wretched life had taken a step backward was almost more than he could bear. He had found himself stuck in this Kafkaesque circle jerk with Mickey, and he couldn't be sure how well or when it would end. But he knew he would have to take the first step. There were no other choices. That's why he had decided that today would be the day he told Mickey he was done being his slave boy. That he would no longer do the shit chores Mickey wouldn't pay a Mexican to do. There was absolutely no work left at Mickey Youngblood's house. Bart had packed and moved everything into the storage space Mickey had rented. And then he had cleaned the place spotless. Even if it meant that their relationship was over—which hurt him to think about—Bart was determined to move on with his life.

When the phone had finally rang this afternoon, Bart had answered it. It was a softer, gentler version of Mickey Youngblood, and it had surprised Bart. His first thought was that Mickey must be sick.

"You feeling okay, Mick?"

"Yeah, fine," Youngblood said hurriedly.

"Where are you?"

"I'm taking the cunt shopping."

"Who?"

"Nicole. It's her birthday. I need to talk to you."

"Great," Pray said, "because I need to talk to you."

"I'll be by in half an hour." And the phone clicked.

And Bart had just stood there with the dead phone in his hand, trying to figure out what had just happened. He loved Mickey Youngblood like most people loved their brothers. And in a lot of ways, he felt closer to Mickey than he did his own brother. But it had been a long, strange road in trying to be Mickey's friend. And Bart had been afraid that once he told Mickey he was done working for him, Mickey wouldn't want to be friends anymore, and that bothered him a lot.

Bart and Mickey had been buddies since Bart was just a scared little twelve-year-old boy locked away in a violent world of insecurity. That world had changed for the better when Bart began to play sports, including hockey, soccer, and baseball. In Little League, Bart played for Dick Youngblood's team, where he first met Mickey. He would go to practice and play in the games, and he soon found himself becoming close to the whole family, often spending weeks on end at the Youngbloods rather than returning to the insanity of his own family life.

When Mickey and his family moved to Montana, Bart had found himself backspinning into his own family, just trying to survive. It wasn't until his junior year in high school that Bart rediscovered some semblance of balance and happiness. And that was when the Youngbloods moved back to the Valley, and Mickey enrolled at Valley High School.

Bart was thrilled to have his old buddy back. They started hanging out together just about every day, before and after school. It was as if a missing family member had returned. Going over to the Youngbloods again provided Bart with some respite from the gruesome existence at home and his grandfather's depression. There was another reason Bart had hooked back up with his old best friend. Mickey Youngblood had developed the reputation of having the best weed in the Valley, bar none. Since Bart was buying sixty bucks worth a week to feed his own growing habit, he started buying from Mickey, who was just a small-time dealer, only selling to his friends to support his own habit.

During the middle of the school year, Youngblood got into one of his trademark tirades against one of the school administrators and got thrown out. But even after he transferred to Chaparral High, their relationship continued to prosper. They partied after school or on weekends, and Bart found himself spending many nights at Dick and Kathy Youngblood's house. During the summer, he spent so much time there he actually felt as though he belonged to a family.

In order to make his way, Bart helped Kathy clean the house. Dick and Kathy even felt comfortable enough to let Bart babysit little Rudy when they were away from the house. The Youngbloods quickly became the family Bart had always wanted. Dick Youngblood became a father figure. He offered his home as a refuge to a kid who didn't have a pleasant place of his own to live, and Bart respected him greatly for it. Kathy Youngblood was kind and offered Bart a semblance of stability his own mother was never able to provide. Where Mickey learned to pick on Bart, Mickey's parents helped to take care of him, to encourage and nurture him.

In school, Bart had always earned above-average grades, but during his senior year at Valley, things changed. He found himself failing to do his homework and not showing up for classes. This resulted from his excessive drinking and drug taking. Due to his deficiency in school credits, he learned he would not be allowed to graduate with his class, and he dropped out of school to work. He quickly took a job as a bagboy at Frank's Market. But after a week on the job, Bart's nose was broken in a fight, which forced him to miss several days of work and resulted in his being fired.

With his schedule freed up, Bart started running around with Youngblood when he was dealing. People would page Mickey—and the boy had his rules, such as never talking business over the phone—and they would come over and tell him what they wanted. Or they would page him with a number, meaning the price of what they were looking for—it was easy to discern the amount of weight from the stated price—and Bart and Youngblood would go meet that person to drop off the pot. Most of the time, Youngblood worked it off on a front. And he only dealt with people he knew personally. The buyer would take the weed and pay Mickey back as soon as they had the chance.

Compared to Bart, Mickey was wealthy, and in sharing Mickey's wealth, Bart had been able to feed his own growing drug habit. He used coke, weed, and pills regularly. He drank alcohol from sunup until passing out at night. When he tried to stop, even if just for a couple days, he suffered from a lack of sleep and the perpetual shakes.

Not long after, Bart's father moved his cow of a wife, her bruised kids, and Bart's half brother, Jimmy, to Brownsville, Texas. Since Bart couldn't get along with the cow, he refused to go. Unfortunately, Bart had also been unable to get along with his unstable mother. So when he didn't stay at the Youngbloods, he found himself living at his grandmother's house. This proved perfect for Youngblood's routine, because that's where he had Bart store his pot. That way, Mickey never had to worry about getting caught with large amounts at his own house, a trick he had learned from his father. He would just stick the stash in a duffel bag and give it to Bart. Mickey knew he could trust Bart not to steal any of it.

But Bart was still unemployed, which meant he spent most of his time without money. To improve his financial situation, he took a job as a busboy at Mac's BrewPub. Everything was working smoothly—he learned important job skills and made enough money to feed and clothe himself—until his drinking did him in again. Unable to get out of bed in the mornings, he found himself regularly oversleeping and arriving late to work. After the third time, he was fired.

But who cares? Bart quickly regrouped, and in a matter of days, he found an opportunity to go into business for himself, all thanks to his good buddy Mickey Youngblood. Bart constantly received phone calls from buddies looking to score weed. One day, it occurred to him that he had direct access to the best, so why not take advantage of it? It was like the center spot on a Bingo board—a gimme, a sure thing—a chance to make a quick buck. It wasn't as if Bart would need a ton of it. If he could just sell to two or three regulars per week, he could make enough money to make ends meet. He wouldn't front it, only take cash upon receipt.

But Youngblood wasn't nickel-and-diming anymore. He was only into selling large amounts. That way, others would be selling for him, with much less opportunity for him to get caught. He got tired of Bart's coming to him all the time for small amounts, so last September Mickey told him, "Why don't you just take a whole one? I mean, you come to me so much, you might as well."

Like, duh, "Okay."

Unfortunately, by January, business died as quickly as it had begun. Those who always called Bart for pot before had suddenly taken their business elsewhere, either finding better bud, or better prices, or both. And it wasn't as if Bart ran across a bunch of new clients while staying at his grandmother's or Mickey's house. Everyone he knew went to Mickey to buy Mickey's weed, not Bart's.

And then there was the problem of smoking more than he could sell. The more Bart smoked, the less he sold, and the more his debt to Mickey grew, with the probability of ever paying him back disappearing in a puff of smoke. To make matters worse, Youngblood was constantly having to bail Bart out for stupid shit. For his birthday, Mickey and a couple buddies had pitched in to buy Bart an old junker car. Unfortunately for Bart, with no money to spare, he couldn't afford to get the car registered. As he drove it around town, its rusty frame and primer paint job quickly became an eyesore magnet for police officers, who constantly ticketed it. When Youngblood, who had moved out of his parents' house and into his new one, received a notice from the DMV for Bart's failure to pay off the tickets, he went full-tilt.

Youngblood had failed to change title to the car out of his own name when he had given it to Bart, so he immediately gave Bart the money and told him to go to court to pay off the tickets. He also told Bart to go to the DMV to register the car in his own name and get it out of Youngblood's.

This created another dilemma for Bart. He was afraid to go anywhere in the car for fear that he would get more tickets and be unable to pay them off. Besides, he still had a serious cocaine problem, so instead of giving the money Mickey had given him to the courts or the DMV, Bart diverted it straight up his nose. The tickets were never paid, and when Mickey received his second notice, he blew through the ceiling. He bitched Bart out for taking advantage of him—for always staying at his place, eating his food, drinking his booze, and smoking his weed—and then not having the decency to pay him back.

To add to Bart's growing dilemma, others were now starting to hang out at Mickey's the way Bart once did, and he quickly felt like he didn't belong. His attitude became so bad that Mickey just stopped inviting him over. It was as if Bart had been cast out of favor, no longer a family friend. Mickey started treating him more as a business partner who was in debt, with the debt never getting paid. Whenever Bart stopped by to party, Mickey would always ask, "Where's my money?" When Bart didn't have a satisfactory response, Mickey would say, "You want an ass kicking?"

Bart would tell Mickey he was trying to find a job and would pay him back as soon as he could. He searched for work, although not as hard as he might have. His friend even drove him down to the Navy recruiting center, where he was quickly rejected for failing the drug screening when it turned up positive for marijuana. But Mickey wasn't buying any of it. He simply didn't believe him.

The pathetic truth was that Bart had never been employed for more than four months at any given time—as a laborer for his father—and the prospects of his now finding employment were grim at best. A week later, he finally came across some money by hustling it off a "business associate." The guy wanted to buy an ounce, but Bart told him he couldn't get it up front and would need the full amount before he could score. When the guy gave him six hundred dollars, rather than getting the weed, Bart just gave four hundred dollars to Mickey and kept the rest for himself. He also made damn sure he never ran into the "business associate" again.

But he still owed Youngblood eight hundred dollars—Mickey's figure, not Bart's—and Mickey would remain appeased for only so long. Two weeks, in fact. Then he really let Bart know how he felt. He started calling Bart's grandmother's house every day, harassing his grandparents, asking for him when he knew he wasn't there. His grandmother told him, "Bart, this young man has been a friend for a long time, but he does *not* run your life. It's time you get a decent job. And figure out what you're going to do. And have him call you on your pager."

But Mickey refused. He just kept calling Bart's grandmother's, even when Bart was out looking for work. Bart told him, "Quit calling my grandparents. You have my pager number." Mickey then started paging Bart incessantly, telling him what to do, sending him on endless errands, having him drive Mickey's brother Rudy to baseball games. Once, Mickey even paged Bart during a job interview. Bart's stepbrother had been driving him around looking for work, and when they got back to Youngblood's, Mickey was waiting for him with an open palm. Bart told him, "Look, I'm somebody you've known for a decade, and you got to stop calling me like every hour looking for money."

An argument ensued. It was at that point that Mickey told him, "Look, either you pay me my money, or you work off the debt. I want some return on my investment." Reluctantly, Bart reported to work the next day. Mickey told him, "I want to sell my house. And I want you to redo my backyard so it looks really nice for the buyers."

"Okay," Bart said skeptically.

"I will knock so much off the debt for each job you do."

Knowing Mickey the way Bart did, this did not sound like such a great deal. But at the time, Bart had no other way of paying Mickey back. He also wanted to get back into Mickey's good graces, if for no other reason than to get more smoke.

Without money, a man in need goes without weed.

Even though Bart was now bound to perform menial labor around Mickey's house, he still considered him a friend and wanted to do a good job for him. His first job was sanding the backyard fence. It was difficult work, and the financial arrangement was a sliding fee based on Mickey's generosity, or lack thereof. Certain jobs required more or less work than others, and Mickey would take it upon himself to decide how much each job was worth and deduct that amount from the debt. His basic attitude was, "You will do this, and I will take this much off," and Bart just did it.

Bart was still trying to find other work, but that proved difficult without a car. The junker had been impounded the month before. Being unmotivated in just about every aspect of his life, Bart found himself in Mickey's yard on a daily basis. He sanded and painted all three fences, planted new grass and all the flowerbeds, yet Mickey was still constantly pissed at his lack of production. As a motivational ploy, one day he told Bart, "For every week you don't pay me any money, I'm going to up your debt one hundred dollars."

"But I'm working my ass off!" Bart told him. "You can't do that."

"Watch me."

To Mickey Youngblood, Bart Pray's pleas were no more than water off a buffalo's ass. The words were meaningless, because the debt wasn't getting paid off. And everybody knew that when Mickey Youngblood's mind was made up about something, it would take more than a stick of dynamite to change it.

Weeks flew by, and Bart worked his tail off, yet the debt would not shrink. Adding insult to injury, while working his ass off, Bart got to watch the party swirl around him. Hank Zitelli, John Barbados, Luke Ridnaur, Patrick Callahan, and all kinds of chicks were constantly in and out. Bart never said a word. He would just watch Barbados or Luke lounge around the house, partying with Mickey, being equals without ever doing an ounce of work. But he never complained. Bart may have hated the way Mickey treated him, but he could only imagine how bad it would get if he told Mickey what he really thought—to fuck off.

Then, out of nowhere, Bart convinced his grandmother to give him four hundred dollars to help with his terrible financial burden. Wanting to clear the debt as soon as possible, he gave it all to Youngblood. Mickey had also reached his point of exasperation. "If you give me any money—a dollar, two dollars—I will not up the debt." Even shysters have their limits. Most of the time, however, Bart couldn't even meet this scaled-down obligation. He had no way of making any money, and the yard work had run out.

He would now find himself back at Mickey's every day, not doing yard work, but cleaning up after Youngblood's drunken parties. Cigarette butts, beer bottles, take-out food cartons, condoms, dogshit, you name it; what else could he do? The parties would end, and Bart would be there, so he would pick up after Mickey. It was the only invitation he got. Unable to give Mickey any money whatsoever, Bart's debt shot right back up. Other times, he performed enough to get the debt back down. By June, it was down to the last two hundred dollars. Bart had been working nonstop since January, and his menial tasks had allowed Mickey to build a small cannabis empire, but Bart needed a break. He pleaded with Mickey not to keep increasing the debt—even if he couldn't give him any money—and Mickey agreed.

For the moment, Youngblood would not increase the debt. But that wouldn't keep him from teasing Bart mercilessly. Wherever he was, whoever was there, Mickey would harass and demean Bart to the point of complete embarrassment. He started calling him "Barty" and tried to make him feel stupid. Bart took a yeoman's worth of abuse but rarely said anything to stop it. He even considered walking away from his obligation, but he was afraid to lose Mickey as a friend. At the last minute, he would always decide to stay, to remain part of the group, even if it was at the bottom of the totem pole.

This afternoon, as Bart had smoked a cigarette and waited for Mickey to pick him up in his front yard, he realized that it was fear that had kept him so close to his erratic friend for so long. Bart had remained Mickey's slaveboy for months on end out of fear of losing him as a friend, because he had no one else. Bart hadn't lived alone with his mother—except for two violently emotional weeks—in his entire life. Bart's father, to whom he was not close, lived in Texas, and they rarely spoke. And Bart was presently sleeping on his grandmother's living room couch. The best he could possibly hope for was to remain in Mickey's good graces.

Youngblood finally showed up a half hour later. Bart was smoking his tenth cigarette, when he saw the red metallic blur of Nicole Babbette's sports car speed up the street and pull over next to the curb. Mickey waved him over.

When Bart climbed inside, Youngblood acted as if he were Bart's new best friend. "Hey, how ya doing, buddy?"

Bart looked at Mickey as if he was stoned. Youngblood slipped it into gear, and they took off.

Bart slid heavily into the passenger door when Mickey turned down Ferndale, and he said, "So, Mickey, you know, I've been thinking a lot about my debt."

"Yeah, hey, you know, I wanted to talk to you about the same thing," Youngblood said, offering him a cigarette.

"No thanks," Bart said, taking in a deep breath. "Yeah, well, you know, Mickey, I don't think I'm going to—"

"Hey, how would you like to …?" Mickey turned and grabbed Bart's arm. "Sorry for interrupting you, buddy. But how would you like to lose the final two hundred dollars off your debt by your birthday?"

Bart jerked straight in his seat. His birthday was just two days away, but he didn't catch what that had to do with his debt. "I don't understand. What do you mean?"

Youngblood punched in the cigarette lighter. "I mean I'll wipe out the last of your debt if you'll run something up to Luke in San Floripez for me."

Bart couldn't believe it. Here he was, finally filled with enough nerve to confront Mickey about the debt, an act that would probably ruin their relationship for good, and Mickey was willing to call them even just for running something up to San Floripez. How easy could it get? "Where does Luke live?"

Youngblood lit his cigarette. "He'll be staying at a hotel. And I'll give you that information later."

Bart felt thrilled at the prospect of getting out of debt with Mickey once and for all. He had worked as Mickey's slave for the last seven months of his life, and in one fell swoop, that was all about to change. Once the debt was paid up, Bart would be able to take his time at getting a real job, without the added pressure of satisfying Mickey Youngblood's daily needs. He could spend the necessary time dealing with himself, getting off his own drug and alcohol habits, so that he would be straight enough to help his mother. And it was his mom who he was thinking about when Mickey whipped around the corner and dropped him back off at his house.

"I'll be back in three or four hours to pick you up."

Bart opened the door. "Whose car will I be taking?" He assumed he'd be taking Mickey's, but Nicole's convertible would be nice.

"You'll be taking Patrick's car," Youngblood said. "I'd be going up there myself, you know, but I'm taking Nicole out for her birthday."

Bart nodded. It had all become very clear. Mickey usually took pot up to Luke in San Floripez whenever Luke didn't come down to pick it up himself. With it being Nicole's birthday, Mickey had previously scheduled events to tend to, so he asked Bart to do it for him. It was just another chore—well, not really. It was Bart's last chore. And he found himself thrilled at the idea that in a matter of hours he would be debt free.

He could already feel the darkness beginning to lift.

Chapter Twenty-Seven

Tuesday—10:37 p.m.

Luke Ridnaur glanced at the red LCD on the clock on the side table next to the bed. It said it was time to clear the room out so he could think. Think about what he was going to say to Barty when he arrived. Think about how he was going to save Bobby Leblanc's life.

He was standing in the middle of room 215 when he clapped his hands together. "All right—time to clear the room. Time for everyone to go home." Groans could be heard everywhere. Luke waved the hotel handbook around as if it were the final word on the subject. "Sorry, ladies, I don't mean to be rude, but according to the guest handbook, it's time for nonpaying guests to leave the hotel rooms."

Rosy looked at Luke as if he was nuts. "Since when did you start reading hotel handbooks?" she asked. "Or anything else, for that matter?"

Luke grinned caustically at the smart-assed comment. "Cute, Rosy. All right, everybody, let's get it together."

"Is Youngblood coming to pick Bobby up or what?" Rosy asked.

"Yes, Rosy," Luke said exasperatedly, "Mickey's coming to pick Bobby up. Bobby gets to go home tonight."

Everyone turned to Bobby and gave him an impromptu ovation. Bobby pirouetted and bowed. Then everyone started saying their good-byes. Everyone, that is, except for Rosy, who got up off the bed and glided over to Luke.

"When's he coming? It's really getting late."

"I told you, Rosy, he'll be here any time." Luke sounded agitated. "Now, I need to get everyone out of here so we can take care of this."

Luke's eyes ferreted the room, as everyone began getting their things together. Rosy didn't move. "Why don't I just take him home myself?" she asked.

Luke's head shook irately. "No! That's not happening, Rosy. Mickey's sending someone to pick him up. Now you need to go."

Luke jabbed his hands onto her shoulders and tried to move her toward the door, but she wouldn't budge. "I thought you said Mickey was coming to pick him up himself."

Luke scratched his chin, thinking about what he had said. "Plans have changed. He's sending someone up to take him home to his brother."

"Who's he sending?"

Luke scowled but wouldn't answer.

"Do you know who he's sending, Luke?"

Luke took in a deep breath, glaring right at Rosy. "Yes, Rosy, I know who he's sending." His eye caught a sock on the floor under the table. He reached down to pick it up and tossed it to Vegas.

Rosy grabbed ahold of Luke's arm, pulling him in closer. "Who's coming?" she whispered. "Is it anyone I know?"

Luke dropped his shoulders impatiently. "No, Rosy, it's nobody you know. Now, can we get going, please? I want to get the room cleared out so I can send Bobby home." He turned to the room and clapped his hands again.

Everyone looked pretty much ready to leave—again everyone except for Rosy. She just stood there with quivering lips, and Luke felt sure she was about to flood the place.

"I just don't feel like this is such a good idea," she said.

"You don't feel like what's a good idea, Rosy?"

"That you send Bobby home with somebody else."

"It's a very good idea." Luke's voice was harsh. "Now, you need to leave." When he turned around, he noticed Cheri, Vegas, Peter, and Bobby had all stopped talking and were staring right at him. "All right—what's going on, guys?"

"We're worried about Bobby," Rosy said. "What if Youngblood's friend doesn't take Bobby home?"

"He will," Luke said, pivoting to face her. "He already told me he would."

"I'm sorry, but I just don't trust him." Rosy sniffled. "I think Bobby should come with us. I'll make sure he gets home safely."

Her eyes were wet, while everyone else's trained on Luke to see what he was going to say next. He was stumped. He didn't have anything to say. All he wanted to do was get everybody out so he could figure out what he was going to say to Barty when he arrived. But he couldn't tell them that. While he considered his lack of options, Bobby stepped up to the plate. He pushed past Luke and right up to Rosy. "Are you crying because of me?"

"Yes." Small brooks trickled down the sides of her face, as she reached into her purse for a tissue.

"Don't," Bobby said, putting his hands around her waist; trying to meet her teary gaze. "Everything's going to be okay. It's almost all over."

She wiped the wetness from her cheek with the back of her hand. "Are you sure?"

"Yes. You heard Luke. Mickey's buddies are on their way as we're talking. Mickey's cool; he's not going to hurt me. They're going to take me home."

She breathed in deeply, trying to keep herself calm. "How do you know?"

"I just know," Bobby said. "Because Luke said so. He said Mickey had called. And they're coming down in a while to take me home. We both know Luke wouldn't lie, right?"

Her lips palpitated while her red and watery eyes fixed on his soft eyes.

Bobby tried to smile her gaze away. "We trust Luke, right?"

Her chin quaked, and tears slid down her face, but Rosy managed to tip her head.

"I'm going to be fine," Bobby insisted. "This will be a good story for me to tell my grandchildren one day. Everything's going to be all right. Okay?"

She tipped her head and pulled away, then reached into her purse and handed Bobby a piece of paper.

"What's this?" He opened it and read it. It was her phone number and e-mail address. He glanced back up. "That is so cool. Thank you."

The rounded curve of a grin flashed across half of her face. "I thought maybe you could call me or something. Not to date or anything, because I ..."

He gazed into her eyes waiting for her to finish, but she never did. "Because what?" he asked.

Rosy swallowed hard. "Because I know I'm not your type or anything."

He smiled as he reached over and pulled her in close. "How do you know that?" he whispered. "You don't even know what my type is."

She blushed several shades of scarlet. She peered over Bobby's shoulder at Cheri, who stood there with her arms crossed below her chest, studying their embrace. Rosy pulled back and winked at Bobby. "I'm going to miss you, stolen boy."

Bobby beamed. "I'm going to miss you too." He leaned over and kissed her cheek.

Her eyes closed. And they would have remained that way forever if Luke hadn't shaken her loose with a loud, obnoxious clap of the hands. "All right, children, I think we've all said enough good-byes. Time to go. Don't want to make the hotel manager mad."

Everybody lined up one last time to say their last good-byes to Bobby. Tears and laughs and hugs were shared by all. Then they filed out of the room, first Cheri, then Peter and Rosy, and finally Vegas. At the last second, Luke reached over and plucked the back of Vegas' shirt collar just before he reached the front door.

"Dude, aren't you going to stay back?"

Vegas stopped and looked at Luke with concerned and bloodshot eyes. "Uh, okay?"

*   *   *   *

By the time Mickey Youngblood had returned to his house three hours later, his story had changed dramatically. Bart had hopped in Babbette's car, and Mickey had sped off. They were heading across the Valley to Patrick Callahan's house to pick up his car. It was getting dark outside, and traffic was heavy. Everybody was in a rush to get home to screaming kids, or to an old lady already drunk and pissed off at the world. That's if they were lucky enough to have an old lady or screaming kids or a home with a bed to sleep in. Bart Pray had none of the above.

"Yeah, Bart, look—I really fucked up," Mickey said in an agitated voice. "And I need your help."

Bart was startled at first. He had never heard Mickey use those words to him before. "What's up, Mick?"

Youngblood took a deep breath and then explained everything. From his history with Rick Leblanc, to the kidnapping of his little brother Bobby, to the kid being holed up with Luke right now at a hotel in San Floripez.

Bart sat there silently listening to everything. He could see moisture in the corner of Mickey's eyes. Mickey wore the same look he had the day he found Zeus dead. It was a sad, defeated, angry look. It was strange too, because Bart could feel a grin breaking out on his own face, and he didn't understand why. Maybe it was because Mickey was confiding in him for the first time in a very long time, and it felt really good. Mickey usually addressed Bart only when telling him what to do or asking him for his money, but here it was as if they were best friends all over again.

"So what're you going to do?" Bart asked.

Youngblood readjusted the rearview mirror. "I don't know. That's the thing. If the kid goes to the cops, I'm looking at going to prison for the rest of my life."

He looked over at Bart, and for the briefest of moments, their gazes touched. In Mickey's intense jade eyes, Bart could sense tremendous pain. In his own heart, Bart could feel Mickey's tremendous suffering. "So what are you going to do, Mickey?"

Youngblood tapped on the brakes as he slowed for a red light. "I can't let the kid go, because he'll go to the cops." Bart nodded as if it all made sense so far. "He needs to be taken care of." The light changed to green, and Youngblood accelerated. Turning to Bart, he added, "And I want you to take care of him."

Bart's face tightened. Without hesitation, he said, "Whatever you need me to do, Mickey."

Youngblood shook his head sullenly. "You'll be even with me. I'll wipe out the debt, and give you an extra four hundred dollars for you to go shopping for your birthday."

Bart couldn't help letting the smile erupt. Not only would he be out of debt for good with Mickey Youngblood, but he would be ahead of the game for his twenty-first birthday. He'd actually be able to buy new clothes with enough left over to take his mother to lunch. Heck, with four hundred dollars burning a hole in his pocket, Bart would have enough to buy her burrito combo dinners for a week, if that's what she wanted.

Mickey didn't say another word until they got over to Patrick Callahan's house. The muteness gave Bart time to reflect on the sword of guilt that sliced through his liver. It was strange too, because it was an emotion that Bart usually reserved for his father whenever his father beat the hell out of him for doing nothing wrong. The guilt here resulted from Bart feeling that he had somehow let Mickey down. After all, he was the one who reintroduced Rick Leblanc to Mickey in the first place, which was in itself strange since Bart had always hated the guy. It used to drive him crazy the way Leblanc would just come over when Bart was younger and bang his sister, and then leave without ever having a nice word to say to anybody. Even Bart's sister hated his guts.

Then the guy had come over and just taken what he wanted from Mickey, ripping him off, breaking his windows, and then he split. It was like déjà vu all over again. Leblanc then threatened Mickey's family and totally fucked up Mickey's life. And for whatever reason, Bart felt it was his fault, as if he were the one who fucked Mickey's life up, in turn, fucking his own life up. He knew that was twisted logic, but he couldn't allow it to happen, regardless. In fact, he figured he could make it work to his advantage.

If Bart did nothing, and Mickey did end up going to prison, then where would Bart be? Maybe he could become a sort of surrogate son to Dick and Kathy. They would have a void to fill, and Bart had always considered them the closest thing he ever had to real parents. But they already had another kid—their younger son Rudy—waiting in the wings, so they'd probably just double up their energies in raising him, and Bart would still be left out flapping homelessly in the wind.

On the other hand, what Youngblood had asked him to do scared the hell out of him. It gave Bart a tremendous responsibility, and he wasn't sure that he was ready for it. The way Bart looked at it, he was the only one who could save Mickey's life right now. Nobody else was going to come out of the woodwork who could, or would, do what Mickey had just asked Bart to do. In a way, if Bart helped to save Mickey's life now, Bart would be saving his own life as well. If he freed Mickey, Mickey would owe Bart forever. Maybe Mickey would even let Bart move back into his house, or buy a new and bigger house and let Bart live there. Either way, Mickey would then be the one in debt to Bart, because Bart would be the owner of one super-gigantic secret.

Youngblood downshifted, and they pulled into the driveway in front of Patrick Callahan's house. Bart turned to him. "I will do whatever you need, Mickey. You can count on me." And he meant it.

Youngblood climbed out and walked around the back, where he opened the trunk. He reached in and pulled out the green duffel bag. He tossed it in the trunk of Patrick Callahan's lime green, Korean compact car, which was parked in the ally next to Callahan's guesthouse. Mickey then gave Bart Luke's phone number at the hotel and went over last-minute instructions.

Now, as Bart sat in that same green battered car outside the gas station, he felt psyched for what he was about to do. He had just spoken to Luke, gotten directions to the hotel, and it was time to go. He turned the key, and the ignition started. He shifted into drive and took off. As he accelerated through the darkness of eastern Lantana County, Bart thrilled at the excitement of having one last job to do for Mickey Youngblood. It was a job filled with utmost importance, one that under no circumstances could he fail, for Mickey or for himself. It was now time to drive to San Floripez to put the dog to sleep.

*   *   *   *

Room 215 had finally been cleared. The incessant pounding in Luke's skull told him he was going to have one helluva hangover in the morning. But he didn't care. He wasn't sure he'd survive the night. He fell back hard in the orange chair and watched Bobby channel-surf from one bed and Vegas watch TV from the other. Somewhere, somehow, Luke had lost control of his life, and he needed to figure out how to regain it. He reached over and poured himself a shot, and he downed it. He then picked up the phone and paged Youngblood, again, but of course, Mickey didn't respond. He never responded when Luke needed him.

The alcohol began coursing through his veins, and he began to feel some peace. The more Luke thought about it, the better it was that Mickey wasn't coming. Bart Pray had no personal stake in any of this. He had no motivation whatsoever to want to hurt Bobby. On the other hand, Mickey Youngblood did. He hated Rick Leblanc with such a passion that it made him want to kill his little brother. But Luke knew that Mickey really didn't have the huevos to do it. Mickey was a pot dealer who liked to blow off steam, but Luke had never actually seen him physically hurt anyone in his life. He'd seen Mickey get in a drunken scrap here or there, but nothing that he and his buddies couldn't handle.

Murdering Rick Leblanc's brother was an altogether different animal.

That freak Bart Pray was an altogether different animal. "And make sure no one's there but you and the kid when I get there." *Fuck you.* Bart Pray was anything but a coldblooded killer. The guy didn't even know how to fight. The only time Luke had ever seen him scrap was at a party at Mickey's, where Pray got all fucked up, started talking shit, and this other dude decked him. As far as Luke was concerned, Bart Pray was the biggest pussy he had ever seen in his life. The guy was not capable of handling his own affairs, let alone hurting a fly. So what was there to worry about?

Luke poured himself another shot.

Bart Pray was one strange dude who had glommed onto Youngblood and wouldn't let go. He had totally pissed Mickey off with that bullshit with the tickets and the car—and owing him all that money—and Mickey had gotten sick of him. Sure, Luke felt bad for the guy to a certain degree. Pray came from an abusive background, but that didn't mean he had to act so goddamned surly and jealous every time he saw Luke, or he might have actually liked the guy. A snoring sound jerked Luke's attention over to the bed, where he could see Bobby snoozing away. From the other bed, Vegas looked like he would soon join him. *Good*, he thought. The room would be quiet when Pray arrived. And if they had to, they could go somewhere else to talk.

He lifted his hands to his head where his temples pulsated like they were about to detonate. He knew he shouldn't drink anymore, so he fired up a blunt instead. When that didn't slow his pulse rate, he poured himself another shot and downed it. When that didn't tranquilize him, he went out onto the balcony and smoked another cigarette. And when that didn't ease his burden, he stumbled back inside, fell back into the chair and stressed. His body vibrated, and his heart pounded against his sunken chest. He found himself wishing that he'd just die of congestive heart failure so he wouldn't have to feel all the pain. His eyes closed, and he kept telling himself that everything would be fine. He pictured himself walking the kid outside and setting him free, and in a matter of minutes, his body started to unbend enough for him to fall asleep.

The severe hammering on his skull woke Luke several minutes later. His eyes flashed open, and his mind felt like mud, and when he jumped up out of his chair, he realized the pounding was not only coming from his head, but also the front door.

Chapter Twenty-Eight

Tuesday—Midnight

Luke Ridnaur watched him silently walk in. Bart Pray wore a short-sleeved dark green shirt, light blue jeans, and leather hiking boots. His hair was dark and slicked back, short on the sides, and long on top. In his hand, he carried Mickey's green duffel bag, and Luke's heart sank into his stomach. He couldn't believe the guy had come all the way up here to machine gun the kid to death. *Jeez Louise.*

Pray pushed past him and into the sleeping room. Luke closed the door and followed him. Pray squinted when he saw Vegas asleep on one bed, and he frowned when he saw Bobby snoozing on the other. "Uh-huh."

Luke frowned right back. *Uh-huh yourself, motherfucker.*

"Who the hell is he?" Pray asked.

Luke pressed his finger to his mouth. "Let's go outside and talk."

Pray shook his head. "Why isn't he taped up?"

Luke glanced over at Bobby, who was sawing logs, and then back up at Pray. "Because he doesn't need to be taped up. Look, Barty, we need to talk. Let's go outside."

Pray scowled, as Luke pivoted and slid the glass door to the balcony open. "Come on."

Pray's head shook irritably. "You're a fucking idiot, you know that?" He followed Luke outside, duffel bag in hand. Luke pulled the glass door shut behind him.

The San Floripez night was warm and filled with the scent of jasmine. "You done fucked up," Pray said. "You're fucking up, man. What are you doing?"

Luke gawked at Pray in disbelief. His head pounded, and he felt as though his stomach were being eaten alive by stress. The night swirled around him like a bad dream that would not end, and now the angry face of a man he had never had a complete conversation with in his life glowered at him menacingly. "What the fuck are you talking about?"

Pray wouldn't take his eyes off the two teens through the glass as he lit a cigarette. He then offered one to Luke. "Who's the other guy?"

Luke took the cig. "That's my friend, Vegas."

"I see." Pray's head bobbed as his jaw tensed. "Where's the shovels?"

Luke's eyes blew wide—the question totally caught him by surprise. "What are you talking about?"

"The shovels, man. What the fuck you think I'm talking about?"

Luke nervously lit his cigarette. "What the fuck do we need shovels for?"

Pray laughed morbidly as a blue ribbon of smoke cleared his nostrils. "What the fuck do you *think* we need shovels for?"

Luke put his hands on the railing and leaned over. He glanced at the muted blue swimming pool in the distance, and he imagined holding Pray's face under the water until he stopped breathing. "Look, man, we got to change this," he said. "We got to do something different, okay?"

Pray stepped over to the railing next to Luke. "What the fuck are you talking about?"

Luke turned to him. "I'm talking about the kid. You can't do this, man."

Pray laughed ghoulishly. "We're going to do this."

"No, we're not!" Luke said it with such ferocity, Pray's brows contorted like those of a jack-o'-lantern. Luke cleared his throat, and lowered his voice. "That's what I'm saying, dude. We need to figure out another way."

"There is no other way."

"Of course there is, man." Luke's voice was rising again. "There's always another way. We can't do this. Mickey, he's just under a lot of pressure. That's all. He's not thinking straight. He doesn't really mean it."

"Of course he means it." Pray winced and took another drag off the cig. "There's no other way, Luke. Mickey fucked up, and he knows it. Now it's up to you and me to fix it for him."

"Look," Luke said, his palms shooting out. "There's no we to this. I'm ... I'm not having anything to do with it."

"You've already got something to do with this. Now quit fucking around. And let's go get the shovels before I get pissed." Pray's shoulders hunched back, and he looked like a bull ready to charge.

"Dude, you got to keep your voice down," Luke said. "We got to figure a way outta this thing quietly."

Pray jabbed his finger into Luke's chest. "Look, motherfucker, Mickey told me you got shovels at your house. We're going to your house, and we're going to get them. Then we're going to take the kid somewhere, and we're going to use them."

Luke frowned because he'd had enough. Pray was talking too loud, and it was too hot outside, and everybody probably had their goddamned windows open listening to their conversation right this very second. And that just wouldn't do. Luke needed some time to think. He needed to try to reason with this asshole, but he obviously couldn't do it here. He didn't want the other guests to know what was going on, and more importantly, he didn't want Bobby to hear what they were discussing. So he did the craziest, most insane fucking thing he could think of by reaching over and grabbing Pray by the shoulders and shaking him.

"You got to shut the fuck up, dude, and listen to me. We'll go get the shovels. But you got to fucking be quiet, okay?"

Pray flashed him a grim grin and tossed his cigarette over the balcony. "Now you're talking."

*   *   *   *

Vegas Parsons opened his eyes right after he saw that dude walk into the bathroom. Then he saw Luke step inside from the balcony, muttering to himself, then walking over to the table where he poured himself a shot. Damn—what had they been arguing about?

Vegas had been dreaming about bitchin' backside one-eighties, when he heard voices and shouting, and his brain told him to wake up. He saw Luke outside with that dude. And they looked as if they were having an argument about something, and he was afraid they were going to fight. Then Luke grabbed the dude by the shoulders, and the dude smiled, and then he headed off into the bathroom. It was really weird.

A drink sounded good to Vegas too, but not the kind Luke was having. Vegas' mouth tasted like the bottom of a birdcage, and he needed some water desperately. He waited until Luke went back outside to smoke a cigarette before he sat up in the bed. He saw Bobby crashed on the other bed, looking like he'd OD'd for the night. The clock on the table said it was a few minutes past midnight, and Vegas knew his ass was grassed.

He was supposed to be home no later than midnight, and he was already late, with no great prospects of getting home anytime soon. When he needed a ride home, he was supposed to phone his mom before 11 p.m., and she would come and pick him up. But he had missed that deadline as well. He knew Luke didn't have a car. So his only chance of getting a ride home this late was from that dude in the bathroom—whoever he was—but the way that guy had been acting, Vegas wasn't sure that was such a good idea either. His more immediate need, however, was to get something to drink.

He climbed off the bed and moved into the vanity area next to the bathroom and flicked on the light. He pivoted toward the sink and turned it on. His hands dipped under the running faucet and splashed cold water on his face, and he felt better instantly. He then cupped his left hand under the water, leaned his head over, and took a sip. The water tasted of metal and chlorine, but his mouth felt parched, and he had no better options, so he drank thirstily. He focused all his attention on the task at hand, so it took Vegas a minute to realize what it was that he was seeing through the mirror's reflection. When he did, he nearly swallowed his tongue.

The bathroom door was cracked open about six inches, and that weird dude sat on the toilet holding a gun cartridge in one hand and a greasy white towel in the other. On the floor next to him, Vegas saw what looked like a black machine gun with a twelve-inch grip, with holes at the end of the barrel, sitting in a green duffel bag. When the dude tipped his head up, he looked right at Vegas, snarled, and kicked the door closed.

At that very second, Vegas decided he would definitely get a ride home from someone else.

*   *   *   *

When Rosy Kinski pulled her dad's car into Peter Melonking's driveway, she felt both happy and sad. She was glad that her night had come to a happy ending, and that Bobby Leblanc was finally going home. She was sad because she figured she'd never see him again.

Bobby had grown on her in a way that very few boys ever had. He was sweet, kind, and super-good looking, but it was those eyes that made her yearn to never forget him. She appreciated the fact he said he wanted to get together with her again, but she knew the reality behind that statement. He was just being sweet. When he got home and back to his Valley girls, she would become nothing more than a long forgotten memory, if that, and that's what made her want to cry.

Peter leaned up from the backseat and gave Rosy a long hug good-bye. They promised to talk next week, and Cheri opened her door and let him out. Rosy had known Peter since first grade, and she was glad he had the chance to come over and party. When he climbed out, Cheri shut the door, and Rosy took off. Another five minutes, and she'd drop Cheri off. Another ten, and she'd be home, and that was the problem.

Although it was getting very late, she was wired and had no chance of sleeping. She couldn't get her mind off Bobby. Cheri must have sensed something too, because she turned to Rosy and said, "I'm glad he's finally going home."

Rosy nodded and smiled. She too was glad Bobby was going home. He was a good kid, and he didn't deserve to pay for what his brother had done. "I just hope he makes it home safely."

"Why wouldn't he?" Cheri asked. "Luke said Mickey Youngblood was on his way."

"I know," Rosy said, squinting at the line of red lights in front of her. "And then what?"

Cheri bounced along with the ride, contemplating as if it were a trick question. "He's going to take him home."

Rosy glanced over her shoulder and accelerated into the fast lane. "Yeah, that's what he said, but I'm not so convinced."

"What do you mean?"

"Well, yesterday, Youngblood tries to get Luke to kill Bobby, right? But today he's going to send someone to take him home? That just doesn't make any sense."

Cheri nodded as if it all made sense to her. "What doesn't?"

God, she's dumb. Rosy sometimes wanted to just slap the reality back into her friend's face. "That Youngblood would change his mind so quickly," she said. "You saw him yesterday. He was still worried about Bobby going to the cops. What changed his mind so quickly? I mean, if he was worried about Bobby going to the cops yesterday, why wouldn't he worry about Bobby going to the cops today?"

Cheri thought about this. "Because Bobby said he wouldn't."

Rosy looked over at her. "That's what he said. But think about it. If you were gone for two days without telling your mom, don't you think she'd want to know where you been? What you've been up to?"

Cheri nodded, her blonde bangs bouncing off her forehead.

"His mother's gotta be going nuts," Rosy continued. "The first thing she's gonna do when Bobby tells her what happened is call the police."

"But she can't."

"Why not?"

"Because Bobby said she wouldn't."

"That's not the point."

Cheri turned to her friend. "Then what is your point?"

Rosy exhaled. "My point is that Youngblood can't be sure." Rosy glanced over at Cheri's blank expression before continuing. "Think about it, Cheri. How would Youngblood know what Bobby is or isn't going to do? Or his mother?"

Cheri's head nodded before dropping her shoulder to her friend. "He wouldn't."

"Exactly. And that's why I'm afraid he might do something."

Cheri shook her head as if she were trying to figure this all out. "Like what?"

Rosy sighed and glanced back at the traffic over her shoulder. "I think after I drop you off, I'm going back."

"For what?" Cheri's voice was higher now.

Rosy flicked the indicator and pulled into the next lane. "To make sure he's okay."

"He's going to be fine," Cheri said emotionally. "Luke said he was going to send Bobby home, and I believe him."

Rosy sighed. "Like I said, it's not Luke that I'm worried about. You know Luke. He's like a feather in the wind. It's not a matter of what he wants to do. But what Youngblood tells him to do. Luke will just bounce from one person to another. Agreeing with whatever anybody tells him. And the way Youngblood pressures him, I just don't trust him."

Cheri threw her hands up disheartened. "I'm sorry, but Luke is a very trustworthy friend. I don't know what you're talking about."

"I'm not talking about Luke," Rosy said exasperatedly. "I'm talking about Mickey Youngblood. I trust him about as far as I can throw him."

Cheri nodded blankly. "Oh, him."

"Yeah, him," Rosy said. "I want to check on Bobby just to make sure he's okay."

"I think you're making a big mistake."

"Why? What could it hurt?"

"Because Luke is our friend," Cheri said. "You and I both know he wouldn't hurt a fly. If he wanted to hurt Bobby, he's had all the time in the world to do it. Luke is a very sweet young man, Rosy. And he's very talented. Did you know he likes to draw? And he wants to go back to school. Luke wouldn't do anything to mess up that goal. He has a future, Rosy. He's just stuck a little bit in his present. Luke wants to shift into the rest of his life; he just needs a little more time. So that's why he's going to make sure Bobby gets home." Cheri's voice cracked with devotion. Satisfied with her logic, she continued, "Besides, you already asked

Bobby if he wanted a ride home, and he said no. You'll embarrass yourself if you go back. And you don't want to do that."

Cheri smiled sweetly, and Rosy appreciated her friend's point of view. Cheri knew Rosy liked Bobby and didn't want to blow any chance she might have of him actually calling her. Time and again, Rosy had offered Bobby the opportunity to leave, but he just wasn't willing to do it. Besides, it was true that Luke wasn't about to ruin his life for his hood friend. Mickey Youngblood might have Luke under his thumb, but Luke was smart enough to know when and where to draw the line. He already assured Rosy that he would take Bobby home, so what else could she ask for? She trusted Luke, and he had never lied to her before. If she couldn't trust a friend like that, whom could she trust? Those thoughts filled the smile of contentment that stretched across her face as she pulled up in front of Cheri's apartment building. Cheri leaned over and gave her friend a big hug good-bye, and then got out. The door closed and Cheri stood on the grass as they waved to each other. Rosy pulled away from the curb and felt a refreshed sense of determination to stop worrying about things.

She had obsessed over Bobby Leblanc for long enough. She had tried her best to help him get away, and he had rejected every one of her efforts. Bobby was a smart kid who was big enough to take care of himself. So was Luke, and Rosy wasn't going to get in the way of any of that any longer. She was going to start minding her own business, worrying about her own problems, and just let the boys be boys.

Chapter Twenty-Nine

Day Four
Wednesday, July 7—12:20 a.m.

By the time Dick dropped Kathy off at home, it was past midnight. He was exhausted but wired by all the coffee he had gulped while sprinting down the coast. He had driven like a maniac the entire trip, and Kathy let him know about it the whole way, before she finally succumbed to fatigue in Lantana.

When Denver Mattson opened the front door, he looked as if he'd been on his own ten-day drunk. What little hair he had left on his head stood straight up on end, like a ragged piece of torn fright wig, and he hadn't shaved for a week. He wore green flannel pajamas under a purple silk robe that hung open revealing a beer gut the size of Texas. A huge swatch of gray-matted hair billowed from the top of his robe, giving him the look of an ancient gorilla.

Dick missed that look, and gave Mattson a big hug to prove it. Mattson growled, pushed him away, and invited him inside. Mattson's living room had always reminded Dick of a winter cabin. The walls were covered in a dark-stained wood. The furniture was chestnut; there was a dark chocolate carpet, and snuff-colored drapes were drawn across the windows. The idea of setting a match to the place had always intrigued Dick, but he quickly tried to clear the negative thoughts from his head. He took a seat on the couch while Mattson stepped into the kitchen and poured himself a drink. Make that a double. "Want one?" he yelled.

Dick leaned back against the cushion and closed his eyes. His long, sinewy arms unfolded along the length of the couch. "No thanks. I need to keep my head clear."

"I never had that problem," Mattson said, as he walked back into the living room. He took a seat in the wooden rocker. A cedar humidor sat on the round glass coffee table separating the two friends. He pushed it over to Dick.

Dick's head shook. "No. Like I said, I, uh, need to keep my head straight."

Mattson stared at him as if he were a lunatic. "For what?"

"So I can figure out what to do."

"That's easy ... Just get ahold of Mickey."

"Oh, yeah, right. I've paged him fifty fucking times. Kid doesn't return any of my calls."

"Can't just cry about it," Mattson grumbled. "Call him again." Mattson strained to lean over and grab the black cordless phone off the coffee table. He tossed it to Dick. Unfortunately, Dick wasn't paying attention, and he had to make a last-second stab just to keep the phone from clobbering him in the head.

He sneered at Mattson as he punched in Mickey's numbers. When he finished, he hung up and pushed the phone back across the table. "He won't call me back."

"Of course he will. Don't be so negative."

"I'm telling you, he hasn't called me back yet. I don't know what the fuck his problem is. He's got to know why I'm calling him."

Mattson lifted his right buttock into the air and nearly incinerated his chair with expended gas. With a deep exhalation, he said, "Just be patient. He doesn't realize he needs you yet."

"How the fuck am I supposed to be patient? My kid's looking at life in prison, for crissakes." Dick again wiped his hand across his wrenched face. "I just can't believe I fucked this up so bad."

"How'd you fuck it up? You didn't take the kid."

"Oh, man, I fucked up by turning my kid into something he wasn't. I fucked up because I should have been here when he needed me. If I wasn't gone, this never would have happened. I'll tell you that right now. If I was here, my son would not be looking at spending the rest of his life in prison. I would have made goddamn sure of that."

Mattson watched the water gather in his friend's eyes as Dick battled for composure. Mattson's big head teetered with a groan when he got up and lumbered back into the kitchen. He returned thirty seconds later with a box of tissues. He tossed them in Dick's lap, then went and sat back down and passed gas with an echo. "Jesus Christ, Dick, get ahold of yourself, will ya? How the fuck could it be your fault? You didn't know Mickey was going to pull this shit. He's the one who fucked up. Not you. Give yourself a fucking break, will ya?"

"Yeah, but I'm the one who made him like that. I didn't ..." The words trailed off as Dick started choking up again. His eyes drew closed, and he inhaled deeply. Struggling for his composure, he glanced up with red and tearful eyes. "Got any water?"

Mattson rolled his eyes and let out a heavy sigh as he struggled back into the kitchen. A minute later he returned, breathing heavily with a glass filled with shaking water in his hand. "Anything else?"

Dick couldn't respond. He couldn't even look up, because he was hunched over, bawling like a baby. His chest and back heaved in violent bursts as he sobbed uncontrollably into his lap. Deep groans seeped out of the back of his chest. Mattson had to turn away, unable to watch the pathetic sight. He gave his friend another sixty seconds, before he cleared his throat into his fist. When the blubbering finally ceased, Dick looked up, and Mattson handed him the water. He then leaned over and picked the box of tissues off the table and dropped it back into Dick's lap.

Dick pulled a tissue out and blew his nose. He leaned his head back and drew in slow, rhythmic breaths, trying to choke back the pain. When his breathing evened, he tilted his gaze back up to Mattson.

"You done yet?" Mattson asked.

Dick took in a lungful of air. "Yeah, thanks." He drank from the glass and then set it on the table in front of him. "You know what the problem is, don't you?"

"Yeah, you got emotional issues."

Dick winced. "No, man, I'm talking about my kid. I mean, you know, what the fuck's his problem? It's like he's got no fucking respect for nothin'. None of 'em do. They all go 'round listening to their gangster rap, not respecting a fuck-ing thing. And look what happens. They don't know how to act. 'Cuz they got no fucking role models. To teach them what the fuck they're supposed to do. That's the problem. It's like, when we were growing up—who was our heavy-weight champion?"

Mattson shrugged.

"No, come on—who was it?"

"I give up, who? Larry Holmes?"

Dick frowned as if that were the lamest answer he'd ever heard. "No, man, come on. Muhammad Ali, right? He was the champ. But he also had a big mouth. And all the parents hated that shit. But he had a cause."

Mattson's head nodded up and down before shaking back and forth. "Yeah? What was it?"

"I don't know," Dick said, "but that's not important. What's important is that he had one, whatever it was. These kids today—what do they got …? They grow up with guys like Mike Tyson as their heavyweight champ … a dirty, cheating, lowlife scumbag if there ever was one. Now what kinda hero is that, you know? He's got no cause. Unless you call raping and beating women a cause. I mean, I don't, but … And what about the music we listened to?"

Mattson gave him a lazy shrug. "What about it?"

"Come on—we had Bob Dylan and Buffalo Springfield. They were rebellious, you know? But with a cause. There was a message there. And we responded to that message. These rapper fuckers our kids listen to spoutin' their mouths off all the time about 'bitches' and 'hos.' I mean—what the fuck is that supposed to mean? They ain't got no respect for nobody."

Mattson rocked quietly studying Dick, and then he said, "You like to hear yourself talk, don't you?"

"What?"

"No, seriously, you're amazing. You know that? The way you like to just rattle on about nothing. I don't know how you do it.'"

Dick's expression said he did not take that as a compliment. "Fuck you."

"Thank you."

"I'm just telling you how it is, okay," Dick said emotionally. "The kids today, they're fucked up. That's all I'm saying. They got all this fucking anger built up inside of 'em. And the only way they know how to get what they want is through violence." Dick hesitated when he noticed the drink in Mattson's beefy fist. For some reason, the melting ice triggered his mouth to water. "That looks good. I think I will have one." He got up and headed into the kitchen.

Mattson's eyes followed him. "You know this ain't over yet."

"What ain't over?" Dick shouted from the kitchen.

"The kid, for crissakes. We just got to get him back. Then everything will take care of itself. As soon as we get him back safely that is."

A minute later, Dick trudged back in with a highball glass in his hand. "Yeah, sure, right. And how do we do that? We can't even get ahold of Mickey."

Mattson polished off the droplets around his ice cube. "Like I said, he'll call. We just got to be ready to act when he does."

Dick sat back on the couch. "How can you be so confident, Denver? I haven't talked to the fucking kid since I left town. I have no idea what's going on with Mickey. I have no idea what he's even thinking."

Mattson coughed into his fist. "I talked it all over with Barnes. Everything's going to be fine."

"You talked what over with Barnes?"

Mattson swirled the lonely ice cube in his glass. He was late for a refill. Arthritic joints creaked as he struggled out of his chair. "Look, once we get ahold of Mickey, he'll tell us where the kid is. We'll go pick him up, take him home, and that'll be that."

Dick got up too. "What the fuck are you talking about? How the fuck you gonna keep a fifteen-year-old kid's mouth shut, huh? Especially after he's been beaten and kidnapped."

Mattson glared at Dick. "You wanna bet?"

"Do I wanna bet what? How the fuck you gonna do it? That's all I want to know. Please, tell me."

Mattson smiled before he galumphed toward the kitchen. "Look, if we can somehow get the kid back to his parents unharmed. Barnes thinks he could work out some kinda deal for Mickey."

Dick followed his friend. "What kinda deal?"

"Yeah, you know, a plea bargain of some sort."

"A plea bargain of some sort?" Dick rolled the thought around his fractured mind. "That's kinda arbitrary, don't you think? A plea bargain of some sort? What the fuck's that supposed to mean?"

Mattson poured himself a drink. With attitude, he looked up to Dick. "You're a smartass, you know that …? Sheldon said he thinks he can get Mickey off for the kidnapping lid."

Dick's eyes rolled to the ceiling. "What's that? Twenty years? Fifty years? What?"

"Calm down. Nine years."

Dick snorted. "Nine years! You fucking outta your mind? You might as well give him the fuckin' death penalty. Mickey couldn't survive nine years in jail, and you know that. Besides, he'd never go for it. That's why he took the kid in the first place, I'm sure of it."

"How do you know?"

"How do I know what?"

"You act so goddamn sure of yourself. How do you know Mickey won't take it? Think about it, Dick. If he ran out of Barnes' place sweating over a life sentence, nine years would seem like a walk in the park. Winter-summer, winter-summer times four. No sweat. He'd still be white and in his twenties when he got out. His asshole might be a little stretched out, but so what? That's the price he's gotta pay."

Dick glowered at the thought. "Not a fucking chance. He'll never do it. I know Mickey. He thinks he walks on water. He thinks … he thinks he's impervious to ever getting caught. I'm telling you, Denver. It's like that video game mentality they all have. Sure, they might get fucking killed. But there's always another game to play after that. To them, life's just another fucking free game. These kids, they don't know any better. They don't realize other people get hurt until it comes back and hits them smack in the fucking face. There's just no way he'll ever do it."

Mattson's eyelids drooped wearily. "Impervious?"

"What?"

Mattson pointed his drink at him. "You said 'impervious.'"

Dick's head shook. "Your ass."

Mattson's face jiggled like an old bulldog's. "Yes, you did. I just heard you." He pushed past Dick and stepped into the living room. Dick turned and followed. "That's where you come in, Dick," Mattson continued. "You got to be the dad, and let him know he's the kid. You got to sit Mickey down and make him understand that's his best shot."

"I can't do that," Dick whined. "I can't tell my oldest kid that his best shot in life is to spend the next nine years in prison. What the fuck kind of life is that? Could you do it? I mean, I—in good conscience—could not do that."

Mattson stopped in front of the rocking chair, and pivoted. "Quit whining, will you? It's really getting on my nerves. You don't have a fucking choice, okay …? If you don't take this matter into your own hands … your fucking kid might never get out of prison alive. The way I look at it, you don't have a fucking choice."

"The hell I don't."

"Then what is it, goddammit?"

"What is what?"

"Mickey, goddammit! What choice do you have besides telling him what the fuck he's gonna do? Look, Dick, I'm not fucking around here, okay? This is our only fucking shot. Sheldon's worried that Mickey's gonna do something much worse than just kidnap the kid, okay? The way Mickey took off outta there, and some of the things he said, made Barnes think he might be thinking of hurting the kid. And if that happens, you know what the fuck's going to happen to Mickey then? He'll be begging for that nine years, trust me. So if you got a better fucking idea, you better speak the fuck up right this minute. Or it might be too fucking late for all of us."

Dick started to speak but stopped. His eyes cocked wide, and his mind spun like a bullet. He stepped over to the couch and started to sit, but then he changed his mind and remained standing. A million ideas pulsed through his brain, but at this point, none of them made any sense. At least what Mattson proposed, no matter how unappealing, made some sense. Dick's head shook as he gazed down at Mattson. "I can't think of any, no."

Mattson exhaled heavily and leaned back in his chair. "I didn't think so. When Mickey calls—"

"If he calls, you mean."

"*When* Mickey calls, this is what we're gonna do."

"Tell me."

"I would if you'd shut up and listen. When Mickey calls, we find out where the kid is, and I'm going to go in there and get him."

Dick shoved his hands deep into his pockets and acted as if he were awaiting the punch line of a joke. When none came, he said, "What, you think this is a mob rescue or something? You think you're Robert De Niro, and this is the fucking *Godfather*? You're talking out of your ass, Denver. Like this is a fucking movie or something. We're not playing around here. What the fuck you think you're gonna do? Have all guns blazing, and then go in there and rescue the kid? You going to play fucking Rambo, or what?"

"If I have to."

"No! That's not gonna fucking happen."

"Then let me fucking finish!"

Dick nodded and sealed his lips. "Finish."

Mattson set his drink on the table. He leaned forward in the chair and planted his feet on the floor. His elbows pressed down to his knees, as his fingers interlaced in front of him. His eyes then shot Dick a look that said he wasn't fucking around.

"Okay, so maybe this is like a fuckin' movie, kinda. A fifties movie. An' I'll be Eddie G. And I'll go in there—with guns blazing—and if I have to fuck somebody up, then that's what I'm gonna do. Because I'm gonna go in there, and I'm gonna rescue the fucking kid. And when we get him out, we'll wipe his ass and give him some money and tell him to keep his fucking mouth shut."

Dick's face softened and his mind flushed with the color of hope. He nodded slowly as he worked the different stages through his brain. "How much?"

"How much what?"

"How much you think it's gonna cost?"

"How the fuck should I know?" Mattson picked up his drink. "How much you got?"

Dick pressed his hand to his chest. "I'm not paying him out of my money."

"How much does Mickey got, then?"

Dick shrugged. "How the hell should I know?"

"You're only his father. Why the hell would I expect you to know anything?" Mattson took a slug from his glass. "We'll have to find out then, won't we? I say we give the kid ten Gs and tell him to shut the fuck up. Give him another ten Gs when he does."

Dick pressed his hand down on the sofa and took a seat. "You think that's enough?"

"For a fifteen-year-old kid? Are you shittin' me?"

Dick nodded skeptically.

"Okay, maybe you're right. Give him twenty Gs up front, and twenty later. Forty Gs would keep my ass shut for an eternity."

Dick got up and headed back into the kitchen. He pulled the bourbon off the counter and refilled his glass. He downed it in one burning swig. He thought about what Mattson was saying, rolling the possibilities around in his mind. If they could somehow get the kid home unhurt, they just might be able to save Mickey's ass.

It was a strange case to begin with. Someone besides Mickey had been holding onto the kid for a couple days, and they had been partying the whole time together. Mickey had been involved in the beginning, but how could anyone prove that? It was not your normal run-of-the-mill kidnapping. This case was different. Barnes just might be able to pull a rabbit out of his ass and get Mickey a good deal, if they could only get the kid home safely. But they still had a long way to go, and they couldn't start until Mickey called them back.

Dick pushed back into the living room and picked the phone up off the couch. He punched in the numbers to page Mickey again. He then took a seat back on the couch and closed his eyes, trying to relax. He tried to picture each move they would need to make, and he prayed that no harm had befallen the kid. As the time dribbled away, he could feel the dread of defeat once again gnawing at the lining of his gut. Mickey was about as likely to call him back as Dick was of inheriting a lot of money from his parents. He was dreaming by even thinking his kid would call him with all the shit he had gotten himself into. That was why Mickey had gone to Sheldon Barnes in the first place instead of coming to him. Either Mickey didn't want his father to know what he had done, or he hadn't called him because he didn't want to get him involved. Either way, they were all going to be fucked if he didn't get ahold of him soon.

His eyelids were heavy, and Dick was having serious problems staying awake. When he peered over, he could see Mattson's eyes were already closed. And the bourbon glass tilted precariously in his fat lap. A minute later, Dick also noticed the jolt in his friend's eyes when they shot open in response to the sudden booming ring of the telephone. The high-pitched jangle caused Mickey's godfather to nearly jump out of his chair and spill his drink all over his lap.

Dick wanted to laugh like hell when he saw the shock envelop Mattson's face; the way he slapped at the ice in his frosted crotch. But instead, Dick leapt out of the couch, grabbed the phone, and answered it. A smile as wide as the crack in Mattson's ass bled across Dick's face the second he heard the beautiful sound of his son's voice on the other end.

"What the fuck you calling me so much about, Dad?"

Chapter Thirty

Wednesday—12:25 a.m.

Vegas sprinted out of the vanity as if his ass were combusting. When he got into the sleeping area, he jumped into the orange chair and curled up into a fetal position. His face was chalk white, and his eyes crater wide. He looked as though he'd seen the Grim Reaper.

The bathroom door snapped open, and Bart Pray charged into the room carrying the AB-10. Luke had started to fix another shot, but when he saw Pray, he froze. He heard a rustling sound and a mild groan, and he turned to see Bobby staring at him from the bed with one blinking red eye. Seeing this, Pray quickly retreated back into the bathroom. When Luke glanced back to the bed, he saw Bobby roll onto his other side and quickly fall back to sleep. Luke didn't think the kid had seen Pray. Exhaustedly, he poured his drink.

Pray reemerged a minute later, this time carrying the duffel bag. He glanced at Bobby, who was asleep on the bed, and then at Vegas, who sat frozen in the chair. He turned to Luke. "Come on."

Luke downed the shot and exhaled the fire. He set the glass down, quickly pushed past Pray, and walked out the door. Pray pivoted and followed.

Luke darted down the corridor to the elevator and punched the button. Pray followed closely behind him, carrying the green bag. When the elevator arrived, they both climbed in. Luke hit the button as Pray pulled the gun out of the bag. He reached into his waistband and pulled out the clip. He shoved it into the gun, which was now loaded. He then jammed the entire AB-10 down the front of his pants, covering it with the front of his green shirt.

They reached the ground floor and exited the elevator. They hurried across the black pavement toward Patrick's lime jalopy. Luke glanced over and couldn't believe how much bigger Pray looked than he'd remembered. With his slicked back hair and the huge mole on his face, the dude reminded Luke of some movie gangster whose name slipped his mind. When they got to the car, Pray popped open the trunk.

"I want you to drive."

Luke guffawed. "What are you talking about, dude? I can't drive a stick."

Pray tossed him the keys anyway. They bounced off Luke's hand and fell to the asphalt. "Dude, I'm not fucking around," Pray said. "I want you to drive."

Luke reached down and picked up the keys. "Dude, I'm not fucking around either. I can't drive stick." He tossed them back.

Pray swiped at them angrily. With his other hand, he grabbed his waist the way Michael Jackson grabs his crotch. He glared at Luke threateningly, but Luke didn't care. The gun wasn't going to make him understand how to drive a stick, so fuck him. He didn't even care if the sonofabitch pulled it out and shot his ass. It would put them both out of his misery.

Go ahead, asshole, make my day.

"Fucking cunt," Pray muttered as he climbed into the car and shut the door. Luke climbed into the passenger's side. Pray pulled the gun out of his waistband and stuck it on the floor beneath his left leg. He started the car, shifted it into reverse, and backed out.

"Dude, I could eat a stillborn fetus," Pray said, as he pulled the battered sardine can out onto County Street. "I need a burrito or something."

"Now?" Luke gawked at him as if he were crazy. "It's one o'clock in the fucking morning."

"What about that place?" Pray pointed to a small taco stand and started to slow. The lights were on outside, but the place was dark inside.

"Dude, it's not even open," Luke said. "Keep going." He gestured with his hand to keep moving, and Pray did.

"How 'bout that one?" Luke cranked his neck to see another restaurant, but there was another closed sign. "Fuck it," Pray said. "Where's your house?"

"For what, dude?"

"So we can get the fucking shovels. What do you think? You need to be able to dig a hole before you do a person. Didn't you know that? It saves time and prevents you from being discovered later."

Luke's head shook at the inanity of Pray's statement. His mouth was dry, and he felt as if he were quickly sinking into a sea of apathy. He needed to get his head around what he was doing. He needed to stall Pray to buy time to think.

But he wasn't sure of the best way to do it, because he couldn't get his mind off the gun.

"Look, man, we don't have to do this. You know that, right? I've got an idea of how we can make this work."

"What are you talking about?"

"The kid," Luke said. "Look, I think if I give him some money and send him home—"

"Dude!" Pray's hand shot up. "The kid's not going home. If he talks, Mickey's going to prison for the rest of his life. So is John. So are you. If you want to fucking go, fine, that's your deal. But I can't let that happen to Mickey. He gave me a job to do. And I'm gonna do it. Now, I'm going to ask you one more time. How do we get to your house?"

Luke rubbed his cold hand across his burning forehead. How had he gotten himself into this? At the moment, he had no solutions, so he pointed left, and Pray turned down Cajun Drive. Luke told him to pull over below the next-door neighbor's driveway. He had no intention whatsoever of letting the madman know which house was his. But he still had to figure out how to get him out of here without waking up the whole neighborhood.

Pray killed the engine, and Luke just sat there. After a silent moment, Pray turned to him and asked, "What are you waiting for?"

Luke just stared straight ahead.

"Yo, fuckhead," Pray said. "I asked you a question."

Still nothing.

"You gettin' the fucking shovels or am I?"

"This is bullshit, man!" Luke screamed. "We're not getting any shovels, okay?"

Pray smiled callously. "Really?"

Luke folded his arms across his stomach. In a belligerent voice, he said, "Really."

The sudden blow to the side of the head stunned Luke so badly, he didn't know what had hit him. His head jerked sideways and slammed off the side window. And at first he thought he'd been shot. But when he put his hand up to his ear, he couldn't find any blood. He twisted to see Pray's fist cocked and ready to wallop him again, and that's when Luke realized he'd been punched. His ears rang, and he felt as if he'd been struck by a sledgehammer. His head shook to see if anything was loose, and he turned back to Pray.

"Dude, don't ever do that again."

"Really? Who's going to stop me?" Pray feigned another punch but pulled it back.

Luke flinched, and his eyes squeezed closed. When he opened them, Pray's dickface glared right at him. "Look, man, you can fucking shoot me for all I care. I don't really give a shit. The bottom line is, I'm not doing it. Okay? That's it. I'm not going to implicate myself in Bobby's murder. I'm just not gonna do it. So you can fucking do whatever you need to do, but I'm not helping you." Luke just sat there, staring straight ahead, one arm folded across his chest, the other one holding his face.

Pray started laughing, and his fist dropped to his side. In a little girl's voice, he said, "Boo hoo, did I hurt you?"

"Yes, it hurt, you fucking asshole."

Pray frowned sarcastically. "Ooh, don't hurt my feelings. So where's the shovels?"

"Fuck, you. I told you, I'm not—"

Luke never saw the second blow coming either, this one landing square in his mouth. His head snapped back and ricocheted violently off the window. He felt sudden dizziness, and his vision filled with a trillion bursting stars.

"There's plenty more where that came from," Pray said, and Luke could hear the echo repeating inside his head. "Now, if you want to sit here and debate it, we can debate it all night long. But we're not leaving without the shovels. So it's your choice, Luke. You can get them, or you can tell me where they are."

Luke rubbed the bloody gash inside his mouth with his tongue. "Fuck you."

"Yeah? Fuck me? Where are they, Luke?"

Luke's head rattled with the realizatioin that Bart Pray was on a one-way mission to mayhem. Youngblood had somehow convinced Pray to kill the kid in cold blood, and he appeared determined not to leave until the job was completed. Pray had pounded Luke twice in the face, and he looked as if he were ready to do it again. The guy was fucking possessed, and Luke didn't want to get into a fight with him here in the car, right next to his parents' house, with that loaded gun on the floor. It was a losing situation that would most likely end up leaving one or the both of them bleeding and dying in the middle of the street, with the entire neighborhood awake and pissed at the disturbance. Luke couldn't do that. His old man would never forgive him. He needed to quietly get the guy out of here and take his chances with him elsewhere.

He turned to Pray. "All right, they're in the fucking garage. On the right side as you walk in. But I don't want you going near the house. Understand?"

Pray sneered. "You're a cunt, you know that." He grabbed the gun off the floor and climbed out of the car.

Luke sulked as he rubbed the sore lump growing on the side of his head. The opposite jawbone near his ear ached, and his lip was swelling like a cow's liver. His ears wouldn't stop ringing, and he wanted to punch Pray's lights out for good. He watched the asshole walk to the rear of the car and stop as if he were confused. Pray peered to the left, toward the neighbor's drive, then over to the distant right, toward Luke's father's driveway. Then he stepped to the left before turning to the right and heading straight toward Luke's drive.

Fuck me, Luke thought, and his chest filled with panic. Watching the fucker carrying the gun like that generated these wild images of Pray going into Luke's house and going postal on his parents. Luke could just see his old man asleep upstairs, and then his eyes popping open, and Pray shooting his ass. The jury was still out on Milsty, but Luke wasn't ready to lose his father yet. They still had too much shit to work out. So he scrambled to find the door handle and flew out of the car. He sprinted up the driveway like a lunatic, because he needed to keep the asshole away from his parents. If the dude so much as thought about going near his house, Luke would bash his fucking skull in with a shovel.

*   *   *   *

Vegas trembled on the orange chair like a flag under fire. He hadn't moved since Luke and that dude left in a huff ten minutes earlier. His chest felt tight, and he had never been scared so shitless in his life. All he kept thinking about was that gun. Luke had told him that some dudes were coming to take Bobby home, and then this one dude he calls "Barty" shows up with a gun. Luke didn't say anything about guns. Luke didn't say shit about shit other than he would call off Vegas' debt if Vegas helped watch Bobby, and that he'd be back in a few minutes. That was it.

Vegas put his hand to his chest, and he could feel himself starting to breathe again. The air felt good. He glanced over at Bobby, who was passed out in the bed, and he couldn't believe that they were really going to do it. He knew he should go over there, wake him up, and get him the hell out of there right now. Keep running without ever looking back. But he couldn't do that.

He just wanted to be home. He wanted to call his mom and have her come and pick him up. He would go wait for her up by the corner and get out of this place forever. But he knew that if she came to the hotel, she would kill him. She would want to know what he had been up to. She would ask questions that he would not want to answer. If he broke down and told his mom what was going on, Luke would kill him. Luke had given him explicit instructions to watch

Bobby until he got back. And if Vegas didn't do what he was supposed to do, and Luke didn't kill him, that "Barty" guy—whoever the hell he was—would.

Then Vegas wondered if it were possible that they weren't going to kill Bobby at all. That maybe that Barty guy was there to scare him. But if that were the case, then why was he in the bathroom cleaning a gun? Maybe he was just assembling it and didn't want anyone to see. Maybe not. Maybe he really was there to kill Bobby. But that was a troubling scenario too. Because Vegas couldn't imagine Luke having any part in that. There's no way Luke would let that guy kill Bobby. It just wasn't his style.

Luke had told Vegas that he liked Bobby very much, and Vegas believed it. He also believed that Luke didn't have what it took to take the life of another human being. That's why Vegas believed they were probably just going to scare him. They were going to show Bobby the gun, tell him to shut up, pretend they were going to kill him, let him beg for mercy, and then tell him they would give him one more chance. As long as he promised not to say anything, they would let him go home.

The more Vegas thought about it, the more he realized it made no sense whatsoever to kill Bobby. He had been partying for three days with all sorts of people who knew about his situation, and with all those witnesses, how could anybody in their right mind believe that not one of them would go to the cops? Besides, if they were going to kill Bobby, why would they have left him alone right now with Vegas? They could both just get up and walk right out, disappearing forever, thereby destroying any plans anybody had of killing anyone. It just didn't make any sense.

And even if it did, why should Vegas worry about it? It wasn't his problem. So why should he be the one to risk his ass for Bobby Leblanc? If Barty were truly there to commit murder, he could just as easily kill Vegas as he could Bobby. That's why Vegas would be better off by just shutting up and sitting tight. Waiting for Luke to get back so he could get the hell out of there.

And that's what he decided to do—be quiet and wait. It was the smart decision, and the best one for Vegas to follow if he wanted to avoid any chance of getting hurt. Yet even the best-laid plans have ways of changing sometimes. Which is what happened the moment Luke startled the shit out of Vegas by banging open the front door and charging into the room.

Vegas' eyes filled with concern when he saw Luke's swollen and red face. He just stood there, hands on his hips, unable to catch his breath. He looked like he'd been in a fight.

"Vegas, you know where Skeleton Jaw is, don't you?"

Vegas blinked, because the question totally caught him off guard. "Well, yeah, of course I do. I've been up there like a thousand times. And it's totally cool, dude, why? What are you gonna do up there?"

"Well, well, just … I want you to go with him, okay?"

Barty stepped into the room. And Vegas glanced up at his dark and threatening face; then at the bag that filled his hand. Vegas quickly turned back to Luke with panic-stricken eyes. "Why? Like what's the deal, dude? I don't want to go up to Skeleton Jaw. I need to get home."

Luke shook his head. "Dude, I just want you to go with him, okay. You can go home later."

"But I don't want to go with him," Vegas said anxiously, tears swelling in eyes. "I need to get home now."

"Dude, like I'm not asking you, okay?"

Chapter Thirty-One

Wednesday—1:00 a.m.

"Ah, Christ, what's this, the fucking old man's convention?" Mickey Youngblood stifled a loud yawn as he peered out the front door of Nicole's parents' townhouse wearing nothing more than baggy jeans and an hourglass torso.

Dick stood on the top step and took a double take at the great shape his kid was in. It had been a long time since he'd seen Mickey without a shirt on, and the kid looked great. When Mickey opened the door behind him, Dick stepped in, followed by Denver Mattson's lumbering girth.

Mickey trailed them inside and closed the door. "It's a little late for you guys to be out, isn't it?"

Dick and Mattson disappeared down the hallway without uttering a word. The Babbette's living room was crowded with brightly colored antiques and tapestries—some expensive, others merely vulgar. The shiny white walls were covered with gaudy gold trim and wainscoting. The place looked like a cross between a Persian museum and a Turkish flea market. Seconds later, Nicole strolled down the stairs wearing a skimpy silk robe, and she greeted everyone. Mickey stood behind his father, wiping the sleep from his eye. "So what the fuck's up, man? It's late. What do you want?"

Dick turned to his son agitatedly. "I told you, I want to know what happened with the fucking kid. What do you think?"

Mickey's eyes rolled toward Babbette, then over to Mattson, then back to his dad. "I don't want to talk about it here."

"Fine," Dick said, glancing around the room. "Then where do you want to talk about it?"

"Let's go outside." Mickey stepped over to the sliding glass door and opened it. Dick pushed outside. Babbette tried to follow, but Mickey stuck his hand out. "What did I say, huh?"

"I want to go with you."

Mickey let out an irritated sigh. It had been such a long day, and he was so exhausted, that he really didn't want to get into it with her right now. He'd been uptight as a motherfucker since his meeting with Sheldon Barnes this afternoon, but after a day filled with reflection and shopping, he had finally found his emotional zone. And he wanted it to stay that way.

After they took off from his lawyer's house, he'd fed the cunt, took her to get her nails done—again, and finished the afternoon off by blowing all his money on the diamond bracelet that was now wrapped around her left wrist. The fucking thing set him back several mortgage payments, but it shut her ass up—for the time being, and she looked great wearing it. Then he cleared out his Montgomery Mutual account of the twenty-five grand he had left over from the insurance scam and collected another ten Gs from Zit and others who had enough to pay him back what they owed him. He needed the money, because he wanted to buy a new car and change his profile a little. Get rid of his Beemer, become liquid as soon as possible.

He then took Babbette out for her twenty-first birthday party celebration with Patrick Callahan at the Lobster Steakhouse, where they pounded lobster, steak, and booze, and where Callahan had zero idea that he was playing the unwitting alibi witness, or that he'd proven instrumental during the unfolding of the evening's events.

Now, Mickey just wanted to sleep. He was exhausted, and he needed to get his old man the fuck out of there. To do that, he needed to first get Babbette out of there. "Let me just talk to my old man alone for a minute, okay, baby?"

"Oooh." Babbette stomped her foot and bit down on her thumbnail.

"Come on, little lady," Mattson said, hooking a meat-slab arm around her. "What do you say we go into the other room and get to know each other a little better?"

Babbette groaned and threw Mickey a dirty look. He returned it. When she turned to leave, he slapped her ass, then stepped outside and shut the door.

The balcony looked more like a sundeck, cozy but quaint, with a small patio table, umbrella and chairs. As soon as Mickey slid the door shut, his father jumped on him like white on rice. "So what the fuck's going on with the kid?"

Mickey's eyes blew wide with surprise at his father's aggression. "It's not what you think, okay? So calm the fuck down."

Dick towered over his kid. "How the fuck do you know what I think? You got a crystal ball stuck up your ass, or what?"

Mickey pivoted away from his father and sidled over to the other side of the green and white table and chairs. "Yeah, I got a crystal ball stuck up my ass. How'd you figure it out?"

"You going to tell me what the fuck's going on? Or are you just going to be a goddamned smartass all night?"

Mickey sneered at his father. "Yeah, okay, Dad. You wanna know what's going on? Fine, I'll tell you. These guys I know, they got into this bad situation that they were having problems getting themselves out of. Okay? And I tried to help them fix it. That's it."

Dick stood there as if waiting for his kid to finish. But he didn't say anything else. "Uh-huh, okay. So you're saying someone else is involved. And it's not you."

Mickey leaned forward and placed his forearms on the railing. "Yeah, no—it's not me."

Dick blinked skeptically. "Okay, so you didn't have anything to do with this, right?"

Mickey's head shook. "No."

"Then who did?" Dick leaned his hip against the table. "If it wasn't you, Mickey, who took the kid?"

"Look, man, don't worry about it, okay? It's none of your fucking business."

"No, motherfucker, I am worried about it." Dick pulled away from the table and over toward Mickey. "I get a call from my lawyer telling me you came over with some cockamamie story about your friends kidnapping some kid. Then when you find out you fucked up and are looking at time, you fucking take off like your dick's liquified. But that's because it's someone else, right? Not you, right? You're not the one whose ass is in a sling."

Mickey said nothing, instead pretending to focus on some unidentified flying object.

"Am I right?" Dick said, angling in next to his son.

Mickey slid over, away from his father.

"Mickey, you can't just run away from your problems. Man, if it's one of your friends, then—fine. Tell me who it is, and let's see what we can do for him. But if it's you, then there's still time to do something. We can get you out of this shit, Mickey. But you got to level with me, okay?"

Mickey huffed as he considered his father's request. He finally looked up. "How?"

Dick's face twisted. "How?"

"How the fuck can you help me, Dad?" Mickey pushed himself up from the railing. "You haven't been around to help me my whole fucking life, but now you're going to come to my rescue, right?"

"Oh, Jesus Christ, here it comes again. Look, Mickey, I'm sorry if you think I didn't give you everyfuckingthing you ever needed when you were growing up—"

"That's not the problem, Dad, and you know it. Come on, man. Sure, you gave me everything I fucking needed. I had more shit than most fucking kids ever dream about. But really—what the fuck good did it do me? I mean it's not like I had a fucking dad when I was growing up. A fucking competitive brother, maybe. But not a father. Not anybody who had any fucking idea how to raise a kid. That's what I really needed, you know." Mickey pivoted around the table. "And you know what the fucking worst part of it was? When I was a kid, and I was in school. Watching all the other dads show up for career day. You know, real dads. With real jobs. But of course, every time my old man would show up. I'd have to lie. My dad? What does he do? Oh, I don't know. Drug dealer? Oh, no way, not my dad. He's … he's a brain surgeon—yeah, a brain surgeon who never pays taxes. That's my fucking dad."

Dick looked speechless. "Jesus Christ. That's really fucking nice. You fucking finished yet?"

Mickey stopped pacing. "No, Dad, I'm not fucking finished yet. What the fuck do you want? Why are you here?"

"I want to help get you out of this fucking problem."

"I don't have a fucking problem, okay? I told you that." Dick just stood there glaring at his son, tight lipped. After a minute, the tactic seemed to fluster Mickey. "Okay, Dad. Fine. What do you want to do?"

"We can start by knocking off all the bullshit, okay? Do you have the kid, or don't you?"

Mickey reached into his pocket and pulled out a cigarette. "I don't know."

Dick frowned. "What the fuck do you mean, you don't know? How can you not know if you have the fucking kid or not?"

Mickey lit the cigarette and said, "Look, this guy's got the kid, and … but there's nothing I can do about it now."

Dick didn't like the answer. He stepped straight up to Mickey and glowered at him. Mickey glowered right back, playing disrespectful chimney in the process. Dick reached over and yanked the disrespect from his son's mouth and threw it on the deck. He then stomped it viciously with his foot.

"Look, Mickey, I'm not some fucking asshole who just fell off the borscht truck, okay? I'm not going away. So where's the fucking kid?"

"I don't know."

Dick's head shook in disbelief. "I repeat—how can you not know where the fucking kidnapped kid is?"

Mickey threw up his hands, and started pacing again. "Look, these fucking dudes had him. But I don't know what they did with him, okay? And now I'm probably totally fucked. I just don't know."

"Totally fucked how?"

Mickey stopped pacing. "Because these dudes probably fucking let him go, okay …? Or he got away, and he's gone to the fucking cops already. Either way, I'm totally fucked, Dad. I'm telling you."

"But you don't know for sure?"

Mickey sighed. "I'm fucked no matter how you look at it. Even if they let him go, he's going to the cops."

"But where is he now?"

"I don't know."

"I don't understand, Mickey. You don't know if he's with your friend or not?"

Mickey went back to pacing. "I don't know where the fuck he is. That's what I'm saying. It's out of my hands, Dad. I'm telling you, my fucking life is ruined."

Dick straightened up and stepped in Mickey's path, forcing him to stop and look at him. "Mickey, look, I want to make sure nothing happens to the kid. First things first, okay? I'll go and get him. We'll get him home. And then we'll worry about what we're going to do from there. Okay?"

Mickey gazed down at his feet.

"So who has him?"

"I don't want to say anything. I've tried all night to reach the guy. But they must have gone somewhere, because I can't get ahold of him."

"But as far as you know, the kid's okay, right?"

"As far as I know." Mickey let out a huge yawn and then squinted down at his watch. "Look, Dad, I'm beat. I'll give him a call in the morning and find out what's going on. And then you can go on your little white horse and pick him up or whatever the fuck you want to do. Okay?"

Dick's head shook. "No."

"What do you mean, 'No?'"

"I don't want to wait until morning," Dick said, "It'll be too late. I want you to get ahold of the guy right now and make sure the kid's okay."

Mickey frowned. "Man, the kid's fine. I told you."

"No, you didn't. You told me you had no idea where he is. You said you weren't sure if your friend even had the kid. Or if the cops were on their way to bust your ass. So call him now!"

"There's nothing we can do about it right now." Mickey pivoted away from his father. "Jesus Christ, Dad, it's fucking late, man. I'm exhausted. If the kid's gone, the kid's gone. If I'm going to fucking prison, there's nothing I can do about it now. Look, I got to get some sleep." Mickey regarded his father expectantly.

Dick didn't stare back at his son so much as burn a hole right through Mickey's face. It unnerved Mickey enough to make him stretch his shoulders and roll his neck, sending a loud crack reverberating into the night. "What are you staring at, Dad?"

"That's what I'm trying to figure out."

"What's that supposed to mean?"

"It means I don't even know who you are, Mickey. You used to be such a sweet fucking kid. What the fuck happened to you?"

"Maybe I spent too much time around you, Dad."

"Oh, I see—so it's my fault you got into this fucking mess? Is that what you're saying?"

Mickey sighed. "Why don't you just fucking go, Dad?"

Dick's arms crossed his chest, as he leaned back against the table and folded one leg across the other. A determined smirk corrugated the right side of his face. "Because I'm not going anywhere until I find out where the kid is."

Chapter Thirty-Two

Vegas Parsons was totally jacked about getting out of room 215, and he couldn't wait to get home. Unfortunately, his expectations quickly diminished when he got into the beat-up lime car with Bart Pray. When they pulled out of the hotel's driveway, instead of going right on Andrade in the direction of Vegas' home, Pray went left. He drove the 1986 four-door with dirty rims up Andrade, turned left on Baseline, and then took a right onto the 267.

The night was sultry, and the winding road up into the Francisco National Forest was dark and foreboding. When Vegas rolled down the window, he could smell sage and lavender in the air. They were driving to a place he had been to a thousand times, partying with friends since his freshman year in high school, but he didn't really want to go there now. In fact, he didn't understand why they were going there at all. When he asked Barty that very question, the dude just told him they needed to go do something. He didn't say what, and Vegas didn't ask. He just shifted in his seat and tried to clear space on the floor for his feet. The car was a stick with bucket seats. Old newspapers, fast food bags, and candy wrappers littered the floorboard.

Every time Vegas thought about going home, he also thought about the green duffel bag he had seen on the bathroom floor. The one that now sat under Barty's feet. What was he going to do with that? If the plan was to kill Bobby, it just didn't make sense that they were driving up to Skeleton Jaw without him. So why have the gun now? Maybe they were going to meet Bobby's brother or some other friends who might be partying up there. Maybe they were going to bring Rick Leblanc and whoever was with him back to the hotel to pick up Bobby. And the gun was for protection because maybe that Barty guy was afraid of Bobby's brother. And then again, maybe not. None of it made any sense, and Vegas was way too beat to think about it anyway.

When they reached the crest of the mountain pass, Vegas told Barty, "Slow down up here." The area was gloomy; the only light emanating from the glow of the moon and stars above. When Vegas saw the sign that said North Pacific Sky Road, he told Barty to "take a left here." Pray took a left. They drove past the sign and took the road to the right.

North Pacific Sky Road was pitch black, but for the car's headlights. A huge awning of thick roadside trees hung over the black asphalt. Their gnarled branches gave it an eerie appearance. It looked like one of those horror movies, and Vegas halfway expected the Headless Horseman to come storming out of the trees, swiping at him with his sword—if Barty didn't shoot him first.

Pray drove slowly, and when they reached the end of the paved road, Vegas told him, "Slow down. This is it." Barty pressed on the brake. Vegas could see the sign for the Century Gun Club up ahead. He wondered if Barty might be driving up there to take some kind of target practice. That would be so weird. It was the middle of the night, and no one was up there, but it wouldn't surprise Vegas to see Barty walk up there and unload on some unsuspecting owl trying to get some Zs on a low-slung branch.

The tires crunched on the gravel as Pray turned around in the gun club's driveway. The sign on the locked gate said, "No Trespassing." Pray drove past the hiking path up into the hill and pulled over on the dirt shoulder. He killed the engine. Through the windshield, Vegas could see the blush from the moon above the canopy of trees that partially obstructed the overhead view. He leaned back and closed his eyes. They both sat there immersed in the same silence they rode with the entire trip. Vegas could hear his heart pounding in his ears. He didn't understand why Barty just sat there. He looked disoriented, as though he were trying to figure something out, but couldn't. Vegas wanted to ask him what it was, but he was too afraid. Afraid of what Barty might tell him. Afraid of what he might do. So he just sat there silently too, waiting.

Suddenly, Pray opened the door. "Let's go."

Vegas glanced over at him. "Where we going?"

"You ask too many fucking questions." Barty got out and slammed the door shut.

Vegas' heart boiled even faster. He didn't like the feel of this at all, but he climbed out of the car anyway. What choice did he have? Maybe if he just did what he was told and didn't ask any questions, the guy would leave him alone or take him home.

Outside, the air smelled of dirt and leaves, reminding Vegas of how much he loved this place. He had his first experience with a girl up here when he was fifteen. She had been a cute blonde named Denise Shirelle, and they had come up with some other friends to party. After a few beers and a couple joints, they both got hot and hammered, and the heavy petting began. If they hadn't started so late, and they weren't both so tired, they would have probably lost their virginity on that hot summer night. As it was, they took care of that the following weekend anyway.

"So where is Skeleton Jaw?" Barty asked, fumbling with the keys before jamming the right one into the trunk lock.

Vegas pointed up the side of the hill. "It's up that path. Why—you going on a hike or something?"

Pray ignored the question and opened the trunk.

Vegas pivoted and stretched his arms into the air. He let out a lung-rattling yawn. It was definitely warm, and he loved that summer feeling. It made him feel young, and he thought again about all the times he'd partied up here, all the friends he'd made, and all the fun they'd had. It was an incredible feeling of happy times and innocence, and it surged through his blood like oxygen. But his goodwill and happy feelings quickly vanished in an explosion of shock and dread. When Vegas saw what was in the trunk, he felt a loud gasp of air squeeze out of his lungs. He looked up at Pray's frightful face.

"Dude, what's up with that? What are we doing here?"

Pray pushed the beam of the flashlight from the trunk up into Vegas' bulging eyes. "Just grab the shovels and follow me."

✳   ✳   ✳   ✳

Luke's brain fried like rice. He couldn't put a complete thought together to save his life. His eyes would barely stay open. That's why he needed another shot; to numb his exposure to the darkness of the night that lay ahead. He leaned back in the orange chair and studied Bobby as he slept soundly on the bed. It was showdown time. Time to make the decision that would reverberate throughout the rest of his life and the lives of many others. Pray had taken Vegas up to Skeleton Jaw to dig Bobby Leblanc's grave this very moment. And Luke was ready to just walk out and put the kid on the train and forget about the whole fucking mess. But he knew he couldn't do that. Pray would kill him. Because Pray was on a mission.

Luke's head pounded with the worst fucking headache he'd ever experienced in his life. He thought seriously about getting some aspirin when he went to the store. Before Pray had left, he told him to go buy some duct tape so they could use it to tie up the kid. Luke told him he didn't need duct tape, just as he told him they didn't need to take the kid up to Skeleton Jaw to bury him, but his pleas fell on Pray's deaf ears. That's when Luke came inside and told Vegas to show Pray the way up there. He knew their time away would give him time to think, time to figure a way out of this tragedy in the making. He still couldn't believe he was considering letting Pray hurt the kid in the first place.

Bobby Leblanc was an angel. The kid had done everything Luke had asked of him over the past three days, and he felt certain he would continue to do so for as long as he was asked. Bobby was looking forward to getting home. When they spoke earlier in the evening, he had told Luke how much he'd grown up since he'd been around him and the others. He thanked Luke for everything he'd done for Bobby and invited him out to visit some time.

It made Luke want to kill himself for being such a shithead for even thinking about what it was he was thinking about. All the kid wanted to do was go home. He had told Luke how he would call all his friends when he got back. There was this hill near his house that he wanted to hike up and sit on top of, so he could watch the sunset and just kind of lay low. He seemed so excited about the prospect of seeing his parents again, of sharing time with them in a whole new light. And he was going to do well in school.

They had talked about it a lot, and Luke had agreed to do the same thing. School was important to Luke. Both his mom and dad had instilled a sort of pride within him to get his shit together and go back. School would be something that could pave the way for the rest of his life, allowing him to turn himself into something important, and he looked forward to that. Luke had always wanted to feel important, and he had grown tired of being stuck in the rut he was in. He wanted to get out. He wanted to be something. He wanted to one day have a family and kids, and he knew that an education would be an important first step toward those goals. But all that would be beyond his reach if he didn't make the right decision concerning Bobby, and time was running out to make it.

He questioned whether he should leave the kid there and go and get the duct tape, taking a chance that Bobby might wake up and take off. Or if he should forget about the tape and just let him go? Either way, now was the time to do it. Before Barty got back to finish the job.

Luke thought again about walking out that door without saying another word to anybody, and never coming back. He could just disappear, and that would be the end of it. If they came back after him later, fine, so be it. That's what he would deserve for being such an ignoramus in the first place.

He thought about taking Bobby out that door with him and making sure the kid never came back either. But he didn't want to do anything rash. He didn't want to make a choice that he'd live to regret for the rest of his life. That's why he figured he could just make a quick run to the store, get the tape, and maybe some aspirin, and a couple candy bars to munch on, and then come right back. Bobby was so knocked out, Luke was sure he wouldn't go anywhere. And the walk over to Frank's Market would be good to help burn off some of the alcohol in Luke's system. The fresh air would help clear his mind. It would help him think straighter. The sugar from the candy would give him a rush and the energy he needed to do what he needed to do.

Luke was surprised by the amount of people shopping at Frank's this late at night. The parking lot sat almost a quarter full, with cars pulling in and out continuously. The entire walk over consisted of Luke listening to his stomach growl while his taste buds were held hostage by the mouthwatering idea of a chewy, peanut buttery chocolate bar. When he was a kid, Luke used to love smashing together a chewy wafer bar with a chocolate bar, then mixing them up with ketchup. The conglomeration was a little tart, but it always seemed to quell his appetite. When he thought about it now, it made his stomach curdle.

He had been fantasizing at the candy section for several minutes when his mind veered back to reality and his need to get back to the hotel to make sure Bobby Leblanc hadn't flown the coop. Luke leaned over and counted out ten peanut butter chocolate bars, scooped them up against his chest, and headed up front.

Only one check stand remained open, and he stood ninth in line, not the most promising statistic for someone in a hurry to save a kid's life. He thought about ditching everything and running back, but he felt the desperate need to feed his craving for sugar. He needed his smokes. He needed to calm his ass down. His neck revolved, as he surveyed his surroundings, and he still couldn't figure out what all these people were doing out so late. It reminded him of when he was a teenager, and he used to go out and get stoned with his friends, and they'd all go down to the grocery store in the Valley and people watch. Everyone out that late always seemed to dress a little differently, each having his own story, and Luke tried to imagine what it might be.

The dark-skinned woman dressed in black at the front of the line looked as if she'd been out working the town. She laughed, and her eyes looked tired, but her exotic beauty and expensive clothes told Luke she was successful at whatever it was she did. The skinny pale guys in leather and nose rings standing behind her looked as if they rocked and rolled with their guitars and stayed up all night snorting meth. The bag woman and old man next to her, whose clothes were filled with holes and smelled about as fresh as an ocean side dump, looked as though they had just crawled out from underneath a rock, a place they'd be returning to right after buying their can of smashed ham. It blew Luke away that people actually ate that shit.

He had heard that in some countries that stuff was considered a delicacy, and he just couldn't imagine why, just as he couldn't imagine people really eating worms, or beetles, or chocolate-covered ants—the chocolate yes, but not the ants. Even a can of mashed ham sounded better than ants, and Luke imagined it all beat the hell out of dog food. When he used to leave food on his plate as a kid, his dad would tease him that if he didn't like what was on his plate, he could always serve him dog food next time. Luke had thought his dad was kidding, but after studying the hungry looks on the faces of the pathetic geriatrics in front of him, he wasn't so sure. What he was sure about was that whatever their nocturnal ventures, none of these people had to decide the fate of a fifteen-year-old boy.

They were lucky too, because the whole thing was driving Luke crazy. None of it felt right. How could he let them murder the kid? He had lived with and fed Bobby for the better part of the past three days. He then promised to send him home, only to then act like a Judas goat leading his flock to slaughter. What an asshole. Why would he even think of doing that? And what would he tell Rosy in the morning? "Yeah, you know, I, uh, yeah, I dropped him off, and, uh, I can't remember where, so don't ask." She'd punch him in the nose and never speak to him again. If Luke did that, he wouldn't want her to speak to him again, because he'd never even be able to look her in the eyes anyway. He'd never be able to look any of them in the eyes again.

He just started hitting it off with Cheri, and he couldn't wait to dig into her shapely little sixteen-year-old body, so he didn't want to do anything to fuck that up either. How could he even think about sex with a dead kid on his conscience? He couldn't, that's how. That's another reason he had to let the kid go.

When Luke reached the front of the line, the tall, thin clerk smiled. He wanted to smile back, but his mouth felt incapacitated. He told her he'd take two packs of Mountain Reds, and she got them for him. He tossed a couple twenties on the counter and wondered when in the hell he had become such an evil bastard. He reminded himself of Mickey Youngblood.

Fuck that. There was no way Luke was going to be like Mickey. The comparison itself was reason enough to let the kid go. Mickey Youngblood had some dark malignancy that allowed him to think of things like killing fifteen-year-old kids, but Luke did not. He had been reared better than that. He knew the difference between right and wrong. And that difference had never, in his entire life, been more prevalent than it was right now. That's why he had to let the kid go. That's why he had to hurry. He would have to hustle back to room 215 before Bart Pray did and get Bobby the fuck out of there. He anxiously watched the woman toss his candy bars and the aspirin and the cigarettes into the bag. And he thought it ironic that he was also buying duct tape—so Barty didn't have a shit fit—even though he was rushing back to the hotel to let the kid go.

Chapter Thirty-Three

Wednesday—1:31 a.m.

Mickey glared at his father as Dick stepped back and pulled a chair out from under the table. Dick glared right back, as he swung the chair around behind him and sat in it. He slowly leaned up and pulled another chair from the other side of the table and arranged it in front of him. He then leaned back in the first chair and kicked his legs up onto the second. He reclined back and folded his arms across his belly. He squirmed until he got comfortable, and then he reached into his pocket and pulled out a pair of sunglasses and put them on. He then sat there and stared at his son, acting like someone getting a suntan at the beach, and it bugged the shit out of Mickey.

"Why don't you just go and pitch a fucking tent?"

"I just might do that," Dick said with a sneer.

His father had some nerve, righteously questioning Mickey about his problem like that. Laying it all out there like an exposed nerve. Rubbing sand in it, and pouring vinegar on it, and then just kicking it back as if he owned the whole joint. Who the fuck did he think he was? If it was a staring contest his old man wanted, Mickey was more than up for it. He could stare down the best of them. After all, he'd learned it from the best. It was like when Mickey was a kid and his old man liked to play the badass around the house. Mickey'd get all pissed or throw a childish tantrum, and his old man would grab him and shake his ass, and, instead of crying, Mickey would just stare his old man down. And his old man would be there, staring right back. Neither one of them would say shit for hours, just staring at each other like a couple mindless lunatics. Then his old man would disappear through the false wall behind his bedroom and hide out in his "office" until the late hours of the morning.

One time when Mickey was ten, he followed his father into his bedroom and snuck through the false door. He found Dick sitting at a desk with about fifty pounds of weed loaded up in duffel bags on a bench right next to it. Mickey discovered that the hidden room was the place where his old man conducted his business. It also provided a great place to hide large amounts of cash without ever having to worry about anyone finding it. The room was filled with computers and a couch, and it looked like a real office with no windows. There was only one way in and one way out, and both of them went through a wooden hatch hidden behind a mirror in the master bedroom closet. His old man had looked over at him from his desk, and Mickey had just stared back. His father didn't say a word, and they didn't take their eyes off each other for an hour. It was the same thing they were doing right now, out on her parents' sundeck.

"You know I can sit here all fucking night and wait for you to answer," Dick Youngblood said, "but I'm not sure we've got all fucking night to wait."

His father continued to stare through those fucking gold aviator glasses that Mickey had grown up hating so much. "What do you want me to say, Dad?"

"I want to know who the fucking kid is, and who he's with."

"His name is Bobby Leblanc," Mickey said, face knotted tightly. "There, does that answer your question?"

Dick placed his hands in his lap. "One of them. Any relation to that schmuck who used to live with you?"

"Rick Leblanc?" Mickey could barely discern a nod from his father. "His little brother."

Dick shook his head disgustedly. "What the fuck's going on, Mickey?"

"Look, Leblanc and I got into a fucking hassle, okay? And it got a little outta control." Mickey splayed his hands, as if his few words should have explained everything.

His father's feet kicked up off the chair. "What kind of a hassle?"

Mickey looked unsure of what he wanted to tell his father. "He threatened me, okay?"

Dick removed his sunglasses and stuck them in his pocket. "What do you mean, he threatened you?"

"He came and broke out all my fucking windows. And now—"

"I don't understand. Hold on a second. What do you mean he broke out all your windows?"

"He came over all loaded one night last week. With one of his fucking butt-buddies and broke out all my windows. You should see it. All the fucking windows in my house are fucking broken."

Dick shook his head, but he didn't say anything.

"Then he called me up and left me a message basically telling me he was going to kill me and my family."

"Wait a minute. Let's go back," Dick said. "This doesn't make any fucking sense. Why the fuck would he do that …? I mean, why would he threaten you and break out all your windows, Mickey? He just did that out of the blue? It doesn't make any fucking sense."

"He did it because … the guy's a fucking moron, okay?"

"Oh, I see. That explains it." Dick's tongue rolled into a ball against his cheek. "The guy's a fucking moron, so he threatens your family. That makes all the fucking sense in the world."

Mickey sighed as he considered how to better explain it. "Because he didn't want to pay me the fucking money he owes me, okay?"

"Oh, so he owes you money? So you were trying to collect a fucking debt?"

Mickey could only shake his head. He wanted to tell his father it wasn't like that, but he didn't.

"So you were trying to collect a fucking debt, and when he didn't pay you back, you fucking picked up his little brother. Real fucking smart, Mickey."

"There's a little more to it than that, okay?"

"But that's what happened, in essence, right?"

Mickey turned to face his father. "Look, we went over there, and we were going to talk to him."

"About what?"

"Would you let me finish?"

"What were you going to talk to him about?"

"What we wanted to do in the first place …" Mickey drew a long breath. "Look, I tried to get ahold of the guy. But he's always ducking and weaving. Rick Leblanc is one slippery motherfucker. And if you don't pin him down, he'll go squeeze under a fucking rock and hide."

Dick sat up in his chair. "So you were trying to pin him down, and then what?"

Mickey turned and started pacing. "I wanted to talk to the motherfucker and get my money."

"What did you want to talk to him about, Mickey? Really? I mean he owed you some fucking money, so what? What the fuck did you have to talk about?"

Mickey's head shook wrathfully. He could feel the mental fatigue, and he didn't want to talk about it anymore. At least not right now. Not with his old man.

But his old man would not back down. The geezer just sat there at the edge of his chair, waiting for the answer he wanted to hear. Mickey knew he could stare it out with his old man until the second coming, but that probably wouldn't get rid of him. So Mickey inhaled deeply and told his father what he wanted to hear. And he didn't hold anything back.

*   *   *   *

Last November, Mickey had a down-line dealer named Danny Kanabi who owed him two grand from a half pound Mickey had fronted him months earlier. The guy split town without paying him back, and Mickey went apeshit. He told Leblanc that if he ever saw Kanabi again, the dude was deadfuckingmeat. Leblanc told Mickey to "save it," because he not only knew the guy, but he knew where he lived. Kanabi had moved up north, and Leblanc said he would help collect the debt. Anything to turn a buck.

So Mickey drove Leblanc up to Desert Port the following Saturday. Mickey stayed in the car while Leblanc went inside to talk to Kanabi. Kanabi told Leblanc he didn't have any money. Leblanc told him he'd better figure something out, because Youngblood was outside in the car waiting for his ass and he wasn't very happy about Kanabi skipping town on the debt. Kanabi didn't have any ideas. Leblanc went out and told Mickey it was a no go. Mickey said he wasn't leaving until he had his money. Leblanc went back in and told Kanabi. And Kanabi all of a sudden had an idea. He said his neighbor sold E, and he could probably get enough to pay Mickey back in tabs. When Leblanc went back and told Mickey this, Mickey said, "Bullshit. I want my money, not some fucking tabs of E." That was when Leblanc came up with the brilliant idea that he'd take the two hundred hits of E, sell them at raves for twenty bucks a pop, pay Mickey back his money, and keep two grand for himself.

Mickey said, "Fine, dude, whatever. I just want my money."

Leblanc went back inside and told Kanabi to get the E because he thought he could get Youngblood to deal. Kanabi went next door and told the Ecstasy dealer he wanted to sell two thousand dollars worth of E to Youngblood and Leblanc. Leblanc waited in the car with Mickey while Kanabi was fronted the Ecstasy.

With his neighbor standing out on his balcony watching, Kanabi brought the E to Leblanc and Mickey down in the parking lot. Leblanc took the stash to look at, then nodded to Youngblood to "Punch it."

"What?"

"Punch it!"

Leblanc smacked Youngblood's leg, which launched his foot into the gas pedal, and they were gone, laughing their asses off all the way back to the Valley. The laughs were short-lived, however, when two weeks later, Youngblood wanted to know where his money was. Leblanc handed him six hundred dollars in cash, and Youngblood threw it on the floor. Youngblood wanted to know where his two thousand was, but all Leblanc would give him were pathetic excuses.

"Dude, you wouldn't fucking believe it. I took the E to a rave in San Bernardino, and they were selling like hotcakes. I unloaded like thirty in an hour. I had six hundred dollars cash in my pocket. I ate none of the profits, dude. None of 'em. I wanted to get your ass paid off. Then a few minutes later—like a couple hot chicks I'd sold to earlier came up to me. And they were all pissed and shit. They told me the fucking E was bunk. I gave 'em their money back. I was like flabbergasted, dude. You wouldn't fucking believe it."

He was right—Mickey didn't fucking believe it. "I want my money," was all Youngblood would say. Leblanc reached into his pocket and handed Mickey another two hundred dollars. Youngblood threw that on the floor as well. Leblanc tried giving him the last one hundred seventy bogus tabs, but Youngblood wouldn't take them either. "I want my money, not this bullshit."

Leblanc told him he got the bullshit. "And if you don't like that, you can fuck yourself."

Youngblood didn't like it, and he didn't hold back. He told Leblanc exactly what he thought of him. "You come over here, take over my fucking house. Don't pay for shit. Rip me off. And now you're going to dis me on this? Fuck you. I want my money."

Leblanc laughed and again told Youngblood to "Go fuck yourself. I made a ton of money for you, Mickey. And now you're going to nickel-and-dime me like this? I just tried to help you collect a debt. Fuck you."

And that was the last time Mickey saw the motherfucker, who never paid him the last twelve hundred back. Two months later, Mickey heard that Leblanc had sold his motorcycle. And instead of paying Mickey back, what did the fucker do? Bought his slut girlfriend an engagement ring. It made Mickey want to puke. And to make matters worse, Mickey then heard that Leblanc had moved into his parents' house with his new fiancée so they could save up to get married. *How fucking sweet!* Ink Stain was finally on his way to fulfilling his lifelong dream of having his own family, but he couldn't pay Mickey back. Fuck him.

"Where's my fucking money?" was what Youngblood wanted to know. He had his new heat—John "Dillinger" Barbados, the lanky gang member, fresh from his stint in prison—calling Leblanc, leaving him long, rambling, slightly menacing messages about getting together and resolving things. But Leblanc never called him back.

In April, the shit exploded for good. That was when Mickey took Nicole out to dinner at Mac's BrewPub. Mac's was a trendy Valley bar and restaurant that sported a reclaimed-barn look with vaulted redwood beams, and it was also where Leblanc's fiancée, Jasmine Violeta, worked, and Mickey knew this. That's why they were there. After a night of eating and drinking, the tab came to over a hundred dollars. Rather than paying it, Mickey wrote a message on the bill, and they left. The message told Violeta: "Have your cuntass boyfriend deduct it from our tab."

When he found out what Mickey had done, Leblanc went nucking futs. The very next day he called Mickey and again threatened him. "You can kiss your money good-bye. This is it, motherfucker. This is the turning point. There is no way you'll ever get your money. If I ever see you … you're dead."

Youngblood told Leblanc, "Go fuck yourself." He would collect his money one way or another, and he had Barbados step up the calls. Youngblood liked the way John worked. Barbados was the kind of guy who would rip you off, go out and sell your stuff, and then tell you he got jacked. But his screw was just loose enough to where Mickey figured he'd give Leblanc something to think about. Leblanc apparently didn't think about it long, because the very next day, when Mickey returned home from a day of flooring with his buddy Bill Lee, he received the shock of his life.

When he went into the backyard, Mickey found his five-year-old Akita, Zeus, his truly best friend in the world, hanging by his collar on the fence. When Mickey pulled him down, he broke down sobbing. He was crazy about that dog.

Zeus loved to bark and jump against the fence when people walked by, and this was made to look like his collar got caught when he jumped, strangling him. But Mickey knew better. He might not be able to prove it, but he knew who had killed his dog.

His suspicions grew stronger when, two weeks later, he received a phone call from Craig Lundgren, an investigator for Modern Insurance Company. Lundgren asked Mickey if he wouldn't mind coming down to the central office so Lundgren could take Mickey's recorded statement in person to clear up some issues that had arisen from Mickey's claim.

Mickey became quite agitated and told Lundgren there were no issues. His tricked-out silver 2000 Japanese car—the '69 Camaro of *The Fast and the Furious* generation—that Mickey had insured for thirty-five thousand dollars had been stolen. Modern made two payments, one for $22,799.03 and another for

$6,503.99, as compensation, and there were no issues. If Lundgren had a prob-lem with that, he could call Mickey's attorney, Sheldon Barnes, and deal with him about it. Then he hung up. It was what Mickey didn't tell Craig Lundgren that would have cleared up the issues.

One night in February, Mickey had taken Babbette out to dinner for sushi. He took the car and parked it on Bryant and Lopshire, and they went into the restaurant to eat. When they returned after dinner, the car was gone. Mickey jumped on his cell, and he called the police to report the car stolen and Modern Insurance to make his claim. He then called Luke at his mother's house. Luke's mom answered, and Youngblood gave her his singsong about how his car had been stolen. He then asked to speak to Luke. When Luke got on the phone, Youngblood gave him the same singsong and asked for a ride. Luke picked them up and drove Mickey and Babbette to Youngblood's house, and they all joked and laughed about getting away with the scam the whole way.

Youngblood knew his car was in the process of being systematically disman-tled so he could sell the rims and other expensive parts, with the remainder of the car being crushed. And that's where he had fucked everything up. Because back in the old days, when he and Leblanc were best buddies, when they acted and played like inseparable twins, Mickey confided some things to him that he never should have. He told Leblanc of his plan.

The plan had been simple and foolproof. The idea was to load the car up, piece by piece, before it was stolen. Mickey had it painted two-tone silver and had a two-tone leather interior. He added florescent lights, mirror glass windows that you could actually see yourself in, and neon lights inside the trunk. He poured in two thousand dollar rims, a sophisticated hydraulics system, and a sound system capable of rattling windows. Mickey Youngblood's ghetto-fabulous street car turned out so hot it ended up in the summer edition of Easy Eurorider, under a headline that read, *Flying Off Into Space With Mickey Youngblood's Wild Ride.*

But like an asshole, Mickey had taken Leblanc with him to buy the insurance. On the way over, he had bragged about how he was going to totally rip Modern off. How he was so clever by overinsuring the car. "But it's just a fucking nip car," Leblanc had told him. "It ain't fucking worth it, Mickey." Leblanc would soon find out how wrong he was.

Months later, Mickey learned that the day after his venture into Mac's Brew-Pub, Leblanc had made a venture of his own. Posing as Craig J. J. Azzizian, Leb-lanc had charged into the Modern Insurance Company office and told the heavyset female receptionist that Mickey Youngblood had filed a false report on the theft of his 2000 nip car. He added that Youngblood had conspired with "Ritchy," the owner of Benders, a body shop in the Valley, to steal the car and file a false claim with the insurance company. Leblanc finished by saying that he was "reporting the false insurance claim because Mickey Youngblood threatened my girlfriend." Lundgren took over from there, and Mickey was up shits creek.

Mickey's payback was to unleash Barbados again. Barbados started leaving Leblanc messages at all hours of the day and night. "Hey, homeboy, how ya doin'? How 'bout you give me a call? I'm at Mickey's house. We haven't talked for a while, ha-ha-ha." The laugh at the end would always be slow and deliberate. "Hey, man. What the fuck? Call me back. I thought we were homeys. You know Mickey's phone number." "Hey, homeboy, don't make me come down there. I'll have my homeboys deal with this like real men."

Leblanc then responded by breaking out Mickey's windows and threatening to kill his family, which now made it Mickey's turn to "bring it all to an end." He looked up at his father's ashen face.

"Well … you certainly fucked that up, didn't you?" Dick said.

Mickey glared at his father. "Well, no shit, Dad. A fucking moron could have told me that. Question is—what the fuck am I gonna do about it?"

"So where's his brother now?"

"I told you—some fucking dude has him."

Mickey's head jerked back as Dick sprang suddenly to his feet. "Who the fuck has him, Mickey?" Mickey ignored his father and stepped over to the other side of the deck. Dick stalked him. "I'm not fucking around, Mickey. Who has him?"

Mickey shook his head as his hands gripped the metal support bar. He leaned over the railing, and his eyes scanned the swimming pool below, the U-shaped complex of expensive townhouses that surrounded it. "It doesn't matter anymore."

"Don't give me that fucking feel sorry for yourself bullshit, okay?" Dick said. "What the fuck's the matter with you, Mickey? You have any fucking idea what's going to happen to you if anything happens to the kid?"

"I'm going to go to prison for the rest of my fucking life. That's what's going to happen."

"So tell me where the kid is!" Dick pleaded. "Maybe I can make something happen."

Mickey slapped the railing. "Like what, Dad? What can you make happen? I didn't want you involved in the first place."

"Well, you should've gotten me involved." Dick stepped right next to his son. "I could have helped you, Mickey. I wouldn't have let you get in this kind of bullshit, that's for sure."

Mickey's hand covered his face. He pivoted away from his father. His chest expanded, and he could feel a wave of darkness surging through him. And then it all cut loose. A fresh torrent of spilled emotion bursting from his eyes. The pain of no tomorrow filling the night. Dick twisted away and slinked to the other side of the table, as if embarrassed by his son's emotive expression. That was fine with Mickey. The time alone would allow him to purge his body of all the stress it had built up over the past several months. Mickey had driven himself into a senseless rage that had stuck to his insides and grown into a massive tumor that now spilled out in tears. He was glad Babbette wasn't there to see him, but he wished he hadn't lost it in front of his father like that.

For as long as he could remember, Mickey and his father never displayed emotions in front of each other unless it came from a place of rage. His dad's display of excitement was limited to his violent outbursts at Mickey whenever he fucked up. Anger and hatred had never been difficult for Dick Youngblood to display. But when it came to displaying any positive emotions, the man might as well have been a rock.

Mickey had grown up not knowing anything about ecstasy or joy, but he sure understood every nuance of how to foam at the mouth, explode, and yell. It was the same when he played in Little League. His old man would never compliment Mickey for making a good play. If he had a couple good swings of the bat, or he made a dazzling play in the field, Mickey didn't hear shit from the old man, because that's what was expected of him. But should Mickey botch a grounder at short, or muff a relay at second, or throw a tantrum and stomp his feet, his old man would practically have a seizure. He'd fly out of the dugout yelling at Mickey, totally embarrassing him in front of his teammates and their parents in the stands. The only coddling Mickey ever got from his old man was in the form of cursing and criticism and indignation when Mickey fucked up. Complementing Mickey for doing something positive just wasn't in his father's makeup. That's why the last thing Mickey would have expected—the furthest thing from his mind at the moment—was for his father to sprint over and grab him in a giant bear of a hug.

The taller Youngblood wrapped his arms around Mickey, holding him tight against his chest. He picked him up off his feet and swung him around in a circle. Mickey could hear his father's heartbeat and the stillness of the night in between his own snuffling. He was calmer now as his father held him, and their heads brushed against each other. Their ears touched, and Mickey's eyes popped open. He imagined the two of them looking like a couple little fags, and he peered up at the glass door and saw Babbette staring at them through the curtains. Mickey squirmed and pushed at his father until he let him go.

Dick straightened up and looked around, trying to figure out what had happened. He glanced over at the glass door, and the curtains were still moving. But Babbette wasn't watching anymore. Dick turned back to Mickey. "Why didn't you fucking come to me?"

"Why didn't I fucking come to you?"

"Yeah. Why didn't you say, 'Hey, Dad, I got this problem. I need some fucking help figuring out what to do?'"

"Why the fuck would I do that, Dad? All you do is criticize me. What the fuck was I going to say? Like I'm really going to fucking tell you that some guy threatened me. And then all you're going to do is tell me what a fucking asshole I am for having the guy around in the first place. It's not like you'd fucking say something supportive of me or anything. I have no idea why you would think I would fucking come to you."

"That's really fucking nice."

"It's the fucking truth."

"Yeah, well, your fucking truth, maybe. Fuck." Dick waved his hand and wagged his head. "Man, all I'm trying to say is, I could have fucking helped you if you'd bothered to say something."

"We're back to that same old question, Dad—how? How the fuck could you have helped me?"

Dick slid around to face him. "If you'd fucking tell me who has the kid, we can go and get him."

"Luke," Mickey Youngblood said. "Luke Ridnaur has the fucking kid."

"Jesus Christ." Dick's eyes began to register. "What the fuck does Luke Ridnaur have to do with any of this?"

"He's got the kid holed up at a hotel in San Floripez. I sent Bart up there to make sure everything's cool."

Dick's face glutted with surprise. "Bart Pray?" Mickey nodded. "You sent Bart Pray up there to make sure everything's cool?"

"Yeah."

"Bart Pray couldn't make a fucking ice cube cool in the Antarctic. What'd you fucking expect Pray to do?"

Mickey laughed pathetically. "Kill the kid."

Dick groaned miserably. "You sent Bart Pray up there to kill the kid?"

Mickey glanced at his watch and then back to his father. "We were going to kill the kid. Then we decided not to. It wasn't worth it. So we decided we were going to hold onto him until we came up with a better idea."

"Great," Dick said, his hands clasping together. "A better idea has arrived. Let's go get him right now." Dick grabbed Mickey's arm and tried to pull him toward the door, but Mickey brushed him away.

"Slow down, Dad, I told you. I tried calling him, but I couldn't reach him."

"You tried calling who?"

"Bart! Who the fuck we talking about? I tried paging him before you guys barged in here. He hasn't called me back yet."

Dick pushed over to the sliding glass door, his hand fidgeting with the handle. "Well, then let's go to a pay phone and give his ass another call."

Dick started to pull the glass door open, but Mickey's hand stopped him. "Dad, slow your ass down. I told you, he hasn't called me back yet. What's the fucking point of calling him if he doesn't call me back? Besides, it's fucking late. And he's probably sleeping."

Dick's face shrunk into a prune. "What the fuck are you talking about, Mickey? He's not sleeping if he's watching a fifteen-year-old kid."

"Then the kid's already fucking got away. Either he got away, or they let him go. Either way, Bart's not calling me back. And there's nothing I can do about it now. I'm sure the kid's already gone, probably."

Dick sniffed. "Probably?"

"Yeah. And the cops are probably on their way to arrest my fucking ass right now. And I'm fucked up the ass. And my fucking life is ruined. Don't you understand, Dad? I know I fucked up. I totally fucked it up, man."

"Because you were afraid of him."

Mickey's face twisted. "What?"

Dick stepped away from the door. "You were fucking scared of Rick Leblanc."

"I was not."

"That's why you fucking kidnapped his brother. Because you were fucking afraid of him."

"I fucking kidnapped his brother because … because the motherfucker still owes me money. He wouldn't return my phone calls. And I couldn't find him to kick his fucking ass. He hid from me like a little cunt. And then when I fucking tried to find him …" Mickey couldn't continue as his jaw began to vibrate. He wrapped his hand around his eyes and breathed in again. "There's no way out."

"There is if we can get the kid, Mickey. Where is he? Where's the fucking kid?"

Mickey's eyes dripped with wetness and anguish. "What the fuck could we possibly do? I can't let him go. His fucking brother would come back and pick up Rudy. And that'd be the end of it. I could just see that asshole waiting outside the house for Mom to come home. No telling what he might do, Dad. The guy's a fucking animal."

Mickey could feel the grave concern wash across his father's face. He imagined the gears of recognition stirring inside his father's head; his father's sudden understanding of what his son had been trying to tell him all along.

"You mean Rick Leblanc knows where we live?"

Chapter Thirty-Four

Wednesday—1:40 a.m.

Vegas Parsons grabbed the shovels out of the trunk, and Bart Pray slammed it shut. Vegas could see they were about a hundred yards from the fence that surrounded the gun range. Pray clicked on the flashlight and told Vegas, "Show me." Vegas hiked along the gravel shoulder, then up the steep trail into the hillside. Pray followed, leading Vegas with the beam from the flashlight. A warm breeze rustled the scrub brush that scraped Vegas' ankles as he weaved his way up the trail.

A half mile up, the area leveled off into a lunar escape. Huge boulders and large, red-colored rock outcroppings filled the landscape. This is where Vegas and his buddies used to come to get stoned and explore, to go bouldering, or to just sit on a rocky outcrop and watch the sun set into the Pacific Ocean. Tonight, the view of Bonita was nothing short of spectacular. With a galaxy of stars now twinkling overhead, Vegas felt as if he were in a movie or a dream. He felt as if he were having an out-of-body experience, that what he was doing really wasn't happening to *him*. He imagined soaring like an eagle down the canyon and over the ocean, and then all the way home, until he looked back and saw Pray huffing and puffing his way up the hill, carrying the bag. Vegas hated that bag. He thought about taking off and running up the trail, until Pray told him to "Stop."

Pray was wheezing, and he leaned against a giant boulder, using his arm as a pillow. After he caught his breath, he straightened up and took several more steps up the trail and then around a patch of scrub brush. Between a giant rocky outcrop lay a dirt area where he dropped his bag. "Start digging," he told Vegas.

Vegas didn't see himself having much of a choice. He threw down one of the shovels and started digging with the other. He broke into a sweat within the first minute. He was drenched within five minutes. After ten minutes, he was exhausted. The shovel constantly clanked off rocks and gravel, and the jolting sensation shot through his arms and shoulders like a jackhammer. He pounded for fifteen minutes without saying anything, because he didn't want to provoke that dude. He didn't want that gun coming out of that bag. His wrists hurt, and he rubbed his shoulder, and sweat dripped down in his eyes, but he had to keep digging. *As long as I keep digging, I'll be all right,* he kept telling himself.

Pray stood there watching Vegas dig every painful shovelful. And so Vegas kept digging. His body ached, and he didn't even want to think about who this hole he was digging might be for, because whenever he did, the answer scared him. He thought it might be for him. He stopped to catch his breath, and he heard a whacking sound. He turned to see Pray using the other shovel to chop branches off the huge, dry rolls of scrub that filled the landscape. The whole thing seemed totally surreal. Vegas was holding a shovel; the other guy had a gun. Bobby was so far away, and Vegas had no idea where it was all going to end. He thought about his parents and wondered why Barty would bring that gun up here if he wasn't planning on using it.

Vegas continued to dig. After digging into the reddish brown sandstone for what seemed like a week, his sweat-drenched face glistened in the soft glow of moonlight.

"That's enough," Pray suddenly told him. "Now stand back."

Vegas turned to see through the shadows the machine gun that was now out of the duffel bag and in Pray's hand. Vegas swiped at the sweat in his right eye with his left arm, and then he froze. He tried looking over at Pray's face, but the flashlight shone directly into his eyes. Vegas shielded the beam with his hand. He tried to get a read on the figure behind the light, and he realized his worst fear had suddenly become a reality.

He thinks I'm Bobby Leblanc.

Images of Mom and Dad and little sister Mandy shot through his mind like a movie reel. The sudden realization that he was never going to see them again paralyzed Vegas. All he could think about was that he was about to die. That the man Luke liked to call Barty was about to blow him away in the world's worst case of mistaken identity.

"He's about to kill me," Vegas heard himself mumble.

Bart Pray ignored him. "Step into the hole."

Vegas glanced back into the ditch he had just dug and told himself that under no circumstances would he ever step into that hole. Ever. So he took a large step forward, away from the hole.

"Stop," Pray told him.

"Look," Vegas said, putting his hands up because it seemed like the thing to do. "I'm not Bobby Leblanc. You've got me mistaken for somebody else."

"I know who you are," Pray said. "I'm not stupid. Now step back into the hole like I told you." He pointed the gun and flashlight at Vegas, and Vegas stepped back.

Wetness welled in Vegas' eyes. "Please listen, Barty—"

"My name's not fucking Barty," Pray said viciously. "Don't ever call me that again."

Vegas gazed at him apologetically. "Sorry, man. I didn't mean anything by it."

"I hate that name. You ever call me that again, and I'll …" Pray's words trailed off as his head cocked at an odd angle toward the hole.

"Look, uhm—what do you want me to call you then?"

"Don't worry about it."

"Okay, I won't worry about it. But my name's Vegas. Vegas Parsons. And I'm not—I'm not Bobby Leblanc. Bobby's about fifteen years old. A little taller than I am. In fact, he's the kid you saw sleeping on the other bed back at the hotel."

Pray didn't respond.

Vegas tried focusing his gaze through the intense brightness. "Look, man, I swear to God I'm not Bobby. Okay? You gotta believe me."

The black barrel of the gun silently raised and pointed at Vegas' chest.

Vegas uttered feebly as his teary gape bent upward into the blackness. He prayed to the heavens that he wouldn't get blasted.

A coyote's yelp from a distant canyon found his ears. As did the plethora of sounds the night had to offer—and laughter. His gaze dropped, and Vegas could see the callous sonofabitch standing behind his flashlight and gun, cracking his ass off, ready to off Vegas. Just like that. The guy thought it was hilarious.

What an asshole, Vegas thought. And then an even more important thought pinched his brain: in the right rear pocket of his swim trunks he had a picture ID that he could hand to Pray to prove who he was. "Wait, stop," he said, his voice oozing with panic. "Look I—I have ID. I can prove who I am. Don't shoot me. Please, don't shoot me."

Vegas knew he sounded like a squeaking pussy to this freak with the gun, but he didn't care. If a little whimpering saved his life, so be it. He jammed his fist into his back pocket and pulled out his wallet. He held it up in front of him with one hand, like the way they do on *Cops*. Just hold it out there, showing the guy he didn't have anything else in the other hand either. Then he scrambled to find his ID, only to drop the wallet and everything else into the hole. He hunched down, stabbed at the wallet, and wiped it off on his bathing suit. He fumbled through the leather slats until he found what he was looking for.

"Here it is! Here it is!" His finger stabbed the card. "My ID. I can prove who I am." He held the card up, flashlight beaming in his eyes. "Vegas Parsons. I'm Vegas Parsons. I'm not Bobby Leblanc. See, it says it right here. Please, you gotta believe me ..." But before he could finish his snivelling, the light went out. And just like that, Vegas found himself in total darkness.

He blinked several times. And he could begin to make out Pray's shadowy silhouette. The dude was still laughing at him. And a minute later, he told Vegas, "I know who you are. You're a big fucking cunt, that's who. Now let's go."

*   *   *   *

Luke had never run so fast in his life. He sprinted through the Frank's parking lot and didn't stop until he had reached the bottom of the steps at the San Floripez Inn. By the time he climbed the stairs, his breathing had turned to wheezing, and he thought he was going to pass out. He flew into the room and over to the bed, where Bobby was sleeping on his back. The kid looked comfortable, and his facial expression was one of peace. It looked as if the kid was having one fucking pleasant dream, and Luke hated to disturb him. But time was running out.

He reached his hand, ready to shake Bobby, when the stone gaze from the whiskey bottle sliced through the back of his head. *Just one more shot*, it told him. *Just one more shot.*

The double shot caught in Luke's throat and nearly gagged him. He doubled over, coughing the entire spray across the room. He coughed so hard, he felt as if his throat were going to forge through his heart. When the coughing spasms finally died down, he considered downing another shot, just to ease the pain from the first one, but he decided to smoke a blunt instead. He went out onto the balcony and started to light it, but stopped. *Fuck that noise.* There was simply not enough time. So he ran back inside, tossed the blunt on the table, and shook Bobby hard. "Dude, wake up—we gotta go."

Bobby groaned and then twisted his body, and then he settled back down on his side. Luke grabbed his shoulder and shook him harder. Suddenly, two bloodshot eyes sprang open. They turned their watery focus on Luke.

"Dude, can you hear me?" Luke asked.

Bobby blinked but didn't say anything.

"If I let you go right now, will you promise not to call the cops on me?" Bobby stretched into a yawn, and his eyes closed, and Luke couldn't tell whether he heard him or not. "Dude, did you hear what I said?"

Bobby's eyes popped back open. "What? Why, what's going on?"

"Just answer the question. I don't have time to fuck around here. If I let you go—"

Bobby's head shook. "No, of course, I won't go to the cops. I told you that." He pushed up on his elbows. "You've been good to me, Luke. I understand what's going on. My brother shouldn't have done these things. I'm okay with it." He glanced around the room, and saw no one. "But I thought someone was coming to pick me up."

"So did I. Now, get up. Let's go."

"Where we going?"

Luke's eyes were methamphetamine wide. "You're getting out of here. Let's go."

Bobby sat up on the bed. "Why? What's going on?"

Luke sprinted over to the table and shoved the blunts and the rest of the weed into his pocket. "Don't ask questions, Bobby—just get up, and let's go."

Bobby's eyes blinked around the room as he tried to gather his bearings.

Luke was practically seeing double. His legs wobbled as he scrambled around the room, checking and double-checking, making sure he was leaving nothing behind. When he spotted Vegas' shorts on the floor, he nearly came to tears. "Fuck."

"What?" Bobby asked.

"I can't leave without Vegas." Luke fell into the orange chair like a deflated carcass. "Fuck! I don't know what to do."

"Why, what's going on?" Bobby shot another look around the room and then over toward the bathroom, but he didn't see anyone. "Where is he?"

"Who the fuck knows?" Luke reached over and grabbed the shorts off the floor. He started to say something, and then he fell back into the chair.

"What's up, dude? What's the matter?"

Luke gazed across the room hopelessly. He stood on the precipice of no return, and he had no idea which direction to jump. If he left now with Bobby, there was no telling what Pray would do to Vegas. Barty would be totally pissed when he got back and found the kid gone. Since Pray was so dedicated to Mickey, Luke was afraid Pray would retaliate against Luke by hurting his friend. Luke couldn't, in good conscience, let him do that. He couldn't leave Vegas

behind. He was going to have to get Bobby out of there and take his chances with
Pray when he got back.

He leapt out of the chair and pulled out his wallet. He yanked out a
fifty-dollar bill and passed it to Bobby.

Bobby's eyes gorged on the the money in his hand.

"I want you to go down to the lobby. No, not the lobby. Fuck." Luke slapped
his hands against his hips and surveyed the room. "Someone could see you down
there."

"What are you talking about?" Bobby asked.

"Nothing. I was talking to myself." And thinking. And trying to get his heart
to calm down. Luke was having second thoughts about everything. So he
snatched the fifty out of the kid's hand. "No, as a matter of fact, I'll walk down
with you. Let's go." He pulled Bobby up off the bed and pushed him toward the
door.

The plan would be for Luke to walk nonchalantly down the stairs with Bobby.
And to take him by the pool or some other out of the way place, where Bobby
could hide until Luke came down and picked him up later. Once he figured out
how to get Vegas out of there. But then Luke stopped. "Fuck."

"What?"

Luke grabbed Bobby's arm, and pulled him back. He wanted to give Bobby
back the fifty, but he didn't think that would be very smart either. If he lets
Bobby go, the first thing he'd do was take off and find a cop, or a cop would find
him. And Luke would be totally rat-fucked. A teenager out this late, all by himself, would be a total sitting duck. But that's what he had to do. Unload the kid,
and Luke unloads his conscience.

He shoved the fifty back into Bobby's fist. "This is what we're going to do.
We're going to walk down the hallway. And I'm going to drop you off by the
pool." Bobby nodded. "If I don't come back in say an hour, then I want you to
take off, okay?" Bobby nodded again. "I want you to head down County Street
about eight or nine blocks. And then take a right on Mariposa, okay? Mariposa.
And then I want you to just keep on walking. And I want you to watch out for
Barty."

Bobby's hand shot up like he was in class.

"What?"

"Who's Barty?"

"Don't worry about it. Just watch out for someone driving a lime-like Jap-car,
okay? You can't miss it. It looks like this really big lime."

Bobby gawked at him blankly.

"Okay?"

"Okay," Bobby said.

"Good—let's go." Luke started to open the door just as Bobby reached to shake his hand, and they banged fists. "Dude, what are you doing?" Luke asked.

"I just, you know, I …" The kid sniffled and Luke began to feel a tingle in his chest. Things were getting really mushy, and Luke didn't want it to end this way.

"Dude, we don't really have time for this shit, okay? You got to get out of here, now."

"I know, man. I just wanted to say thank you for everything, that's all."

"Dude, send me a thank-you card. Now let's go."

Luke reached for the door again, when Bobby thrust his arm out and hugged him. Luke gave him the straight-arm shimmy, and pushed the kid away. "Dude, another time. Okay? Now can we go?"

The kid's eyes veered around the room one last time. He inhaled deeply as a determined energy permeated his face. "Yeah, sure. Let's go."

"Finally, Jeez Louise." Luke's head shook as he pushed him aside and grabbed the door. Unfortunately, at that exact instant, the door bolted inward and slammed Luke's hand cruelly.

"Ow!" Luke yelled, jerking his hand back and shaking it violently. His knuckle screamed, and he thought he might've broken it. He glanced over at Bobby who stood frozen; jaw agaped; eyes wide as devil lakes.

When the door burst inward, a pair of bloodshot eyes protruding through a mound of reddish-brown dirt got shoved into the room. The eyes belonged to Vegas, and they bugged wide as saucers. His body was covered from head to toe in earthen smudge marks. He looked like a cross between a cartoon character and one of those refugee kids in the photos pleading for food sponsorships.

Bart Pray pushed in behind him, carrying the green duffel bag. When Luke saw this, he nonchalantly reached over and snatched the fifty out of Bobby's hand, and tucked it into his back pocket.

Pray flushed with anger. "What're you doing, Luke?"

Pray watched Luke squirm for an answer. "Dude, I'm just, uh, you know …"

"Yeah, I know," Pray said, muscling Vegas out of the way. "Were you going somewhere?"

Luke's head shook enthusiastically. "No way, dude. I would never do that."

Pray slammed the door shut behind him. "Where were you going, Luke?"

Luke stepped back into the living area. "Dude, I swear—nowhere."

"Bullshit."

Bobby couldn't stop gaping at the dirt caked on Vegas' shoes. Dirt and sweat had formed muddy red streaks down his chest, legs, and arms.

Pray pushed everyone into the sleeping area and threw the duffel bag down onto the bed. The zipper wasn't zipped, and the bag slung open, and the barrel of the gun stuck straight out. Luke's eyes ballooned, and he twisted and shot Pray a "what the fuck are you doing, asshole?" look. Pray glanced down at the bag and grinned callously. He then reached down and quickly zipped it up. He hauled up the bag and moved back into the bathroom.

But it was too late. The cat was out of the bag. Bobby had seen the gun.

Luke watched Bobby's eyes bug and his jaw smack the floor. Vegas had seen it too. "I need to get a ride home," he announced nervously.

"It'll have to wait," Luke snapped, his eyes not leaving Bobby's.

Bobby breathed heavily at what he had just seen. "Why does he have a gun?"

"Dude, it's okay, man," Luke said. "Don't worry about it. Everything's gonna be totally cool, okay?"

"No, it's not okay." Bobby gazed at Luke with complete dismay. "You knew what was going on the whole time."

"Dude, that's not true."

"You knew he had a gun. And you weren't going to say anything about it."

Luke's head shook manically. "Dude, I'm telling you, that's just not true."

"You're in on it, Luke. Just like the rest of them." Bobby's voice edged with panic as he glanced over at Vegas and then back to Luke. "Look, Luke, I'm sorry for what my brother did. That was so uncool of him. But you know what? My parents will pay for everything he destroyed of Mickey's. I swear to God. They will pay for every cent of it. Please, don't let him shoot me."

Luke was about to respond inanely, when Pray blasted out of the bathroom. His eyes were inflamed, and his finger stabbed through the air at Bobby. "Shut your fucking mouth." He whirled to Luke. "Tape his fucking mouth shut now."

Luke shook his head, but he didn't say anything.

Pray's crazed eyes combed the room until he spotted what he wanted. He pushed over to the dresser, squatted down, and picked up a white sock off the floor. He stood and rotated toward Bobby. Suddenly, his left hand reached around and gripped the back of the kid's head, while his right hand stuffed the sock in Bobby's mouth, tightly.

Bobby's eyes burst wide, as muffled gurgling sounds leaked from his throat. Luke charged over, and slapped his hands on Pray's shoulders. He yanked him away from the kid. "Look, dude, you've got to try to keep your fucking cool. Come on, we all gotta keep cool."

Bobby started freaking out. His face puckered, and whimpers spewed from his insulated mouth. His body vibrated uncontrollably, and Luke feared the kid might have a seizure. He knew he had to cool Bobby down, now. He had to cool himself down as well.

"I'm sorry about all this, Bobby." Luke's hands waved through the air like a mime. "The gun's just in there to scare the hell out of you, okay? That's all."

"Yeah, man," Pray chimed in, maliciously. "Just to scare you."

Luke saw Pray smiling, and he tried to match it. Bobby gazed back at the smiling jerks, scared shitless.

Pray said, "And that's what's going to happen to you if you tell anyone what happened. Okay?"

Bobby nodded as a chain of tears began streaming down his face.

Pray turned to Luke. "Now tape him up."

"Don't be ridiculous," Luke cried. "We're going to leave and walk outside into public. And you want to tape him up? Are you fucking crazy?"

"I ain't doin' nothing," Bobby whimpered inaudibly through the sock; tears staining his face. *"I'm not going to say anything, I swear."*

Luke watched Pray's big old head revolve slowly, as if he was contemplating the situation. Bobby's eyes bulged pleadingly at Luke. And Luke pleaded back. "Dude, I swear to God, we're going to make sure you get home, okay? We're going to take you to meet some people who will take you home. So just be cool. Take a deep breath, and calm down."

Luke watched as Bobby took several deep breaths and tried desperately to calm himself. The river of tears did soon dissipate. Bobby's breathing began to even out. His chest wasn't heaving as violently as it had just a minute ago. He appeared much more at ease; the story having been sold to Bobby, just as Young-blood had sold it to Luke.

"Barty was just teaching you a lesson," Luke continued. "He'll be cool from now on. Won't you, Barty?" Luke patted Pray on the shoulder like they had been buddies for years.

"Yeah, real fucking cool," Pray said, snarl-smiling. "So you'll keep your fucking mouth shut if I don't tape you up, right?"

Bobby nodded slowly, reminding Luke of an Easter pig with tears trickling down its cheeks and an apple stuffed in its mouth. Luke reached over and pulled the sock from between Bobby's jaws.

"I swear to God I won't say anything," the kid said, flexing his chops. "I will be totally cool. You can trust me."

Luke and Pray glanced at each other, and smiled insincerely. When they turned back to Bobby, he too was smiling. And wiping the wetness from his cheeks with the backs of his hands. Everybody just smiled at each other, and the moment looked like a goddamned smile-a-thon.

Chapter Thirty-Five

Wednesday—2:48 a.m.

It was balmy and late. A slight breeze rustled the fronds of the king and queen palms that lined the hotel property. The city appeared asleep except for the two teenage boys and the two young men slipping through the parking lot of the San Floripez Inn.

They were silent because Bart Pray carried a green duffel bag with a loaded machine gun inside. And it was what that bag contained that scared the hell out of Bobby Leblanc. The only thing that kept his legs moving was the fact that deep down in his heart, he knew Luke Ridnaur would never let him down. He knew that the whole routine back in the hotel room was an act, a performance to try to scare him. That gun would never come out of the bag to really hurt him, and there really wasn't anything to worry about. Luke had said as much straight to Bobby's face. "Dude, I swear to God, we're going to take you home."

Bobby believed him then, and he still did now.

So, the story had changed a little. And they were now taking him "to meet some dudes who are going to take you home." If that's what Bobby needed to do to get home, he could live with it. He'd be more than happy to rendezvous with a flock of gay Peruvian goat herders, if it got him any closer to his parents' house. Luke had never failed him before, so Bobby couldn't fathom why he would now. They had known each other for a long time, and Luke had even met Bobby's parents. They had built an incredible bond over the last three days just by hanging out and talking about stuff. Bobby had really come to trust and appreciate the guy. Luke had made a special effort to act as a buffer between Mickey and Bobby. Luke had given Youngblood a rash of shit in Bobby's defense, and Bobby appreciated it tremendously.

Bobby truly believed they were just trying to scare him, and it worked. He was petrified. Bobby would never tell a living soul about anything ever again. He would be allowed to go home, to see his family, and he'd play the mute for the rest of his life, if that's what they wanted him to do. He would do whatever it took to get home, whatever it took to keep that weird dude with the mole on his face from taking his gun out of that bag.

As Pray approached the car, he tossed something through the shadows that bounced square off Luke's chest and fell to the ground. Luke grimaced. The jangle sounded like keys.

"You drive," Pray said.

"Dude, we've been through this." Luke rubbed his bruised chest. "I told you, I don't know how to drive stick."

Pray muttered, "Fucking cunt," and he angrily stooped over and picked up the keys. Then he marched around the car, and climbed behind the wheel. Luke climbed in the passenger's side and rode shotgun. Vegas climbed in behind him, with Bobby riding behind the driver.

The battered lime menace backed out of the space and pulled around the black asphalt of the parking lot. After stopping for a passing car on Andrade, Pray turned left.

"So where we going?" Bobby asked groggily.

There was no response. Pray's eyes remained fixed on the road ahead. Vegas was a statue, focused straight ahead at the back of the seat that crammed his long legs into his chest.

"You know where we're going, Luke?" Bobby asked.

Luke sat upright, then he glanced over his shoulder. "Vegas, where we going up here?"

Vegas leaned up between the seats. "Take a left up here."

Pray took a sweeping left at the next light without stopping.

Luke's head swiveled again. "Vegas, where is it that we're taking Bobby?"

The reflection of headlights from an oncoming car bathed Vegas' face in a hard glow of yellow-white light. His eyes were glossy and wet, and his mouth and lips were dry and cracked. "We're going to Skeleton Jaw."

Luke's eyes shifted to Bobby. "That's where we're meeting the people who are taking you back to the Valley."

Bobby fell back into his seat. Sedated, exhausted, and sleep deprived, he could scarcely muster a nod. He was so completely fucked up, he was numb. He could barely feel his legs in the tight back seat, and a tingling sensation, bigger than the one in his head, ran down the length of his arms through to the ends of his fingertips. He had been on a three-day drinking and smoking and pill-popping binge like none other in his young life, and his body displayed the devastating results.

Even though he was only fifteen, Bobby Leblanc had experienced more than his share of party time. Pot smoking had become an obsession. He had chased the high of smoking pot from the moment he woke up in the mornings to the time he took off his sneakers and fell asleep at night. Tranquilizers had also become an addiction. Fostered by a brother who liked to trek across the border with his hoodlum friends and buy the friendly little blue pills by the jarful for about a buck apiece, over the counter. Rick would then lay fistfuls on his younger brother upon his return. And Bobby took them. And he searched for drugs to steal from his mother. Who had the greatest collection of pills Bobby never saw, because she also was great at hiding them and at hiding all evidence of her psychological weaknesses from Bobby so he would not get any ideas of how not to act.

Bobby's exposure to pharmaceuticals had led him to an addiction that resulted in his consuming most of the thirty blue pills during the three days of his captivity. He had smoked a ton of pot each day, while averaging several beers and shots of the hard stuff. His stay with Luke had become a nonstop party. And it was no wonder he felt so out of sorts, so completely drained and lethargic, as the car ride carried him deeper into the darkened foothills above San Floripez.

The low-slung trees and scrub brush that rose from the blackened hillsides posed a menacing backdrop for Bobby's trip into the unknown. To the side of the road, a sign basked in the car's headlights read 267, and Bobby wondered who the hell was going to meet him up here. Then, a low, rumbling, buzzing sound seized his attention. On instinct, he patted his pockets, checking for his pager. Then he remembered Youngblood had taken it from him on Sunday.

"What's that?" He heard Luke ask. For the longest second, nobody said anything. Then Luke gazed over at the driver. "You know what that sound is?"

Pray turned to Luke, his face a display of irritation. "It's my fucking pager."

Luke pumped his head. "Aren't you going to see who it is?"

"It doesn't matter who it is."

Luke thought about that for a moment. "What if it's Mickey?"

Pray shot him that look again, and Luke said nothing else.

The serpentine road plus a heavy dose of nerves gave Bobby's stomach a queasy feel. His eyes closed, and he tried to imagine where they were going to meet these people. And who were these people they were supposedly going to meet? The ride up the swerving 267 proved deafeningly quiet. The only noise was the sucking sound of wind pouring in through the cracked rubber seal that lined the driver's window. It was the same sound that Bobby's mind made as he pondered the illogic of the moment. It was completely unrealistic to believe they were going to meet anyone up here. Luke and Vegas and this other dude weren't taking him to meet somebody to take him home. And they weren't taking him up here to scare him either. They were driving him up to a deserted location to kill him. They were going to leave him up here for the buzzards and the maggots, and Bobby's heart arrested with panic.

He pulled himself up against the back of the driver's seat, and his voice cracked with alarm. "I swear to God, my parents will pay Mickey back. Please don't do this. Please, Luke! I don't want to die!"

Pray's neck rotated like Linda Blair. "Shut your fucking ass!"

Bobby cringed and shrunk back into his seat. Bloated whimpers bellowed from his throat, and the waters burst the dam. Rivers of tears streamed out of his swollen eyes. He was going to die, and he couldn't believe it.

Luke twisted, and in a much calmer voice, said, "Calm down, little man. Everything's going to be all right. We're going to take you home."

Pray shifted drastically in his seat, his eyes focused on the road. He wore the face of a man who wanted to tear someone's heart out.

Luke recognized that look. "Hey, dude, be fucking cool, okay?"

"Don't tell me to be fucking cool. I told you we should've taped him up."

Luke said nothing; shrinking away from Pray like a dog retreating from a fire hydrant.

They continued their ascent into what looked like the heart of a forest, in dead silence; and Bobby's snuffling whimpers. After one particularly nauseating turn, Vegas leaned up in his seat. "You take a left up here." Pray slowed before taking the left, and then he took a quick right down a deserted road. There were no signs of life, and Bobby hadn't seen a car in the last ten minutes. It was so dark he could barely make out the silhouette of large trees that drooped down, giving the road a creepy horror look. Fright bumps popped up all over his arms. He rubbed them up and down with numb fingers, trying to bring life to his cold and dirty skin. The night air was hot, yet Bobby could feel shivering in his spastic limbs. He wondered if this was the feeling of impending death.

"Is that it?" Pray said, pointing straight ahead into utter darkness.

Vegas leaned up in his seat and gazed through the windshield. "Yeah." He leaned back just as quickly.

The car pulled up into a fenced off driveway. As they turned around, Bobby could make out a sign standing up the hill ten yards off the road that said something about a gun club. Pray pulled the car along the dirt shoulder of the dark narrow road and killed the engine. "Get out," he said, opening the driver's door. "Let's go."

Vegas leaned up between the seats, his face drenched in perspiration. "I think I'll just stay down here in the car."

Pray angrily twisted in his seat. "I said, let's go! All of us."

Vegas glanced at Bobby, then quickly away when Bobby tried to meet his gaze. He opened the door and climbed out. Bobby did the same.

Outside the car, Pray popped the trunk. He reached in and grabbed a white, plastic Frank's bag. Inside the bag, he found a roll of duct tape, which he dropped in the duffel bag. He wadded up the plastic bag and threw it in the bushes. He lifted the duffel bag out of the trunk, zipped it closed, and shut the trunk. He twisted to Vegas.

"You lead the way."

Vegas started walking up the dark narrow road, away from the car. Bobby followed him, followed by Luke, with Pray, carrying the duffel bag and flashlight, bringing up the rear. They walked about thirty yards before disappearing into the rock formation. They headed south, up and over the rocks. Even with Pray's pointing the way with the flashlight, Bobby still had a tough time seeing his way up the hill.

The path was narrow and uneven; it cut through dense strands of manzanita and scrub oak. Large roots and rocks jutted out from the earthen path, causing Bobby to trip practically every other step. Halfway up the ridge, he fell. When he tried to get up, he felt himself being dragged and then pushed from behind by Pray, which made him stumble and fall all over again. When he got up, he brushed off his hands and knees, and he fell back in line behind Luke.

The thought of having no idea where they were going freaked Bobby out again. They were hiking up a dark path into some mountain area where there was no way his brother or anyone else was going to find him. There were no lights whatsoever, other than the flashlight in Pray's hand. Bobby could scream his little heart dry, and no one would ever hear him. He hadn't seen a house for ten miles back down the 267. All this talk about meeting someone to take him home was bullshit, and he couldn't believe he had fallen for it. They weren't meeting anyone. Not up here, anyway. Nobody ever came up here.

Bobby squinted and surveyed up the trail through the darkness and the thick bush. He thought about taking off—and running and screaming and hiding—but what good would any of that do? *They* had the only light and the only gun, and there were three of them against just him. They'd probably catch and shoot his ass before he could get away. Besides, Bobby was so exhausted, he couldn't run and hide, even though his life depended on it. Bobby Leblanc was about to die for being the brother of Rick Leblanc, sentenced to death for running away from his problems at home. But why?

Everybody had domestic problems. It was part of growing up. So why did Bobby have to be the one to pay? Weren't his brother and parents at least a little bit responsible for the mess he'd gotten himself into? He loved his brother to death, but Rick had made a mess of his own life and had pretty much fucked Bobby's up too. Rick had been cut loose on the streets, joining gangs and selling drugs, at a very young age. At twelve years old, he'd started slashing tires and stealing cars. Two years later he was arrested for attacking someone with brass knuckles. At fourteen, Rick became the national karate champion, and then he brought home a nine-millimeter handgun and got thrown out of the house by his father. At fifteen, he ran away from home for good. And from that point on, he moved from one household to another, living with girlfriends or karate instructors, always begging for someone to understand him. But Rick never got settled, never had a place he could call home. And Bobby blamed his parents for that.

He loved his mother beyond belief, but she had a rough side to her that made you want to crack your teeth against a cement curb. The woman grated on you with an air of superiority that Bobby tried to ignore. Their lives had turned into a battle of wills, and his parents' two wills were kicking Bobby's ass. They came down on him so hard and so often that he nearly suffocated. Bobby's life amounted to an overstructured prison sentence that gave him no time to be who *he* wanted to be. His mom helped him choose his classes, his meals, his bedroom décor, and his lifestyle. She made every effort to account for his every activity from the time he awoke in the morning to the time he slept at night. And when Bobby decided to cross the line, his father was there to play hardball and knock him back around.

Max Leblanc used to do the same thing to Rick. While growing up, all Rick had ever wanted was a place to eat and sleep, and a home with enough structure to help him deal with life without suffocating him. His father never provided that for him during either one of his marriages. The man was a workaholic whose solutions to their dysfunctional family existence included sending Rick to counseling, encouraging Rick to take his Ritalin, moving into an apartment with Rick, and taking Rick to the store every day to learn a trade that Rick was bored stiff learning.

Bobby's father worked too much and never took the time to try to understand what his first son's needs really were. Receiving no substantive nurturing from his mother or his father and stepmother, Rick turned to the streets. But the streets provided zero structure, and with it came the compunction for Rick to live life fast and furiously 24/7. He had to party and fuck and go crazy on anyone who dared to venture into his distorted path toward self-destruction. All his actions, all the crazy-assed trouble he got himself into, served as a cry to his father and his mother, and indirectly, to Bobby's mom, and they all failed to hear it.

Bobby's mother made no effort whatsoever to make Rick feel at home, and neither did Rick's father. The only time he dealt with Rick was out of a place of anger whenever Rick acted out. Whenever Rick tried to move back into the house, his father would always read him the riot act first thing. Max Leblanc would impose restrictions on Rick that everyone knew he could never and would never accept. By nightfall, Rick would always be back out on the streets. By rejecting Rick at home, Bobby's mother and father played an indirect part in creating the angry forces that fueled not only Bobby's kidnapping, but also his death march up this hill. Not having a stable home environment caused Rick to go crazy on the streets, where he spun out of control on drugs and alcohol and violence, and he built up this intense anger toward his family that bubbled over during the time he lived with Youngblood. When they had their falling out, Rick then focused all that anger and hatred into terrorizing Youngblood, and Youngblood retaliated by grabbing Bobby.

But what spread dread deepest through Bobby's heart, even more than the failures of his parents and brother, were those of his own. Bobby had simply refused to grow up. He had neglected to accept the responsibility for who and what he had become. Bobby would have never been in the position he faced if he had been doing what he should have been doing, rather than following in his brother's footsteps. Bobby had gone off the deep end both at home and in school, and he got into fights regularly. His brother had done the same thing when he was growing up.

At a young age, Rick had grown street-tough and street-wise, stealing cars and dealing dope, and strong-arming small-time drug dealers. While Rick led practically the entire Lopshire Division on high-speed auto chases through the Valley, Bobby lounged around his parents' house, watching TV and playing video games. Rick was a natural athlete, while Bobby was uninterested in athletics. Rick hung out in tattoo parlors, snorted crank with Hell's Angels, and sold drugs by the pound. Bobby had to battle his mother just to get out of the house to smoke pot in the park down the street. He sold little dime bags to friends to support his own habit.

Although raised from relatively divergent backgrounds, Bobby and his brother ended up steering toward the same broken path. After getting thrown out of two schools for fighting, Rick stopped going altogether. He partied and sold drugs and terrorized the Valley all through his teens. Bobby also got thrown out of two schools, but the only thing he terrorized were boxes of donuts whenever he got the munchies. Bobby thought and acted as if he were tough, but the reality was that he couldn't fight his way out of a wet paper bag. And he knew it. He was the gentle, poetic soul, where Rick was the dark street pugilist. Where Rick, fueled by the anger he held toward his family, trained intensely to become an American karate champion, Bobby lounged around the house, smoked pot, played video games, and talked a lot of shit to his mom. Where Rick attacked people who crossed him with a violent vengeance, Bobby got his ass kicked more times than he won. That's why Rick survived and even thrived on the streets, while Bobby got browbeaten by his mother at home and was now being serenaded with the song of the executioner.

The biggest irony to Bobby's miserable end rose from the pangs he held in his heart for his mother. He couldn't believe how much he missed her. Where he had avoided her like the plague before his internment, he now reveled in the idea of being with her, of cradling into her arms, of letting her kiss him. It was funny, too, but the older Bobby had gotten, the less he let his mother near him, let alone kiss him. Mothers loved to smother their babies in kisses and hugs, and his mom was no exception. Only, she took it to an extreme. Bobby was in high school, yet she insisted on treating him as if he were a little boy, always trying to kiss him and tuck him into bed, and it drove him ballistic. He would be stoned out of his mind, wanting to be left alone, and he'd yell at her, telling her to get out of his room. But now he missed it. He missed his mom's touch, the softness of her hair, her soothing voice when he needed to be comforted.

He also missed Anja Johannson. His mind sped with all the things he wanted to tell his ex-girlfriend. He wanted another chance to show Anja how much she really meant to him. He wanted to kiss her beautiful face, to make love to her the way she deserved it. He wanted to sweep her away on his magic carpet and fly her to the heavens without ever looking back. It shattered his heart to think he might never have that chance, that he would never again gaze into the blueness of her oceans.

He thought about his sister Lisa. And his beautiful niece Koya, who adored him beyond belief. He was very close to Lisa, and she'd bring Koya over. And the little girl would always ask, "Where's Unco Bobo?" She couldn't say Uncle Bobby, but she loved her Unco Bobo. And he loved her. She'd come up to his room and ask him to help her draw. He'd pull out some paper and give her a couple pens, and she'd crawl down on the floor and start drawing. Her work was primitive, but she'd finish it and proudly hand the drawing to Bobby, and he'd hang it up on his wall. He had a whole wall filled with her beautiful little drawings. He felt the sting of sadness in his chest, and he wondered who would help her draw when he was gone. And what would his mom tell little Koya now when she came over and asked, "Where's Unco Bobo?"

Bobby sniffled and wiped away the tears draining down his face. He took a deep breath and forced himself not to weep. If this really was the end, he knew he had to face it like a man. He couldn't be a pussy, and he couldn't cry. *No matter what happens, I will not cry,* was what he kept telling himself—but then he saw it. And it startled the hell out of him.

The most spectacular view of coastline Bobby had ever seen in his life stood right there before him. They had reached the top of the path, and he didn't even realize it at first. He had been chugging so hard and was so completely distraught that he didn't notice the terrain change from a scrub path to this vast gaping maw of rock that Vegas had referred to as Skeleton Jaw.

It was unreal.

As a million stars twinkled overhead, this intense moonlight swept across these huge sandstone formations that protruded from the earth like stone soldiers guarding the gates to heaven. And that's when Bobby gazed upward and prayed for another chance. He cried in his heart and to God—if there truly were such a thing—to lend him a hand and carry him away. He had paid his price and was scared shitless. He'd spent a lifetime saying his prayers at home and trying to be kind to old ladies, and he would relish one more opportunity to remain alive.

But his cries went unheeded. And his eyes widened with imminent gloom the moment Pray shoved him from behind, launching him back into reality and up the rocky path. It was only seconds later, when the sweet thunder of voices resonated down the path, that Bobby heard what he believed to be the sound of his brother's voice.

Chapter Thirty-Six

Wednesday—3:22 a.m.

At first, it sounded like the voices of a man and a woman. Bobby wasn't sure that anyone else had heard them, because they all just continued up the trail until Vegas stopped at a big flat L-shaped rock. Vegas climbed up on top of it for a better view. Bobby did the same. He heard them again, only this time the voices were followed by laughter, and one of them was definitely female. Everyone else must have heard them too, because they all stood frozen in place. One by one, their gazes bent up the path.

Vegas breathed heavily and jumped off the rock. As his eyes grew wider, the voices drew nearer. "I can't go any farther," he said.

"Shut up," Pray snapped.

The voices grew, and this was obviously a hiking trail of some sort, and those voices were apparently coming from hikers, a man and a woman, who were probably up there for a reason. Which meant there was no way these guys were up here to kill Bobby, especially if those hikers were here to take him home.

Luke and that dude had both insisted they were taking Bobby to meet some people who were going to take him home, and Bobby hadn't believed them at first. But here they were, and Bobby felt embarrassed by the fact he ever doubted Luke's word. He wanted to apologize, but Luke was too busy ogling up the trail. Bobby felt so excited by the prospects of going home that he wanted to somersault all the way down the hill. He was going home, and that's all that mattered. He couldn't get his mind to stop singing it.

He couldn't wait to run off to that unkempt sliver of land near his house where they had built a small fort; they used to smoke joints there and watch the sunset. He would get to see his mom again—and his dad, his brother and sister, and his favorite little niece in the whole world. He would draw pictures with her and buy her a whole new art set. He was going to be the best uncle little Koya ever had. Bobby relished the idea of holding her little body in his hands and letting her sleep on his chest. He never realized he had so much to live for, so much to be grateful about.

He realized something else too. His parents had been right about him all along. Maybe their methods were a little lame, and maybe they screwed up with Rick, but in the end, they were right about Bobby. He had spent a lifetime trying to grow up to be somebody he wasn't. It seemed like the right thing to do—take off, run away, and ignore the responsibilities he faced as a kid growing up. That's what Rick had done, and that's what Bobby was doing at the time he got picked up. He had had a fight with Anja once where she told him to quit trying to be Rick Leblanc. Bobby laughed in her face. He laughed in all their faces, because that's what Rick would have done.

Bobby and his parents had spun apart and had practically become adversaries, and he was determined to change all that. He might have been Bobby Leblanc— the not so infamous Leblanc brother—but that was okay. When he got back, Bobby would learn to be at ease in his own skin. He would learn how to recognize and appreciate being just a kid growing up in a supportive and loving household. Every family had problems, and each member needed to learn to deal with those problems and communicate the solutions in a loving, heartfelt way. Bobby was going to try to learn to do that with his family. He was going to learn how to love his parents the right way.

For the first time, he thought how cool it would be to go back to work for his father and to allow him to groom Bobby to take over the family business, the same way Bobby's father had been groomed by Bobby's grandfather. And then again, maybe not. But that was the point, right? It was a whole new ballgame, and Bobby could do whatever he wanted.

He might even become a famous actor. He loved drama, and he had always wanted to act. He had a funny side to him that could entertain a room full of people anytime he found himself in a room full of people. Bobby was determined to become everything he should have been, and that meant with Anja Johannson as well. He would work hard to give her the world. He would become the loving son his mom deserved. He didn't want to be a hood like his brother. That wasn't Bobby Leblanc. As Michael Jackson used to sing, "I'm a lover, not a fighter." *That* was Bobby: The lover of beautiful women. He really wasn't a fighter. He hated fighting. He just wanted to sit back and appreciate the fact that he really did have everything in the world; he no longer had the need to be like Rick.

He took in a deep breath, and he smelled sage and love in the air. Millions of stars shimmered beneath the night's blackness, and the voices turned into two hikers, a man and a woman, coming down the trail, laughing and talking. Bobby squinted, trying to see who it was until Pray slid over right in front of him, blocking his view. Vegas worked around Pray to also get a better view.

Pray whispered, "I want you guys to shut up and keep walking." He signaled for everyone to follow him. Bobby glanced over at Luke's concerned face, and then he climbed down off the rock.

"Be cool," Pray said. "Allow them to walk by."

Everyone stood there huddled behind Pray, as a man and a woman in their late twenties hiked down the hill. When they approached, they all exchanged hellos. Both Luke and Pray shot Bobby "shut the fuck up" looks, causing Bobby to swallow all the words that filled his throat. He could clearly see that the man was not Rick; the woman he did not recognize either. And the dread of realization settled heavily into Bobby's chest.

As the couple continued down the hill, Pray reached back and grabbed Vegas by the arm. He yanked him up the path, and Vegas tripped over a rock. He got up and started hiking up the hill, then stopped and turned around. Pray stopped and faced him. Vegas' eyes were bloodshot, and it looked as if he'd been crying. "I can't go on."

"Don't start this bullshit," Pray said depravedly. "Turn around, and let's go."

"I can't," Vegas cried, "I'm telling you, I can't go any further. You're going to have to do it without me."

Bobby flashed Luke a distressed look. And Luke's eyes flickered off in the other direction.

"Get your ass moving," Pray told Vegas. "I'm not fucking around."

But Vegas stood his ground. He refused the order to move up the hill. And Pray lunged toward him. He shoved Vegas with both hands to the chest. Vegas tripped and fell backward, smacking the ground hard. He sprang to his feet. And Pray charged at him again. Vegas pivoted quickly. He then scrambled up a few more steps before spinning around to face his tormentor.

"No, you know what. I'm—whatever you guys are doing, man, I don't want anything to do with this." Vegas whined, and his eyes dripped with tears. "I'm just … I'm not going any farther! You can do whatever you want! I'm just not … I can't do it." He turned to Bobby and snuffled and wiped the moisture from his eyes with the back of his arm. A dirty wet smudge spread like red mud across his face. "Good-bye, Bobby."

Bobby's breathing hastened and his gaze met Vegas' wet eyes. Tears began streaking down Bobby's face. They stood across from each other, crying and saying good-bye; rivers of tears spilling everywhere, afraid to speak the unspeakable.

Vegas then pointed up the path to a rock formation surrounded by waist-high brush. To Pray, he said, "It's right over there."

And then, without warning, Vegas bolted.

Like the crafty midfielder that he was, Vegas dodged would-be tacklers, and sprinted past Pray and around Luke, and then he was gone—running down the hill toward the two hikers.

Pray didn't know what hit him. "Shit. What the fuck's he doing?"

The three twisted and watched Vegas sprint down the hill and out of sight. Pray dropped the bag and cupped both hands to his mouth. "Honk the horn if anyone comes up, you fucking schmuck ..."

His voice trailed off, and Bobby's first thought was to take off after Vegas. But his mind raced with a thousand fears, and he was far too wasted to walk straight, let alone run for his life. And even if he did, where would he go? He had no idea which path Vegas had taken. So he'd have to hide in some bushes, and then what? Wait until daybreak? They wouldn't let him get away. They'd be out here searching for him all night if that's what it took. This place was deserted. Those hikers were freaks of nature, two lovers out copulating under the stars. There was nobody else out here. Bobby couldn't imagine anybody coming up here in a million years to find him now.

He glanced over at Luke, who was staring at Pray, who looked utterly befuddled. His head hung at an odd angle out in front of him, and he gazed up the hill. Then he swiveled his hips, and he gazed back down the hill. His eyes searched aimlessly, and then he repeated the process. It was strange behavior, but Bobby didn't mind so long as the gun didn't come out of the bag, which, at the moment, it hadn't.

Although the couple and Vegas had completely disappeared, Bobby again thought about running. But Pray continued to daze and gaze in their direction. And it occurred to Bobby that maybe Pray thought he had recognized them. Maybe everything really would be okay once Pray figured out what he was doing. Then they'd head back down the hill, and Bobby would get his ride home.

Luke glanced over and Bobby could feel the warmth of Luke's concern wash over him.

And then Pray flicked the flashlight back on and continued walking up the hill. "Let's go; let's just go. Forget about him."

Luke trailed Pray, and Bobby just stood there, confused about what was happening. He watched Pray stop after a few steps and shine his flashlight beam across a cyclopean red and brown rocky outcropping to the right of the path. Pray hiked past a waist-high patch of scrub, and his eyes darted around as if he were looking for something. Bobby had no idea what they were doing, but he followed Luke as he headed over toward the bushes, where he stopped suddenly and tried to light a cigarette. Luke's hands were trembling, and he kept staring down at the cigarette, but he couldn't get it lit.

Pray waved the flashlight across the sandstone outcropping, and Bobby stood up on his tiptoes and leaned over the scrub, trying to see what was going on. The flashlight beam zigged back across the giant boulder and hovered across the rocks, and then down to the sandstone floor in a circle. Bobby watched it cross over a mound of what looked like freshly dug red clay. Next to it stood a long hole in the ground, about two feet deep and seven feet long, which looked a lot like an irrigation ditch.

Bobby scratched his head because he had no idea what Pray was looking at, or what they were doing. And then he caught, out of the side of his eye, the reflection of the flashlight beam off something metallic. When he stepped around the bush for a closer look, the reflection became two shovels, and Bobby could feel his heart seize with understanding.

He was about to pay for his brother's sins with his life.

Chapter Thirty-Seven

Wednesday—3:00 a.m.

"Yes, Dad, that's what I've been trying to tell you the whole fucking time."

Dick Youngblood looked appalled. "How the fuck does Rick Leblanc know where we live?"

Mickey gazed at his father as if the answer should have been obvious. It took Dick a second to catch his son's drift. "You mean he ...?"

Mickey nodded. "Yeah."

Dick fell into the chair, totally discouraged.

"But that's not even the worst of it, Dad."

Dick glanced up apprehensively.

"I think he knows about our whole routine."

Dick's face shifted into a paroxysm. "You think?"

"Look, Dad, he used to sell for me, okay. What the fuck? He lived with me and he figured out what was going on. What can I say? And he knows where you live. He knows what you do. He knows what I do. He knows where Mom and Rudy live. He knows everything ... Fuck." Mickey swallowed hard. "Now you can see what I've been up against."

Dick's mouth contorted, as he looked up at Mickey in shocked disbelief. His son had told Leblanc too much, and now it was obvious why the guy had been so brazen in his actions against Mickey. Leblanc knew that if Mickey tried to retaliate, Leblanc would just go to the cops and reveal the Youngbloods' entire operation. "So what's he going to do when he finds out his brother's been kidnapped?"

Mickey threw out his hands and started pacing. "I don't know, Dad. That's the million-fucking-dollar question, isn't it? What's anybody gonna do when they find out about anything?"

Dick looked dazed. "So what are we going to do?"

Mickey exhaled gravely before he answered. "I don't really have a choice, Dad. I've got to make sure the kid doesn't go home and blab his mouth. Even Barnes told me I should dig a fucking ditch for the kid."

Dick's brow furrowed. "Shelly told you that? What the fuck would he tell you something like that for? There are other ways of shutting a kid up besides just fucking offing him."

Mickey turned to face his father. "There are?"

"Yeah, there fucking are."

"Like what?"

Dick started to answer, then suddenly he looked like a man at a loss for words. Mickey flashed him a sarcastic grin. "Tell me, Dad—what should I do?"

Dick sat there rocking back and forth, considering their options. He let out a deep sigh and then glanced up at Mickey. "I told you. If we can get the kid back, I'll talk to him. I'll sit him down and make damn sure he understands that he has to keep his mouth shut."

Mickey scoffed. "Dad? I fucking talked to him, okay? We all talked to him—okay!"

"And?" Dick's palms turned over. "What the fuck did he say?"

"He said he wouldn't say anything. But that doesn't—"

Dick jumped out of his seat. "What else do you fucking want, Mickey?"

"What?"

"The kid said he wasn't going to say anything. What the fuck else do you want?"

"Just because he said it doesn't mean he's going to do it. You know that as well as I do. As soon as he gets home, he's going to shoot his fucking mouth off."

"How the fuck do you know, Einstein? I guarantee you, when I finish with him, the kid's not going to say a goddamned thing to anyone!"

Mickey gave his father a dismissive wave. "How can you be so fucking sure?"

"Mickey, you got to trust me. I'm your father for crissake. Just pretend I know what the fuck I'm talking about, all right." Mickey studied his father, searching his face for the answer. "I'll take care of it," Dick said. "I'll make sure the kid never talks to anyone again. Just tell me where he is."

Mickey slowly nodded as he considered his father's request.

"Besides," Dick continued, "it's not like this is this cut-and-dry kidnapping, you know what I mean. The kid had a chance to leave—isn't that right?"

Mickey nodded.

"So you took him. You let him go with Luke. And he had a chance to go home, but he didn't. That certainly ain't no kidnapping for ransom. That's a kidnapping, all right. But it's not for ransom. So that ain't no life sentence, Mickey—do you hear what I'm saying?"

Mickey nodded, this time more enthusiastically.

"So I go pick the kid up. Give him a few bucks—"

"How much?" Mickey interrupted.

Dick frowned. "It doesn't matter how much. Maybe twenty grand. I don't know."

"Twenty fucking grand!" Mickey yelled. "For what? Are you fucking crazy?"

Dick lowered his voice. "No, Mickey, I'm not fucking crazy. It's gonna cost you something to keep the fucking kid's mouth shut, okay?"

Mickey spun around and kicked the table. "I'm not paying him twenty fucking grand, I'm telling you that much right now."

"Mickey, just shut up for a second, okay ...? Hear me out."

Mickey's jaw tightened, but he didn't say anything.

"We're going to have to pay him something—"

"Fine, we'll pay him something. I'm just not gonna pay him twenty fucking grand."

"Fine," Dick agreed, "we'll pay him whatever the fuck you want. The point is that he's not gonna say anything, okay. And then we'll take you down to Shelly's. And he'll negotiate you a deal before you turn yourself in."

A look of utter disbelief encased Mickey's face. "What the fuck are you talking about, Dad? I'm not turning myself in. What kind of fucking deal am I supposed to get? What the fuck's the matter with you? Are you outta your fucking mind?"

"Mickey, I'm not going to argue with you. Let's go give Bart a call. And see what's going on with the kid."

A loud yawn escaped Mickey's mouth. "Dad, I'm exhausted. We'll call him in the morning. I'm going to bed. Good night."

Mickey put his hands on his hips and leaned back, trying to stretch his back. He took one last glance beyond the townhomes and into the Valley night. The moon stood nearly full with a light breeze rippling the decorative trees that landscaped the complex grounds. The faint whir of traffic from distant freeways filled the back of Mickey's ears as he walked back inside. He held the sliding glass door open for his father, but Dick just stood there glaring at his son. *Tough shit*, Mickey thought. If his dad didn't like it, fuck him. Mickey was tired, Babbette was pissed at him, and it was time to go to bed.

"Good night, Dad," he said, and his father just stood there. Mickey started to pull the door closed, but his father suddenly charged him. Dick reached up and grabbed the door, and yanked it back open without getting his hand crushed. He then pushed his way inside and immediately yelled, "Denver, let's go."

Mickey gawked stupidly at his father. A minute later, Mattson lumbered into the room, followed by Babbette. She asked, "Mickey, are you ready to go to bed?"

Mickey yawned and nodded, and then he headed toward the front door.

"Let's go," Dick said to Mattson, "we're going to make a phone call."

Mattson tipped his head and hustled toward the front door. Mickey opened the door and stood there waiting for them to leave. Mattson and Dick both started out, when they suddenly stopped. They stepped back inside, each grabbing one of Mickey's arms, and then they tried dragging him out. But Mickey flexed his muscular back and threw his arms out, and easily deflected the old men away. Dick and Mattson nearly fell down the stairs for their troubles.

"You're a goddamned fool," Dick yelled, stumbling to regain his balance. "You're not only blowing your own life, Mickey. But you're blowing everyone's around you who gives a shit about you. Everyone in this family cares about what happens to you. What the fuck's the matter with you ...? We gotta go get the kid. Now let's go."

Mattson's fat old head bopped up and down in agreement.

"Are you coming to bed?" Babbette asked from the front door.

"In a minute," Mickey snapped. "I'll meet you inside."

She leaned forward and gave him a peck behind the ear. Before she could get away, Mickey twisted and wrapped her in his arm. He jerked her close and afflicted his lips upon hers. When he stopped, she stepped back, and her eyes flicked wide with delight. She licked her lips and gave Mickey a wanton smile that said everything. And then she pivoted and headed inside. Mickey revolved and faced the two old men at the bottom of the steps. As he gazed at their wrinkled and caring faces, he came to a painful realization. His old man was right about what he had said.

Mickey had picked up Bobby Leblanc because he had no other tools to use against Rick Leblanc. The guy was a fucking madman who had terrorized Mickey without recrimination or fear. He poisoned Mickey's dog and then hung him on the backyard fence to make it look like an accident. He tried to destroy Mickey's house. He threatened Mickey and his family, and the threats worked. Mickey had insurance investigators by the dozens climbing up his ass. Rick's tactics had forced Mickey to plan the uplifting of the entire life he had built for himself, with the intent of moving it to some still as of yet undetermined location.

Rick Leblanc had made Mickey think of guns. Mickey bought guns, carried guns, and had people around him carry guns for him, all because of his former best friend. And now, Mickey wanted to kill the asshole's kid brother, and it made Mickey sick to think about.

"If we can just get the kid back," his father kept repeating, as they sped down Henry Avenue all the way to Victoria Boulevard, where Dick screeched a right. He floored it more than a half mile before turning and then flying into a driveway, the front end of his car slamming into the cement slope, the rear undercarriage gouging the asphalt, sparks flying and the car lunging to a stop in front of a row of newspaper stands.

They all hopped out, and Mickey told his dad the number. Dick sprinted over to the pay phone and punched in the numbers. The pager sound beeped, and he hung up. He then walked over to his car, leaned back against it, and let out a deep sough. Mattson pulled his fat ass over and rented space on Dick's rear fender next to him. Mickey watched old sausage fingers then reach into his pocket and pull out the second fattest doobie he had ever seen. Dick handed Mattson a lighter, and Mattson fired it up. And the three of them kicked back by that convenience store pay phone, just like old times, and waited for Bart Pray to call them back.

Chapter Thirty-Eight

Wednesday—3:32 a.m.

Bart Pray could see the terror spring from the kid's eyes the moment he saw his grave. The kid's face went from casual curiosity to pure panic in no time flat. It made Bart laugh to himself, because that was the same expression he used to wear when his stepmother chased after him with the sprinkler key. He'd be running away screaming bloody murder for having committed some minor infraction, thinking he was about to get his head bashed in. Then he'd slow down and glance back to see her leaning over the rusted-out dryer that sat out on the front lawn, huffing and puffing away, because her asthma would be acting up from smoking too much, and her liver failed from drinking. He knew she'd never be able to catch him in a hundred years.

Bobby Leblanc didn't have that same pleasure, because he had Bart Pray standing behind him, anxious to put the dog to sleep. The kid begged for his life, pleading to be spared for his "brother's sins." He screamed and coughed and promised, "My mother will pay for Mickey's house. And whatever else he wants. Please just don't hurt me." He sobbed hysterically as rivers streaked down both sides of his face. It was so pathetic that Bart almost found himself wanting to feel sorry for the kid. But the crying and the tears sounded like fingernails scraping the chalkboard of his mind. It make Bart want to scream and curse and break things. It agitated his brain and freaked his mind out so completely that it scared him, because it made him think of his father.

Bart's dad was such a complete fucking lunatic with Bart and his siblings that he could never tolerate crying or screaming or begging of any kind. The madman instantly flew into a rage and beat his kids with fists and kicked them half to death with work boots. The guy went completely psycho, and that's who Bart had become this very instant while listening to Bobby beg for his life. Bart simply did not possess the tools to handle the stress. It ran in his family like dark hair, only for the Prays, it was violent hair-trigger reactions. Which made Bart want to reach over and rip the kid's mouth off. But instead, he turned to Luke. "Tape him up and shut his fucking ass up."

Luke watched Bobby dispiritedly. "Look at him, dude. He doesn't need to be taped up."

Bobby's head and body convulsed with violent spasms. Primal sounds erupted from his mouth and chest. And it all drove Pray nuts. His face contorted, and he grabbed Bobby by the neck and threw him down on a huge boulder. "Shut the fuck up!" Pray turned to Luke. "Now tape his fucking mouth and hands so he doesn't try anything."

"He doesn't need to be—"

"Do it!"

Luke stood frozen, and Pray's eyes spun with rage. He reached into the bag, pulled out the roll of duct tape, and tossed it to Luke.

When Luke approached Bobby, Bobby said nothing. He just sat there against the rock, sniffling and defeated, offering no resistance whatsoever.

"Hurry up," Pray demanded.

Luke fumbled with the tape, scraping his thumb along the ridge, until finally peeling off an eight-inch strip. "You know I won't hurt you," he said, wiping wetness from his eye with his shoulder.

Bobby sniffled softly. "I know you won't."

Luke signaled for Bobby to get up off the rock. "Put your hands together."

Bobby did as he was told. He climbed off the rock and pressed his hands together in front of him. "Now turn around," Luke said. He grabbed Bobby's arm and gently swung him around.

Bobby put his hands together, behind him, palms in. When he glanced up, the moon's illumination washed over his face revealing a look of desertion and mistrust. Luke slapped the tape against Bobby's left wrist. With his other hand he jerked and wrapped the roll around Bobby's hands twice, and then strung it up through the middle. Suddenly, Luke stopped and threw his hands up in the air. "I can't do it. I can't finish the job."

Pray cringed and angrily charged up to him. He ripped the tape out of Luke's hand and turned to Bobby. Pray then jerked and yanked and tightly wrapped the tape around Bobby's wrists, over his hands, and all the way down to his finger-tips. Bobby groaned when Pray ripped off the last piece. Tears began to slide down the tape and his skin. Pray turned and started to tromp away before realizing he wasn't finished yet. He pivoted and marched back up to the kid, unraveling another huge section of tape. His right hand then reached behind Bobby's head, grabbing his hair and jerking his head back. He then took his other hand, slapped it across Bobby's face, and then brutally wrapped the tape around the kid's mouth and head.

When he finished, Bobby stood there whimpering uncontrollably, his chest rising and falling, his eyes as wide as the moon overhead. He battled to suck in enough air through his two nostrils to breathe.

"Go sit on the rock," Pray demanded. Like a wounded hero, Bobby staggered back over to the rock and fell on it.

As Pray twisted and treaded over to the duffel bag, he again felt the vibration from his pager. It had been buzzing ever since they were halfway up the 267, when he flipped the sound off in the car. It was starting to piss him off. He had a dog to put to sleep, and he didn't have time to fuck around with his pager. He was getting paged so much, he wanted to throw it against a rock and end all the confusion. He hadn't checked to see who it was because he wanted to remain focused on what he had to do.

He reached into his back pocket and pulled it out. He shined the flashlight across the readout and saw phone numbers he did not recognize. Seven calls from three different numbers, and they were all spaced less than eight minutes apart. When he found out who it was, he was going to kill them. It did strike him that it might be Mickey calling.

He wouldn't kill Mickey.

He glanced up the trail and then back down, and again he felt the feather of confusion floating in his mind. Where was poofy hair? The kid had taken off and disappeared, and he was the only person who knew where they were and what they were up to. Pray had dropped the keys on the floorboard of the car, and he feared poofy hair might try to drive out of there, leaving them stuck without a ride back to the Valley. He wondered if he should run down the hill after poofy hair. But what if Luke and the kid took off? Then he'd be totally fucked. They'd all be gone, and Pray would be wandering around in the wilderness with Mickey's gun and someone busting his balls on his pager.

Pray didn't want to continue this anymore. What he wanted to do was follow poofy hair down the hill and say it was all just a big joke. And it was, kind of. He wondered if the quaking kid on the rock had a sense of humor.

And what about those two people they saw? What did they know? What had they seen or heard? And what if they were going to the police right now as his mind spoke? When they had gone to Callahan's house to pick up Patrick's car,

Mickey told Bart that the safest way to handle this would be to leave no witnesses. Dead men tell no tales, or some shit like that, and Bart couldn't remember if he was supposed to off Luke as well. If so, how was he going to fit them both into the same grave? The ditch hardly looked big enough for the kid, let alone somebody as gangly and geeky as Luke. And what about that puffy-haired dude who ran back to the car? What was Bart supposed to do with him? The bitch of it was—he couldn't remember. His mind felt as if everything he ever had in it had somehow leaked out, leaving his head empty and afraid.

He was ready to turn around and drag everyone back down the hill, when his pager went off again. Who the fuck was it now? It was going off like every few minutes now, and it had to be Youngblood, because no one else would be that fucking persistent this late at night. It was past two in the morning, and Mickey had a wild stick up his ass about something. The guy was fucking obsessed again, and it reminded Bart of the old days when Mickey used to try to collect money from him. He would page Bart and call his grandmother incessantly at all hours of the day and night, and it drove Bart nuts. But he didn't think Youngblood was trying to collect money from him now.

They had a deal. Bart was to off the kid, and the debt would be cleared. Mickey would also give Bart money for his birthday, which was now really tomorrow, since it was past midnight, and technically very early Wednesday morning. So what did Mickey want Bart to do? Reverse field? If Bart reversed field, what would he do about the kid seeing his grave? Should he take him back down the hill to find a pay phone to call and see what Youngblood wanted? That hardly made any sense.

Bart glanced over at the vibrating mummy in jeans who sat on the rock, and wondered if he was going to piss himself. Then he thought maybe Luke, standing on the other side of the scrub brush, shaking like a leaf and smoking a cigarette, was the one who was going to piss himself. Pray again glanced down at the pager. The latest number was the same as the two previous pages. Three in a row from the same location, just a few minutes apart. What did that mean? Bart hoped that Mickey wanted him to abort plans, but he knew better. Bart knew the only thing Mickey Youngblood would obsessively call him about this late at night would be to find out if he had finished the job. To see if Bart Pray had once again come through in the clutch, just as he had with sanding the deck and picking up the dogshit.

Bart had been a pantywaist his entire life, hiding behind the violence of his familial upbringing. He had been a lifelong victim of his own circumstances, and now, he was acting like a big sissy just by thinking about aborting plans.

His life depended upon his finishing the job. Youngblood's life depended upon it. That's why Mickey had been paging him. Because he needed Bart Pray as no one had ever needed him before. It had always been just the opposite—Bart needing someone else. But now look at him. Someone finally needed him, and all he wanted to do was run like a little girl. What was up with that? He certainly didn't want Mickey thinking he was weak like Luke, afraid to commit one way or another. Bart had spent a lifetime being afraid. Afraid to shit and afraid to get off the pot. Afraid to commit the smallest infraction at home. Afraid of being beaten like the hated stepchild he was. But not anymore.

This was Bart Pray's big chance. He finally felt a purpose in life. It was now so totally obvious what he needed to do, that he found himself laughing. He looked over at the panting kid on the rock, and he knew the only way to free himself would be to put the dog to sleep. To not be afraid of taking the risk of being different, by having the strength to move forward without fear of repercussions.

Mickey needed him to do that.

So it was with sheer determination that Bart focused on Bobby's pleading eyes, his taped face begging Luke for salvation. Bart could hear his promises to be quiet. Promises that his parents would pay for Rick Leblanc's madness. *Too fucking late*, Bart wanted to tell the kid. *Your brother has caused too much damage. And now you must pay for the crimes Rick Leblanc has committed against Mickey Youngblood.* Bart could feel the fuel of hatred and rage from Mickey Youngblood surging through his veins, as he reached down and picked up the shovel. It was time to put the dog to bed.

"Please, no ..." Luke yowled tearfully, knees crashing into the earthen floor. He watched with pure horror as the shovel glistened and rose high into the night; Bart Pray chopping it down like an axman, metal crushing into Bobby's skull.

✳   ✳   ✳   ✳

Vegas Parsons stopped where the sandstone trail intersected with the scrub path. He leaned back against a giant boulder and glanced up the path, making sure no one was following. He thought he was alone, at least for the moment. There were voices and the rattling of keys below him, and he figured the passing couple was about to get into their car. He slid his hand to his chest and sucked in deeply, trying to catch his breath. He could feel the thumping of his heart against his hand, and he couldn't believe how scared he was. He couldn't believe he just took off like that and didn't get shot. He totally caught Barty and Luke off guard when he bolted. It was no surprise they didn't follow him, since he was the only one who knew his way around Skeleton Jaw.

He hiked down another twenty feet to where the path leveled out above the road. He could hear giggling sounds, and he ducked beneath a row of boulders. He could see the couple kissing and playing grabass down by the car Barty drove them up in. Vegas wondered if they hadn't finished what they had come up here for. He felt like a peeping Tom, watching them as he pinned her back against the car, and they started making out. His unwieldy hands slipped under her top, and she did nothing to discourage the fondling. Vegas debated whether to move down for a better view, but he quickly decided against it. He would be out in the open, and he didn't want to take a chance of their seeing him until he decided what he was going to do.

He wanted to go sit in the car, put his hands over his ears, and forget about the nightmare he found himself in—but he knew that wouldn't save Bobby Leblanc's life. Bobby's only chance was for Vegas to go to those two horny people down there and see if he could borrow their cell phone and call the police. If they didn't have a cell, maybe they would drive him down to a pay phone or the police station. That idea sounded even more appealing, considering where Vegas was. If they drove him to a phone, Vegas would be that much farther away from Barty, reducing the risk of getting his ass shot off too.

Vegas heard a slapping sound, and through the dark, he could see the woman playfully pushing away from the guy and running across the road. The dude sprinted after her, and he caught her seconds later hiding behind the rear bumper of some kind of SUV that Vegas hadn't seen when they drove up. He spun her around and clamped his mouth onto her neck as if he were Count Dracula.

The problems with going to the police were many. First, there was no guarantee they'd get back in time to save Bobby. Even if they called, the nearest cop could be thirty minutes away. Bobby's journey was coming to an end real soon, and he needed more immediate help. The U.S. Air Force probably couldn't get here fast enough to save Bobby now. Vegas thought that maybe he could get that guy to go up there after Barty. Yeah, right, like the guy wouldn't be asking a bunch of questions that Vegas just couldn't answer. And then the dude would really want to leave his hot and horny chick in the SUV while he goes up the dark trail to confront a madman holding a machine gun. Oh, yeah, that would really fly. And Vegas was going to fuck Britney Spears real soon.

He heard the door slam, and Vegas looked over to see the guy staggering back around the SUV before climbing in on the driver's side and shutting the door. A warm wind fluttered through the manzanita leaves, and Vegas could feel his heart racing like thieves. The moment to do or die was here, and he felt paralyzed with fear. If he brought someone to help save Bobby, that someone would want to know what had happened. They would ask Bobby about the people who brought him up here, and they would ask who dug the ditch. Vegas feared a tough time explaining his way out of the fact that he had dug Bobby Leblanc's grave. And that he had been the one to lead the foursome back up the trail to the gravesite for Bobby's execution. Vegas knew he could be implicated for the planning of Bobby's murder, and he could not allow that to happen.

The rear lights flashed red, and Vegas could hear the engine turn over. A darkened smoky burst spewed out the rear of the SUV. And the headlights brought the trees and hillside to life. Vegas had no desire to be implicated, but he also knew he could never live with himself if he just let Bobby die. Bobby was a good kid, who would have been a good friend if it weren't for the extraordinary circumstances of their meeting. Vegas couldn't imagine ending up in the kind of situation where someone else decided your fate. He couldn't believe that Luke had let everything get so out of hand. Luke had been totally stressed, but he had had no intention of hurting Bobby. He truly and honestly wanted Bobby to go home, but he just sort of let Mickey dictate things. Vegas felt hamstrung by the same circumstances.

Bobby should be allowed to live, but Vegas wondered what would happen to him and his family as a result? Luke had told him a hundred times that Youngblood and his father had underworld connections, and Vegas believed it. Mickey Youngblood moved lots of pot, and his father supplied it, orchestrating the shipment of truckloads of BC bud, disseminating it across the western United States. It took power and heat to make that kind of business work. Vegas didn't want that kind of power and heat to come searching for his ass later on down the road. He had a sister and parents to worry about. He couldn't be stupid and make a move that would jeopardize his family.

He climbed out from behind the cover of rock and sauntered down the path to where it emptied out at the side of the road. There was a dirt shoulder to his right where the lime-colored bucket was parked about eighty yards down. Directly across the asphalt, revved the SUV. The guy was about to take off. If Vegas were going to do anything to save Bobby Leblanc's life, now was the time. He pulled his hands out of his pockets and thought about yelling and waving his arms, but that might attract the wrong kind of attention. For all he knew, Barty could be huffing his ass down the trail right now, ready to blast Vegas the moment he spotted him.

Vegas could hear the car shift into gear and then the release of the emergency brake, yet he made no effort to speak with the people inside. He knew it would be the death knell for Bobby Leblanc, but he just couldn't get himself to take the risk. He couldn't risk being implicated for Bobby's murder, and he couldn't risk his family being injured by Mickey Youngblood. Besides, even if Vegas got away cleanly and went to the cops, they would arrest Barty and Luke, and Luke would be put away for a very long time. There would be no telling if Luke would ever get out. And with him would go Vegas' one reliable source to the sweetest bud he'd ever smoked.

The skunk bud that Mickey Youngblood's father imported was the bud to beat all bud. It was the stoniest, best-tasting, most ass-kicking pot Vegas had ever smoked. And he couldn't risk losing that connection. If he got help and saved Bobby Leblanc's life, even if he faced no legal problems himself—which was doubtful—Youngblood and Luke would go down. And the incredible bud Youngblood sold to Luke, who used Vegas to spread it through the inner pipeline of San Floripez's high school bud trade, would be shut off forever. Vegas simply could not allow that to happen.

He was so dependent upon the taste and power of the magical bud that he could never survive being without it. His parents would try to shut off all inroads to smoke, and Vegas would go crazy. He didn't want to go crazy. He liked his life. He liked being able to get up in the mornings and get stoned and forget about the bullshit of the coming day. He liked to stay stoned. Until he did the same thing the following morning. Vegas Parsons wanted to remain stoned out of his mind for the rest of his life. And that was why he stood there; hands shoved back into his pockets, when the SUV pulled away in a cloud of dust and sped off. He watched the two red taillights slide through the darkness before vanishing around a grove of droopy eucalyptus trees.

Vegas felt an emptiness inside his chest where his heart should have been. He felt the remorse of having betrayed someone dear to him. He considered Bobby a friend and couldn't believe he hadn't the strength to honor their friendship. Bobby had been good to Vegas and fun to be around. They had talked about getting together again, partying, and picking up babes. That was never going to happen now. Bobby was going to die, while Vegas walked away from the whole thing. He felt like a piece of shit and wished he were up there instead of Bobby, that Bobby were down here, away from Barty.

When Vegas reached the car, the door was unlocked. He climbed in through the driver's side, into the back. He pulled the door closed and crawled over behind the front passenger's seat. He pictured Bobby sitting next to him only a half hour earlier, and a wave of emotion enflamed his chest. His head felt light. He couldn't believe he was never going to see Bobby again, and he imagined if it had been him. He imagined what his own mom and dad and sister would feel like when they realized he was never coming home again. It made him want to bawl, and he did.

Bursts of sobs filled the back seat. Vegas could feel the pain dripping down his face and all over his shirt. He had failed to be a friend and led Bobby to his death. He was a terrible person unworthy of this world. His body shuddered as his sobs turned into animalistic groans so raw, Vegas felt as though his entire body were bleeding. He grabbed onto the back of the front seat and forced himself to breathe the air in, to fill his lungs with the life that he had helped to take away from Bobby Leblanc.

Minutes later, the pain subsided, and Vegas could begin to live with himself again. He could stand the pain of being alive, but his mouth was bone-desert dry. He searched around on the floor until he actually found a half-empty water bottle. He opened it and drank thirstily. He felt dirty as he drank, as if his hands were permanently stained with blood. And he didn't stop drinking until he had finished the water. Until he had heard the unmistakable sound of gunfire echoing through the starlit night.

Chapter Thirty-Nine

Wednesday—6:00 a.m.

The nightmare would not end. Even when Luke opened his eyes to the exhaustion of the new day, the memories from the night before attacked him like kamikaze jets, torpedoing his fractured brain. It was like being strapped to a chair, with his eyes pried open, and force-fed over and over the images of the diabolical forces that generated so much destruction on that hilltop just a few hours before.

"I'm starved," Pray muttered, interrupting Luke's morbid thoughts while driving south on the 203, up the El Camino Pass. Barty's face looked soggy with exhaustion. His eyes were swollen and red. The guy didn't smoke or drink anything the night before, and he was running on pure adrenalin. His whole demeanor had lightened up once they had gotten on the freeway and started heading home. But he was still a fucking asshole as far as Luke was concerned.

The drive up the grade was dark and steep, the traffic sparse. Luke could see the sleepy, colored lights of Lantana County in the side rearview mirror. If he never saw Lantana or San Floripez again, it would be fine with him. He never wanted to go back to his dad's house or see the area near the Francisco National Forest ever again. He never wanted to see Bart Pray or Mickey Youngblood or Vegas Parsons again in his life. And if Luke never spoke to Rosy or Cheri ever again, that would be fine too, so long as he never had to explain what happened on the top of Skeleton Jaw to anyone, ever.

The horrific images continued to wash over his mind like nuclear sludge. The images of Bobby's duct-taped face—his hands tied behind his back—his eyes wide with terror. The image of Bobby begging Luke not to allow Barty to hurt him. They all made Luke want to cry. His heart had sunk into the abysm when he had turned to Pray, begging him to leave the kid alone.

"We can't do this," Luke had cried. "We got to let the kid go. Please, don't shoot him ..."

Luke watched helplessly as his cries for mercy went unheeded. As Pray picked up the shovel and cracked it down across Bobby's face in one bloody swoop. Pray slammed Bobby twice more before the kid's body crumpled to the sandstone floor. Crimson flowed from Bobby's face and skull. He didn't move, and Luke couldn't tell if he were dead or alive. Pray then kneeled down and picked Bobby up under his arms and dragged his limp body over to the hole. He laid Bobby out lengthwise before dropping him into the shallow grave.

Luke cried and pushed himself up onto his knees and begged for some kind of mercy for Bobby Leblanc. "Please don't shoot him. Don't shoot the kid. Please!" But his cries found deaf ears.

Pray had become a vehicle in overdrive, and there was nothing but clear road ahead. He pulled the AB-10 out of the bag and held it at his hip as if it were Saint Valentine's Day—and he unloaded. Sparks glittered through the night. Bullets flew everywhere, ricocheting off rocks and boulders, striking Bobby in the head and chest and leg. Bobby's body bounced and sprayed blood, and Luke sobbed like a mother who'd seen her baby die right before her eyes. A terrible mother. A mother who had had her baby in her arms, yet who had failed to protect it out of her own selfish interests. And fear.

And that's what Luke couldn't understand. When was it that he had become such a chickenshit? When was it that he had lost such total control of his life that he let them march Bobby Leblanc straight to his death? Luke had planned everything almost perfectly and had been totally set to send Bobby home—and then he lost it. When had that happened?

The later the evening wore on, the more the pressure built for Luke to do something—so the more he drank, the less coherent he had become. Once they had gotten down to the hotel, and he had gotten those cheeseburgers in him, he began a downward spiral through the bottle of whiskey that still had him on his knees as the El Camino Pass leveled off, and Pray started heading through Barksdale.

Luke's stomach grumbled the sounds of gastrointestinal warfare, with the acids winning and his stomach lining being eaten alive. Last night, he had allowed the alcohol and pot smoking to cloud his mind so completely that he had basically stopped functioning. Luke was not thinking clearly when they rode up to Skeleton Jaw, and it only got worse from there. He knew the difference between right and wrong, but when the time had come for him to make the correct decision, his mind had been so fucked up he couldn't get his priorities straight. He couldn't discern what was in *his* best interest.

At the time, for reasons he did not yet understand, Luke believed that eliminating Bobby's voice was his best shot. Now, he believed just the opposite. He should have had trust in the kid to do what he had said he was going to do. Luke shouldn't have let Mickey's distorted logic sway him to the dark side. He should have had the cajones to repel Bart Pray's murderous actions. Luke was a coward, and he knew it. His actions had sealed the verdict.

Last night, Pray had twisted around and pointed the gun at Luke. Luke was sure Pray would have shot him too if the gun hadn't jammed when he was doing Bobby. But it had jammed, and Pray reached down and lifted Bobby's body up by the shoulder and threw the gun down in the hole underneath him. Then he walked over to Luke, who hadn't yet finished vomiting his guts into the sandstone earth, and he said, "Come over and help me cover the body."

Luke climbed up on one knee and stood. His legs were wobbly as he grabbed a shovel and stabbed it into the dirt pile. He threw a couple shovelfuls onto Bobby's lifeless body and felt the bubble rise up inside of him. He dropped the shovel and barfed again.

Pray leaned on his shovel, laughing his ass off. He told Luke that he was nothing but a big old BFC, and how he wished Mickey could see him right now. Luke retched into the night listening to Pray chastise him about what a big fucking cunt he was because he couldn't "throw a little dirt on the kid without puking like a little girl."

That's what Luke felt like when he got up and slurred a "fuck you." He started walking and then tripped over a rock, almost smashing his skull into a boulder before hitting the earth again. He dragged himself up off the rock, but the best he could do was get up on his knees before he got sick again. Only this time it was dry heaves. There was nothing left.

And Pray howled. And then he finished throwing dirt in the hole and covered it with the branches and twigs he had pulled from a pile off to the side. When he had finished, Pray walked over with the flashlight in one hand and the two shovels hooked through the straps of the duffel bag in the other, pointing the flashlight beam directly in Luke's watery and bloodshot eyes, laughing and teasing him. "Get up," he told him. And then he headed down the hill.

Luke scrambled to his feet, knowing that Pray had the only flashlight. They sprinted their asses off all the way down to the car, both repeating, "Let's go, let's go, let's go." They found Vegas, thirty minutes after they'd last seen him, sweating, and crunched up in a mute ball in the backseat. Pray died laughing. He then grabbed the keys off the floor, threw the shovels and the duffel bag into the trunk, and slammed it shut. Their pants and shoes and shirts were covered in dirt, as they climbed in the car. Pray lit a cigarette, and they peeled out of there.

They headed back down North Pacific Sky Road. When they turned right onto the 267, Luke noticed Pray adjusting the rearview mirror, and staring at his reflection like a man proud of his work. "That was the first time I ever did somebody. I didn't know he would go so fast."

Luke rolled down his window and panted into the hot night like a carsick Dachshund. He felt the rumble of nerves well up from inside, before kecking all over the side of the car. Vegas ducked in the back seat. Pray screeched with laughter. And the nauseating smell, redolent of the crimes he'd committed, demoralized Luke.

He pulled his head inside and again saw Pray staring into the rearview mirror, this time at Vegas. "This never happened. You were never in this car. You never saw the kid before. You understand?"

Vegas nodded terrified.

"If you say anything, you're dead."

Vegas swallowed an "Okay."

Luke twisted in his seat. "Seriously, Vegas, it's important for you to be quiet. You were not there."

Vegas repeated the mantra. "Dude, I had nothing to do with this whole thing." Vegas understood.

Pray got Luke to give him directions to Luke's house. When he pulled over at the bottom of Luke's driveway, Luke refused to get out. "I'm not keeping the shovels at my house, dude."

"But they're your shovels," Pray said.

"I don't care."

"Fine." Pray slammed the car into reverse and pulled into Luke's driveway. He downshifted, when Luke panicked and told him, "Stop." He wasn't letting the child killer near his house. He got out and grabbed the shovels from the trunk. He walked them up the drive and snuck them into the garage. He then ran back down to the car, praying his father hadn't seen him.

They drove back to the San Floripez Inn. When they pulled into the parking lot, Luke told Vegas, "You gotta stay here. I'm going to the Valley to stay with my mom." When Vegas got out, Luke handed him a twenty. Vegas looked up at him blankly. "So you can pay the phone bill when you check out."

*　　　*　　　*　　　*

Pray exited at Triangle Drive. The first thing he did was pull into a McDoogle's and order three McDickheads. Luke had left his appetite at Skeleton Jaw, so he asked only for water. He got out, used the pay phone, and woke his mom's ass up. "Mom, I got to get a key to the house. I'm almost there."

Helen Parker did not sound thrilled to hear from her son. She didn't understand why he had to come so early. They were going to Luke's cousin's wedding together, but that wasn't until later in the week. "Chris will be home," Helen said, letting out a deep yawn. "If not, the key is under the mat."

Pray dropped Luke off at his mother's house, and Luke found the key his stepfather had left for him under the mat. Luke opened the door and let himself in. He found Chris reading in the living room and wanted to confess everything to him right then and there. Instead, he went into the spare bedroom and fell back onto the bed. He lay there very still with his forearm across his forehead, and he tried not to think about Bobby Leblanc.

When his stepfather left, Luke moved to the kitchen and consumed many fluids. He felt dehydrated and sick. He then crawled into the bedroom and kicked back until Pray dragged him from his coma with an eleven o'clock phone call. "We need to talk," Pray said. They agreed to meet at their mutual friend Corie Benjamin's house. Youngblood would also be there. Luke had a thing or three he wanted to tell Mickey, so he agreed to meet Pray.

He again phoned his mother at work, but he couldn't talk and broke down crying. He sobbed like a baby, repeatedly telling her, "Something terrible has happened. It never should have happened." She tried calming him down, but Luke was inconsolable. He kept saying, "My life is over. Nothing matters anymore." His mother questioned him, trying to find out what was wrong, but Luke just wailed.

When he hung up, Luke marched over to Corie Benjamin's house. Pray was already there. Corie pulled out a few brews and some bud, and they took severe bongloads. Luke and Pray never acknowledged each other the whole time they were smoking. Pray just sat there on the couch with his head up his ass as usual, nursing his beer. Luke's nerves were shot, and even though he had promised himself he'd never drink again after last night, he cracked open the beer.

I will quit later, he told himself for the umpteenth time, but right now he was so stressed out, he needed the pot and the booze to stop shaking. He thought about Bobby's parents and wondered what they were going through right now.

He couldn't imagine the pain Bobby's mother must have felt in not knowing where her son was. It was terrible to think about, but the beer was good. It tasted crisp, and Luke's throat had been dry. He was happy to be out of San Floripez, away from the terrible sounds that kept hammering through his head: the repeat from the gunfire, the clicking sound of the gun jamming, the last bit of air gurgling from Bobby's lungs. He tried not to think about it, but he couldn't help himself. Luke's mind was out of control.

He had been such a coward for not helping Bobby. Instead of groveling down on his knees, he should have gotten up and grabbed one of the shovels and whopped Pray with it. Just knocked his ass out, laying him flat in the dirt. If Luke had any huevos at all, he would have dotted that fucker good, and when the cops had showed up, told them it was all in self-defense. That Pray had burst into the hotel room, waving the machine gun around, and had kidnapped them all. The cops would have believed him, and Bobby and Vegas would have corroborated Luke's story.

But when they were on the hill, Luke didn't know where Vegas had gone, or whether he'd even come back. And with Luke's string of bad luck, Pray would probably have disarmed him anyway and whapped Luke with his own shovel. Then what would Luke have done? Shot Pray? He couldn't do that. He couldn't shoot anybody. Luke wasn't a killer. That was for guys with long hair and scars across their faces. Guys named Guido and Luther, not guys named Luke Ridnaur. So he did nothing except watch Pray kill the kid, and now Luke felt a good rat-fucking coming on. Which was what he told Youngblood when he arrived with Babbette.

"It's all because of you, Mickey. We didn't have to kill the kid. You know that, right? You totally fucked it up, dude."

Youngblood took a long swig of his beer, and belched. "Don't fucking worry about it."

"No, dude, I am worried about it. Bobby was my friend. He wasn't going to say anything. He shouldn't have had to die."

"Oh, poor baby," Pray's mocking voice said, as he walked back in the room carrying three more beers. He handed one each to Mickey and Babbette, keeping the third for himself.

Youngblood made it clear that he wasn't there to talk about whether they should have offed the kid or not. He worried about coordinating the stories between the three participants. He reviewed with Bart and Luke all the details of what to say if the police ever came and questioned them. They had to agree where they had dropped the kid off, what they had said to him, and where they went when they were finished. Youngblood explained in methodical detail each and every point, and Pray acted as if he wanted to ejaculate after every word. He nodded and smiled and acted seriously, as if the world's welfare hinged on Mickey's words.

Luke's anxiety grew as he listened to Youngblood tell him what Luke was going to say and do, what he was going to tell the cops. Luke couldn't believe how meticulous Mickey's plan was, as if he had spent a lot of time going over every detail. As if Dick Youngblood had been up all night telling Mickey what he was going to say and do. And Pray just nodded his fat head, as Luke felt ready to explode. Luke danced from one foot to the other, nodding while Youngblood made up excuses for why they had called each other on the phone a million times. Finally, Luke had to cut him off.

"All you had to do was communicate with me, Mickey. But you never did through the whole process. You kept telling me you couldn't talk about it over the phone. Fuck, we needed to talk about it, dude. We needed to think about what we were doing. If we had communicated, we would have come up with something better."

Luke had tried paging Youngblood a thousand times, but Mickey never returned any of his calls. When they finally did speak, Mickey told him they'd take the kid home later. But later never came.

"You used to complain about how Leblanc never talked to you when you tried to meet with him to collect your money," Luke said. "Well, same for you, Mick. When all this shit came down, you never tried to get ahold of Leblanc either."

Youngblood just swigged his beer and gawked at Luke as if he were an idiot.

Pray then stepped in front of Luke, his demeanor all tough and confident. "You're a hypocrite, Luke. You had your chance to do something the whole time. You held onto the kid for two days. You fucking helped march him all the way to his death. How can you even talk?"

"I was too fucked up to do the right thing," Luke said, his hands balling into fists. "What's your excuse?"

"What's my excuse?" Pray looked at him sharply. "It certainly isn't because I was too fucked up."

Pray laughed, and Luke didn't blame him one bit. Luke's argument was so weak that he had even lost interest in it. Luke knew he was weak, and his weakness had cost Bobby Leblanc his life. But Luke wasn't depraved, and that's exactly how Mickey had acted the entire time. By staying away from the kid, by using Luke as his buffer, Mickey had never allowed himself to get close enough to Bobby to realize that he was a human being who deserved a lot better than he got.

When Luke finished whining at Youngblood, Mickey just stood there stone-faced and erected. Luke had seen that sarcastic look a million times and wanted to knock it off him. That smug look typified Mickey Youngblood and his attitude around others. He didn't give a shit about Luke. Mickey didn't give a shit about anything but covering his own sweet-smelling ass. It was an attitude he'd inherited from his father, an attitude that said he was better than everyone else, that we all might be shit, but the Youngbloods were the kings of shit.

"Don't look at me like that, Mickey," Luke said, and he meant it. What was Youngblood going to do, shoot him? "You're a fucking asshole for killing the kid. He just didn't have to die."

Youngblood's face warped. "Shut your fucking mouth."

"No, Mickey, shut your fucking mouth. I don't have to listen to you. I'm done taking orders from you. In fact, I'm done with you in my life, period."

Youngblood looked as if he wanted to hit Luke, and Luke glared right back. Then Pray stuck his chest into Luke, and climbed right up into his face. Luke backed away, and Youngblood laughed. And Luke wanted to punch Mickey's lights out; pay Mickey back for taking advantage of him, for setting Luke up to take the fall for Bobby Leblanc's murder. And so that's what Luke did. He closed his eyes, and hauled off and punched Mickey with everything he had.

Unfortunatley, Luke missed his target. Excruciating pain shot from his balled fist to his brain, as he realized it wasn't Mickey who he had hit, but Bart Pray. And it sent the assbite sprawling. Pray's head jerked back, and he staggered into the coffee table, toppling over it and onto the floor. His head cracked off the marble stand with a sickening thud. Blood began spilling from his nose and skull. Pray's face registered with shock, as his eyes woozily blinked up at Mickey who stood there laughin' the load at him.

Chapter Forty

If life were depressing, it was news to Bart Pray. He couldn't have been more excited if he had just won the lottery and got blown by Pamela Anderson all in the same month. Where Luke and Youngblood and everyone else acted morose and deflated about what had happened, Bart felt exhilarated. Where others moped and schemed and planned how to keep everything quiet, Bart Pray wanted to tell the world about what he had done. He had never accomplished so much in so little time and felt so good about it. He finally felt the value of what it was like to be a successful human being. He had gone from taking it up the ass with abuse from Youngblood and all his friends to taking charge of his own life and becoming Mickey Youngblood's hero.

Just for killing a guy. How cool was that?

Bart played it cool, laying low the morning he drove back to the Valley from San Floripez, but he played the cat's meow the following day, his twenty-first birthday. He crashed over at Patrick Callahan's guesthouse, resting up from all his dirty work. Early in the afternoon, Callahan had called from work and wished him a happy birthday. He said they were going to have a party for Bart, and he'd be home early from work. When Callahan arrived, Bart asked him to take him shopping for new clothes.

Mickey had been by, and Bart felt like a new man with a pocket full of money to burn. He was finally out of debt, and he wanted to go on a shopping spree, the first of his life. They took off to Skater Store, and he bought clothes, spending more than half of the four hundred dollars Youngblood had given him for his birthday. He bought two pairs of pants, three shirts, and a pair of shoes.

Callahan had asked Bart where he got all the money from, and Bart had told him he got it from Youngblood. Bart's debt had been cleared, and he felt like a free man.

"How did that happen?" Callahan had asked.

Bart told him the story. He told Patrick Callahan how he cruised up to San Floripez and took care of the problem.

"What problem?"

"The problem with Bobby Leblanc."

Callahan looked at Bart as if he'd taken the wrong turn down a one-way street. "What are you talking about?"

"I killed Bobby Leblanc," Bart Pray said proudly. "Luke Ridnaur and I took him to a ditch and shot him. We put a bush over him after he was dead."

"Why'd you do that?"

"Some things are better left unsaid."

That night, they partied like animals. Bart was treated like an idol. He went from depressed dogshit detailer to the toast of the Valley in one fell swoop. Everybody who was anybody in the Mickey Youngblood pot distribution hierarchy paid their respects to the newfound king of freedom. Mickey even made a short appearance; wished Bart a "Happy fucking birthday," and then he disappeared just as quickly.

Bart loved playing the hero. He loved the fit of his new skateboarder pants, shirt, and shoes, and he turned into a babe magnet at his own party. Julie Newmann, with her black-framed glasses and Shirley Temple curls, glommed onto Bart as if he were made of gold, not letting go until Callahan tossed her ass out the next morning on his way to work.

Bart felt intoxicated with happiness. He saw Larry Haynes carrying two bottles of champagne, and Larry nearly dragged him to the ground when they hugged. Chuck Connelly handed Bart fifteen of his favorite tranquilizers as a birthday present. Eddy Barbados, John's brother, buddied up and pulled out a Cheech and Chong doobie the size of a football. Thirty of Mickey Youngblood's closest friends paid tribute to Bart Pray, drinking and smoking and pill popping to their hearts' desires into the wee hours of the morning.

Barbados told Bart that he had heard that Mickey's father had stopped by and was looking for Bart. Bart had no idea why.

"And I hear the kid's father has been all over the Valley looking for him," Barbados said. "So has his brother."

Bart swallowed hard and finished his beer.

Patrick Callahan said, "I heard rumors that money was being offered to take care of Rick Leblanc."

"Beat him up? Or kill him?" Barbados asked.

Callahan shrugged. "I don't know."

"Well, who made the offer?"

"Mickey Youngblood."

Dick Youngblood then pushed his way through the raucous crowd. He acted edgy and flustered when he trudged up to the trio. "Where's Mickey?" Bart told him he had no idea. Dick glared at the birthday boy. "You're the fucking hero of the party. You're ripped off your ass. And you don't know where my son is?" Dick shook his head disgustedly and pushed back through the congested living room.

"Tough crowd," Callahan said. "What the fuck was that all about?" Bart shrugged, and Patrick Callahan polished off his beer and belched with the ferocity of a small nuclear explosion. "I can't believe you fucking guys did this shit, man," Callahan added. "I mean, like what the fuck are you going to do?"

"What the fuck are *we* going to do?" Barbados said, jabbing his finger into Callahan's chest. "I was going to ask you the same thing."

Callahan's head shook with incomprehension as he grabbed Barbados' finger and removed it from his sternum. "What do you mean?"

"I hear you're the one who supplied the vehicle used in the murder. I wondered how you were going to keep that quiet."

"What the fuck are you talking about?" Callahan croaked as he spilled beer all down his front. He bowed away, slapping at his shirt trying to get the beer off him, his Irish cackle rising above the room's party din. He laughed and smiled, and then he looked up at Barbados and Bart, and they weren't laughing or smiling. "What's up guys? What the fuck? Why are you looking at me like that?"

Pray chuckled. "Dude, you realize we took the lime-mobile the night we drove to Skeleton Jaw, don't you?"

Callahan's smile transformed into a puddle of chalk. "What are you talking about?"

"Mickey took me over to your house to pick up your car. He gave me the gun. And then I went up to San Floripez."

It took Callahan several seconds to realize the direct implications of what he had just heard. When he did, he said excitedly, "No way, dude. Mickey told me you needed my car to help him move."

Bart and Barbados cackled like two hyenas in on the same joke. Callahan looked as if he were going to be sick.

"Dude, don't worry about it," Pray said. "I promise I won't tell anyone, if you don't. We'll keep it just between us."

Pray winked and Barbados snickered. And Patrick Callahan suddenly looked like a man who had just learned of his complicity in the murder of a kid he had never met.

*   *   *   *

Mickey Youngblood's heart and mind ached beyond comprehension. He had lain low since everything came down, but now he felt the world starting to crash in around him. He had collected what money he could from those he could find who owed him, but he still didn't know if he had enough. He didn't know how long he'd be looking over his shoulder. But he could live with the uncertainty, because in his line of business that's what you did sometimes—lay low until the heat died down, and you knew it was safe to move on. It was the overwhelming sadness of doing something so totally stupid that he thought might do him in.

Youngblood had been running from Rick Leblanc ever since the guy had moved in with him a year ago. Mickey had butted heads with one of the Valley's all-time dickheads, getting into a ball-dangling, throat-slashing game of chicken that they had both lost big time. Only Rick Leblanc didn't know it yet. But Mickey did, and he harbored enough remorse for two lifetimes and wanted to wash it all away as he climbed into Nicole's parents' black marble walk-in bathtub. Babbette awaited him wearing nothing more than devilish eyes and a mischievous smile, and Mickey acted as if he barely noticed. He hung ice-water-shriveled, and he could see Babbette's expression of bitter disappointment.

Mickey couldn't help it. His mind wasn't right with hers. And he wasn't sure it ever would be until he could figure out how to reconcile certain issues within himself. He had ordered the execution of Rick Leblanc's fifteen-year-old brother to bury the word of the kid's abduction six feet under ground, and Mickey felt his insides split in half as a result. He no longer feared revenge from Rick Leblanc, but he dreaded retribution from a higher source. He felt as though he had committed the ultimate mortal sin and now must pay the ultimate price. He thought his body would burn in hell, but he had problems enough dealing with the heat Babbette generated by rubbing her glistening body all over him in the 103 degrees of her parents' bathtub.

Mickey Youngblood had been afraid that Rick Leblanc would hurt his family—in particular, his little brother—if word got out about his nabbing Bobby. So Mickey did a terrible thing.

But he now understood it had all been a lie. And he stood ready to face the repercussions of what he had done. Although he couldn't quite imagine what they might be yet.

He heard himself mumble, "Should I turn myself in?"

Babbette massaged her humongous soapy plastic globes with lascivious hands. "Into what, baby?"

Mickey tried to imagine what might have happened if he had let the kid go. If Bart Pray had never become involved. They had had the kid for two and a half days, and there would have been hell to pay at home when Bobby got back. His manic mother and father would have climbed up the kid's ass like suppositories. Bobby would have eventually seen his brother, and Rick would have wanted to know what had happened, where Bobby had been, and who had been involved. The kid would have eventually cracked, and someone would have wanted revenge. The cops would have been called, and Mickey would have gone down. That's why he had to do what he did. There was no other way. He had to send Bart Pray in to finish the job, and now he was going to have to pay for it.

"I should turn myself into the police," he said.

"Why would you do that?" Babbette said, reaching over and taking his limpness into her hand. "You just going to hand your cock over to Rick Leblanc? Did Rick Leblanc turn himself in to the police when he broke out your windows?"

Mickey shook his head meekly. She arched her back and leaned down. Her mouth cracked and her tongue rode his glans like a desiccated lollipop. And then her eyes gazed up. "How about when he threatened your family? Or when he killed Zeus?"

Mickey shook his head and took the back of hers into his hands, pulling her to her feet. He pressed his lips against hers, and he grabbed her rounded ass and rubbed that spot just above the cheeks that she loved so much with his thumbs. She was right, of course. Rick Leblanc had never so much as offered a "thank you" to Mickey in all the time he had known him. The guy had leeched as much as he could from Mickey, before Mickey had to throw his ass out. Then, when Mickey tried to collect his money, Leblanc terrorized him, killed his dog, and threatened his family, without ever considering what Mickey might be forced to do in response. Mickey had had no intention of hurting Leblanc's little brother anymore than he did of seeing his own brother get hurt. But when push had turned into shove, what choice did Mickey really have?

Babbette bit and kissed along the fine line of blond hair below Mickey's belly, and he could feel the vindication rising from within.

"You've got to stop feeling the blame, Mickey," Babbette said. "It wasn't your fault. You're a hero. Don't you realize that? You did what you had to do. You protected your family."

Her long cherry nails dug into the flesh of his sculpted abs, and she once again took him into her mouth. Only this time, he felt rock strong, and they both groaned their pleasure. Mickey had done what any red-blooded American would have done: he protected his family. He played like President Bush and took a preemptive strike. He ordered the murder of Bobby Leblanc to end the war before it got totally out of hand. He was a smart man who took care of business the way it should have been taken care of, and he should have no regrets whatsoever.

Business was ugly sometimes, and you had to take risks to make gains. Mickey was a man willing to take risks, and he felt the power of that man taking over.

That man lifted Nicole Babbette out of the tub and spun her around. He leaned her over the railing and admired her flawless shape that awaited him. He pulled and pushed slowly inside and rode her into the night. Once again, he felt what it was to be Mickey Youngblood. Any doubts he might have had evaporated when he heard Babbette's angry screams of climax, the eight-inch letters tattooed above her ass spelling "Mickey" bouncing up and down, paying tribute to his newfound virility.

* * * *

"Dude, what I'm saying is—what if something did go wrong?" John Barbados handed Mickey and Babbette ice-cold brewskis. They stood in the middle of Barbados' mom's living room, and chugged them.

Youngblood said, "Dude, what I'm saying is—nothing went wrong."

Youngblood and Babbette had been playing it loose and on the road, spending the weekend in the desert, hanging low at a modeling convention, not being seen. They were now back in town and staying at her parents' townhouse. Her parents were on the road again, and Babbette had her run of the place. They had just stopped by Barbados', so Mickey could collect money from John's brother Eddy.

"What—you don't think anything can go wrong?" Barbados asked while belching weakly and blowing it on Babbette.

Nicole squealed and Youngblood thought that was hilarious. So he belched up a lung and blew the whole mephitic mess onto Barbados. Barbados ducked and tried to escape the toxic cloud, with no luck.

"Grow up," Babbette yelled, "you guys are so gross."

Youngblood laughed like a strumpet and told Barbados, "Dude, I told you. I planned everything to perfection. What's going to go wrong? Nothing."

"I don't know, dude. I heard Rick Leblanc and his old man have been plastering the town in like missing posters and shit."

"So what?" Mickey whined. "Let them plaster their little hearts out. What the fuck do I care?"

"You don't understand," Barbados said. "They've got people out looking for him. They're asking lots of questions. I heard the police are looking into it."

"Let them look," Youngblood said. "What the fuck are they going to find?"

"You tell me," Barbados asked.

Youngblood wasn't worried. The only ones who knew he had any connection to the kid were Luke, Barbados, Pray, Babbette, Mickey's dad, his dad's best friend, and his lawyer. And none of them were going to say anything.

His dad was the one who told Mickey to go hide under a rock. He helped Mickey devise a plan to stay loose and to be ready to run at a moment's notice. His dad wasn't going to talk.

And the kidnapping took place in Denver Mattson's van. After Pray had returned it, Mattson took the van to one of those do-it-yourself car washes, and scrubbed everything down, intentionally vacuuming away all remnants of Bobby Leblanc ever having been in it. If Mattson said anything, he'd be considered a suspect.

And Sheldon Barnes wouldn't say anything. He was Mickey's attorney, and everything Mickey had said to him was privileged. Babbette wouldn't say anything, because Mickey fucked her and would fuck her up good if she ever did. But she wouldn't anyway, because she knew who buttered her bread.

And Bart Pray killed the kid, so he wasn't going to say shit. And nobody but Pray heard Mickey discuss the plan or saw Mickey give the AB-10 to Pray, so it was just Pray's word against Mickey's. And who were they going to believe?

Luke wouldn't say anything, because he drove the van that kidnapped the kid, held Bobby Leblanc for three days at his house, then marched him to his death.

"And you're not going to say anything," Youngblood said, pivoting to Barbados. "Because you beat his ass up when we picked him up. Then you stuck the gun in his ear and threatened him. What the fuck are you talking about? You're not going to say shit."

"Yeah, okay. So?"

"So nobody's going to say nothing, and there's nothing to worry about."

Barbados' forehead furrowed with worry. "So maybe there's other ways they could find out."

"What other ways?" Youngblood asked. "There are no other ways, John."

"But I mean, what if there were?"

Youngblood's mouth crimpled. "Like what?"

"I don't know," Barbados said. "What if ... What if maybe they found the body?"

"What if who found the body?" Youngblood smirked at the idea. "Impossible."

"How do you know, Mickey? It could happen. And if it did, what would happen to us?"

"Nothing," Youngblood proclaimed. "How could it? They buried the kid in a ditch. Barty and Luke both said so. They buried him in a ditch in some out of the way bumfuck place up in the mountains. And nobody's ever going to find him."

Youngblood was out of breath and his mouth was dry, and he asked for another beer. Barbados grabbed three more out of the fridge; came back and passed them out. They all drank heartily and Mickey felt the comfort of knowing he had made the right decisions about everything. He had been cool with Babbette throughout the whole ordeal, and they were getting along better than ever. He had kept his feet loose, and his ear to the pavement, and so far everything was cool. He hadn't heard from Rick Leblanc, and there was nothing on the news about the kid's disappearance. He looked forward to someday going into a legitimate business with his father, but he felt bad about having deceived him.

Mickey felt bad, because he had seen the hope spilled across his father's face. And Mickey had fed that hope by lying to him. The night they left Babbette's, they had gone and paged Pray. But Mickey knew Pray wouldn't call him back until the job had been completed. That meant Dick waited with Mickey in vain, and the pay phone never rang.

Mickey had wanted more than ever to please his father, but he knew that would be impossible. Once Mickey had told Pray that Mickey was looking at life in prison, he could see something change in Pray's eyes; a newfound desire to complete the job right. When he saw that, Mickey knew there would be nothing to worry about. He knew he had beaten the system again, and he felt good about it. He had made the correct decision each and every time he had had to. He possessed this innate ability to stay out of trouble, something he had inherited from his father, and he had done it once again.

He finished his beer and saw Barbados eyeballing him. "What? What the fuck did I miss?"

"I just don't know how you can be so sure they won't find the kid. That's all."

"Because I'm sure, okay? Because I made all the right decisions."

Barbados beamed sarcastically. "So you're sure then?"

Mickey glanced over to Babbette and then back to Barbados. "Of course I'm sure. Why? What the fuck?"

Barbados sneered, as he reached over to the table and grabbed the front page of the newspaper. He handed it over to Babbette and waited to see her expression.

Babbette's smile suddenly shriveled and went sallow. She gawked nervously at the paper and quickly handed it over to Youngblood. When Mickey glanced at it, he gasped as if his balls had been caught in a lawn mower.

The lower right hand corner of the front page of *The Valley Times* featured a photograph of Bobby Leblanc from his high school sophomore yearbook. The caption underneath it read, "Bobby Leblanc, a fifteen-year-old Valley boy, was shot execution style as he lay bound and gagged in a shallow grave."

Mickey blanched a lighter shade of pale, and he looked as if he were going to be sick. "I'm so outta here," he said. And he was.

Babbette frowned and hustled after him out the front door. "I'm hungry," she whined. "When are we going to eat?"

Made in the USA
Lexington, KY
28 February 2010